S0-AFZ-726

The Calling

A sense of urgency was building; adrenaline was coursing through my veins.

At the corner of Eighty-seventh and Central Park West, I stumbled to a sudden stop, my heart hammering. There it was.

The house had four stories, and I could glimpse granite facing behind a tangle of thick, gnarled wisteria vines. Three stone steps led to the front door, where a doorbell was embedded in a stone carving of a gorgon's head. It was exactly what I'd seen in the vision.

A thin, icy cloak of fear settled around me. . . .

• • •

SWEEP

SWEEP

Cate Tiernan

Volume III

THE CALLING

CHANGELING

STRIFE

speak

An Imprint of Penguin Group (USA) Inc.

All quoted materials in this work were created by the author.
Any resemblance to existing works is accidental.

The Calling

SPEAK
Published by the Penguin Group
Penguin Group (USA) Inc., 345 Hudson Street, New York, New York 10014, U.S.A.
Penguin Group (Canada), 90 Eglinton Avenue East, Suite 700, Toronto, Ontario, Canada M4P 2Y3
(a division of Pearson Penguin Canada Inc.)
Penguin Books Ltd, 80 Strand, London WC2R 0RL, England
Penguin Ireland, 25 St Stephen's Green, Dublin 2, Ireland (a division of Penguin Books Ltd)
Penguin Group (Australia), 250 Camberwell Road, Camberwell, Victoria 3124, Australia
(a division of Pearson Australia Group Pty Ltd)
Penguin Books India Pvt Ltd, 11 Community Centre, Panchsheel Park, New Delhi - 110 017, India
Penguin Group (NZ), 67 Apollo Drive, Rosedale, North Shore 0632, New Zealand
(a division of Pearson New Zealand Ltd)
Penguin Books (South Africa) (Pty) Ltd, 24 Sturdee Avenue, Rosebank, Johannesburg 2196, South Africa

Registered Offices: Penguin Books Ltd, 80 Strand, London WC2R 0RL, England

Published by Puffin Books, a division of Penguin Young Readers Group, 2001
Published by Speak, an imprint of Penguin Group (USA) Inc., 2008
This omnibus edition published by Speak, an imprint of Penguin Group (USA) Inc., 2011

5 7 9 10 8 6 4

Copyright © 2001 17th Street Productions, an Alloy company
All rights reserved

Produced by 17th Street Productions,
an Alloy company
151 West 26th Street
New York, NY 10001

17th Street Productions and associated logos
are trademarks and/or registered trademarks of Alloy, Inc.

Speak ISBN 978-0-14-241022-6
This omnibus ISBN 978-0-14-241955-7

Printed in the United States of America

Except in the United States of America, this book is sold subject to the condition that
it shall not, by way of trade or otherwise, be lent, re-sold, hired out, or otherwise
circulated without the publisher's prior consent in any form of binding or cover
other than that in which it is published and without a similar condition
including this condition being imposed on the subsequent purchaser.

The publisher does not have any control over and does not assume any
responsibility for author or third-party Web sites or their content.

BOOK SEVEN

SWEEP
THE CALLING

Prologue

A wolf, silver-tipped fur, ivory teeth glinting in the candlelight, padding across a dark, polished marble floor to a stone table. The room huge, black candles flickering in wall sconces. Leaves and vines in ornate plaster molding. A cougar, muscles rippling beneath a tawny pelt, bounds toward the table, golden eyes glittering. Black drapes covering tall, narrow windows. A great horned owl, its wings and talons outstretched, hovering over the stone table. The air rank with the smells of the animals. A viper coiled on the table, fangs exposed. An eagle, an enormous bear. A jaguar, tail lashing. The air crackling with dark power. An elaborate silver candlestick with black candles burning on top of an ebony cabinet. A hawk circling. An athame set with a single bloodred ruby. A jackal, a weasel, both greedy with hunger. The wolf ravenous. All closing on the great round stone table where a wolf cub lies bound, its eyes wide with terror, its small body trembling. One by one the candles gutter out. The darkness becomes thicker, complete. And the wolf cub howls.

*   *   *

I bolted upright, my heart hammering. I could still hear the echo of the cub's agonized scream, and the darkness around me . . . was only the darkness of my bedroom in the middle of the night. I was in my own room, in my own bed, yet the dream was still with me, vivid and terrifying.

Hunter, I need you! Without thinking I sent a witch message to my boyfriend, Hunter Niall.

I felt his instant response: On my way.

I glanced at my alarm clock. It was just past three A.M. I padded downstairs in my flannel pajamas to wait for Hunter.

It took him only ten minutes to arrive, but it felt more like ten hours as I paced the living room nervously. The nightmare wasn't even close to fading. It still seemed present, as if all I had to do was close my eyes and I'd be right back inside it.

I looked out the window as I felt Hunter approach, crunching across the crust of old snow on our lawn. His pale blond hair stuck up in spikes around his head, and my magesight showed me the traces of pink the cold wind had whipped into his pale, chiseled face.

"What happened?" he asked without preamble as I opened the front door.

"I had a dream." I pulled him inside, opened his coat, and buried my face against his sweater-covered chest.

He stroked my hair back from my forehead. "Tell me."

I told him, standing within the circle of his arms, speaking in a whisper so as not to wake my family. As I spoke, the images from the dream seemed to hover in the air around me, the wolf slavering, the owl's yellow eyes searching, searching. I wanted to hide from those yellow eyes, wanted to stop them from hunting me out.

Stop. It's not real, I told myself.

"I don't know why it scared me so much," I finished lamely. "It was just a dream. And I wasn't even in it."

But Hunter didn't say the comforting things people usually say. Instead he was silent a moment, tapping his fingers gently on my shoulder. At last he said, "I think I should report it to the council."

My heart contracted. "The council? You think it's that serious?"

He shook his head, his green eyes somber. "I don't know. I'm not experienced in interpreting dreams. But there are things in it that worry me—a lot."

I swallowed. "Oh," I said in a small voice.

"Morgan?" I heard my dad's sleepy voice coming from the top of the stairs. "Are you down there? What are you doing up at this hour?"

I turned quickly. "Just getting something to drink," I called. "Go back to sleep, Dad."

"You too," he mumbled.

Hunter and I looked at each other.

"I'll call you," he whispered.

I watched him disappear back into the darkness. Then I went back up to my room and lay there, sleepless and full of dread, waiting for the dawn to come.

1
Prophecies

March 2, 1977

I dreamt of Ireland again. As always, the dream left me with a longing that makes no sense. It's just an image, deceptively simple, innocent really: a small child's dress of cream linen, blowing on a line against an open blue sky. Behind it the grass slopes up to the base of Slieve Corrofin, with the great rock at the peak in the shape of a lizard's head. I remember the locals calling it the Ballynigel dragon, though I reckon that was more for the tourists than anything else.

So why does Ballynigel still haunt my dreams? And what do I make of the fact that the dream returns when I am eighteen, two nights before I'm to marry Grania? If, as we are taught, everything has meaning, then what does this mean? Am I being warned away from the marriage? No, that seems impossible. I've been dreaming of that dress since I was eight.

Besides, Grania is three months pregnant with my child. And she's a good match. Her family is one of the wealthiest in Liathach, our coven. More to the point, her mother is the high priestess of Liathach and has no other children, and Grania has no ambition to lead the coven herself. She's happy to let me take that role. I've always known that one day Liathach would be mine to lead. Being Greer MacMuredach's son-in-law will make the passing of power that much easier. Together Grania and I will raise a dynasty full of true Woodbane magick.

—Neimhidh

At eight-thirty the sky still held the paleness of early morning as I drove south on the New York State Thruway. There were almost no other cars on the road, and the world seemed still and hushed in the chill January air. In the back-seat of Das Boot, my enormous '71 Plymouth Valiant, Bree Warren, Robbie Gurevitch, Raven Meltzer, and Hunter's cousin, Sky Eventide, were crammed together. All were sleep-ing—Raven half collapsed against Sky, Bree snuggling with Robbie. The only other person awake was Hunter, who sat in the passenger seat beside me. I glanced at him, saw his chiseled profile intent as he studied a map. Sometimes I won-dered if Hunter ever lived a moment without that focused intensity. Did he even sleep intensely?

Maybe I would find out over the coming weekend. The six of us were about to spend four nights in New York City. I'd never spent that much time with Hunter, and something deep inside me thrummed with pleasure at his being so close to me. Things were still new between us, but I knew without question that I loved him. Most of the time I felt pretty certain that he loved me, too, although sometimes I got insecure about that. I had told him how I felt weeks ago, but he had never said it back to me. Who knew—maybe he just didn't feel it was necessary. I hadn't had the nerve to ask him.

"Morgan, you'll need to take the Palisades Parkway to the George Washington Bridge, then get the Harlem River Drive to the Franklin Delano Roosevelt motorway," he said, sounding very British.

"We call them *highways* here," I said, unable to resist ribbing him.

"The *highway*, then. It will take us straight down the east side of the city."

"I know." I'd never driven to New York City before, but I'd gone with my family plenty of times. From Widow's Vale, about two hours north, it was a pretty direct route.

"How fast are you going?"

I glanced at the speedometer. "Seventy-five."

He frowned. I smiled. Responsible Hunter. At nineteen, he was the youngest member of the International Council of Witches, a Seeker, charged with ferreting out witches who used their power inappropriately and administering punishment. It was a serious job. Too serious, I sometimes felt. Since I'd met Hunter, I'd seen more of Wicca's dark side than I cared to.

About two months earlier I'd learned that I was in fact not the biological child of the people I'd always thought of as my parents. Rather, I was adopted and a blood witch, the descendant of one of the Seven Great Clans of Wicca. What's more, I was heir to an incredible legacy of power.

Magick had brought me searing grief. It had made me question absolutely everything I'd ever believed to be true. But magick was also the most amazing gift: an opening of the senses, a surfacing of ancestral memories, an exhilarating connection to the earth, and a strength I'd never imagined possible. And it had brought Hunter into my life. Hunter, who I loved more than I'd thought possible.

"You're almost up to eighty," Hunter said, sounding disapproving.

I slowed down to sixty-five. "There's no one else on the road," I pointed out.

"Except perhaps a police officer," he warned. I felt his green eyes on me, and when I glanced at him, he smiled. "Pity we don't travel by broomstick anymore," he said.

"Did we ever?" I asked, honestly curious. "It sounds like fun."

Hunter shrugged. "Really? I suspect it would be awfully uncomfortable—hard seat, no heat or air-conditioning, bugs constantly flying into your mouth. . . ."

I glanced at him again and saw the glint of amusement in his eyes. I felt a rush of delight that made me break into a goofy grin. "I guess I'll stick to driving for now."

We rode in silence for a while. The haze of thin clouds in the sky was starting to burn off, the sky settling into the pale, crystalline blue so typical of winter skies. There were a few more cars on the road now.

Hunter was the reason we were all going to New York City. Hunter, my dream, and the ancient boiler in Widow's

Vale High, which had broken down the Wednesday before Martin Luther King Jr. Day, miraculously extending a three-day weekend to five days.

As it turned out, the council had taken my dream very seriously. They considered it a prophetic vision and had ordered Hunter to investigate. "They think the animals in your dream were actually members of a Woodbane coven called Amyranth," Hunter had told me when he'd gotten the council's directive.

"Amyranth?" I frowned. Where had I heard that name before?

Of the Seven Great Clans, the Woodbanes were known for their tendency to covet and abuse power. But there were also Woodbane covens, like Belwicket, the one my birth parents had belonged to, that had forsworn evil.

"Amyranth is not one of the good ones," Hunter told me. "It's one of the worst. It's the only coven believed to practice the forbidden magick of shape-shifting. Actually, another coven, Turneval, also used to shape-shift. But Turneval was disbanded in the early seventies, after their core members were stripped of their magick by the council. Amyranth has avoided the same fate by operating in deep secrecy. Members usually maintain membership in another coven; Amyranth is their secret coven." He gave me a sideways look. "Selene Belltower was a member of Amyranth."

"Oh." *That's* where I'd heard the name Amyranth before. I shuddered involuntarily at the thought of Selene. "So we're talking very scary."

Hunter had been sent to Widow's Vale last fall to ferret out a group of Woodbane witches who were using dark magick to destroy their opponents and increase their own power. Their local leader had been Selene Belltower, the mother of Cal Blaire, Hunter's half brother and my first love. Though I was Woodbane myself, Selene had wanted to drain me of my power, and she'd used Cal to get to me. When that plan had failed, Selene had kidnapped my younger sister, Mary K., forcing Hunter and me into a horrible showdown with her, just before Christmas. She'd nearly killed Hunter and me both, and I worried that Mary K. might still be suffering some subtle bad effects from having been her captive.

Cal had stepped in front of me and taken the bolt of dark energy she'd aimed at me. Now Cal was dead, killed by his own mother. Although he'd used and betrayed me, in the end he'd given his life for me. I was still coming to terms with that: both with the fact that the beautiful boy I'd loved so much was gone and that he was gone because of me.

Selene had also died that night—and though I certainly hadn't meant to kill her, I was haunted by the fear that my magick had somehow contributed to her death. I'd never seen death up close. It was so final and empty and awful. Seeing Cal and Selene alive one minute, dead the next had changed something inside me. For all of Selene's and Cal's formidable powers, they were as mortal as anyone else. Ever since that night I'd looked at everyone I knew and loved with a new awareness. We were all so fragile, all capable of being so easily extinguished. I couldn't help thinking of that again as I drove on this beautiful morning.

"Are you all right?" Hunter asked softly. "If you grip that wheel any more tightly, you're going to wrench it off the steering column."

"I'm fine." I forced my hands to relax.

"Are you thinking about Selene and Cal?" Hunter guessed. He was very sensitive to my emotions. No one had ever read me with such precision. Sometimes it made feel vulnerable and exposed. Sometimes it was weirdly comforting. At that moment it was a little of both.

I nodded as we whizzed past an exit. No love had been lost between Hunter and Cal. They'd never known each other except as enemies. But Hunter knew I'd loved Cal and was doing his best to be respectful of that. More than anyone, he understood how much coming into my powers had cost me.

"Let's talk about something else," I said. "Can we go over the details of this vision one more time? I'm still not clear on what it is we're supposed to do."

"*We're* not supposed to do anything," Hunter said. "You're staying out of this. I don't want you taking any risks, Morgan."

I felt a prickle of annoyance. We'd had this argument several times in the two days since the council had contacted Hunter. Because I was the one who'd had the dream, the council had asked that I accompany Hunter, just in case he needed to consult with me. I, of course, wanted to go. It was my dream, after all. Besides, I loved the idea of spending time in the city with Hunter.

Hunter hadn't been so keen on the idea, though. "It's too dangerous," he'd told me flatly. "For you of all people to go walking into a nest of Woodbanes . . ."

He explained that the council believed Selene had been acting on behalf of Amyranth; it was possible I still was a target. I couldn't pretend that prospect didn't frighten me. But

Selene was dead now, nothing bad had happened to me in the weeks since her death, and I was starting to feel safer. Safe enough that my desire to go with Hunter outweighed my fear.

"The council thinks I should go," I'd argued.

"The council are a bunch of—" He broke off, pressing his lips together in irritation. My eyes widened. Was he really about to bad-mouth the International Council of Witches?

"They don't always consider the risk to individuals," he said after a minute. "They're not out here, doing the legwork. Anyway, you can't go," he went on. "You've got school. Your parents aren't going to let you take two days off to go down to the city just because a bunch of witches in London think you should." He was right about that, I had to admit.

But then the school boiler had broken down, and Bree had suggested that we combine Hunter's mission with a road trip to her dad's New York City apartment. After a long discussion my parents had said I could go, and after that even Hunter couldn't come up with any more good reasons for me not to. I smiled, thinking about it. It must have been fate.

By late Wednesday night our road trip had expanded to include six members of Kithic, our coven. Sky was coming along because she and Hunter, who were cousins, always looked out for each other. Raven wanted to be with Sky, and Robbie had come to be with Bree.

Traffic thickened as we headed down the Palisades Parkway toward the George Washington Bridge. I slowed. "So the animals in my dream were actually Amyranth witches in their animal forms—have I got that right?"

"Right," Hunter confirmed. "We think so. We know they use animal masks in some of their darker rites. It's rarer for a witch to actually be able to take on animal form, but they are capable of that as well. The council thinks that the wolf cub on the table must represent the child of the witch who appeared as the wolf."

My mouth fell open. "But—I mean, it looked like the cub was about to be sacrificed. Are you saying a mother—or father—is out to kill their own child?"

Hunter nodded. "That's the theory," he said quietly. "The most likely scenario is that the victim's power is going to be drained. Which usually means death."

"What else?" I asked after a moment, trying to match his calm.

"Well, now we get to what the council doesn't know," Hunter said. "First of all, we aren't sure which cell of Amyranth is planning this event."

"How many cells are there?"

Hunter blew out a long breath. "Four that we know of. One in San Francisco—that was Selene's group—one near Glasgow in Scotland, one in northern France, and one in New York City. We've managed to get spies into the other three cells, but unfortunately, the one in New York is the one that the council knows the least about. Basically, all we know is that it exists. We don't know the identity of any of its members, can't even connect it to any specific incidents of dark magick. It's the most shadowy of all the branches."

I tried to make sense of all of this. "So the council doesn't know who the wolf really is."

"Or who the cub is," Hunter said. "We believe that he or she is a young witch in terrible danger. But we have no idea who this witch is or why he or she has been chosen as a victim."

"And your job?" I asked.

"As I said, we've already got agents inside the other three Amyranth cells, who will find out as much as they can," Hunter said. "Since we have so little information about the New York coven, I'm to try to fill in the gaps, find the witch who's targeted, and, if it turns out the target is here in New York—"

"We've got to find a way to protect him," I said, finishing his sentence.

"*I've* got to find a way to protect him," Hunter amended. "*You've* got to relax and enjoy the city. Shop, see museums, eat bagels, visit the Statue of Liberty."

"Oh, come on. You're going to need help," I argued. "I mean, you've got nothing to go on. Where do you even begin to find this stuff out? Can we scry or something?"

"Don't you think the council has already tried all the methods of getting information by magick?" Hunter asked gently. "We're at a dead end. It's a matter of legwork now. And you can't help me on this." He laid his fingers gently on my lips as I started to protest. "You know it as well as I do, Morgan. It's simply too dangerous for you." He looked troubled. "Which reminds me of the other thing the council couldn't figure out."

"What's that?" I whacked the horn impatiently. Traffic had slowed to a crawl, even though we were still miles from the exit for the bridge.

"We don't know why you're the one who was given this dream."

A cold finger of fear traced its way down my back. I swallowed and was silent.

"Gurevitch, get your elbow out of my ribs," Raven murmured. There was a general stirring in the back, then Robbie leaned over the blue vinyl bench seat. "Morning," he said to us. "Where are we?"

"About five miles north of the city," Hunter answered.

"I'm starving," Robbie said. "How about we stop for breakfast?"

"I brought muffins," Bree announced. I glanced in the rearview mirror and saw her holding up a large white paper bag, managing to look both sleepy and cover-girl beautiful. Bree was tall and slim, with dark eyes and sleek, mink-brown hair. She and Robbie, our good friend since elementary school, had recently started going out—sort of. Robbie was in love with Bree, but when he'd told her that, she'd gotten "all squirrelly," as Robbie put it. Yet she continued to see him. What, exactly, she felt for him was a puzzle to me. Not that I was any expert on coupledom. Hunter was only the second guy I'd gone out with.

"Got any lemon poppy seed?" Raven asked as she rooted through the muffin bag. "Want one, Sky?"

"Yeah, thanks," Sky said, yawning.

Sky and Raven were a study in contrasts. Sky was slim, pale, blond, with a penchant for androgynous clothing and a delicate beauty that belied her considerable power. Raven, Widow's Vale's resident goth girl, favored a bad-girl wardrobe that left very little to the imagination. Her current outfit featured a tight black vinyl bustier that revealed the circle of flames tattooed around her belly button. A purple stud in her nose flashed as she turned her head. The interesting thing was that Raven, who had set a record for seducing guys, was now seeing Sky. And Sky was in love with Raven. It was definitely an attraction of opposites.

Hunter took a cranberry muffin from Bree and fed me a chunk of it as I navigated the torturous bridge traffic. "Thanks," I mumbled through a sticky mouthful, and he reached out to wipe a crumb from the corner of my mouth. Our eyes met and held, and I felt the blood rush to my cheeks as I saw the desire in his gaze.

"Um, Morgan?" Robbie said from the backseat. "The road is that way." He pointed through the windshield.

Still flushed, I wrenched my attention back to the road and tried to ignore what being so close to Hunter was doing to all my nerve endings. But I couldn't help wondering what it would be like to stay with him in Bree's father's apartment.

Mr. Warren was a successful lawyer with clients in the city and upstate New York. I knew his city apartment was in the East Twenties. Even if we weren't going to have the place to ourselves, being in a New York City apartment with Hunter seemed wildly romantic. I pictured us in the master bedroom, gazing out at a night view of the Manhattan skyline.

And then what? I asked myself with a twinge of alarm. Hunter, sensing it, took his hand off my thigh. "What's wrong?" he asked.

"Nothing," I said quickly.

"Are you sure?"

"Um—I'm not really ready to talk about it," I said.

"Fair enough." I could feel Hunter deliberately turning his senses away from me, leaving me to examine my own thoughts in peace.

Cal had been my first boyfriend. He'd been so beautiful, so charismatic and seductive. Not only that, he'd introduced me to magick and all its beauty. He'd told me we were *mùirn beatha dàns*, soul mates. And I'd wanted to believe him. Every fiber of my being had wanted to be with him, yet I hadn't felt ready for the final step of going to bed with him. Now I wondered if part of me had known all along that Cal was lying to me, manipulating me. It made my grief for him into a more complicated thing, layered with resentment and anger.

But Hunter was different. I loved him, trusted him, and was completely, soul-shakingly attracted to him. So why did it scare me to think about actually sleeping with him? I glanced in the rearview mirror, studying my friends. Robbie was a virgin like me, but I was pretty sure that wouldn't last long, now that he and Bree were together. He wanted her desperately. I didn't know about Sky, but I knew that Bree had lost her virginity in the tenth grade, and Raven—well, I couldn't imagine Raven *ever* being a virgin.

What was wrong with me, that I was seventeen and still so inexperienced?

"You'll want to take the next exit," Hunter murmured, and I was grateful for the gentle prompt. I merged into the traffic on the Harlem River Drive, and we swept across the top of Manhattan to the FDR Drive and the East River.

Quite suddenly the open view of the winter sky disappeared. The air became tinged with gray, and billboards and tall brick projects rose to my right. The traffic, already slow, became stop and go; impatient drivers leaned on horns. A van in front of me spewed a cloud of black exhaust. I caught a glimpse of lead-gray river water to my left, with industrial buildings on the far side. A taxi driver yelled unintelligibly at me as he passed on the right.

I felt a surge of raw, boisterous energy. We were in the city.

2

Searching

March 3, 1977

My wedding garments are laid out. The white robe embroidered in gold with the runes to summon power. The belt woven of gold and crimson threads. The groom's wristbands, beaten gold set with rubies, that I inherit from Grania's father. Everything is spelled with charms for strength and fertility, with protections against whatever might harm us, with blessings for wealth and long life.

I wonder about love, though. Grania teases me, saying that nothing truly touches my heart, and maybe she's right. I know I don't love her, though I'm fond of her.

Yet my mind lingers on last summer's fling with that American Woodbane, Selene. Now, I know that wasn't love, but Goddess, it *was exciting, the most intense experience I've ever had. And that includes all the times I've been with Grania. Still, Grania is a pretty thing and very pliant. And she's strong in her magick. Our children will be powerful, and that's the most important thing. Power. Woodbane power.*

So why do I hesitate as I prepare for our wedding? And why do I keep dreaming of that damned white dress?

—Neimhidh

Bree's father's apartment was on Park Avenue and Twenty-second Street. Bree gave directions, and I maneuvered Das Boot off the FDR, across Twenty-third Street, and finally onto Park and into the garage beneath the building.

The garage attendant gave me a strange look as we pulled in. With its two front quarter panels covered with gray body filler, its slate blue hood and shiny new metal bumper, Das Boot was not looking its most sophisticated.

Bree cranked down her window and spoke to the guard. "We're guests of Mr. Warren in apartment thirty-sixty," she said. "He's arranged for a guest pass."

The guard checked a computer screen and let us in. The garage was filled with BMWs, Jags, Mercedes, and top-of-the-line SUVs.

I patted Das Boot on its piebald fender. "You're good for this place," I told it. "They need to see how the other half drives."

"It's the perfect city car," Robbie assured me. "No one would ever try to steal it."

Loaded down with bags, we walked to the elevator. Bree

hit the button for the thirtieth floor, and I felt Hunter clasp my hand. This was so glamorous, like something in a movie.

Raven smiled at Sky. "This is very cool. I love the city."

Sky smiled back at her. "Think I could persuade you to visit the Cloisters?"

"Hell, yes," Raven said. "It's a medieval museum, right? I love that stuff."

The elevator opened, and we walked down a narrow hallway to the apartment at the very end. Mr. Warren opened the door before we knocked. Like Bree, he was tall, slender, and very good-looking. He was dressed in an elegantly tailored suit and silk tie.

"Come on in," he said. He pointed to a little video monitor by the door that revealed the thirtieth-floor hallway. "I saw you arrive." He pecked Bree on the cheek, then gave me a smile. "Hello, Morgan. Haven't seen you in a while."

"Hi, Mr. Warren," I mumbled. He had always made me a little nervous.

He hit a button, and the scene on the monitor switched to the garage. Another button showed us the building's lobby and doorman. "I've told the security people that you'll be here through Monday," he said. "Did you have a good trip?"

Bree stretched. "Perfect. Morgan drove. I slept most of the way. Oh, Dad, you've met Robbie, Raven, and Sky. And this is Hunter Niall, Sky's cousin. I've mentioned him to you."

I wondered what, exactly, Bree had told her father. Did he know that Hunter and Sky were witches, that his own daughter practiced Wicca? Probably not, I decided. Mr. Warren was a pretty hands-off parent. Half the time he was in New

York City instead of Widow's Vale, and even when he was home, Bree didn't have a curfew, didn't have to be home for dinner by a certain time, didn't have to call to say where she was. My parents had been a little leery of letting me come on this trip because of that.

Mr. Warren glanced at his watch. "I'm afraid I've got to run, kids. Meeting. Bree, I've left a couple of extra keys in the kitchen. Show everyone around and help yourself to whatever's in the fridge. You can sleep anywhere except my room. I've got a dinner out on Long Island tonight, so I won't be back until quite late." He brushed her cheek with a kiss and reached into the hall closet for his coat. "Enjoy the city!"

When he was gone, Bree smiled and said, "Come on, let me give you the grand tour."

The grand tour took all of two minutes. Mr. Warren's apartment consisted of a decent-size living room whose windows looked out over Park Avenue, a master bedroom, a small study, an even smaller guest room, a bathroom, and a tiny efficiency kitchen.

Everybody oohed and aahed, but I couldn't help feeling disappointed, and I suspected the others did, too. Bree had told us the apartment had only two bedrooms, but somehow I'd expected something bigger, grander. Privacy was going to be tough.

"Nice," Robbie said at last. "Great location."

"One bathroom?" Raven sounded incredulous. "For seven of us?"

Bree shrugged. "It's Manhattan. Space is at a premium. Actually, this place is huge by Manhattan standards."

"I like the decor," Sky said. "It's simple."

That was an understatement, I thought. Like the Warrens' Widow's Vale house, the apartment was austere. The walls were white, the upholstery, muted neutrals. The furniture was light and spare, with an L-shaped couch, a coffee table, and a flat-screen TV the only furniture in the living room. One painting hung on the north wall, an abstract block of brown fading into tan against a white canvas. There were no knickknacks, no photographs or vases. The room didn't feel very lived in.

We dropped our bags in a pile next to the couch. Hunter stood by the windows. In faded jeans that hung loose on his hips and an oversize wheat-colored sweater, he looked vaguely bohemian and wholly beautiful. The light made his eyes turn a deep jade. In the time that I'd known him, I'd spent an inordinate amount of time thinking about Hunter's eyes. Sometimes they were the color of spring grass, sometimes the color of the sea.

"What's the plan, then?" Sky asked Hunter.

"It's just after ten," Hunter said. He hadn't bothered to check a clock. His witch senses included an uncanny sense of time. "I need to call on some people," he went on. Briefly he explained his mission to the others.

"Oh, right," Raven said sarcastically. "No problem."

"Hey, I lost a needle in a haystack last week," Bree chimed in. "Think you could find that for me? You know, when you've got a second."

"Do you want help?" Sky asked Hunter quietly, and I had to suppress an irrational surge of jealousy. She's his cousin, I reminded myself. They look out for each other.

Hunter glanced at me with a very slight smile, and I knew

he'd noticed my reaction. "No," he told Sky. "Not for this part of it, anyway. It will be easier for me to get people to talk if I'm on my own. We'll meet back here before dinner. Say, six o'clock?"

"Works for me," said Raven. "There are some stores near St. Mark's Place I want to check out. Anyone want to come?"

Sky, Bree, and Robbie signed on for the St. Mark's excursion. I decided to stay at the apartment, my excuse being that I wanted to rest for a bit after the drive. Actually, I had a secret mission of my own in the city. I needed to come up with a plan of action.

When the others had left, I went to the wide double window that looked out over Park Avenue. I could feel the city humming beneath me, people in cars and buses and taxicabs; pedestrians and bicycle messengers. I felt a twinge of regret that I wasn't down there on the streets with the others. But I had work to do.

I opened my backpack and took out a book bound in dark red cloth and a dagger with an intricately carved ivory handle. They were part of my inheritance, the Book of Shadows and the athame, or ceremonial dagger, that had belonged to my birth mother, Maeve Riordan. The rest of her witch's tools were back in Widow's Vale, hidden in my house.

I settled myself on Mr. Warren's living room floor and opened the Book of Shadows to an entry dated April 1982, a few months after Maeve and Angus Bramson, my birth father, arrived in America. They'd fled Ireland when their coven, Belwicket, was destroyed by something called the dark wave, a deadly concentration of dark energies. Maeve and Angus were the only survivors.

With nothing left in Ireland and a clear sense that they were being hunted, Maeve and Angus came to New York City. Eventually they left the city and settled upstate, an hour or two north of Widow's Vale, in a tiny town called Meshomah Falls.

The entry on the page I'd turned to talked about how unhappy Maeve was in her Hell's Kitchen flat. She felt Manhattan was a place cut off from the pulse of the earth. It made her grief for all she'd lost that much sharper.

I held the athame to the page covered with Maeve's handwriting. Slowly I passed the age-worn silver blade over the blue ink, and as I did, pinpricks of light began to form a different set of words entirely. It was one of Maeve's secret entries.

I have been staring at this gold watch for hours, as though it were a gift from the Goddess herself. I never should have brought it with me from Ireland. Oh, it's a beautiful object, passed down through the ages from one lover to another. Were I to cast my senses, I know I could feel generations of love and desire radiating from it. But it was given to me by Ciaran. If Angus ever saw it, it would break him.

Ciaran gave it to me the night we pledged ourselves to each other. He said that if you place it beneath the house, the tick of the watch will keep the hearts beating within steady and faithful. Is my holding on to it a selfish hope that Ciaran somehow will find his way back into my life? I must not even think such thoughts. I've chosen to live my life with Angus, and that's all there is to it.

Next month Angus and I will leave this dreadful city for a new home upstate. I must end this heartsick madness now. I can't bring myself to destroy the watch, but I won't take it, either. Angus and I will move on. The watch will stay here.

Ciaran had been Maeve's *mùirn beatha dàn*, but he had lied to her, betrayed her. And then, years later, long after she'd rejected him, he had found her and Angus in Meshomah Falls, where he'd trapped them in an abandoned barn and set fire to it. She was pure goodness, he pure evil. How could she have loved him? It was unfathomable. Yet . . . yet I'd loved Cal, who had nearly killed me the same way Ciaran killed Maeve.

I needed to know more. I needed to understand, as much to silence my questions about myself as to know Maeve more fully.

When we'd made the plan to come to New York, it had dawned on me that while we were there, I'd be only a subway ride from where Maeve and Angus had lived. If I could find their apartment, then maybe, just maybe, I'd find the watch. Maeve had said she was leaving it behind, after all. I knew the odds were heavily against its still being there—it had been almost twenty years ago, and even if she'd hidden the watch, surely someone would have found it. Still, I couldn't let the idea go. I wasn't even sure why I was so obsessed with the watch. Morbid fascination? I needed to see it, hold it.

Of course, I realized that anything touched by Ciaran was tainted, even potentially dangerous. Which was why I hadn't mentioned the watch to Hunter or anyone. Hunter would never approve of my doing anything remotely risky. But I had to try to find it.

I tucked the athame and the Book of Shadows back into my pack. At home I'd tried scrying with fire for Maeve's old Manhattan address. All I'd seen was a vision of the inside of a dingy apartment. Granted, most witches considered fire the most difficult medium with which to scry, but I had a natural connection to it, another gift from Maeve. But what the fire revealed was only a second cousin to what I asked for, close but not quite right. Was I doing it wrong?

It was doubly frustrating because just before Yule, I'd undergone a ceremony called *tàth meànma brach* with Alyce Fernbrake, the blood witch who ran Practical Magick, an occult store near Widow's Vale. *Tàth meànma* is a kind of Wiccan mind meld, where one witch enters another's mind.

Tàth meànma brach takes it one step further: it's an exchange of all you have inside you. Alyce gave me access to her memories, her loves and heartbreaks, her years of study and knowledge. In turn I gave her access to the ancestral memories that flowed through me from Maeve and her mother Mackenna before her.

I came out of the *tàth meànma brach* with a much deeper knowledge of magick. Without it I'd never have stood a chance against Selene. It had focused me, connected me to the earth so powerfully that for almost two days afterward I'd felt almost like I was hallucinating.

Since then I'd gotten more used to the infusion of knowledge I'd received from Alyce. I wasn't conscious of it all the time. It was more like I'd been given a filing cabinet chock-full of files. When I needed a certain piece of knowledge, all I had to do was check my files.

Of course, the knowledge in those files was specific to Alyce. For example, I now had a wonderful sense of how to work with herbs and plants. Unfortunately, scrying wasn't Alyce's strong point. That meant I had to resort to more mundane means to find out where Maeve and Angus had lived.

In Mr. Warren's study I found a Manhattan phone book. I got the address for the city's Bureau of Records, then consulted a subway map Mr. Warren had left out for us. The bureau was near City Hall. The number 6 train would get me there.

I'd just put on my coat and scarf and grabbed one of Mr. Warren's spare keys when the door to the apartment opened and Bree came in.

"Hey," she said.

"Hey, yourself. Where is everyone?"

"I left them in an East Village art gallery. There's some kind of performance going on involving a stone pyramid, two dancers dressed in aluminum foil, and a giant ball of string. Robbie was mesmerized," she said with a laugh. "Are you going out?"

I hesitated. I didn't want to lie to Bree, but I didn't want to tell her about my quest for Maeve's watch, either. I was afraid she'd try to talk me out of it. "I was going to run a few errands," I said vaguely. "And I thought we could use some candles for Saturday night's circle. You're sure your dad doesn't mind us having a circle in his apartment?"

"He probably wouldn't, but he'll never know," Bree assured me. "He's seeing some woman who lives in

Connecticut, and he's going out to her place this weekend."
She pulled out her wallet and checked for cash. "I'm going to
stock up on some food—if I know my dad, his idea of food in
the house is one wedge of gourmet cheese, a jar of imported
olives, and a bag of ground coffee."

Bree's prediction was accurate except for the cheese,
which was nonexistent. "Why don't we go together?" she
suggested. "I know all the good stores in the neighborhood."

"Sure," I said. I realized I was glad of the chance to spend
a little normal time with Bree, even though it would delay my
trip to the Bureau of Records.

Bree and I had been best friends since we were little kids.
That, like nearly everything else, had changed this past fall
when Cal Blaire came into our lives. Bree fell for him, Cal
chose me, and we'd had a horrible fight and stopped speaking to each other. For a hideous couple of months we were
enemies. But on the night that Cal tried to kill me, Bree had
helped save my life.

Since then we'd begun to rebuild our friendship. We
hadn't yet found our way back to being completely easy with
each other. On the one hand, she was the friend I knew and
loved best. On the other, I'd learned there were parts of Bree
I didn't know at all.

Besides, I was different now. Since I'd learned I was a blood
witch, I'd been through experiences that were both amazing
and horrifying. Once Bree and I had shared everything. Now
there was a huge part of my life she could never understand.

We walked toward Irving Place. The wind was brisk
and cold. I gave myself a moment to adjust to being on
the streets, massive buildings towering overhead, people

hurrying by. It was as if New York moved at a pace faster and more intense than the rest of the world. It felt both intimidating and wonderful.

"Pretty cool, huh?" Bree said.

"It feels like we're light-years away from Widow's Vale."

"We are," Bree said with a grin.

"So . . . things are good between you and Robbie?" I asked.

"I guess," she said, her grin fading. We went into a supermarket. Bree grabbed a basket, headed for the deli counter, and ordered macaroni salad and sliced turkey breast.

"You guess? You two seemed pretty much in sync on the drive down."

"We were," she said. She shrugged. "But that doesn't mean anything."

"Why not?"

She gave me a look that made me feel like I was seven.

"What?" I asked. "What's wrong with Robbie?"

"Nothing. We get along great. That's the problem."

We moved to the aisle with chips and sodas, and I tried to make sense of what Bree had just said. I'd seen Bree break up with dozens of guys for all kinds of reasons. One was too self-absorbed; another too controlling. One bad-mouthed everyone; another couldn't talk about anything except tennis. One guy was such a lousy kisser that Bree got depressed just looking at his lips.

"Okay," I finally said. "Maybe I'm dense, but what is the problem with a relationship in which the two people get along great?"

"Simple," she said. "If you love someone, you can get hurt. If you don't, you can't."

"So?"

"So . . . Robbie wants us to be in love. But I don't want to fall in love with Robbie. Too risky."

"Bree, that's ridiculous," I said.

She grabbed a bottle of Diet Coke and turned to me, anger flickering in her dark eyes. "Is it?" she said. "You loved Cal, and look where it got you."

I stood there, stunned. She could be so cruel sometimes. That was one of the things I hadn't really realized about her until our falling-out.

"I'm sorry," she said quickly. "I—I didn't mean that."

"You did," I said, struggling to keep my voice calm.

"Okay, maybe I did," she admitted. The hand that held the basket was trembling. "But I also meant that loving some-one—really opening your heart to them—is just asking to have your heart smashed and handed back to you in little pieces. I mean, love is great for selling perfume. But the real thing, Morgan? It just trashes everything."

"Do you really believe that?" I demanded.

"Yes," she said in a flat voice. She turned and strode down the aisle.

"Bree, wait," I called, hurrying down the aisle after her.

I caught up to her at a rack full of assorted potato chips. She was staring at them with a frown, apparently concentrating on just which flavor was the most desirable.

"Is this all because of your parents?" I asked in a tactful, subtle way. Bree's parents had split up when she was twelve. It had been ugly—Bree's mom had run off to Europe with her tennis instructor. Bree had been shattered.

Now she shrugged. "My parents are just one example among many," she said. "Look, it's not really that big a deal. I'm just not into the whole love thing right now, that's all. I'm too young. I'd just rather have fun."

I could tell the subject was closed, and I felt a pang as the realization of how far apart we'd been pulled hit me yet again.

I sighed. "Listen, there's somewhere I need to go. I'll be back in a couple of hours."

Bree looked at me, and I could read regret on her face, too. Once she would have asked where I was going, and I would have invited her along.

"I'll get the candles and some salt for the circle," she said. "Sure you'll be okay on your own?"

"Yeah," I said. "I'll see you later."

3

Witch Dance

September 6, 1977

My son was born ten days ago, and I know I should be the proud, happy da. The boy is big and healthy—but Goddess, he's a loud, needy little bugger and Grania's still so fat. When will she get back to normal? And when will someone pay some bloody attention to me for a change?

Tonight, after little Kyle screamed his lungs out for three solid hours ("Poor wee thing has colic," Grania said, as if that made it bearable), I couldn't take it anymore. I went out to the pub and had myself a few pints and a good sulk. On the way home a bony old cat dashed straight in front of me and I toppled onto someone's rubbish left out for the trash man. I didn't even think about it. I muttered a spell and blasted the damn cat. I couldn't see it die, just heard its scream in the darkness. Now

I feel a fool. I know better than to vent my spleen in such a childish way.

—Neimhidh

I found my way to the Lexington Avenue subway line, bought a MetroCard, checked my route with the map posted in the station, and was soon speeding south beneath the city streets. I'd ridden the subway a couple of times before with my family. My sister, Mary K., hated it, but I loved the speed, the relentless rhythm. It felt like I was surging through the city's veins, being propelled by the beat of its heart.

I emerged from the subway at the City Hall stop. With a bit of asking around I found the Bureau of Records and the fifth-floor office where records of the city's rental properties were kept.

The air smelled of old paper, the floors of ammonia. A wooden bench lined the wall by the door. Half a dozen people sat on it, a few reading, the rest staring into space with glazed eyes and blank expressions.

I walked up to the counter at the front of the room. Behind it were stacks of shelves filled with ledgers bound in black. A clerk stood behind a computer on the counter.

"Excuse me," I began.

She pointed at a sign that said Please Take a Number. So I took a number from a dispenser and sat down on the bench next to a man with a thick mustache. "Have you been waiting long?" I asked.

"I've spent less time waiting in line at the DMV," he told me.

I took that as a yes, but since there were only seven

people ahead of me, I figured the wait couldn't be too long. I was wrong. The clerk not only moved in excruciatingly slow motion whenever she was actually helping anyone, but she seemed to need lengthy breaks between finishing with one person and calling the next.

The minutes ticked on. I tapped my fingers on my leg, trying not to let dark images creep into my mind—images of Cal being struck by the bolt of dark magick, of his body lying there on the floor of Selene's study. Since that horrible day, those pictures often came to haunt me in moments when I wasn't actively thinking about something else.

I distracted myself by reciting—under my breath—the properties of all the healing plants I knew. After that I went through rocks and minerals. Then I began counting the tiles in the floor, the cracks in the ceiling, the scuff marks on the plastic chairs. If only I'd thought to bring a book.

It was almost two hours later when my number was called. "I'm trying to find the address of an apartment that was rented by Maeve Riordan and Angus Bramson in 1982," I explained.

The clerk looked at me like I'd just asked her to sprout wings. "That's not possible," she said. "This system doesn't find apartments by the tenants' names. You give me the address, then I can tell you who lived there."

"All I know is it was somewhere in Hell's Kitchen," I said.

She tapped fuchsia nails against the counter. "Then you're out of luck," she told me. "There are hundreds of apartments in Hell's Kitchen. I can't be searching every building listing for the Bransons."

"It's Bramson and Riordan," I corrected her, trying not to

lose the few shreds of patience I had left. "Isn't there some kind of quick computer search you can do?"

She glanced at her computer. "Program's not set up that way."

I glanced at the rows of ledgers behind her. There were dates on the spines. "Do you think I could look through the 1982 books?" I asked.

"Not without a note from my supervisor, and she's on vacation for the next two weeks." The woman gave me a malicious smile. "Why don't you come back in February?" she suggested.

"I won't be here in February," I protested.

She started typing on the keyboard. I'd been dismissed.

I turned toward the door. Then I turned back again. If this woman wanted to play a power game, I decided angrily, I'd be happy to play, too. And I'd win. I hesitated only a moment, though I knew I was about to do something I wasn't supposed to do. Well, city employees weren't supposed to be totally unhelpful, either, I reasoned.

I licked my lips and glanced around. The only person still waiting on the bench was a worn-looking elderly man who dozed as he sat. He wouldn't notice anything.

I used a very simple spell, one of the first that Cal had taught me, one I had used to retrieve Maeve's tools. "I'm invisible," I whispered. "You see me not. I am but a shadow."

The spell didn't really make me invisible. It simply made me unnoticeable, trivial. When I used it, people would focus on other things instead of me. I jumped up and down a few times to see if it had worked. The clerk didn't react, so I summoned my nerve and walked behind the counter. I hesitated when I reached for the first 1982 volume. Even if the spell made me unnoticeable, I wasn't sure it would do the same for the book.

I focused on the clerk's computer. Electricity was a form of energy and, as Hunter had taught me, energy was fairly easy to manipulate. I sent out my own energy, focusing until I picked up the emanations from the motherboard. Then I sent my energy into it, forcing the electric current into a series of irregular spikes.

"Damn, what is wrong with this machine?" the woman muttered.

Quickly I flipped open the 1982 book to the addresses in the West Forties and began scanning the cramped columns. On the seventh page I found it: Bramson. 788 W. 49th Street, Apt. 3.

I glanced at the clerk's computer screen. Lines were flickering madly across it. Quietly I replaced the book and started out of the office.

The clerk looked up as she heard me open the door. "You," she said, sounding surprised. "I thought you'd left."

I smiled at her. "You were a real help," I said. "Thanks."

I hurried out, enjoying her look of blank confusion.

As I waited for the subway that would take me back to the apartment, I wondered if the clerk's computer had recovered. Even if it was permanently fried, I had no regrets. Okay, I'd used my magick on an unsuspecting person, something I wasn't supposed to do—but she'd deserved it. Besides, I hadn't hurt her.

I knew, of course, that if Hunter ever found out what I'd done, he'd be angry. But this situation had been special. Using magick to get my birth mother's address seemed justified. No real damage had been done, and I'd gotten the necessary results.

I felt good. My magick was growing stronger and more sure, and I loved it.

That evening we ate dinner at a bustling diner on lower Second Avenue. All six of us were squeezed into a booth with red vinyl seats. Hunter was on one side of me, Robbie on the other.

"So, what does everyone want to do tonight?" Bree asked.

"I've always wanted to walk across the Brooklyn Bridge," said Robbie. "It must be gorgeous at night when you can see all the lights of Manhattan."

Bree waved a dismissive hand. "Excellent way to get mugged. Besides, it's freezing."

"Actually, I've got a lead I need to pursue," Hunter said. "There's a club not too far from here, a bit of a hangout for witches, and I'm told one of the DJs might know something about Amyranth. How would you all feel about going to a dance club?"

Raven grinned at Sky. "I could live with that."

Sky nodded, Bree said, "Sounds good," and Robbie said, "Cool."

I was the only one who seemed to have mixed feelings about going. On the one hand, I was dying to go to a cool New York club, especially one where other witches hung out. But on the other, I was terrified I'd be rejected at the door, or if I actually got in, everyone would know I was from the boonies. Besides, I've always been too self-conscious to enjoy dancing.

"I have one condition, though," Hunter went on. "If we go to this club and someone asks where you're from, just say upstate. Also, no one says anything about Selene and Cal. I don't want any of you associated with what happened to them."

Raven made a face. "Do you have to get all cloak-and-dagger on us?"

I saw Sky stiffen. Hunter, though, merely said, "We don't take risks with each other's safety." His voice was quiet but firm.

Raven looked away. "Forget I said anything."

"Fine," Hunter agreed, and let the subject drop.

The club was in the East Village, just beyond Avenue C. On the way over, Hunter hooked his arm through mine, and I felt absurdly happy. When we reached Avenue C, he nodded toward a large industrial building with big, opaque glass windows. "That's it," he said.

A husky guy in black jeans and a black leather jacket stood in front of a rope at the door. I was suddenly nervous again. "What if they don't let us in?" I asked.

"They'll let us in," Hunter said with the assurance of the effortlessly beautiful.

It occurred to me that I was the only one in our group who might have trouble. Bree was gorgeous, and Robbie was, too. Raven definitely made a fashion statement. As for Hunter and Sky, in addition to their luminous blond hair, fine, even features, and cheekbones to die for, they had a certain indefinable cool. I'm not ugly or anything, but I don't stand out, either. My hair, which I actually like, was in a single, messy braid. Plus I'd dressed for the cold, not a trendy club.

But the time for worrying was over. We were suddenly at

the door and the bouncer was opening the rope for us, with a nod to Hunter.

I felt a burst of triumph. I almost blurted, I did it. I got in! Oh God, I thought, I'm such a nerd.

"I didn't realize you were the club type," I said to Hunter.

"I'm not," he assured me with a smile as we walked into an enormous room. Near the door was a bar that opened onto a vast dance floor where two DJs were spinning house music. At the far end of the room I saw an area with cozy bench seats. Hunter pointed to it. "The café serves cappuccino and pastries. Want something?"

I shook my head. "Not yet."

We checked our coats. I gazed at my clothes doubtfully. Faded brown cords, one of my dad's oversize wool sweaters, heavy, winter hiking boots. Clearly I hadn't been thinking straight when I'd packed for this trip.

"There's someone I need to talk with," Hunter said in my ear. "Do you mind if I leave you on your own for a few minutes?"

"No, of course not," I said, though I did mind. I was feeling more insecure and provincial by the second.

Hunter blended into the crowd. I tried not to feel irked by the fact that Sky went with him, no questions asked. I stood there, trying to look casual and feeling completely out of my element.

I walked back to the edge of the dance floor. In an effort to stop focusing on my insecurities, I opened up and let my senses explore.

There was a thick, throbbing feel to the air. After a moment I realized it wasn't just the music—the club was actually pulsing with magick. I'd never felt anything like it before. There must be dozens of blood witches here, I thought. I could pinpoint a few of them even in this crowd, not so much because of what they were doing, but because power streamed out from them in a way that was almost tangible.

Most of the blood witches I knew must keep their power damped down, I realized suddenly. But not these people. Not the tall, thin African American man with the shaved head who stood on a low stage, dancing. The skinny kid in the oversize green suit. The sleek, blond woman in the low-cut, slithery dress and her dance partner, a rangy, loose-limbed guy with a beard. I frowned. Wow. There seemed to be some kind of weird psychic duel going on between the two of them. I could practically see the crackling energy that passed between them. Another woman, with long gray hair and the most extraordinary amber jewelry, danced by herself. She was surrounded by an aura of deep, vibrant green—it was so strong that I wondered if even those who weren't blood witches could see it.

Cal came to my mind again, unbidden. He would have loved this, I thought sadly, all these beautiful witches using their magick so freely. He would have felt at home here.

Robbie came up to me, looking slightly stunned. "Is it just me, or is there something weird in the air here?" he shouted over the throbbing drums and bass.

Well, that answered my question. "It's not you," I told him. "It's magick. A lot of these people are blood witches."

"I think I'm a little out of my depth," he murmured.

"Me too," I admitted. Seeing the downcast look on his face, I asked, "Where's Bree?"

Robbie gestured silently toward the café. I spotted Bree talking to a tall, handsome man with copper-colored hair. As we watched, she turned to a younger guy, maybe seventeen or so, and with a hand on his arm she drew him into the conversation, giving him a teasing smile.

Robbie groaned. "Tell me the truth, Morgan. Am I a masochist or simply out of my mind? I mean, why do I even bother?"

"I know it looks bad," I said, trying not to get angry at Bree, "but I really don't think it means anything."

"Well, it feels awful," Robbie said. "It—" He was cut off when a girl wearing body glitter, a gold sports top, and tiny little gold shorts took his hand. "Dance with me?" she asked.

Robbie gulped, nodded, and let himself be led out onto the dance floor.

My senses were wide open now, trying to process the stunning array of magick. One guy in particular caught my eye. He was probably nineteen or twenty, with a muscular body and glossy, dark brown hair that fell to his shoulders. He was heading toward Raven, who stood near me, and there was something reckless and confident in his eyes. He wasn't exactly gorgeous, but he was very sexy. And I could sense his power from yards away. He was strong.

Then, to my shock, he stopped in front of me. "Don't I know you from somewhere?" he asked with a frown.

Was that a pickup line? I wondered, slightly panicked. Or did he really know me? Come to think of it, there was something vaguely familiar about him, too. . . .

"Um—I've never been here before," I said cautiously.

"Hmmm. Well, stop looking so impressed," he said with a

grin. "These New York witches all think they're so hot. It's not healthy to encourage them. Besides"—his eyes raked me appraisingly— "I reckon you're worth the lot of them."

Before I could figure out how to respond to that, he walked past me to Raven, stopped in front of her, and said, "There you are, love. I've been waiting for you."

Raven glanced at him in surprise. His grin got even wider, and he pulled her onto the dance floor.

I recognized a familiar presence behind me. Sky. There was nothing sloppy about Sky's being or her power. Everything about her was clear, precise, and honed, like an elegant arrow.

"So, what do you think of this place?" Sky asked.

"It's . . . intense."

She looked at me and laughed. "That's a good word for it. There are more blood witches here than you may ever see in one place again. Some of them highly eccentric."

"What do you mean?" I asked. Sky knew so much about the world I'd only recently come to be part of.

She nodded toward a woman spinning in place to the beat, one arm stretched high overhead. "That one, for instance. She'll only cast spells that involve using nightshade. And he," she said, gesturing toward a small, dark-haired man at the bar, "spent years living in a cave on the coast of Scotland."

"Why?"

"Teaching himself to work with the sea. He's remarkable at scrying with water. And he has a strong affinity for the ocean and its creatures."

"Sky, *ma chère*." A tall, elegant woman in a silver gown came up, kissed Sky on both cheeks, and began a rapid exchange in French.

I watched, slightly awed.

"That's Mathilde," Sky said as the Frenchwoman moved on. "Sorry I didn't introduce you, but she was in a hurry. She's got an amazing greenhouse on her roof. Every herb a witch could want."

"How do you know all these people?" I asked.

"Some I know from Europe. Others I met coming here with Hunter," she explained. "This is a good place for him to make connections."

I glanced around but didn't see Hunter's blond hair anywhere.

Sky answered my unasked question. "He's upstairs, talking to some people. Trying to get leads."

A shout drew our attention back to the dance floor, where a space had opened around Raven and her partner. They were doing some kind of dance that involved a lot of athletic gyrating and shimmying.

I glanced at Sky. Her face was blank, neutral, but her eyes never left Raven and her partner. As if conscious of her gaze, the wild guy looked straight at her and laughed.

I felt sudden sympathy for Sky. "Don't let them upset you." As the words left my mouth, I was shocked at my own presumptuousness. Me, consoling Sky?

But she simply gave me a rueful half smile. "I'll get over it. Raven has to be who she is."

She nodded toward Robbie and the gorgeous girl dancing with him. Robbie looked mystified by the attention.

"He still doesn't understand how attractive he is," Sky said. "I wonder if Bree does."

Bree was still standing in the café, three men around her, but her gaze was focused across the floor on Robbie.

"Maybe she's starting to," I said.

Hunter came up behind me then, and I felt a thrill along my nerve endings as he rested his hands lightly on my hips. "How are you doing?" he asked.

"I'm a little overwhelmed," I answered, turning to face him.

He gave me an apologetic smile. "I should have prepared you."

"No, it's okay. Sky's orienting me. It's . . . fascinating. I just didn't expect it."

"Yes, well, meet your people," he said wryly.

"Did you talk to the DJ?" Sky wanted to know.

Hunter nodded. "If he knows anything, he's not telling. But I did find someone who used to date a member of Amyranth. He'll talk to me, but not here. I've arranged to meet him tomorrow at a ridiculous hour of the morning, at the most inconvenient, out-of-the-way place he could think of." He gave Sky a grin. "Sorry. I know you're not a morning person. But I really need you with me. This one sounds like he might give me some trouble."

Sky nodded. "Fine. Just promise you'll buy me a coffee."

My rational, mathematical self told me I was being silly—Hunter was keeping me out for my own safety—but I couldn't help feeling irked at the way they both just took it for granted that Sky was the one who helped Hunter, that the two of them were a team, while I was just a bumbling novice who had to be kept out of harm's way. It wasn't fair—especially not now. It was *my* dream that had started this, after all.

A black light flared above us, turning Hunter's white shirt neon purple, his hair a bright silky lavender. He kissed me lightly on the mouth. "I've got to go now, but I'll be back. Dance, why don't you?"

"Oh, thank you very much," I muttered. "You know how much I love dancing. Especially alone."

But he was already moving past me to have a quick whispered conference with Sky, which did nothing to improve my mood. Then he headed off toward the stage. The tall African American man pointed at Hunter with a knowing grin, then made his way down from the stage to talk to him. I had to admit, it was impressive seeing how at ease Hunter was with so many people. I knew I could never extract information from strangers like that.

Sky drifted back toward me, and I had the feeling that Hunter had told her to look out for me. My irritation deepened. Luckily I was relieved of the need to make awkward conversation by Robbie, who came up to us looking sweaty and exhausted. "Man, that girl can move," he said, waving at his partner. He blinked in surprise as a waitress approached him with a glass of wine balanced on a round tray.

"The lady over there"—she indicated a tall woman with long, ebony hair who was dressed entirely in leather—"sends it to you with her compliments."

"Uh, tell her thanks, would you?" Robbie sounded flustered. "But I don't drink."

"I'll tell her," the waitress said reluctantly. "But if you don't want to offend her—and I'd advise you not to—you won't send the wine back."

Robbie smiled weakly at the woman in leather and took the glass of wine.

I gave a low whistle. "You're getting a lot of attention tonight." I peeked covertly at Bree and was glad to see that she hadn't missed the exchange with Leather Woman, either.

She'd stopped even pretending to flirt with the guys around her and was just standing there, looking sulky.

Robbie, however, didn't look pleased. "It's a little freaky. Two witches have asked me out tonight."

"You have something against us?" I teased him.

"Not you," he said seriously. "But apart from the fact that I'm in love with Bree, I want a relationship of equals, not someone who can put spells on me without my even knowing."

I winced. When I was just getting acquainted with Wicca, I'd given Robbie a spelled potion to help heal his acne, which had been really out of control. It had done the job—in fact, it had more than done the job; it had gone so far as to correct his terrible eyesight—but Robbie had been upset with me for doing magick on him without telling him.

"What is his problem?" Sky said suddenly. Her eyes were on Raven and the long-haired guy. "Is he a complete exhibitionist?"

I looked, too. The guy had taken off his shirt. His body was thin but looked hard and well muscled.

Raven sent an amused glance toward Sky, as if to say, Do you believe this? Her dancing partner put his hands on her butt and pulled her close, and then pinwheels of colored light were raining down around them, and Raven was laughing, trying to catch one in her hand. The guy traced a sign in the air, and three of them rested on her palm.

I couldn't suppress a gasp. I was half appalled at his recklessness, half delighted by his clever, beautiful magick.

"Oh, man," Robbie muttered. "What is that?"

"It's showy and irresponsible, that's what it is," Sky said, sounding angry. "That cocky little bugger. Anyone could be watching him."

Raven and the guy were dancing close now, grinding pelvises. "That's enough," Sky said, and strode toward them. I saw her take Raven's arm and say something in her ear.

"Maybe I'd better go find Bree," Robbie said with a sigh. "If she hasn't already left with someone else."

"She wouldn't do that," I told him.

"You don't think so?" Robbie's smile was sad as he moved away. It made me want to shake Bree. She really liked Robbie. Why couldn't she just let things happen with him?

I headed for the café and got a Diet Coke. Then I looked around for Hunter. Nowhere in sight. I sighed, too, and tried not to feel too much like a wallflower.

A woman in a short black dress sauntered up to me. "Don't be so self-conscious, *chica*," she said. She was beautiful, with coffee-colored skin and black hair that framed her face in waves. "All this energy spent thinking you are not beautiful enough, not good enough. It's a waste. You must take all this healing energy you have and make a salve for your own heart, no? Life is too short to be so hard on yourself."

I stood there, blinking stupidly. She was gazing into my eyes, into my soul, and I felt stripped, vulnerable.

"Um . . . excuse me," I said. "I have to go."

I shut down my senses and bolted for a door marked Exit. I didn't plan to go far. I just needed to be out of there, away from all that magick for a few minutes.

I thought the door would lead to the street. Instead I found myself in a small courtyard planted with skinny oak saplings. I wasn't alone. A man with short-cropped, silver-flecked dark hair stood in the yard, staring up at a big square of the night sky. Even with my senses shut down I felt a surge of energy—deep, vital energy, not the fractured, hectic kind that ruled inside. Whether it was from the man or the giant orange moon, I couldn't be sure.

I sat down on a bench at the edge of the courtyard and gazed up at the moon, wondering what he was seeing. As I looked, I felt my frazzled nerve endings begin to relax. The moon was so eternal, so familiar in this place where everything else was so strange. I breathed deeply, and peace began to creep back into my body.

"The moon is our anchor," the man said without looking at me.

Ordinarily I would have been startled by these bizarre words coming from a total stranger. But at that moment my only thought was, Yes. I didn't feel the need to respond aloud, and he didn't seem to expect me to.

I stared at the moon, letting it anchor me.

4

Glamor

July 15, 1981

I write this on the ferry crossing the Irish Sea. I'm part of a delegation from Liathach, bound for western Ireland, to the very village where I was born, Ballynigel. We're going, as clansmen, to pay a visit to the Belwicket coven. I don't remember any of them at all. I'm very curious to see a Woodbane coven that forswore evil more than a hundred years ago. Bright magick and dark, the Woodbanes have never feared either. How Belwicket could have given up fully half of our ancient, essential powers, I can't fathom. But that is what we're going to observe. And we'll see whether there is anything in Ballynigel strong enough to resist us. We can't—won't—risk opposition. If we find it . . . there has been talk of the dark wave.

Mother stands near the bow with Greer, probably gossiping about the bairns. The two grannies are both mad for little Iona, and a sweet thing she is, though every bit as much trouble as her brother, Kyle. I take it as a good sign that Greer invited me to be part of this mission. Finally she is admitting me to Liathach's inner circle of leaders.

Grania, of course, didn't want me to go. "You can't leave me with two little ones to care for all on my own," she kept telling me. But I can and I have. The dream is still with me, and I long to see Ballynigel again.

—Neimhidh

I gazed up at the winter moon. I could feel my own power coursing through me, untainted by questions of whether I'd misused it or whether I was worth the sacrifice of Cal's life. It was as if my world had silently, subtly slipped into perfect balance. A few yards away from me the dark-haired man stood silent. He hadn't looked at me once, but I felt a strange connection between us, as sure and strong as if he'd thrown me a rope.

Where are you? Hunter's witch message almost made me jump. Reluctantly I stood up. The man nodded, as if acknowledging that I was leaving, but didn't say a word. I returned to the club, feeling I'd just been given a strange but lovely gift.

I found my friends gathered on a semicircular leather couch in the bar area. The showy witch Raven had been dancing with sat next to her on the very end of the couch.

Sky looked up as I approached. "Morgan, this is Killian," she said, her voice perfectly neutral, which made me wonder what I'd missed.

Killian gave me a grin, held out his hand, and said, "Enchanted."

Hunter made room for me beside him. Killian's dark eyes flickered between us, and I wondered if he could tell that just sitting next to Hunter made my whole body feel more alive.

Bree was looking at Killian with a calculating expression. "So you're another Brit?" she asked.

"Yeah, we're all over New York, a ruddy plague of us," he admitted cheerfully.

His accent was different from Hunter's and Sky's. I was glad when Robbie asked, "Which part of England?"

"Oh, I've done the whole miserable U.K. Born in Scotland, went to school in London, spent time in Ireland, summers in Wales and the Shetlands. And in all those places it rains too bleeding much. I'm still damp." He held out his arm to me. "Can you see the moss?"

I couldn't help laughing, liking him. He was definitely appealing. His features weren't perfect, like Cal's had been, and he didn't have Hunter's classic, chiseled bone structure, but he had energy. There was something wild, almost animal, about him. I wondered which clan he belonged to. But I knew I couldn't ask. Among witches, that question was considered very intrusive.

Killian got to his feet. "I'm going to get a beer. Anyone want one?"

"You're twenty-one?" I asked, surprised. He didn't look any older than the rest of us.

"Almost twenty," he admitted with a grin, "but I age well."

As he spoke, he drew a sign in the air, and the planes of his face became softer and fuller. Lines appeared across his forehead, and a crease deepened between his brows. Anyone would have thought he was pushing thirty. "Now . . . beer, wine, scotch, anyone?"

"I'll have a beer, too," Raven said, looking smitten.

"A Sprite would be great," Robbie said.

"Sprite it is," Killian said graciously, but I could sense mockery.

"He's good," Bree said as Killian started off for the crowded bar.

"It was just a glamor," Sky said dismissively. "A trick of the eye."

Bree looked at me. "What do you think of him?"

I shrugged, unsure of how to answer. On one level, I couldn't help liking him, his cheerful irreverence and the fact that he seemed to be having such a good time just being Killian. But there was also something about him that alarmed me, something dangerous in his raw, animal spirits. And there was the fact that when he cast that glamor, I felt pure envy. I knew I had the power to pull off magick like that, yet my lack of experience held me back. Alyce didn't know how to cast glamors, and neither did I.

Hunter gave me an odd look. "What's bothering you?"

"I don't know." I shifted in my seat, annoyed with myself for being so competitive. A good Wiccan would be able to simply enjoy Killian's power for what it was.

"I'm not sure I trust him," Hunter said thoughtfully. His eyes followed Killian as he scored the two beers and Robbie's soda.

Raven lit a cigarette and blew smoke through her nostrils at us. "What is your collective problem?" she asked. "So Killian shows off a little with his magick. All it means is he's different."

"That's one word for it," said Sky, her voice acid-edged.

Killian returned then, his glamor dissolved, and gave Robbie and Raven their drinks. "How long are you going to be in the city?" he asked Raven.

Raven started to answer, only to be silenced by a warning look from Hunter. "Uh, I'm not sure," she said.

"So, will I see you again?" he persisted.

"Maybe," she said. She slid a quick glance at Sky, as if to ask, How far will you let me push you? before she added, "Why don't you give me your number?"

He gave her a wide-eyed look. "Would you believe I'm staying with friends and I can't remember their number? How about you give me your number?"

It was a transparent lie, and I wondered why he told it, especially since he didn't make any real effort to be convincing. I could feel Sky reaching a silent boil. Raven must have felt it, too, because she shrugged, downed her beer, and got to her feet. "Same here," she said. "Can't remember it. Guess I'll see you when I see you."

Killian held out his hand and pulled her to him. Then he gave her a quick kiss, teetering on the edge between friendly and sexual.

I glanced at Sky in alarm. Her face was set, her nostrils flared.

"Raven, we're leaving now," Hunter said loudly.

Raven looked at Killian and shrugged. "Gotta go."

Killian's dark brows rose. "Must you?"

"Yes, we must," Hunter said. We retrieved our coats and trailed out of the club into the frigid streets.

We started back to the apartment. Sky and Raven walked ahead, maintaining an icy distance between themselves and us. Robbie slung an arm around Bree's shoulders, and they walked on like that, quiet and compatible. Whatever ups and downs they'd had during the evening, they seemed to have ended it on an upward trend.

Hunter was quiet, too, and walking slowly enough that we fell behind Robbie and Bree after a block or two. "Thinking about your job?" I guessed.

He nodded in a distracted way.

How could he focus so intensely on something so nebulous, so unformed? I couldn't—especially not when I was around him. I felt the familiar rush of insecurity. Did he even love me? He'd never said he did.

Of course he does, I told myself. He's just not as obvious about it as Cal was.

Feeling suddenly sad, I pulled my jacket tighter. Above us white stars blazed through a clear black night. The moon was gone, dropped somewhere behind the Manhattan skyline.

"Cold?" Hunter asked, pulling me against him.

"I'm not so sure I want to go to that club again," I told him. "The amount of magick flying around was almost too much."

"It was intense, that's true. But it's good to be exposed to lots of magick, coming from lots of sources. Besides just increasing your general knowledge, it will help you to recognize and deal with dark magick. Which, as you know, is especially important for you."

I felt my chest tighten. We'd already talked about this

more than once—about the fact that Selene had been part of a larger conspiracy, that her death probably didn't mean I was safe from other members of her coven or from other factions altogether. I'm going to be looking over my shoulder for the rest of my life, I thought bleakly.

Hunter pulled me to a stop under a streetlight. It cast harsh shadows on the planes of his face, making his cheekbones look razor sharp. "Don't worry," he said gently. "I'm looking after you. And you can look after yourself pretty well, too, you know. Besides, if Amyranth knows about you at all, they'll know you're high on the council's radar right now."

I thought of Killian. "Maybe I need to learn the art of magickal disguise."

"That's the least of it." Hunter frowned at me. "Why are you so eager to be casting glamors, anyway? I could see it in your eyes tonight. They went round with envy when Killian did his little parlor trick."

"It's not just envy," I said, thinking it through aloud. "It's knowing that I have the power to be like those other witches, except I don't know how to use it. It's like being given the key to this fabulous palace and seeing all these gorgeous rooms lit up inside but not knowing how to get the key into the lock."

"Is that bad?" he asked. "You've only been practicing magick for two and a half months. And learning to wield magick properly is a lifetime's work."

Oh Goddess, how sick I was of hearing that! I started walking again.

Hunter reached out, caught my arm, and pulled me toward him. "Morgan. You know that I want you to be able to put that key in the lock, don't you? I'm not trying to keep you out of the palace. I want you to come fully into your power, to be able to use every bit of magick in you." His fingertips stroked my face, and I felt myself moving toward him. "I just don't want you or anyone else getting hurt in the process."

"I know," I breathed as he gently lowered his head to mine. Then his arms wrapped around me and our mouths met and I felt all the tension of the evening melt away. I opened myself to Hunter, and it was like a river of sapphire light poured into me, like he was washing me in his magick and his love. I felt my own heart open and my power moving, streaming through my body, twining with his. It felt like that spot on the Manhattan sidewalk was the center of the universe and the night and all its stars spun out from us. In that moment, in that place, I had no doubts, no insecurities.

Love, I thought. The ultimate magick.

Hunter and I were the last ones to get back to the apartment. Inside we found Robbie in the kitchen, emptying a bag of popcorn into a bowl, Bree taking sheets and blankets from the linen closet, and Sky and Raven standing at opposite ends of the living room. Mr. Warren was nowhere in sight.

Robbie consulted his watch as I hung up my jacket. "Where have you two been?" he asked, sounding like a disapproving parent.

"We . . . got a little lost," Hunter said, flashing me a quick, secret smile that made my cold cheeks turn a shade more pink.

Raven grabbed a handful of popcorn. "So, where's everyone sleeping?" she asked.

No one answered. Sky stared out the window, Robbie concentrated on the popcorn, and Bree murmured something about pillowcases and returned to the linen closet.

Hunter's green eyes locked on me, and I found myself looking away, unaccountably shy all over again. Was it possible that we'd actually wind up in the same bed? Even if we did, I was fairly sure no one was going to be doing much fooling around—the apartment was just too cramped. I was secretly relieved. I wasn't quite ready for that. But my heart was pounding at the thought of sleeping with some part of my body touching Hunter's. I longed to be with him for a few peaceful hours without the confusion of consciousness. I longed to wake up in his arms.

I wondered what Bree and Robbie wanted to do. They seemed to be getting along now, but I wasn't about to discount what Bree had said in the market.

Bree, holding an armful of linens, cleared her throat. "Well, the living room couch folds out to a double bed. The bed in the guest room is a trundle bed, so it has another mattress under it, and there's a couch in the study." She flashed an overly bright smile that proved she felt every bit as nervous as I did.

Raven made an impatient noise. "Let's get it over with already. How do you want to split it up?"

Again no one answered. Finally Hunter spoke up. "The way I see it, Mr. Warren's being kind enough to host us. Whatever we do shouldn't upset him."

Bree's eyes lingered on Robbie with a mix of desire and regret. "I'm not sure my dad would notice if we mixed it up," she admitted, "but it's probably a good idea not to find out.

Better to keep the girls and guys separate."

I tried not to look disappointed and told myself that Bree and Hunter were right.

"Robbie and I can take the study," Hunter volunteered.

Robbie walked over to the pile of luggage in the living room and picked up his pack and a small green stuff sack. "Air mattress," he explained.

"Morgan and I can take the guest room," Bree said. "That's the room I usually sleep in when I come down here, anyway."

"Sounds good," I said, surprised and pleased that Bree had chosen me for her roommate.

"That means Sky and I have the living room," Raven said.

Sky said, "I think I'll go out for a walk. Don't wait up for me."

Raven stared at her in disbelief. "Oh, come on! I can't believe you're still upset. I was just flirting with him. It was harmless."

"That's not how I saw it," Sky said, her voice tight.

Raven made a face. "Oh, Jesus."

"Look, we'll just rearrange," Hunter said, sounding weary. "Robbie and I can share the foldout in the living room. Sky can have the study."

"And where does that leave me?" Raven demanded, one hand on her hip.

Bree took the air mattress from Robbie. "You can sleep in the guest room with me and Morgan," she said. "Really, it will be totally comfortable."

"Brilliant," said Hunter. "Then everybody's happy."

I don't think anyone actually believed that, but we all went off to our agreed-upon quarters.

For the next fifteen minutes Bree and Raven and I

worked on inflating the air mattress and getting sheets and blankets on all three beds. I was fighting a sense of crashing disappointment. How did my romantic getaway with Hunter turn into a sleepover with the girls?

Bree grabbed a robe from behind the door and announced she was going to take a shower, leaving me in the guest room with Raven. I pulled my nightgown out of my pack. It was a simple white cotton gown cut straight across the chest with skinny ribbon shoulder straps. Actually, it was Mary K.'s; she had loaned it to me. I didn't even own a nightgown.

"You want to wear this," Mary K. had assured me. "Trust me, Hunter will love it."

Hunter's not even going to see it, I thought grumpily.

Raven had changed into a loose black T-shirt with the neck and arms cut out. She was sitting on the air mattress, examining the black polish on her toenails. "Sky can be a cold bitch sometimes," she muttered.

"Maybe," I agreed. "But I think your flirting with Killian was hard on her."

Raven snorted. "She knows that didn't mean anything."

"Then why was she so freaked?"

"I don't know," Raven said irritably.

I wondered how far into this conversation I should go. Though we were in the same coven, Raven and I had never exactly been friends. She was a senior and hung out with a much tougher crowd than I ever had. The idea of me, who'd been kissed by all of two boys, giving Raven Meltzer romantic advice was a joke.

I was brushing out my hair when Raven said, "So tell me—

what's your theory? On Sky, I mean."

Okay, it was definitely a weird night. I chose my words carefully. "Sky cares about you, and you hurt her. I think her coldness is the way she reacts to being hurt. If I were you, I'd give her another chance," I said. Then, before things could get any weirder, I grabbed my toothbrush and headed for the bathroom.

Robbie was already standing in line, listening to the sound of the shower. I wondered if that meant Hunter was alone in the living room but didn't have the nerve to ask.

"Bree's still in there," Robbie reported, rolling his eyes at the bathroom door. "I think she's washing every strand of hair on her head individually."

"That's okay—I'll wait." A daring idea suddenly occurred to me. "Robbie . . . how would you feel about switching places with me a little later tonight?"

Robbie's eyebrows rose. "Morganita, you sly dog!"

"Not for the whole night or anything. Maybe for an hour or so."

"I dunno," Robbie said. "That means you get an hour with Hunter, and I've got that same hour with Bree and Raven."

"We'll wait till one," I said. "Everyone should be asleep. You can just slip in next to Bree. Raven will never know."

Robbie eyed me doubtfully. "What if Raven wakes up?"

"Then just explain you were sleepwalking and stumbled into the wrong room."

"Yeah, that's believable."

"Oh, come on, Robbie. Please."

"Shhh," he whispered. "Okay, I'll do it."

My heart skipped a beat as Hunter walked toward us,

toothbrush in hand. He was wearing a long-sleeved black T-shirt over gray sweats that just seemed to emphasize how long and lean he was.

I felt his eyes on me, taking in the white nightgown and my hair brushed out and hanging loose, and I knew that Mary K. had been right. I could feel Hunter's senses reaching out to me, wanting me, drawing me toward him.

Robbie must have sensed the electricity between us. "I'm going to hang in the kitchen," he said. "But if Bree ever gets out of the bathroom, I'm first."

Neither Hunter nor I said anything until he left. Then Hunter came close. "You look beautiful," he said in a husky voice.

"Thanks. Um—you too," I said in my eloquent way. My hands, ridiculously, trembled a little, and I folded my arms so he wouldn't notice. I debated whether or not to tell him what Robbie and I had been planning. But before I'd worked up my nerve, he spoke in a rush.

"Do you think I could possibly persuade you to change places with Robbie for a little while tonight?" he asked. I heard the anxiety in his voice, the fear that I might say no, and I loved him so, so much.

"I already asked him," I said, my heart hammering.

Hunter blew out his breath and grinned. His eyes danced with emerald green light. "Great minds . . ." he said, and bent to kiss me. Just then the bathroom door swung open and a cloud of steam floated out.

"Whoops," Bree said.

Hunter and I pulled apart. "Robbie," I called, grateful for the steam that hid my red cheeks. "The bathroom's yours."

An hour later we were all tucked in. I was too excited to even consider sleep. Periodically I extended my senses, identifying the patterns of the people in the apartment. Bree was sleeping, and so were Raven and Sky. Hunter and Robbie were both wide awake.

Finally it was one A.M. Moving quietly so as not to wake Bree and Raven, I made my way out of the guest room. In the living room a single candle flickered. Hunter and Robbie were sitting on opposite ends of the couch, waiting for me.

"Bree," Robbie whispered. "Is she—"

"Asleep," I told him. "Be careful you don't startle her. Any sign of Mr. Warren?"

Hunter shook his head. "Not yet."

I was keenly aware of his being just a few feet from me. My heart began to beat faster, and that funny anticipation feeling—that mix of pleasure with just a thread of uncertainty—began to hum through me. I waited till Robbie had gone, and then I sat beside Hunter.

"I was afraid you wouldn't come," he said. He reached out and closed one hand over mine. "I thought you might fall asleep."

"Almost did," I teased.

"Did you really?" he asked.

"No," I admitted, suddenly feeling vulnerable and unsure. It occurred to me again that Hunter had never told me he loved me, though I'd told him I loved him. Was it just a guy thing, not being able to say the words? Or did he not feel the same way? Hunter was honest to a fault, and I was certain that he cared about me. But maybe it wasn't love, and that's why he'd never said the words. Could Bree be right about love? Maybe Hunter was about to break my heart and hand it back to me in little pieces.

Maybe I shouldn't be here now, I thought, feeling a tickle of panic. Maybe I should just go back to my own bed, not get close to anything I can't handle.

Then Hunter turned over my hand and began to gently stroke the underside of my arm. His touch sent shivers of delight racing through me.

"You were like a vision, you know," he said, his voice soft and low. "Standing there in the hall in that innocent gown, your hair shining, holding a toothbrush of all things. I just wanted to run away with you."

"Really?" I whispered. "Where to?"

"I don't know. Didn't think it through that far." He brushed back a strand of hair from my face. "You know, I never had second thoughts about becoming a Seeker. It seemed necessary, fated. But lately . . ." His voice trailed off on a note of longing.

"Lately what?"

"I wish there were a way to take a break from it. I wish I could just steal away with you for a while."

My heart was pounding like a drum. I fought desperately to keep things grounded, realistic. "My parents probably wouldn't be too keen on that idea," I said.

"Right. Parents," he said. "They probably wouldn't approve of this, either." He bent forward and kissed the side of my neck.

Chills raced through me. The energy flowing between us felt so strong and right and good. I didn't want to walk away from it. Not anymore. Gently I lifted his head so that I could put my mouth on his. He wrapped his arms around me.

At first our kisses were soft, searching, as if we were just getting to know each other. Hunter's hands slid along my nightgown, caressing my waist, my side. Every inch of my body was alight with desire. Everything in me streamed toward Hunter. I slid my hand under his shirt, felt the smooth skin of his chest over a hard sheath of muscle. Gently he pushed me backward so we were lying on the foldout bed. He pulled back for a moment, and I saw his face in the light from the window, intent as always. But now, this time, he was totally focused on *me*. His lips came down on mine again, harder now, more urgent.

Then, without warning, Hunter broke away.

"What's wrong?" I asked, breathless.

"Don't you sense him?"

And then I did. It was Mr. Warren, coming down the hall.

"He can't!" I groaned. "It's not fair."

"But he is." Hunter held me close with one arm. He ran his other hand along my face and kissed me gently. "We'd better call it a night."

"No! Can't we do a spell to make him think he's dropped his keys and has to go back down to the garage, or—"

Hunter swatted at me lightly. "You know better. Come on, now. Go give Bree and Robbie some warning."

I got up with a groan. I could hear Mr. Warren's footsteps coming down the hallway. "Okay." I leaned forward and gave Hunter one last kiss. "To be continued," I promised.

5

Gifts of the Mage

July 16, 1981

We've been in Ballynigel less than twenty-four hours, and everything has changed. I know now why I kept dreaming of this place, why I've felt drawn back here, as though there were an invisible string connecting it to my heart.

I first saw Maeve Riordan yesterday. She was not among those who welcomed our boat. She was off gathering moss for a poultice and didn't come back into the village until we were in a meeting with Belwicket's elders. We were in the house of Mackenna, their high priestess, beginning to ask those questions whose answers would determine Belwicket's fate, though they didn't realize it, poor sods. And in walks Mackenna's daughter, a girl of nineteen with a mud-streaked skirt and a basket overflowing with drippy moss.

I had the strangest sensation that I'd waited twenty-two years to see her. It was as though my life were slightly unreal until that moment. She seemed fey—a luminous creature—and at the same time utterly familiar, as if I'd known and loved her my whole life.

Everything about Maeve enchants me. The light that dances in her eyes, the rhythm of her speech, the sound of her laughter, the grace of her hands, and, of course, the magick that sparkles around her. She has a great deal of raw power—as much as Selene, I think. Selene was a different package, though. She'd been honing her magick for years, had studied, sacrificed, undergone a Great Trial, even. In Maeve it's simply a matter of her birthright. She takes it for granted, doesn't yet realize how much power courses through her.

Of course, there is the matter of Belwicket having forsworn the old Woodbane ways. Still, I'm certain we'll get past that. She feels the same way about me that I do about her—I can see it in her eyes. I will show Maeve how to realize her true power. I'll convince her that my way is the right one.

So this is what love feels like, the love that lasts for all time. When it happens, there are no questions, no doubts. I know that now. And I know the dress on the line . . . it can only have been hers.

—Neimhidh

Friday morning, I woke to unfamiliar sounds filtering through the guest room door—Mr. Warren making coffee while having a heated phone conversation about depositions.

On the mattress next to me Bree stretched and opened her eyes. "Sleep well?" she asked with a drowsy smile.

I blushed. "Yeah. How about you?"

She shrugged. "Fine," she said in a neutral voice.

Raven's eyes shot open, ringed with black eye makeup she hadn't washed off. "What time is it?" she demanded.

"Just after nine-thirty," Bree answered. "We should get moving. I want to go to Diva's this morning. It's in SoHo. You guys should come, too—they've got great clothes, and they're really cheap."

I could feel that Hunter and Sky weren't in the apartment; they must have already left for their meeting with the mysterious contact Hunter had met last night. "Uh—okay," I agreed. Maybe I could find an outfit that was slightly more appropriate for the city.

Raven shook her head. "I'll pass. Not my kind of place," she said.

"Okay." Bree got up, took her robe from its hook, and went out into the kitchen.

Raven rubbed her temples. "I feel like hell. I need a shower," she said, and padded off to the bathroom.

I got dressed, my thoughts on Hunter and how good it had felt to be with him last night, how I wished it could have lasted longer.

I quickly plaited my hair into a braid and glanced in the mirror on the closet door. In a black turtleneck and jeans, I was presentable. I went out into the living room, where I found Robbie folding up the sofa bed. He was dressed in jeans and a blue plaid flannel shirt, and his hair was still mussed from sleep.

"Morning," Robbie said. "Hunter left a note for you." He pulled a folded piece of paper from his pocket and handed it to me.

Morgan—
  I'll meet you back at the apartment by 10:30.
                                    —Hunter

Of course, the thing that I noticed was that he'd signed it Hunter. Not: Love, Hunter or even Yours, Hunter. Just plain Hunter. Very romantic.

Mr. Warren rushed out of the apartment, briefcase in hand, and Bree came into the living room. "What's up?"

I showed her Hunter's note. Bree made a face. "I wanted to go the coffee shop downstairs and get some breakfast. But I guess we'll wait."

So we waited. Raven emerged from the guest room in yet another skintight black outfit. She seemed a little annoyed that Sky was still out. Bree and Robbie weren't talking, I noticed, and Robbie was doing his best to pretend he was okay about it. He headed out, saying a little too casually that he wanted to do some exploring on his own. First, though, we agreed that we'd all meet up for lunch at a deli on the Upper West Side at two that afternoon.

Ten-thirty came and went. By eleven Hunter and Sky still hadn't come back, and Bree and I were dying to get out, get food, do something besides sit around the apartment. And I was getting worried.

Finally I sent Hunter a witch message. But after ten minutes he hadn't responded. My pulse rate picked up a little. Was he okay?

"Well?" Raven asked.

"Nothing," I said, trying to keep my voice calmer than I felt.

"That boy has really got to join the twenty-first century and get a cell phone," Bree said.

I sent another, more emphatic witch message to Hunter, trying to determine if he was okay.

After a moment I got a response from Sky: We're fine. That was it. Hunter didn't bother to reply at all. Again I couldn't help a surge of irritation. Maybe I wasn't being rational about this, but it sure felt like I was being shut out.

"I just heard from Sky," I told the others. "They're okay. But I don't think they're going to be back for a while."

"Then let's shop," Bree said.

Raven yawned. "I'm going back to bed," she announced. "I am not a morning person."

Half an hour and two pastries later, Bree and I stood on the cast-iron steps of Diva's on West Broadway. I'd been there once before, but even if you lived in Widow's Vale and had never been to the city, you knew about Diva's. It was a mecca for the young and broke.

Bree led the way inside the huge warehouse of a store. Rap blared from the speakers. There were stacks of T-shirts in every color of the rainbow; pants in reds and blues and petal pinks; sweatshirts in olive green, neon yellow, and baby blue.

Bree started poking through the vintage racks and found a man's long-sleeved black shirt with gray pearl buttons. "Maybe I should buy this for Robbie," she mused. Unlike the rest of us, Bree had a generous allowance.

I couldn't keep my mouth shut. "Bree, do you or do you not like that boy?"

She looked at me, startled. "I told you. I'm completely crazy about him."

"Well, then please stop treating him like crap!" I said. "It's painful to watch."

Bree put the shirt back and calmly moved on to a rack of trendier clothing. "If you want to know the truth," she said, "it's Robbie who should be treating me better."

"What?" I stared at her.

"At the club last night," she said. "He danced and flirted with all those women."

"Three, and they all came on to him," I argued.

"Don't blame them. It's Robbie's responsibility to say no," said Bree. "If he really wants to be with me, why did he encourage them?"

"Maybe because he wasn't getting any encouragement from you?" I suggested. "Come on, Bree. You had your own little entourage over by the café. What kind of message did that send? Besides, you know none of those women mattered. Robbie doesn't care about anyone except you. Can't you see that?"

Bree held up a slinky black cocktail dress. "I know Robbie's trying," she acknowledged. "But so am I." She frowned, put the dress back, and moved on to a rack of pants. "This is just the way relationships go."

"Only because you steer them that way."

Bree sighed. "I don't want to talk about this right now. I'm hitting the dressing room. Are you going to try anything on?"

"I'll meet you in there," I told her. Obviously the conversation was over.

I quickly scooped up a couple of V-necked T-shirts and a few camisoles. Camisoles were my official choice for underwear.

Having nothing to put in the cups, I'd given up on bras.

There was a line for the dressing rooms, so I shouted for Bree. She yelled back that I should share her room.

I found Bree wearing a stretchy bronze-colored top with black knit hip-hugger pants. She looked amazing. "Think Robbie will like this?" she asked.

I groaned and slid down onto the floor of the tiny cubicle. I decided to try one more time. "Listen, I know for a fact that Robbie loves you. And you obviously care about him. Why can't you trust that and stop trying to undermine all the good stuff? Why can't you just let yourself love him and be happy?"

Bree rolled her eyes. "Because," she said with absolute certainty, "in real life things just don't work that way, Morgan."

Didn't they? I wondered. I thought again about Bree's mom walking out on her and her dad. That had to be the root of all her warped ideas about love.

Or did Bree really know something I didn't?

Twenty minutes later Bree and I left Diva's, each of us carrying a neon pink shopping bag. Bree had bought the bronze-top outfit, a chartreuse day pack, and a black T-shirt for Robbie. I'd gotten a cobalt blue tee and a lilac camisole, which pretty much shot my clothing budget.

"What's next?" I asked, cheered by our retail therapy.

Bree looked thoughtful. "There's a fabulous shoe store right around the corner, and there's a shop close by that specializes in African jewelry. There's also an aromatherapy place off Wooster," she added.

"Let's check that out."

We hadn't gone more than a block when my witch senses

began to tug at me. "Bree, can we go this way?" I asked, pointing down Broome Street.

She shrugged good-naturedly. "Why not?"

I followed my senses the way a spider follows its own silken thread and found myself in an alley off Broome Street. Hanging over a narrow doorway at the end of the alley was a square white banner with a green wheel printed on it. In the center of the green wheel was a purple pentagram.

"The Wheel of the Year," Bree said. "The diagram for the eight Wiccan sabbats."

The feel of magick grew stronger with every step we took. When we reached the shop, a sign on the black cast-iron door made me smile: Gifts of the Mage: Specializing in Books of Magick and the Occult. And beneath it in smaller letters: Welcome, Friends.

I pushed open the door, causing a brass bell to ring, and stepped into a cool, dim, high-ceilinged space. I didn't see the sort of general Wiccan supplies that Practical Magick stocked, but a wall of cabinets behind the counter held essential oils in bottles that looked positively ancient. A deep balcony ran around the walls halfway up, with more bookshelves and shabby armchairs in alcoves.

Bree walked toward mahogany shelves stacked with tarot decks. "Oh, they have a reproduction of that gorgeous Italian deck I saw in the Pierpont Morgan Library," she said.

My witch senses were still prickling. Was there something here that I was meant to find? I glanced up at the black metal staircase that led to the balcony floor.

"Alyce recommended a book on scrying," I told Bree, "but she didn't have it in stock. Maybe I can find it here."

Already absorbed in tarot decks, Bree mumbled an okay.

Following the store directory, I climbed the stairs to the balcony and began to search for the divination section. The scent of old leather tickled my nose. I could almost feel centuries of spells whispering to me. *Find me, invoke me. I'm yours, I'm made for your power.* I passed sections labeled Oracles and Emanations, Amulets and Talismans. It felt good be among so many books filled with so much knowledge.

I rounded the end of the aisle and came face-to-face with a large section labeled Divination. Just beyond it, at the end of this next aisle, I saw a man seated in an armchair next to a potted tree of some sort. I stopped, confused by the feeling of familiarity that swept over me.

Then I realized he was the same man who'd been in the courtyard of the club the night before. He was reading a book, looking as relaxed as if he were in his own living room. He wore a tweed jacket over a white shirt and faded jeans. Cropped salt-and-pepper hair softened a hawkish weathered face.

He glanced up, showing me deep-set brown eyes, and acknowledged me with a courteous nod. "We meet again," he said.

"Do you work here?" I blurted.

"No." He seemed surprised by the idea. "I teach myth and folklore at Columbia. This is just one of my more pleasant sources for reference materials." He had a faint accent, which I hadn't noticed before. Irish or Scottish, maybe—I wasn't sure. He marked his place in the book and closed it. "Was that your first time at the club, last night?" he asked.

"Yes." Sometimes I am such a brilliant conversationalist, it's really overwhelming. Why was I so tongue-tied around this man? I asked myself. It certainly wasn't a crush thing. He had to be nearly as old as my dad. And yet I felt an affinity with him, a familiarity, an attraction.

He regarded me with curiosity. "What did you think of it?"

I thought about the beautiful illusion Killian had created for Raven.

"It was a little intense, but also cool," I said. "I'd never seen witches use their magick just for pleasure."

"Personally, that's what I've always liked best about magick—using it to create beauty and pleasure in the midst of the trials life forces us to undergo."

He made a sign over the potted tree, and I watched its leaves fade, shrivel, and fall off. From the soil a green shoot grew. It was as if I were watching a movie on fast-forward. No natural plant could grow so quickly, but in the space of a minute or so a lilac bush grew against the trunk of the dead tree, and pale lilac blossoms opened, filling the air with sweet fragrance.

It was incredibly beautiful. It was also a little unnerving. It broke all the laws of nature. What would happen to the lilac? It was an outdoor plant that needed a winter's frost. It couldn't survive in a pot in a store. And I couldn't help feeling a little sorry for the healthy tree that had died for a witch's pleasure.

And what would Hunter think of this? I wondered. He'd probably consider it an irresponsible, not to mention indiscreet, use of magick. Something the council would frown on.

"The world can always use more beauty, you know," the man said, as if he'd read my doubts. "Adding beauty to the world is never irresponsible."

I didn't know how to answer. I suddenly felt very, very young and ignorant.

He seemed to sense my discomfort. "So, you came here looking for a book?"

"Yes." I was enormously relieved to remember I had a concrete reason for being there. "I'm looking for a book on scrying by Devin Dhualach."

"A good name, that," the man said. "Devin means bard, you know, so hopefully he can write. And Dhualach is an old Irish name that comes down to us from the Druids. If he's true to his ancestors, he may indeed have something useful to say about scrying."

"I—I'll just look at these shelves under divination," I said, suddenly shy and nervous.

"Good idea." The man smiled and went back to his book.

I found the Dhualach and sat down cross-legged on the floor to look through it. There were chapters on scrying with water, fire, mirrors, and *luegs*, scrying stones or crystals. There was even a macabre chapter on throwing bones, snake vertebrae being very highly recommended. There was nothing, though—at least nothing I could see on a quick skim— that dealt with how to control the visions, how to fine-tune them so I could see exactly what I needed to see.

The man from the courtyard glanced up from his book. "Not finding quite what you're looking for?" he asked.

I hesitated, aware that I had to be careful. Yet it didn't feel like he was prying. It was more that he recognized me as another blood witch and sensed my power. It wasn't the first time that had happened. David Redstone had recognized what I was the first time he saw me, even before I knew myself.

I noticed that he was looking at me oddly, as if he'd suddenly remembered something but wasn't sure whether or

not he should mention it. Then he said, "You scry with fire."
It was an acknowledgment rather than a question.

I nodded, and my nervousness dropped away. It was as if
I'd just walked through a door into a room where we were
acknowledged peers. Witch to witch. Strength to strength.
Power conduit to power conduit.

"The fire shows me things, but I feel like they're often random. I don't know how to make it show me what *I'm* looking for," I admitted.

"Fire has a will of her own," he said. "Fire is ravenous,
fighting control, always seeking her own pleasure. To tame
her is a lifetime's work, a matter of coaxing her to reveal
what you want to know. I could show you, but"—he looked
at the shelves around us and smiled—"a bookstore is hardly
the place to play with fire."

"That's all right," I said, trying not to sound disappointed.

The lines around his eyes crinkled. "Perhaps I can explain
it through another medium. The principle's the same."

He reached into an inner pocket of his jacket and drew out
a piece of clear, polished crystal, cut in the shape of a crescent
moon. It wasn't big, maybe three inches across, but its surface
was faceted and etched with runes and magickal symbols.

He held the crystal out to me, and I took it in my right
hand. The crystal was surprisingly light, as if it belonged to a
slightly altered gravity.

"I assume you know that you must ask the medium to give
you a vision and that you must be specific. If what you want
is to see your kitten tomorrow, specify tomorrow." I wondered how he knew I had a kitten. Then again, it wasn't
uncommon for witches to have cats. "In your mind's eye

picture that animal or person and send the image into the stone, asking it to accept it." His voice was soft, almost hypnotic. "The key is you must then use your power to feel the energy in the crystal—or the fire—and send its light into the future, searching for what you seek. That's really all there is to it."

"You make it sound simple," I said.

"Most things are, once they're familiar. Why don't you practice with the crystal first?" At the doubt in my eyes he said, "Hold on to the crystal if you like. I need to go downstairs and check a few books for my syllabus. Just leave the crystal by the chair when you're done with it."

I sat there debating as he went down the stairs. I didn't want to try anything complicated in the store, but maybe I could do something simple. I'd been worried about Mary K. ever since that awful night Selene kidnapped her, using her as the bait to get me. She didn't seem to remember anything about being at Selene's house—in fact, she seemed to have believed the cover story we gave my parents, which was that she had gone to the movies by herself because she was depressed. But lately she'd been having nightmares.

I'd finally learned not to underestimate anything Selene did. Rational or not, there was a part of me that worried that though Selene was dead, her magick somehow still had a hold on my sister.

Holding the crystal, I silently asked the stone to give me the vision I sought. I pictured my sister at home, sitting at the table, and asked the crystal to accept that image. I nearly dropped the stone as Mary K.'s image appeared inside it, tiny and perfect and three-dimensional. I watched her sitting at the table, then I asked the crystal to show her to me one week from now.

A stone's energy pattern is as distinct as any person's or animal's. The energy in this particular crystal was cool, glowing green-white, surging and swelling like a tide. For several breaths I let my energy ride its swells. Then I sent it surging into the future.

The image in the crescent changed. I saw Mary K. and her friend Jaycee walking out of the Widow's Vale Cineplex. The vision was so perfect and detailed, I could even see the missing X in the marquee.

Then I felt something odd, almost like a cold draft on the back of my neck. I wheeled around in alarm. Was someone watching me? Even in a place frequented by other witches, I knew it wasn't a good idea for me to work magick in public. But I could see no one else on the balcony, and when I extended my senses, I couldn't feel anyone nearby.

Focusing on the crystal again, I realized I was starting to feel tired, which was pretty common whenever I moved into a new level of magick. Knowing I wouldn't be able to maintain the spell much longer, I thanked the stone for its help and withdrew my power from it. The glowing green-white light inside it faded, and the vision of Mary K. winked out.

I'd done it. I'd called up a vision and seen exactly what I'd asked to see. This was the way magick was supposed to work.

I stood up. Then, feeling light-headed, I sat down in the chair. I was vaguely aware that Bree must be wondering where I was. I told myself I'd just sit long enough for my pulse to return to normal. But a wave of exhaustion totaled me. My limbs felt heavy. My head began to nod. I couldn't keep my eyes from drifting closed.

*　　　*　　　*

Everything shadowed. The owl hovering over the stone table. Razor-sharp talons and golden eyes. The jackal's high-pitched laughter. Venom dripping from the viper's fangs. The jaguar, claws unsheathed. Hunger that could never be sated. The weasel, crawling so close, its claws scrape the table. Candles burning low, casting shadows on the walls. Golden eyes, green eyes, glittering, intent. All of them fixed on the wolf cub. All of them waiting. The cub's terror, sharp and pungent. The red ruby set in the hilt of the athame, glowing with power. The eagle's scream. And the silver wolf. The one they all wait for. It leaps to the table and opens its great jaws. The cub howls.

"Are you all right?" I felt someone gently shaking my shoulder.

My eyes flew open. The man from the courtyard was standing over me, his eyes shadowed with concern.

"What happened?" he asked.

"I—I must have fallen asleep," I said, feeling shaken and embarrassed. I was soaked with sweat. "I had a dream."

"What sort of dream?"

"Just a bad one." Even though I felt sick and disoriented, I knew I couldn't risk saying more. Especially if the council was right about what the dream meant.

"Dreams are funny," the man said thoughtfully. "They have their own internal logic. They mix past and present and future and then some things that I believe belong to our collective unconscious. Things that may have nothing to do with you specifically."

"Maybe this wasn't specific to me," I agreed. After all, no one had ever explained why I was the one who had this dream, but the fact that I'd had it twice now unnerved me.

I drew in several deep breaths, then got to my feet. So far, so good; walking seemed possible. I glanced at my watch. It was after one. "I'd better find my friend," I said. "Thanks for all your help."

"You're sure you're all right?"

"Yes."

As I started to walk away, he touched me lightly on my arm. "I'm sorry. I haven't even had the manners to ask. What's your name?"

"Morgan," I answered without thinking.

He held out his hand to me. "Well, Morgan, may your magick always bring you joy."

I found Bree on the first floor, holding a tarot deck in a bag. "I was going to send out a search party for you," she said. "We're supposed to meet everyone for lunch in forty-five minutes, remember?"

I bought the book on scrying, and we left the store and headed for the subway station on Spring Street. It was only later, as we emerged from the subway on the Upper West Side, that I thought about the fact that I'd given the man my name. Had I committed some sort of breach of security?

No, I decided. After all, I'd only given him my first name. But I wished I'd thought to ask what his name was.

6

Healing

August 19, 1981

Maeve and I have pledged our souls to each other. We left
the village just after dark and went out beneath the cliffs. She
and I share an affinity for fire, so it was child's play to kindle a
raging bonfire with our minds—the concrete expression of the all-
consuming nature of our love. Dancing and licking at the night
like an animal, it was a thing of beauty, red and yellow and
orange, with a dazzling white-blue heat at its heart. I am so
happy, I am nearly delirious. At last I am fully alive.

I even gave her the watch that Da gave to Ma, the one I've
carried with me all these years. Funny that I never thought to
give it to Grania. But then, I never loved Grania.

There is only one thing more to do. I haven't yet made love to
Maeve, though Goddess knows, I want it more than I've ever
wanted anything on this earth. But I want no lies between us, so

first I must tell her about Grania and the children. It will be difficult. But our love will get us through. I have no fear. Nothing can quench our fire.

—Neimhidh

Murray's was a crowded deli on Columbus Avenue, sandwiched between a shop selling computer accessories and a flower stand. The spicy smells of corned beef, pastrami, and sauerkraut suddenly made me realize that I was starving.

Bree and I made our way over to the small, square table where Raven and Robbie sat. Seconds after we pulled up chairs a waitress dropped four huge menus on the table.

"No Sky or Hunter," Raven announced.

"They never showed up at the apartment?" I asked her, starting to worry all over again. I knew Hunter and Sky could take care of themselves, but having the dream a second time had left me with a feeling of dread. Was he just late now, or was he not going to show at all?

"No," Raven answered, "but I recorded a message for them on Bree's dad's answering machine, telling them to get their witchy butts up here."

Bree looked both amused and horrified. "Great. I'm just imagining one of my father's clients calling and getting that message."

The waitress returned. "What'll you have?" she asked.

"Uh—we're waiting for friends," Robbie said. "Could you come back in ten minutes?"

She gestured at the line that had formed near the door. "I got people waiting for tables," she told us. "Either you're ready to order or you should let someone else sit down."

"Let's just order," Bree decided.

So we ordered corned beef and pastrami sandwiches and sodas. Raven got a Reuben. The food came immediately, and I'd eaten half my sandwich when I felt Hunter and Sky nearby. I turned around to see them walking through the door.

Hunter was wearing his leather jacket and a bottle-green scarf. His cheeks were red from the cold. "Sorry we're late," he said as they reached the table.

Raven rolled her eyes. "Nice of you to show up."

Robbie, ever the gentleman, managed to round up two more chairs and bring them over to the table. Sky sat down next to Raven.

"Are you hungry?" I offered Hunter the uneaten half of my sandwich.

"No. Thanks," he said, sounding distracted. He didn't take the chair Robbie had brought for him. Instead, he knelt by my side. "There's something I need to talk to you about," he said in a low voice. "How about if you wrap up your sandwich and we take a walk?"

"I'm full," I said. I was glad of the chance to talk—I wanted to tell him about having the dream again.

I left money for the check and made arrangements to meet the others back at Murray's in half an hour. Then Hunter and I set off. By unspoken agreement we headed toward Central Park, stopping only to buy two takeout coffees, defense against the cold.

We walked down a side street lined with gracious brownstones, past the Dakota, where John Lennon had lived, and finally stopped to sit on a low wall overlooking Strawberry Fields, Lennon's memorial. Because it was so cold, there weren't many visitors to the teardrop-shaped garden that day. But on the circular mosaic imprinted with the word *Imagine* someone had left a bouquet of white and yellow daisies.

"Did you know that Strawberry Field was actually the name of an orphanage next door to John Lennon's boyhood home?" Hunter asked. "His aunt, who raised him, used to threaten to send him there whenever he misbehaved."

"I'll have to remember that tidbit for my dad," I said. "He's still a big fan."

"My parents had all the Beatles' albums," Hunter remembered. "My mum used to play the second side of *Abbey Road* on Sunday mornings. 'Here Comes the Sun.'" He hummed the tune softly for a moment. "Goddess, it's been ages since I thought about that." He shook his head as though trying to shake off the pain of memory.

"At least you know they're alive now," I said, trying to sound positive. The dark wave had demolished Hunter's parents' coven when he was only eight, and his mother and father had been in hiding ever since. For years he hadn't even known for sure whether they were dead or alive. Right before Yule, Hunter's father had actually contacted him through his *lueg*. But the dark wave had overwhelmed the vision, cutting it off before Hunter heard what his father was trying to tell him. Since then we hadn't dared try to contact them again, for fear that it would lead the darkness to them.

"I know they were alive three weeks ago," Hunter corrected, his voice tight. "Or at least Dad was. But anything could have happened since then, and I wouldn't know. That's what kills me—not knowing."

Aching for him, I put my arms around his waist. For the most part Hunter kept his grief for his family hidden well below the surface, but every so often it would well up and I'd see how it always was with him. How part of him would never rest until he knew for certain what had happened to his parents.

I felt a gentle glow of white light in the center of my chest. One of Alyce's healing spells was opening to me. "Will you let me try something?" I asked.

Hunter nodded. I unzipped his jacket halfway. I took off my glove, undid one button of his shirt, and slid my already cold hand against his smooth, warm skin. He flinched, then I felt him opening himself to the white light that was flowing through me.

I began a whispered chant. " 'The heart that loves must one day grieve. Love and grief are the Goddess's twined gifts. Let the pain in, let it open your heart to compassion. Let me help you bear your grief. . . .' "

I couldn't continue. Suddenly I knew exactly what it would feel like to have my parents and Mary K. ripped from me. It was beyond excruciating. It was more than could be borne. I cried out in grief though I managed to keep my hand on Hunter's chest, managed to keep the healing light flowing.

"Shhh," Hunter said. "You don't have to do any more."

"No," I whispered. "I have to finish the spell. 'Then may your heart ease and open to greater love. May the love that flows eternally through the universe embrace and comfort you.' "

Gradually I felt the white light diffusing and, with it, Hunter's pain. My eyes met his. There was something different in them, a new clarity. I felt something that had bound him dissolving. "Thank you," he said.

"Courtesy of Alyce," I told him shakily. "I didn't realize quite how much it hurt. I'm sorry."

He kissed my forehead and pulled me against him. When I'd stopped trembling, he said, "Would you like to know why we're sitting here freezing our bums off instead of eating lunch?"

"Oh, that."

"Yes, that," he said. "First, I'm sorry for not answering your messages. It took us a while to find our contact, and then when we finally tracked him down, he was absolutely terrified. He led us through a maze of elaborate safety precautions. If I'd answered you and he'd noticed, he might have thought I was betraying him."

"It's all right," I said. "I was just worried about you. Did this guy have any information?"

"Yes," Hunter said, "he did."

He paused. The sun, which hadn't been strong that morning, disappeared behind a band of thick, white clouds.

"So?" I prompted after a moment.

Hunter's green eyes looked troubled. "I found out who the leader of the New York Amyranth cell is. Apparently the members of the coven wear masks that represent their animal counterparts when they need to draw on the power of that animal. Their leader wears the wolf's mask. My contact didn't know them all, but he confirmed that there are also coven members who wear the masks of an owl, a viper, a cougar, a jaguar, and a weasel."

"So my dream—"

"Was of the New York cell of Amyranth," Hunter finished. "Yes."

I shuddered. "Hunter, I had the dream again," I told him.

"It was just about an hour ago, while I was in an occult book-store down in SoHo."

"Goddess!" Hunter looked alarmed. "Why didn't you contact me?" Before I could answer, he let out an exclamation of annoyance. "Stupid question. I wasn't answering your messages. Morgan, I'm sorry."

"It's okay," I said. "I mean, it was scary, but this time I knew what it was. I'm not sure why I had it again, though."

"Perhaps because we're in New York," he said. "Or perhaps . . ." He trailed off, looking still more troubled. Then he reached out and took my hand. "There's something I've got to tell you. Something I learned today. It will bring up painful thoughts for you."

Icy fingers of dread walked up my spine as I sensed the weight of whatever news Hunter was carrying. I gave him a weak smile. "Go for it."

"The name of this wolf-masked leader is Ciaran," he said.

"Ciaran?" I felt sick. "It—it can't be the same Ciaran. I mean, surely there's more than one Ciaran in the world."

"I'm sure there is," Hunter agreed. "But this Ciaran is a powerful Woodbane witch in his early forties who comes from northern Scotland. I'm sorry, Morgan, but there really isn't any doubt. He's the one who killed Maeve and Angus."

I realized I'd never had any idea of what happened to Ciaran after he set the fire that killed my parents. "I guess I assumed he was back in Scotland," I said lamely. "But he's here in New York City?"

Hunter nodded, his eyes on my face. I sat there, trying to process this new information. Ciaran—alive. Here. Within my reach.

Within my reach? What the hell did that mean? I asked myself bitterly. What would I do if I ever came face-to-face with him? Turn and run the other way, if I had any brains at all. He'd been more powerful than Maeve and Angus together. He could crush me like an ant.

"We also found out that Ciaran has three children," Hunter went on. "Two of them, Kyle and Iona, still live in Scotland. But the youngest is here in New York. You're not going to believe this." He paused. "It's Killian."

"Killian?" My jaw dropped. "The witch we met last night?"

Hunter nodded grimly. "He was all but sitting in my lap, and I didn't realize he was the one."

I downed the last gulp of my now cold coffee. "That's too much of a coincidence."

"There are no coincidences," Hunter reminded me, stating one of those Wiccan axioms that I found so annoying and cryptic.

I thought of the terrified wolf cub in my dream. "That means Killian is Amyranth's intended victim?"

"That's what it looks like," Hunter said.

"Oh God. First Ciaran kills my mother and father; now he's gunning for his own son."

"Ciaran gave himself to the darkness a long time ago," Hunter said. "It's all of a piece. A man capable of killing the love of his life is capable of killing his own son, too."

"What else did you find out? Do you know where he lives? What he looks like?"

"None of that. I've just told you everything." Hunter crumpled his empty coffee cup and launched it at a trash container a good fifteen feet away. The cup went in.

He hopped down off the wall and helped me off. "I've got to try to find Killian and see if I can suss out why Amyranth wants to drain his power. Maybe he has some sort of special ability they need. In any case, he may have valuable information about the coven, and if I play my cards right, he could become a valuable ally for the council."

"I'm going with you," I said impulsively.

Hunter was suddenly holding my upper arms and scowling at me. "Morgan, are you crazy? You can't come with me—especially now that we know Ciaran is the leader of Amyranth. The last thing I want is for him to become aware of your existence. I wish to God you'd stayed in Widow's Vale. In fact, I should take you to Port Authority right now. You can catch the next bus back upstate. I can bring your car and your things back in a day or so."

In a flash we had reverted to our old antagonistic relationship. "Let go of me," I said, furious. "I don't take orders from you. When I go back to Widow's Vale, I'll be driving my own car, thank you, and I'll go when I'm ready."

For a long moment we just glared at each other. I saw Hunter struggling to keep his temper in check.

"If you stay," he said between his teeth, "you've got to give me your word that you'll keep a low profile. No flashy magick on the street. In fact, while we're in the city, I want you to avoid any magick that isn't absolutely necessary. I don't want you drawing any attention to yourself."

I knew he was right, much as I hated to admit it. "Okay," I said sulkily. "I promise."

"Thank you." Hunter's grasp relaxed.

"Be careful," I said.

He kissed me again. "That's my line. Be careful. I'll see you tonight."

I hurried back to Columbus Avenue. As I neared the restaurant, I passed a father carrying his little son on his shoulders. The boy was laughing, as if it were the greatest treat in the world.

It made me wonder about Killian and his father. Was there ever a time when they were close? What would it be like to be the child of a father who was devoted to evil?

Maybe, I thought, it explained Killian's recklessness. Maybe he was running away from the darkness. That, I thought with a sigh, I could certainly understand.

Bree and the others were on their way out when I got back to Murray's.

"Perfect timing," Bree said as she stepped out of the restaurant. "Do you want to come to the Museum of Modern Art with me and Sky?"

"I opted out," Raven said. "I'm going to see a movie down in the Village." I didn't know Raven well enough to be sure, but she was talking more loudly than usual, and I had a feeling it meant that things between her and Sky were still tense.

I glanced at Robbie. He looked so miserable, I was certain that he hadn't been invited on the museum trip. I tried to remember: Was Bree always this ruthless in relationships? Or was Robbie getting special treatment because he was the one she actually cared about? Either way, her behavior made me uncomfortable.

"No thanks," I said, my voice curt. "I'm not in the mood."

Bree shrugged. "Okay, we'll see you back at the apartment."

I started for Broadway. Since I was unexpectedly on my own, it occurred to me that now would be a good time to see if I could find Maeve and Angus's old apartment. I thought of the promise I'd made Hunter, to refrain from anything that might draw unwelcome attention to me. But looking for my birth parents' old apartment wouldn't do that, I reasoned. I'd just have to make sure I avoided using magick during the search.

A ray of late-afternoon sun emerged from the clouds as I walked, and that bit of brightness seemed to lift the mood on the street. Two skateboarders whizzed by while a woman assured her reluctant poodle that it was a beautiful day for a walk. I suddenly realized that Robbie was trailing behind me.

"Robbie," I said. "Where are you going?"

Robbie gave an overly casual shrug. "I thought I'd hang with you. Is that okay?"

Robbie looked so miserable and abandoned that I couldn't say no. Besides, Robbie was special. He'd been with me when I found Maeve's tools.

"I'm not going to a very scenic part of the city," I warned. "Um—I was kind of trying to keep this quiet. You know, discreet."

Robbie raised his eyebrows. "What, are you going to score some dope or something?"

I swatted him on the shoulder. "Idiot. Of course not. It's just . . . Maeve and Angus had an apartment in Hell's Kitchen before they moved upstate. I want to find it."

"Okay," Robbie said. "I don't know what the big secret is, but I'll keep my mouth shut."

We walked on in silence. I was the one who finally broke it. "I think your restraint is admirable," I told him. "If I were you, I would have decked Bree a long time ago."

He grinned at me. "You did once, didn't you?"

I winced at the memory of a horrible argument in the hallway at school. An argument about Cal. "I slapped her across the face," I corrected him. "Actually, it felt awful."

"Yeah, that's what I figured."

I tried to think of a delicate way to put my question. "Did things go—okay—between you two last night?"

Robbie took a deep breath. "That's what's so weird. It was great. I mean, as great as it could be with Raven snoring right next to us. We just cuddled. And it felt good to be together, totally warm and affectionate—and right. It was sweet, Morgan, for both of us, I swear."

"So, what changed this morning?" I asked.

"I don't have a clue. I woke up, said good morning to Bree when I saw her in the kitchen, and she snapped my head off. I can't figure out what I did."

I thought about it as we waited at the bus stop. I wondered how much I could tell Robbie without betraying what Bree had told me. After about ten minutes of waiting, a bus finally lumbered to a stop. We managed to snag seats together, facing the center aisle.

"Maybe you didn't do anything wrong," I said, grateful for the blasting heat. I loosened my scarf and peeled off my gloves. "Or maybe what you did wrong last night was to be right."

Robbie massaged his forehead. "You just lost me."

"Okay, maybe last night things were every bit as great as

you thought they were," I said. "And maybe that's the problem. When things are good is when Bree has trouble trusting them. So that's when she has to mess them up again."

"That makes absolutely no sense," Robbie said.

I gave him a look. "Did I ever claim Bree was logical?"

We got off at Forty-ninth Street and began walking west. "We're looking for number seven-eight-eight," I told Robbie.

He glanced up at the building we were passing. "We're nowhere near."

We waited for the light on Ninth Avenue to turn. Ninth Avenue looked pretty decent, with lots of restaurants and small shops selling ethnic foods. But as we kept walking west, Forty-ninth Street became seedier and seedier. The theaters and little studio workshops were gone now. Garbage was piled by the curb. The buildings were mostly residential tenement types, with crumbling brickwork and boarded-up windows. Many were spray-painted with gang tags. We were in Hell's Kitchen.

I knew that this neighborhood had a long history of violent crime. Robbie was wide-eyed and wary. I cast my senses, hoping to pick up any trace Maeve might have left. At first all I got were flashes of the people in the neighborhood: families in crowded apartments; a few elderly people, ailing and miserably alone; a crack junkie, adrenaline rocketing through her body. Then I felt the hairs along the back of my neck rise. In the worn brickwork of an abandoned building I saw vestiges of runes and magickal symbols, nearly covered over by layers of graffiti. It didn't feel like Maeve's or Angus's work. That made sense; they had renounced their powers completely when they fled Ireland. But it was proof that witches had been here.

"This is it," Robbie said as we came to a soot-streaked redbrick tenement with iron fire escapes running down its front. The building was narrow and only five stories high. It seemed sad and neglected, and I wondered how much worse it had gotten since Maeve and Angus had lived in it nearly twenty years ago.

I couldn't pick up any trace of my birth mother, but that didn't mean there wasn't something inside the building. If only I could get into the actual apartment where she'd lived. Three low stairs led to a front door behind a steel-mesh gate. A sign on a first-floor window read Apartments for Rent, Powell Mgmt. Co. I rang the bell marked Superintendent and waited.

No one answered the bell or my pounding on the steel gate. Robbie said, "Now what?"

I could try a spell, I thought. But I wasn't supposed to use magick unless I absolutely had to. And this didn't qualify as an emergency.

"Can I use your phone?" I asked Robbie. I called the management company on Robbie's cell phone. To my astonishment, the woman on the phone told me that apartment three was available. I was so excited, my voice shook as I made an appointment to see the place the next day. It was meant to be, I thought. Obviously.

"I hate to bring this up," Robbie said when I hung up. "But you look like the high school kid you are. I mean, why would anyone show you an apartment?"

"I'm not sure," I told Robbie. "But I'll find a way."

7

The Watch

August 20, 1981

This morning at dawn I took Maeve for a walk along the cliffs. We were both still floating on the joy of last night. Yet I knew I had to tell her. I expected it to shock, possibly hurt her, but I was certain she'd forgive me in the end. After all, we are mùirn beatha dàns.

Maeve was going on about where we'd live. Much as she loves Ballynigel, she does not want to stay here her entire life; she wants to see the world, and I would love nothing more than to show it to her. But her happy ramblings were like blows to my heart. At last, when I could stand to wait no more, I told her, as gently as I could, that I was not yet free to travel with her, that I had a wife and two children in Scotland.

At first she only looked at me in confusion. I repeated what I'd said, this time taking her hands in mine.

Then her confusion was replaced by disbelief. She begged me, weeping, to tell her it wasn't true. But I couldn't. I could not lie to her.

I pulled her close to kiss away her tears. But she would have none of me. She yanked her hands from mine and stepped away. I pleaded with her to give me time. I told her I couldn't afford to enrage Greer—not if I wanted to take her place. But I swore I'd leave the lot of them as soon as I could.

She cut me off. "You will not leave your wife and children," she said, the anguish in her eyes turning to fire. "First you betray me with lies. Now you want to destroy a family as well?" Then she told me to leave her, to get away.

I couldn't believe she was serious. I argued, cajoled, begged. I told her to take time to consider. I said we'd find a gentle way to go forward together, that, of course, I would provide for my family. But no matter what I said, I could not dissuade her. She who had been so soft, so yielding, was suddenly like iron.

My soul is shattered. Tomorrow I return to Scotland.

—Neimhidh

When we got back to Ninth Avenue, Robbie took off on his own. I went back to Bree's father's place. We hadn't made any group plans for the evening, and the apartment was empty. For a while I couldn't settle down. I was too revved up—from the news about Ciaran being here in the city, from having found Maeve's old building. Was the watch still there? I wondered. If it was, would I be able to find it? I tried to scry for it, but I was too wired to concentrate. Finally I curled up with the book on scrying that I'd bought in SoHo and read for a while.

The sun had almost set when I sensed Hunter walking down the hall. I couldn't quite believe my luck. Were we really going to have a chance to be alone together in the apartment? I rushed into the bathroom and quickly brushed my teeth and my hair.

But the moment Hunter opened the door, I realized this was not going to be a romantic interlude. He walked in, took off his scarf and jacket, gave me a curt nod, then went to stare morosely out the window.

I went to stand beside him. Despite his mood, I immediately tuned in to our connection. I couldn't have defined either of them, but this was completely different from my connection with the man in the bookstore. Hunter touched everything in me. It was a delicious tease to stand near him, not physically touching, and let myself feel how his presence stroked my every nerve ending into a state of total anticipation.

He reached out and caught my hand in his. "Don't," he said gently. "I can't be with you that way right now."

"What happened?" I asked, feeling a twinge of alarm. "What went wrong?"

"My finding Killian. I didn't. Either he got wind of the fact that a council Seeker is looking for him or Amyranth has already snatched him because I can't find him anywhere."

"Did you try—"

Hunter began to pace the length of the living room. "I

found his flat, rang his doorbell and his phone. I went to the club, found out the names of some of his friends, and asked them. I've sent him witch messages. He doesn't answer any of them. I even took out my *lueg* and scryed right on the street. That's how desperate I was for a lead—any lead. And none of it has done a bit of good," he finished bitterly.

He dropped onto the couch and ran a hand through his hair. "I simply don't know where to go next with this. I'm going to have to contact the council again."

"Want me to try scrying?"

"I've scryed my way to Samhain and back again and I haven't seen a trace of Killian."

"I know. But I scry with fire," I reminded him. "I might get a different result."

He shrugged and reached for a thick, ivory candle on the coffee table—one that Bree must have bought the day before—and pushed it toward me. "Be my guest," he said, but his voice was skeptical.

I settled myself cross-legged on the floor. I focused on my breathing, but my thoughts didn't slip away as easily as they usually did. I wondered if I'd be able to transfer what I'd done with the crystal to fire. Whether this time I'd be able to control the vision.

"Morgan?"

"Sorry," I said. "I got distracted. Let me try again. You want to see where Killian is right now?"

"That'd be a start."

"Okay." Again I focused on my breathing. This time I felt my mind quieting and the tension draining from my muscles. I stared at the candle's wick, thought of fire, and the candle lit. I let my eyes focus on the flame, sinking deeper into my meditative state until the coffee table, the room, Hunter, even the candle itself faded from my consciousness. There was only the flame.

Killian. I let a picture of him as he'd been at the club fill my mind—confident, cocky, laughing, with that heady mix of danger and delight in his own power.

I focused on the fire, asked it to give me the vision that I sought, to show me Killian as he was right now. I asked it to let me in, and I sent my energy toward it. I couldn't touch it the way I'd touched the crystal. The fire would burn me. But I let my power flicker beside it, calling to its heat and energy.

Something inside the flame shifted. It danced higher, blazed brighter. Its blue center became a mirror, and in it I saw Killian in profile. He was alone in a dark, dilapidated room. There was a window across from him, casting reddish light across his face. Through the window I could see some sort of gray stone tower, partly cloaked by a screen of bare tree branches. Killian seemed frightened, his face pale and drawn.

I sent more of my power to the flame, willing more of the vision to appear, something that would give a clue to his location. The flame crackled, and Killian turned and looked straight into my eyes. Abruptly, the connection was severed. I pushed back a surge of annoyance and focused on the flame again. Again I asked for the vision of Killian as he was now and sent my energy to dance with the flame.

This time there was no vision. Instead, the flame winked out, almost as if someone had snuffed it. I blinked hard. The rest of the room came back into focus.

Hunter was watching me, his eyes inscrutable. "I saw him," he said in an odd tone. "And I wasn't joining my power to yours. I've never been able to do that before, see the vision of the one who's scrying."

"Is that a problem?" I asked uncertainly.

"No," he said. "It's because your scrying is so powerful." He pulled me up on the couch beside him and wrapped his arms around me. "You are a seer." He kissed each of my eyelids. "And I'm awed. Even humbled—almost."

"Almost?" I couldn't help being thrilled that I'd managed to pull off a feat of magick that had stymied Hunter.

"Well, you know, humble isn't exactly my style," he confessed with a grin.

"I've noticed."

"Nor is it Killian's," he said, his tone serious again. He blew out a breath and leaned back against the couch. "At least we know he's alive. He didn't seem hurt, either. He looked scared, though. That room he was in, do you have any sense of where it is?"

I shook my head. "None."

"I wonder," Hunter said, "why the vision was snuffed out so quickly and why it didn't come back. It's almost as if someone didn't want you to see."

"Maybe Killian himself," I said. "He looked at me, remember? Maybe he felt me scrying for him. Do you think he's got enough power to cut off a vision?"

"I'd guess that he's not lacking in power," Hunter said with a sigh.

"There's got to be a way to find him," I said.

"Hang on a minute," Hunter said. "The window across

from him. Did you notice the church steeple you could see through it?"

"Oh!" I exclaimed. "That's what it was."

"Yes. And there was reddish light on his face, so I'm pretty sure the window must have been a westerly one. Also, wherever he is must be far enough west that the sunset isn't blocked by lots of tall buildings."

"Wow." I was impressed by his deductions.

He looked intent, eager. "I'm thinking maybe I could find a building that satisfies those conditions—far west, with a westerly window, opposite a gray stone church."

"That sounds like a lot of legwork."

"Maybe tomorrow I can come up with a way to narrow the search. Listen, there's one more contact I want to try to track down tonight. I'm not sure when I'll get back."

I glanced at my watch. It was six. "Are you telling me not to wait up?"

Hunter looked genuinely regretful. "I'm afraid so." He put on his jacket and scarf and kissed me. "I'll be back as soon as I can."

Robbie was the first to show up at the apartment. After we'd split up, he'd gone down to the Village, where he'd dropped in on one of the chess shops near Washington Square Park. "Got beat by a seventy-year-old grand master," he reported with a satisfied grin. "It was an education."

Bree, Raven, and Sky showed up a few minutes after Robbie—Raven must have hooked up with the other two at some point during the afternoon. Bree was irritable and out of sorts, but Raven and Sky seemed to be getting along again. We ordered Chinese food, and then Raven and Sky went out to look up some goth friends of Raven's while Robbie, Bree, and I watched a Hong Kong action movie on pay-per-view. An exciting Friday night in the big city.

Whenever it was that Hunter returned to the apartment, I was asleep.

On Saturday morning I woke up before Bree. Raven wasn't in the room; extending my senses, I realized that she was in the study with Sky. Quietly I pulled on jeans and a sweater. I found Hunter in the kitchen, washing up a plate and cup. "Morning," he said. "Want me to make you a cup of tea before I go?"

"You know better," I said, and reached into the fridge for a Diet Coke.

"Ugh," he said. "Well, I'm off on a long day of looking for gray stone churches and westerly windows."

"It sounds like it could take you a week," I said. "There must be hundreds of churches like that in the city."

He shrugged, looking resigned. "What else can I do? Whether Killian is hiding his own tracks or someone else is doing it for him, I'm not getting anywhere trying to find him by magick." He picked up his jacket. "What are you going to do today?" he asked.

I helped myself to one of the Pop-Tarts that Bree had thoughtfully stocked up on and tried to look nonchalant. "Robbie and I thought we'd wander around the city for a while." It wasn't a lie—I knew better than that with Hunter. But it wasn't the whole truth, either.

Hunter gave me a searching look but didn't question me further. "I'll see you this evening for our circle," he said.

*   *   *

"We'll be the perfect young couple," Robbie said as we walked down Forty-ninth Street. "I mean, you've got a ring and everything." He glanced at the fake diamond ring we'd just bought at a tacky gift shop and shook his head. "Whoa. It's a little freaky to see that thing on you."

"Yeah, well, imagine how I feel wearing it," I said.

Robbie laughed. "Just think what a promising future we're in for, starting out in a tenement apartment in Hell's Kitchen."

"That's all Maeve and Angus started with in this country," I said. I felt suddenly very sad. "The entries from her Book of Shadows at that time were all about how she couldn't bear living in the city. She thought it was full of unhappy people, racing around pointlessly."

"Well, it is, sort of." Robbie gave me a sympathetic glance. "And didn't they come here straight after Ballynigel was destroyed? Of course she was depressed. She'd just lost her home, her family, nearly everyone she loved."

"And she'd given up her magick," I added. "She said it was like living in a world suddenly stripped of all its colors. It makes me sad for her."

We reached the building. It seemed even more dilapidated today. Robbie grinned at me. "Well, Ms. Rowlands. Are you ready for your first real estate experience?"

"Hey, my mom is a Realtor," I reminded him. "I probably know more about leases than the rental agent."

Still, I could feel my heart race as I rang the super's bell. I was about to see my birth parents' apartment! What would it be like? Would I be able to find the watch?

"Who is it?" asked a woman's voice over a crackly intercom.

"It's Morgan and Robbie Rowlands," I called back. "I spoke to the management company yesterday about the apartment for rent. They said you would show it to me today at noon."

Robbie tapped his watch. We were on time.

"All right," she said after a hesitation. "I'll be right there."

We waited another five minutes before the steel gate was opened to reveal a short, heavyset woman in her late sixties. I could see the pink of her scalp through gray pin curls.

She looked at me and Robbie, and I saw the suspicion in her eyes.

"The apartment's this way," she grumbled.

We followed her up a flight of stairs and down a narrow hallway. The paint was peeling, and the place reeked of urine. I hoped it hadn't been this bad when Maeve and Angus lived here. I couldn't bear the thought of my mother, who'd had such a profound love of the earth, walking into this ugliness every day.

The woman took a ring of keys from the pocket of her housedress and opened a door with the number two on it. "The rent's six-seventy-five a month," she told us. "You don't find prices like that in Manhattan anymore. Better grab it fast."

"Actually, we came to see apartment three," I said. "The management company said it was available."

She gave me a look that reminded me of the look I'd gotten from the clerk in the records office. "They were wrong. I got someone living in apartment three," she said. "It's not for rent. This one is. Do you want to see it or not?"

Robbie and I exchanged glances. I was fighting intense disappointment. All this for nothing. We weren't going to get into Maeve's apartment. I wasn't going to find the watch after all.

"We'll look at it," Robbie said. As the woman lumbered toward the stairs, he nudged me and whispered, "I didn't want this woman realizing we were poseurs and calling the police or something."

She let us into a dark, railroad-flat apartment, not much wider than the narrow hallway. "This is your living room," she said as we entered a small front room. She tapped the steel bars that covered the window. "Security," she told us proudly.

The kitchen had a claw-foot bathtub, a small refrigerator desperately in need of cleaning, and a family of large, healthy cockroaches living in the sink. "Just put down some boric acid," the woman said casually.

Then she took us into the last room, a tiny decrepit bedroom with a window the size of a phone directory.

"You two got jobs?"

"I work in . . . with computers," Robbie said.

"I waitress," I said. That had been Maeve's first job in America.

"Well, you'll have to put all that in the application," the woman said. "Come down to my apartment and you can fill one out."

I was wondering how we were going to get out of the application process when I felt something in the tiny bedroom calling me. I studied the stained ceiling.

"There used to be a leak," the woman admitted, her gaze following mine. "But we fixed it."

But that wasn't what had caught my attention. I had felt a magickal pull from the corner of the ceiling. Looking more closely, I saw that one of the panels of the dropped ceiling was slightly askew. Whatever I was sensing was behind that panel. The watch? Could it possibly be, after all these years? I had to find out.

"I told you, we fixed the leak," the woman said loudly.

I bit back an irritated reply. I needed a moment of privacy. How was I going to get rid of this woman?

Frustrated, I raised my eyebrows at Robbie and nodded toward the living room. Robbie shot me a "Who, me?" look.

I nodded again, more emphatically.

"Um—could I ask you a question about the living room?" Robbie said hesitantly. "It's about the woodwork."

"What woodwork?" the woman demanded, but she followed him, anyway.

As soon as they had left the room, I shut the door and quickly turned the lock. I had to reach that ceiling panel. There was only one way. I climbed up on the narrow window ledge and balanced precariously.

Thank the Goddess for low ceilings! I thought as I found I could just reach the panel. With my fingertips I pushed up against it. The panel moved a fraction of an inch. I stretched and pressed harder. The magickal pull was getting stronger. I felt a faint warm current against my hand. I stretched, groaned softly, and gave another hard push.

The panel lifted up and I fell off the ledge onto the floor with a thud.

"Ow," I mumbled. Quickly I climbed back up onto the ledge. I heard the superintendent's footsteps hurrying across the apartment. Then she was twisting the doorknob, trying to open the door.

"Hey, what's going on in there?" she yelled, pounding on the door. "What are you doing? Are you okay?"

"I'm sure she's fine," Robbie said quickly.

"Then come out of there!" the woman shouted, pounding harder.

Just ignore her, I told myself, heart racing. I stuck my fingers through the open panel. Empty space and a wooden beam. Then my fingers closed on smooth fabric encasing something hard and round.

"You come out right now or I'm calling the police!" the woman shouted.

I didn't hesitate. This was absolutely necessary magick. If he ever found out, Hunter would understand.

"You will forget," I whispered. "You never saw us. This did not happen. You will forget."

It was as simple as that. One moment the woman was screaming and threatening, the next I heard her ask Robbie, "So you want to see the apartment? You know, you're the first one I've shown it to."

I put the panel back in place, then jumped down from the ledge, clutching the watch. Apartment three must be directly upstairs, I realized. Maeve must have hidden the watch beneath her floorboards. I unfolded the green silk and felt a protective spell whispering from the material. The watch case was gold, engraved with a Celtic knot pattern. A white face, gold hands. A tiny cabochon ruby on the end of the winding stem. I stared at it, and tears rose in my eyes. It represented so many things to me, things both wonderful and horrible.

But there was no time to think about that now. I tucked the watch into my pocket and unlocked the door. Then I went out to get Robbie.

"You're not going to believe what I found in there!" I said when we were about a block away from the apartment. "You've got to see this watch." I started to take it from my pocket.

Robbie was walking fast, his eyes on the sidewalk. "Just put it away," he said.

"What?" I was startled at his angry tone.

"I don't want to see it," he snapped.

I stared at him. "What's wrong?" I asked. "Is this about Bree?"

Robbie turned on me, his eyes blazing. "No, Morgan. This is about you. What the hell happened back there? One minute that old lady was calling for you to get out of the bedroom. The next minute she couldn't remember ever having seen us before."

"I did a little spell," I said. "I made her forget."

"You did what?"

"Robbie, it's okay," I said. "It was temporary. It's already worn off."

"How do you know that?" he demanded. "How do you know that spell didn't rewire her brain? How do you know she won't think she's going senile when she suddenly remembers the two people she blanked on? Elderly people find that kind of thing a little upsetting."

"I know because I made the spell," I said, keeping my voice calm. "What are you so freaked about, anyway?"

Robbie looked enraged. "You don't get it, do you? You messed with someone's mind! You've lucked into these amazing powers, and you're abusing them. How do I know you won't do something like that to me?"

I felt like he'd knocked the wind out of me. When I found my voice, it sounded high and tinny. "Because I gave you my word that I wouldn't. Come on, Robbie, we've been friends since second grade. You know I'm not like that. This was a special circumstance."

He looked at me like I was a stranger, a stranger who frightened him. "The Morgan I know wouldn't screw around with some poor old lady. You played her like she was a puppet. And I feel like a jerk for having been part of that whole charade. I feel dirty."

I tried to calm the butterflies in my stomach. This was serious. "Robbie, I'm sorry," I said. "I had no right to make you part of that. But this watch belonged to Maeve. I had to get it. Did you really think I could leave it there? It was my mother's. That makes it my birthright."

"Like your power?" he asked, his voice shaking.

"Yes. Exactly like my power." Every so often words come out of your mouth with a cool, resonant certainty and you know you've hit a bone-deep truth. There's no taking it back or denying it. That's how it felt then, and Robbie and I both stood there, suspended for a moment in the awful implications of what I'd just said.

Maeve had given up her magick, but there was nothing on this earth that would make me give up mine.

"So this birthright of yours." I could see him fighting for control, trying to keep his voice steady. "It gives you the right to manipulate some woman you don't even know?"

"I didn't say that!"

"No, it's just what you *did*. You were flexing your power. Well, I'm starting to think maybe your power isn't such a great thing."

"Robbie, that's not true! I—"

"Forget it," he said. "I'm going to see if I can get in on another chess game. If I'm going to be totally overwhelmed, at least it's going to be by something I understand."

He stalked off down Ninth Avenue, leaving me with Maeve's watch and a sick feeling in the pit of my stomach.

8

Spy

August 27, 1981

I've been back in Scotland almost a week now. And a bleak, colorless landscape it is. Was I ever happy here? Grania met me at the door with bawling babies clinging to her skirts and a list of complaints. It had been pouring for ten days straight, and the thatching on the roof was leaking, making the entire house reek of mildew. Oh, and little Iona was cutting a tooth and couldn't I make a tincture for the pain? It's a wonder she didn't ask me to stop the rains. The thing is, Grania's not without power of her own. Before the babies came, she was a promising witch. But now she's the martyr, and it's all up to me. I wasn't home half an hour before I left for the pub, and I've spent most of my time there ever since. I can't face my own home. Can't face life without Maeve.

Last night was the worst yet. The little ones both had a bug. Kyle was feverish. Iona couldn't keep down anything she ate. With Greer still in Ballynigel, I was called on to lead a circle. I came back to find Grania shrieking like a harpy. How could I have left her with two sick kids? Didn't I care about my own children? I didn't have it in me to lie. "No," I told her. "Nor do I care for you, you fat cow." She struck me then, and I nearly struck her back. Instead, I told her she was a shrew and a chore just to look at. Made her cry, which of course drove me even farther round the bend. Finally I took her to bed just to get her to stop the waterworks. It was awful. All I wanted was Maeve in my arms.

Today Grania's playing the victim for all it's worth, and I find myself wishing I could stop her pathetic whining once and for all. It would cost me the coven, though. She's still Greer's daughter, with a certain inherited position here, no matter how undeserved.

I have so much rage in me that everything I see is enclosed in an aura of flaming red. I am furious with Maeve for her self-righteous rejection of me. Furious with myself for marrying Grania, when I should have known Maeve was out there, waiting for me. And furious with Grania for having the wretched luck to be who she is.

She just came in to tell me that she already feels a child stirring within her from last night's mockery of lovemaking. "It *will be a boy," she said, a sickly hope on her face. "What shall we name him?"*

"We shall call him Killian," I answered. It means strife.

—Neimhidh

I was grateful no one else was in the apartment when I got back. I was still trying to pull myself together after Robbie's accusations. After the shock had come anger. How could he have thought I'd hurt that old woman? How could he accuse me of such awful things? I'd assumed Robbie was strong enough not to be freaked by things he didn't understand. Instead, he'd gotten totally hysterical. He hadn't even listened when I'd tried to explain.

Yet I couldn't help feeling a twinge—more than a twinge—of guilt. There'd been some truth in what Robbie had said. Plus I'd broken my promise to Hunter to keep a low profile.

I drew out the watch that Ciaran had given to Maeve. The gold case gleamed softly in the light coming through the living room windows. I pulled out the ruby-tipped winding stem and wound it to the right, deasil, feeling the resistance of the spring inside. Would it work after all these years? Yes, there was a soft, even ticking.

Had it been worth my trouble? I wondered, thinking about the argument with Robbie. Yes. I could no more have left the watch in that awful apartment than I could have left Maeve's Book of Shadows in Selene's house.

Sitting cross-legged on Bree's father's couch, I tried to find a way through the murk. I wasn't going to lose Robbie, I told myself. Especially now that I'd sort of lost Bree. We both needed to calm down, and we probably both needed to apologize. And Robbie needed to realize that I was still the same Morgan he knew and trusted.

But you're not, a voice inside me said. You're a blood witch, and no one but another blood witch will ever understand.

Again I thought about why I'd wanted the watch so badly. Was it simply because it had been loved by Maeve? Or was I fascinated by the fact that it had been given to her by Ciaran, her *mùirn beatha dàn*, the man who eventually became her murderer? I felt my jaw tensing with anger as I thought of him, and I had to will myself to relax.

Then my senses tingled. Hunter was approaching. I took a few deep breaths to calm my conflicted heart. I wasn't ready to discuss this with Hunter, both because I was certain he'd side with Robbie and because I knew he wouldn't approve of my having anything connected to Ciaran.

I tucked the watch away in my pocket and went to the door.

"Hey," I said as he came in. "How was the rest of your day?"

Hunter pulled me to him. "Spectacularly lousy. How was yours?"

"So-so. You didn't find that building?"

"Not yet, no. I'm going to keep looking. I just wanted to stop in and tell you I wouldn't be here for tonight's circle." Hunter arched one blond eyebrow. "Anyone else here?"

"Nope. Just you and me."

"Thank the Goddess for that," he said. He held me tight, and I felt that familiar shift as our energies aligned in perfect synchronicity. "Mmm," I said. "This is nice. I think I've had enough of the group experience."

Hunter laughed. "You didn't expect we'd get on each other's nerves living in such close quarters? Try growing up in a coven where everyone's been able to read your emotions from the day you were born. There's a reason New York is teeming with witches run away from home."

He took off his jacket, and we went into the kitchen. I got myself a Diet Coke from the fridge.

Hunter wrinkled his nose. "How can you drink that vile stuff?"

"It's delicious. And nutritious."

"You would think so," he said darkly. He sighed. "I'm up against a brick wall, Morgan. Killian was here, and now he's gone. I've been—what do they say? Not beating the bushes."

"Pounding the pavement?" I suggested helpfully.

"Whatever. Not a trace of him anywhere. It's almost as if he never existed." Hunter ran himself a glass of water from the tap. "I didn't imagine him, did I?"

"If you did, then we shared the same arrogant hallucination."

A corner of Hunter's mouth lifted. "You didn't find him—attractive?"

"No," I said, realizing with some surprise that I was being totally honest, not trying to save Hunter's feelings. "I liked him. I thought he was fun. But he also seemed kind of stuck on himself."

"Personally, I think he's a pain, but that doesn't mean he isn't worth saving."

"That's big of you," I teased, but the worried look in Hunter's eyes scared me. "You think Amyranth has him already, don't you?"

He didn't reply, but his lips thinned.

"Look, why don't we just put off the circle for a night?" I suggested. "We could all help you search for him."

Hunter's answer was swift and firm. "No. Especially now that we know Ciaran's involved. I don't want you anywhere near this."

"Do you think he already knows about me? I mean, that Maeve and Angus had a daughter."

Hunter looked absolutely miserable. "God, I hope not."

I took some deep breaths and tried to fight off the feeling of dread.

I felt Hunter's hand close around my wrist. "I'm going to leave soon. But first . . . come with me. Let's just . . . be with each other for a little while."

I nodded. We went into the guest bedroom and lay down on my narrow mattress. I let Hunter hold me loosely in his arms. I wanted to clasp him to me, to stave off all the desperation and fear charging through me. I wanted never to let him go.

"We can't hold on to each other forever, you know," he said, echoing my thoughts.

"Why not?" I asked. "Why can't we just stay here and keep each other safe?"

He kissed the tip of my nose. "For one thing, I'm a Seeker. For another, none of us can guarantee another's safety, much as we'd love to." He kissed me again, this time on the mouth. I could feel his heart beating against mine. Someday, I thought, when all this is over, we'll be able to be like this all the time. Warm, close together.

Someday.

* * *

By the time I'd changed, set out candles and salt, and purified the living room with the smoke of cedar and sage, Hunter was gone and everyone else had returned to the apartment.

Though Bree and Robbie seemed to be keeping their distance, Sky and Raven had come in together. Packages were put away. Plans for later that evening were discussed. When everyone had finally settled in, we gathered in the living room for our circle. It felt odd to be there without Jenna, Matt, Ethan, Sharon, and the other members of Kithic. I wondered briefly what they were doing back in Widow's Vale.

Since Sky was the only initiated witch among us, she would lead the circle. But first, at Hunter's request, I filled everyone in on the Killian situation.

"Let's work a spell to lift obstacles and send power to Hunter," Sky suggested.

We pushed the few pieces of furniture against the walls and rolled up the rug. Sky traced a wide circle with chalk on the wood floor. On each of the four compass points she placed one of the four elements: a small dish of water for water, a stick of incense for air, a crystal for earth, and a candle for fire. One by one, we entered the circle. Sky closed it behind us.

"We come together to honor the Goddess and the God," she began. "We ask their help and guidance. May our magick be pure and strong, and may we use it to help those in need."

We joined hands, each of us focusing on our breathing. Bree stood on one side of me, Robbie on the other. I opened my senses. I could feel the familiar presences of the others, feel their heartbeats. They were all precious to me, I realized. Even

Raven. The circle bound us as allies in the fight against darkness.

Slowly we began to move deasil. I felt power moving through me. I drew energy up from the earth and down from the sky.

Sky had us visualize the rune Thorn, for overcoming adversity. Then she led us in a chant for lifting obstacles. The circle began to move faster. I could feel the energy humming, rising, flowing among us, getting stronger. Sky's pale face was alight with the purity of the power she was channeling. She traced a sigil in the air, and I felt the power lift and rise above the circle.

"To Hunter," she said.

Abruptly the air changed. The thrum of power was gone. Suddenly we seemed like a bunch of teenagers, standing around a New York City living room instead of the beings of power we'd been just moments before.

"Good work," Sky said, sounding pleased. "Everyone, sit down for a moment. Ground yourselves."

We all sat down on the floor.

"Something real happened there," Robbie said.

Bree looked worried. "How do we know that energy went to Hunter and didn't get picked up by the Woodbanes?"

"I bound it with a sigil of protection before I sent it out," Sky answered.

"So now he should be able to find Killian?" Raven asked.

Sky shrugged her slender shoulders. "There are no guarantees, of course. Killian seems to have a gift for making himself scarce. But hopefully what we just did will make it a little easier for Hunter." She glanced around at the circle. "We'd better clean up."

For the next twenty minutes we cleaned up and debated

what everyone was going to do with the rest of the evening. Raven wanted to go to another club—a normal, nonwitch one, this time—while Robbie wanted to hear some obscure band that was playing in Tribeca, and Bree wanted to go to a trendy pool hall down near Battery Park. I, of course, was wondering if Hunter was going to show up, but it seemed wimpy to say that aloud. And I was tired. Maybe it was the fight with Robbie or the circle, but I felt drained.

We were still trying to make a plan when the apartment door opened and Hunter walked in, one hand gripping Killian's elbow. Killian looked sullen, and Hunter looked irritated. It was clear that Killian had not come of his own free will.

We must all have been staring openmouthed because Killian's sullen expression turned to one of delight. He grinned and said, "I am pretty amazing, aren't I?"

"Are you all right?" I asked, unable to reconcile his cheerful presence with the Killian of my vision.

"Tip-top," Killian replied. "How about you, love?" He flicked his thumb at Hunter. "Must be rough, hanging out with Mr. Doom-and-Gloom here. Sucks the joy right out of life."

"Shut up and sit down," Hunter snapped.

Killian first helped himself to a soda from the fridge and then flopped onto the couch.

"He was in Chelsea," Hunter said, "hiding out in an abandoned apartment building."

"Who said anything about hiding?" Killian protested. "I just wanted some time by myself. No one asked you to come barging in, Seeker."

"Would you rather your father found you first?" Hunter snapped.

Killian gave an overly casual shrug. "Why should I care if my father finds me? As long as he doesn't try to send me to bed early." He held up his hand as Hunter started to speak. "And please, don't start up with that idiocy about him wanting to drain my power. I mean, honestly, where do you get all this? Is that what the council spends its time on—dreaming up daft conspiracy theories?"

I couldn't make sense of it. Had my vision been all wrong? Or had Killian been held somewhere and escaped? Was Killian powerful enough to manipulate my scrying?

Hunter glanced at Bree. "Do you think your father would mind if Killian stayed the night?"

"I guess not," Bree said, but she didn't look happy about it.

"Right, then," Hunter said. "He can sleep in the living room with me and Robbie."

"Oh, joy," Killian caroled.

Robbie dug out another green stuff sack from the mound of gear in the living room and tossed it to him. Killian caught the air mattress, then dropped it on the floor and fixed his gaze on Raven. "I knew we'd meet again. How about if you and I sneak off for a quick pint, get to know each other better?"

"That's enough," Sky said.

Killian shrugged and grinned at me. "Touchy bunch you hang out with. Everyone always taking offense. Are you as bad as the rest of them?"

"Are you playing us off against each other?" I asked, not able to muster quite as much outrage as I should have. There was just something about him that appealed to me. I felt like we were coconspirators. It was a completely alien feeling for me, but I liked it.

Killian's grin grew even wider. "Well, it would provide a little drama."

"Oh, I think you have plenty of drama in your life," Hunter said. "Anyway, you're not going anywhere tonight. I worked too hard to find you—I'm not going to risk you running off or getting captured."

"As if you knew anything about it," Killian said with contempt.

"Would you excuse us for a minute?" I said, motioning for Hunter and Sky to follow me into the study for a quick huddle.

"I think you all ought to go out and leave me here with Killian," I said.

"Are you mad?" Hunter demanded.

"He and I kind of . . . get along," I said. "I don't understand it," I added quickly, "but he's not flirting with me, the way he does with Raven. Bree and Sky both flat-out dislike him. And Hunter, the two of you just irritate each other. I think I might be able to get him to talk if you'll all just leave us here."

"It's too dangerous—" Hunter began.

"I know he's a pain," I said, "but I don't sense any real danger from him."

"Morgan can take care of herself, you know," said Sky. "And it's true. Killian doesn't have that antagonistic streak with her, while I think the rest of us could cheerfully strangle him."

"All right," Hunter agreed at last. "But I'm going to be in the coffee shop in the building. If anything feels dangerous or even a little bit dodgy, I want you to send me a message immediately."

I gave Hunter my word, and five minutes later Killian and I were alone in the apartment. We sat on opposite ends of the couch, watching each other. I tried to figure out why I liked someone so obnoxious. It wasn't sexual attraction. It was something else, something equally as strong. Despite his being clearly amoral and self-centered, there was something oddly lovable about Killian. Maybe it was that he genuinely seemed to like me.

"Are you all right?" he asked. The gentleness in his voice took me by surprise.

"Why wouldn't I be?"

"I don't know," Killian said. "I don't know you very well, do I? But I sense you're feeling weaker than you're used to. Drained, maybe."

Be wary of him, I told myself. "I'm just tired," I said.

"Right, it's been a long day." He glanced at the green stuff sack on the floor. "I could turn in, I suppose, behave myself and make the Seeker happy."

"He's just trying to protect you," I said.

Anger flickered in Killian's dark eyes. "I never asked for protection."

"You need it," I said. "Your own father is trying to kill you."

Killian waved his hand. "The Seeker was going on about the same thing. Let me tell you, right? It's not likely my dad would go after me. He's got much bigger fish to fry, as the saying goes." Killian looked over his shoulder at the kitchen. "Now, there's one thing the States is lacking, a good fish-and-chips joint. I could use some right now, in fact."

"You're out of luck," I said testily. "Back to the subject. Your father is the leader of Amyranth?"

Killian got up and walked over to the window. He leaned his palms against the sill and stared out into the darkness. "My dad is a very powerful witch. I respect his power. I'd be a bloody madman not to. I stay out of his way. He's got no reason to want me dead."

He hadn't answered the question, I noticed with interest. "What about your mother?" I asked.

Killian laughed mirthlessly and turned to face me. "Grania? The bird's got generations of magick in her blood, but does she appreciate it? Not at all. She gets her real power from being a victim. No matter what happens, she suffers. Nobly, dramatically, and loudly. I tell you, I completely understand why my dad left that house. I couldn't wait to get out myself."

"So you came to New York to be with him?" I asked.

"No," he said. "I knew he was here, of course. And there were certain . . . connections for me in the city because of him. But Dad's a heartless bastard. We're not what you would call close." He polished off his soda and looked at me. "What about you? What's your story?"

I shrugged, not wanting to lie about myself, but knowing I shouldn't tell him anything of my real story.

"You're a blood witch," he stated.

I nodded. That much I couldn't hide from him.

"Quite powerful, I can sense that," he went on. "And for reasons that are unfathomable to me, you're quite fond of that bore of a Seeker."

"That's enough," I said sharply.

Killian laughed. "Right. Didn't take me long to find your sore point, did it?"

"Are you always this much fun?" I asked, irritated.

Killian put his hand over his heart and looked to the ceiling. "May the gods strike me dead," he said with mock solemnity. "Always."

"If you weren't running from your father, then who were you running from?" I asked, unable to give it up. "And don't tell me you weren't running."

He looked at me again. All of a sudden the mirth went out of his eyes. "All right," he said, leaning forward. "It's like this. I don't really believe the Seeker is right about me being an Amyranth target," he went on in a hushed voice. "On the other hand, it is true that Amyranth isn't exactly pleased with me. See, I'd all but joined the coven. Never went through with the initiation, but I was in deep enough to learn some of their secrets, the minor ones at least. Then I . . . decided that I didn't want to join. But Amyranth isn't the sort of coven you just walk out on. And my dad took the defection a bit personally."

"It sounds like it took courage to defect," I said, genuinely starting to like him. "What made you do it?"

Killian gave another of his casual shrugs. "I just wasn't into their whole agenda."

"Why not?" Finally, I thought, we were getting somewhere.

But he just winked at me. "Too much homework," he said with a laugh. "Took up all my quality time. New York is a blast. Don't you think it's kind of a waste to spend all your time feeling like one of the witches in a bad production of *Macbeth*?"

I couldn't tell anymore if Killian was being honest or just playing with me. "I think—"

I never finished my sentence because suddenly my witch

senses were on red alert, shrieking in alarm. Killian felt it, too. He was on his feet in an instant, his gaze sweeping the apartment.

"What the hell is that?" I whispered. The sense of menace was so sharp, it was almost physical.

"Someone's trying to get into the apartment," he said.

Instantly I sent a message to Hunter. Then I ran to the video monitor in the hall and pressed the button for the doorman. "Did anyone come past you?" I asked him, trying to keep my voice normal. "Did you send anyone up to this apartment?"

"Bollocks to that," Killian muttered. He peered through the peephole in the door and did a scan of the hallway. "No one there," he reported a moment later. His face was pale. "But someone is definitely paying attention to us. Someone unfriendly."

Something thumped hard against the living room window, and I jumped about a foot in the air. Killian and I both spun around. I got a brief impression of feathers in motion.

"Oh, thank God!" I said, weak with relief. "It was only a pigeon. I thought someone was trying to climb in the window."

The front door flew open, and Hunter burst in. "What is it?" he asked breathlessly.

I ran to him. "Someone's out there," I said, resisting the urge to bury my face in his chest. "Someone's watching us."

"What?" His eyes widened. "Tell me what happened."

My words tumbled over one another as I told him how Killian and I had both felt the hostile attention, how we'd been unable to pin down where it was coming from or who it was. Killian didn't say anything, just nodded every now and then. His face was still pale, but I figured that was normal, after what we'd sensed.

Looking grim, Hunter began to prowl through the apartment. I could tell that his senses were fully extended, and I felt something else besides—probably some Seeker spell he was using to get the danger to reveal itself.

"Nothing," he said, walking back into the living room. "Which doesn't mean that there wasn't something very real trying to get in. Only that whatever it was seems to be gone now." He looked at Killian. "Anything else you noticed that might help us?"

Killian shook his head. "No. Nothing," he said, sounding almost angry. Then he added abruptly, "Look, I'm knackered. I'm going to sleep." Ignoring the air mattress, he stretched out on the couch and rolled over, presenting his back to us.

A moment later the door opened again and the rest of our group came into the apartment. Apparently they had gone to some club where a terrible band was playing and everyone else was in their fifties. There was a good deal of loud discussion of just whose bad idea it had been. Throughout it Killian lay on the couch, eyes closed. He seemed to be asleep, though I didn't see how it was really possible, given the noise level in the room.

After a few moments I retreated to the guest room and crawled into bed. It had been a long day, and in spite of everything on my mind, I fell asleep quickly.

When I woke just before ten the next morning, Hunter was cursing.

Killian was gone.

9

Connections

November 11, 1981

I thought it would get easier. Isn't time supposed to heal all wounds? And if not time, what about the healing rituals our clan has used for hundreds of years?

Why is it that I see Maeve's face when I wake and when I sleep and when I lie in bed with Grania? Maeve, behind every door, around every corner, in every invocation to the Goddess? There is no longer any joy for me in this world. Even my own children cannot hold my interest or attention, and that's probably a kindness. If I really let myself see them, I see them as the things that made Maeve reject me. If not for them, she and I would be together now. I can't forget her. And I can't have her. And the rage does not ebb.

It's funny. Fat, old Greer, of all people, was the one who saw *what was happening. She didn't mince words. "Your soul is sick-ening and your heart shriveling," she told me. "There's a black, twisted thing inside you. So use it, boy."*

At first I was so out of my mind with pain, I didn't under-stand what she meant. It was not hard to figure out, though. Who better to call on dark magick than one whose own soul has sunk into darkness?

—Neimhidh

Hunter was staring out the living room window at a leaden winter sky, his jaw tight with frustration. Raven was still sleep-ing, and Robbie had gone out to get bagels.

Bree sat cross-legged on the living room floor, doing a yoga stretch. "Look, I know you're trying to protect Killian, but personally, I'm not sure his being gone is such a loss."

From the couch Sky said, "I know what you mean."

Hunter's eyes focused on me. "I want to go over what happened last night when you and Killian sensed that hostile presence. I know you think you told me everything, but tell me again. Even the littlest details, no matter how unimpor-tant they might seem."

I sat down on the couch. "We were in the living room, just talking, when we both felt a presence. Killian said something was trying to get into the apartment. I sent that message to you then, and we both searched with our senses. Then I went to the intercom and called the doorman to see if he'd seen any-one. Killian did a scan of the hallway. And then there was a big thump at the window that nearly scared us both to death—"

"You didn't mention anything about a thump last night," Hunter said sharply.

"That's because was it nothing. Just a pigeon. And then right after that you showed up."

Hunter frowned. "A pigeon?"

"What?" I said. "What's wrong?"

"Pigeons aren't nocturnal," Hunter said. He looked tense. "What exactly did you see?"

I felt a stirring of alarm. "Um, it was just a blur. Feathers. Brown and gray, I think. About this big." I held up my hands to make a shape the size of a large cantaloupe.

"That's too big to be a pigeon," Hunter said instantly. "I suspect it was an owl."

My mouth went dry. "You mean . . ."

He nodded. "I mean one of the shape-shifters from Amyranth."

There was a long silence. I tried to still the flutterings of terror in my stomach.

"At least we can be reasonably sure we were right about Killian being their target," Hunter said. "Obviously Amyranth followed him here."

"He knew," I said, suddenly understanding why Killian was so subdued after the "pigeon" incident. "He didn't tell us, but I'm sure he knew exactly what it was."

Hunter blew out a long breath. "Now the question is whether Killian cut out on his own or whether Amyranth somehow managed to spirit him away. But it all comes down to the same thing. Somehow we've got to find him before anything happens to him."

I thought about Ciaran's watch, wondering if we could

somehow use it to figure out where Ciaran was. "Hunter," I said, feeling nervous. "I need to show you something. Come with me for a minute."

Bree and Sky both gave me questioning looks as Hunter followed me into the guest room. Wishing I'd been straight with him from the start, I took the watch from my jacket pocket and handed it to him.

One blond eyebrow arched as he unwrapped the green silk covering. "Where did you get this?" he asked, his eyes unreadable.

I told him the whole story then.

Hunter listened silently. Then for an endless stretch he just looked at me. I didn't need my witch senses to know that I'd disappointed him—by acting so rashly, by having kept the whole thing secret from him, especially once I knew Ciaran was the Amyranth leader.

"I'm sorry," I said. "I should have told you."

"Yes. You should have." He sounded weary. "Nevertheless, the watch might be a valuable aid. Let's see if it will help us." He wound the stem a few turns. "Since you're connected to Maeve and it was hers, you need to be the one to hold it."

I took the watch from him and held it in my hand. Intuitively we both slipped into a meditative state, focusing on the rhythm of the watch's ticking.

Hunter chanted a few words in Gaelic. "A spell to make visible the energies of those who once held the watch dear," he explained.

I felt a warmth along the watch's golden case and a rush of tenderness wound through with what I'd come to recognize as my mother's energy.

"Maeve cherished it," I told Hunter.

He sketched a rune in the air, and I recognized Peorth, the rune for hidden things revealed. "What else?" he asked.

Something flickered along the surface of the shiny, gold case. A bit of green. Maeve's wide green eyes, then her russet-colored hair. I felt my throat go thick with tears. The last time I'd seen a vision of Maeve, it had been of her trapped in the burning barn. Dying.

Here she stood in an open field, her eyes lit with joy and love. The image changed. This time it showed Maeve in what must have been her bedroom. A small space tucked under the eaves with a narrow bed covered by a brightly colored quilt. Maeve stood in a white nightgown, gazing from her window at the moon, a look of yearning on her face. I was sure she was thinking about Ciaran.

Now show me Ciaran, I entreated the watch silently. But there was only Maeve, and her image lasted just a moment before fading away.

I looked up at Hunter. "Not much help, I'm afraid. Just my mother from back before I was born."

"Are you okay?" he asked.

I nodded, wrapped the watch back in its green silk, and returned it to my jacket pocket.

"Well, there's one more thing I can try," Hunter said. He reached into his back pocket and drew out what looked like a playing card, only on it was an image of the Virgin Mary, shown with a spiky golden halo and a little angel over her head.

"The Virgin of Guadalupe," Hunter explained. "When I finally found Killian in the abandoned building last night,

I found this in there with him. I've traced it to its source."

"Huh?" I wasn't following this at all.

Hunter smiled. "Want to come with me and see where he got it?"

My day suddenly looked brighter. I was going to spend it with Hunter!

In the living room we had a brief confab about plans for the day. Sky and Raven were going to the Cloisters. Bree and Robbie were still undecided. We were all going to meet that night for our one real restaurant splurge.

Hunter and I walked across town to the West Village. Hunter led the way to a small store just west of Hudson Street. The shop's crowded window was filled with candles in colored glass jars, crosses, rosaries, statues of the saints, gazing crystals, herbs, oils, and powders. We stepped inside, and I smelled an odd blend: frankincense and rosemary, musk and myrrh.

"This is weird," I whispered to Hunter. "It feels like a cross between an outlet for church goods and a Wiccan store."

"The woman who runs this place is a *curandera*," Hunter explained in a low voice. "A Mexican white witch. Central American witchcraft often has a good deal of Christian symbolism mixed in with the Wicca." He rang a bell on the counter. My eyes widened as a beautiful, dark-haired woman stepped out from the back room. It was the witch from the club, the one who'd told me that I needed to heal my own heart.

"*Buenos días*," she said. Her eyes lingered on me, and there was a silent moment in which we each recognized and acknowledged each other. "Can I help you?"

Hunter held out the card with the Virgin on it. "Is this from your shop?"

She studied it for a moment, then gazed up at him. "*Sí.* I sometimes give these cards to those in need of protection. How did you trace it to me?"

"It carries the pattern of your energy."

"Most witches wouldn't be able to pick that up," she said. "I put spells on my cards so that they can't be traced." She looked at him more carefully. "You're from the council?"

He nodded. "I'm looking for a witch called Killian. I think he's in danger."

"That one is always in danger," she said, but her eyes were suddenly wary.

"Do you know where he is?" Hunter asked.

Silently she shook her head.

"If you see him," Hunter said, "would you contact me?"

She gazed at him again, and I had the feeling that she was reading him the way she'd read me. "Yes," she said at last, "I will."

Hunter hesitated, then said, "Do you know anything about Amyranth?"

"*Brujas!*" she said, shivering. "They worship darkness. You don't want to go near them."

"We think they may have Killian," Hunter said.

Something unreadable flickered in her eyes. Then she scrawled a name on a piece of paper and handed it to Hunter. "She once had the misfortune to be the lover of Amyranth's leader. She has been trapped in terror ever since. I don't know if she'll talk to you, but you can try. Show her my card."

"Thank you," Hunter said. We turned to go.

"There's something you've been putting off, Seeker," the woman said.

Hunter turned back to face her, startled. "Do it now," she urged him. "Do not hesitate. Otherwise you may be too late. *Comprende?*"

I was baffled, but Hunter's eyes widened. "Yes," he said slowly.

"Wait, I have something that might help you." The woman disappeared into the back room and reappeared with what looked like a large seedpod. "You know what to do with this?" she asked.

"Yes," Hunter said again. His face had turned pale. "Thank you."

"*Hasta luego, chica,*" she called to me as we left.

"What was that all about?" I asked when we were outside.

Hunter took my arm and steered me west, toward the Hudson River. "She's befriended Killian," he explained. "She's been trying to help him. I'm fairly certain she's the one who told him to hide out in that building in Chelsea. The church across the street was called Our Lady of Guadalupe."

"But what was she talking about at the end?"

He was silent for almost a block. Then he said, "She's very empathic. She can pick up on people's deep fears and worries."

"I noticed," I said, thinking back to what she'd said to me at the club. "And?"

"And . . . she picked up on my worry about my mum and dad. She gave me a safe way to contact them—I think. With this." He stared at the seedpod.

"How does it work?" I asked.

"Indirectly, as I understand it," Hunter said. "I've never used one of these before—they're rather a specialty of Latin witches. It's supposed to work something like a message in a bottle, but with a very low-level finding spell on it that will seek out the person you're trying to reach. The spell is so slight that with any luck, it will slip right under the radar of anyone who might be watching. The drawback is that with such a weak spell, the message could take a while to reach its destination—and anything might happen to it along the way." He sucked in a deep breath. "But I have to try it."

"Are you sure you should?" I asked hesitantly. "I mean, the council told you to leave it to them. I know I'm not the council's biggest fan in general, but maybe they're right about this. It seems too dangerous for you to do on your own."

"They've had no success," Hunter said. "And I've been getting the feeling that time is short—that I've got to contact Mum and Dad now. I hope I'm wrong, but I don't dare wait any longer and find out too late that I was right."

The wind rose as we drew closer to the river. "This way," Hunter said, leading me to a small commercial pier. There was a metal gate with a lock on the pier, but Hunter spelled it, and it popped open. We walked through the gate and past a bunch of industrial drums and crates.

Hunter knelt by the water, a smooth sheet of lead gray. Carefully he opened the pod. I watched as he drew sigils that glittered softly on the air before disappearing into the pod. He sang a long Gaelic chant, something unknown to me. Then he closed the pod and wrapped it in more spells. Finally he threw the pod into the water. We watched it bob on the surface for a few moments. I gasped as it finally sank beneath a swell.

Hunter reached out and took my hand, and I tried to give him my strength. "I've done what I can," he said. "Now I just have to wait—and hope."

10

Signs

December 14, 1981

Greer has been dead a month now of a heart attack, and if anyone suspects that I helped to hasten her death, they dare not accuse me. Liathach is mine now. Andarra, Grania's father, doesn't quite understand that. He's still grieving. He came to tonight's circle and chanted the opening invocation to the Goddess and the God. His eyes filled with confusion when I thanked him for it and took over. I had to. He wanted to spend the entire night sending on Greer's soul, which I believe we took care of immediately after her death. She had so many dealings with the taibhs, the dark spirits. Doesn't he know they came for her in the end?

It's almost Yule, the time of the return of the God, an appropriate time for me to take over Liathach. Greer was *a power, I'll grant, but she wasn't bold enough. She was always worrying about the council. It's time to turn the tables. Now Liathach will come into its own, and the council will fear us.*

—Neimhidh

Hunter came back to the apartment with me, then went off to look for Ciaran's former lover. Bree had gone for a pedicure, and Robbie and I were alone in the apartment. I was glad—I wanted to try to work things out with him. But to my dismay, when I came back into the living room after using the bathroom, he was pulling on his coat.

"Where are you going?" I asked, feeling forlorn.

"Museum of Natural History," Robbie said briefly. He'd barely spoken to me since our argument.

"Want company?"

"Not really."

"Okay," I said, trying not to show how much that hurt. "But Robbie? I've been thinking a lot about what you said yesterday. I need to talk to you about it. Um—can I walk you to the subway?"

After a moment he nodded, and I put my coat back on. We walked up to Twenty-third Street. Robbie's plan was to take the bus across to Eighth Avenue, where he could pick up the C train. The wide cross street was jammed with buses, trucks, and taxis. An ambulance and a fire truck, sirens wailing, tried to make their way through the gridlock. Talking—or rather, hearing—was almost impossible.

"Want to stop in a coffee shop?" I shouted over the commotion. "My treat."

"Not really," Robbie said again. He stepped forward as a bus pulled up to the stop.

I gritted my teeth. "Okay," I said. "We'll talk on the bus."

Fortunately the bus wasn't too crowded. We got a seat together. "I want to apologize to you," I said. "You were right—I shouldn't have messed with that woman."

Robbie looked straight ahead. He was still angry.

"This being a blood witch and having power, it's still kind of new to me," I went on. "I'm not saying that excuses what I did. Only that I'm still getting used to it, still trying to figure out when I should and shouldn't use magick. And the truth is, the power is a kick. I get tempted to use it when I shouldn't. So I'm probably going to screw up now and then."

Robbie folded his arms across his chest. "Tell me something I don't know."

I sighed. "You're not making this easy."

He looked at me coldly. "You can make it easy. Just cast a spell on me."

I winced. "Robbie, listen. I promise I'll be more careful. I give you my word that I'm going to be more conscious and try not to abuse my power. And I'll never put you in a bad position again."

Robbie shut his eyes. When he opened them, the anger was gone and in its place was sorrow. "Morgan, I'm not trying to punish you. I just don't know how to trust you anymore," he said. "I don't know how we can be friends. I don't want to lose you, but—" He raised his hands in a gesture of helplessness. "You've got all the power. The playing field is nowhere near level. That makes it pretty hard to have a real friendship."

I felt my hope draining away. I'd assumed that we would talk and everything would be okay again. Robbie and I had never stayed angry with each other before. But Robbie was right. Things were unequal. I was operating in a different realm now, with different rules.

He got off the bus, and I followed him down the steps into the subway station. The train came, and we got on it.

"So, my being a blood witch means I've got to lose your friendship?" I bit down on my lip to keep from crying as the train moved out of the station.

"I don't know," Robbie said. "I don't know what to do about it."

We hurtled through several stops, during which I did my best not to break into tears. Things with Bree would never be the same. And now I was losing Robbie, too. Why did being a blood witch mean I had to give up my best friends?

The subway came to a stop at Seventy-second Street, and I glanced at the map. The next stop was Robbie's.

"I don't want to give up on our friendship," I said stubbornly. "I need you. I need Robbie who's not a blood witch and who knows me better than almost anyone. I—" I wiped my nose. "Robbie, you're one of the best people I've ever met. I can't bear to lose you."

Robbie gave me a long, complicated look—sympathy, love, and a weary exasperation all bound together. "I don't want to give up on us, either," he said just as the subway rolled into the Eighty-first Street station. "You want to come see some dinosaurs?"

"Sure." I managed a shaky smile.

We got off the train together, but as we walked through

the turnstiles, a cloud of intense exhaustion dropped down over me. Then came vague nausea.

"Uh . . . Robbie? I think I need to bail on the museum."

"After all that? You won't even see dinosaurs with me?"

"I want to, but I feel really wrung out all of a sudden. I think I just need to sit down for a while."

"You sure?" he asked.

I nodded. I wanted to give Robbie a hug, but by this time I was focusing on not throwing up. He hovered uncertainly for a moment. Then he said, "Okay. See you later," and walked toward the museum.

I crossed the street to the park and sat down on one of the benches. The nausea hadn't let up. If anything, I felt worse, weak and disoriented. I shut my eyes for a second.

When I opened them again, I was no longer looking at the wide steps and columns of the museum. The scene in front of me had changed.

A blur of gray-brown branches. Across from them, a tall, narrow house obscured by snaky, tangled wisteria vines. Sirens and an emergency light flashing, cars speeding by. A doorbell hidden in a stone gorgon's head. Screams and the sound of a struggle. A man's voice, familiar but somehow terrifying. Blurry figures wearing animal masks. A bound figure, lying on a stone table.

I felt something nudging my ankle, and I snapped out of the vision with a cry, startling the poor dog who was sniffing my shoe. The dog's owner pulled it away, giving me an indignant look.

Goddess, what was that? I wondered. I'd never had anything like it before—a waking vision, something that just came to me with no prompting. It was clearly connected to the dream I'd had. But it was different—more real somehow. Was I seeing Killian being tortured by Amyranth?

I had to talk to Hunter. I sent him an urgent witch message. Then I sat there, shaken, waiting for him to answer. But there was no response. Hunter, now is not the time to ignore me, I thought. I tried again, letting my fear permeate the message.

Still nothing. I felt a flicker of fear. It wasn't like him to ignore an urgent summons. Had something happened to him? After waiting another minute I tried Sky. But she didn't respond, either. Were my messages even getting through?

Trying not to give in to panic, I found a pay phone and pulled out the phone card my parents had given me for emergencies. I punched in the number of the apartment. No one answered, but I left a message just in case Hunter or Sky came in.

Next I called Bree's cell phone. Bree picked up at once. "Speak," she said loftily.

"It's me," I said. "Where are you?"

"In a cab, stuck in traffic." She sounded irked.

"Bree," I said, "I think I saw Killian."

"What? Where?"

I told Bree about the vision I'd just had. "I'm sure Ciaran's got him, only I can't figure out where they are. I've got to find that house," I finished. I thought of how Hunter had used what we'd seen when I'd scryed to find Killian. Maybe Bree and I could do the same thing. "I need your help."

"Okay." Bree sounded hesitant. "Um—what can I do?"

"You know the city better than I do," I said. "Think about

what I described and help me figure out where it might be."

"Oh, I get it. Cool idea," she said. "Um—okay, you say you saw a blur of branches?"

When I said yes, Bree said, "It sounds like this house you saw was by a park. Maybe Central Park."

"Right. Makes sense," I said, feeling a flicker of excitement.

"Okay, now, where, exactly, were the trees?"

I closed my eyes and tried to call up the vision. "I was standing on a corner. The house was across a narrow street from me, and the blur was in my right eye. I think the trees were across a wide street from the house. Yeah, the house was on a corner. The front door faced a side street. . . . At the corner there was a wide avenue, and the trees were on the other side."

"Now we're getting somewhere. Okay, let's think. . . . Describe the avenue. How wide was it? And which way was the traffic going?" Bree pressed.

"Jesus, Bree," I said, frustrated. "I wasn't paying attention to traffic patterns."

"Think," she insisted over the blare of horns. "Could you see any cars at all?"

I forced my mind back to the siren and the flashing emergency light. The light was on top of an ambulance. I followed it in my mind until a blue SUV passed on its left. . . . "It was at least four lanes wide, and the cars were going both ways," I said. "It was two-way traffic. Hey!" I knew most of the avenues were one way. That narrowed it down a lot.

Bree's voice rose with excitement. "It sounds like the house is somewhere on Central Park West. Two-way traffic . . . a wide avenue with a park on one side . . . a fancy house . . . I can't think of anyplace else in Manhattan that looks like that."

"Bree, you're brilliant," I said fervently.

"Where are you now?" she asked.

"Right by the Museum of Natural History."

"Perfect," Bree said. "Why don't you just walk along Central Park West and see if you can find anything that looks familiar?"

Bree was right—it was perfect. I might be within a few blocks of the house right now. I might actually find Killian—and Ciaran. I felt my chest constrict with fear.

"Morgan? Are you there?" Bree asked.

"I'm here," I said. "Listen, I'm going to look for this place. Can you try to track down Hunter? Tell him I need him now!"

Bree hesitated a moment. "Morgan, promise me that if you find it, you won't go in there by yourself."

"I'm not planning on it," I said, feeling a rush of warmth at her concern. "Bree—thanks for your help."

I hung up and made one more call, this one to Robbie's cell. After all, he was somewhere just across the street. But all I got was his voice mail. Robbie had turned off his phone, and I didn't have time to search the museum for him.

I tried Hunter one more time. Still nothing. Was he okay? I just had to trust that he was. And I had to trust in the fact that there were no coincidences. Fate was guiding me. I took the fact that I was on Central Park West as a sign. I was being guided to find Killian.

Focusing my eyes straight ahead, I saw the park in my peripheral vision. The blur of branches in my right eye was very much like what I'd seen in the vision.

I started walking north, and my senses began tingling.

They were charged the way the air is charged before a summer rainstorm. Everything was about to break wide open. I passed a vendor selling hot roasted chestnuts, a dog walker with half a dozen yapping dogs pulling him along. The winter wind was at my back, sweeping up Central Park West, propelling me. A sense of urgency was building; adrenaline was coursing through my veins.

At the corner of Eighty-seventh and Central Park West, I stumbled to a sudden stop, my heart hammering. There it was.

The house had four stories, and I could glimpse granite facing behind a tangle of thick, gnarled wisteria vines. Three stone steps led to the front door, where a doorbell was embedded in a stone carving of a gorgon's head. It was exactly what I'd seen in the vision.

A thin, icy cloak of fear settled around me. I was standing in front of the place where Amyranth held Killian.

11

Fated

The rumors are true. She lives. Ballynigel was razed to the ground by the dark wave, yet Maeve Riordan and that fawning blue-eyed half-wit, Angus Bramson, managed to survive. Goddess, I've lost track of the number of times I've wished them both dead and in everlasting torment. Especially her. In the space of two enchanted weeks she opened my heart and destroyed my entire life. My marriage became a hollow sham, my home a prison. Grania hates me. The children . . . well, they respect my power, at least.

I'm leaving Scotland, leaving Liathach. The coven has grown in strength and magick as never before. We took part in the destruction of Crossbrig, which gained Liathach their much coveted Wyndenkell spell books. But the Liathach witches are *weak, fearful. They've been ruled too long by Grania's family. They think I've led them into danger. They want to retreat. Well, let them. But I won't be a part of it.*

I don't care about leaving Liathach. I should have done it years ago. All that matters is that I find Maeve. She has done the impossible. She survived the dark wave. I've scryed, and I've seen her. I know that she still holds me in her heart, that we are still meant to be together. I can't live without her another day. Now I must find her.

The only question is whether it will be to tell her how much I love her . . . or to kill her.

—Neimhidh

The house was old, a part of the city left over from the nineteenth century. The worn stonework had a faded elegance, and the thick tangle of wisteria vines reminded me of the Briar Rose fairy tale. A sleeping princess hidden behind a wall of thorns . . . But Killian was no fictional princess, and I was no rescuer prince. Now that I'd found it, what on earth was I going to do?

I crossed the street to another pay phone and called Bree again. She'd just gotten back to the apartment.

"I found it," I told her. "It's right on the corner of Central Park West and Eighty-seventh. Have you heard anything from Hunter?"

"Nada," Bree answered. "Any idea where he might be?"

Nothing immediately jumped to mind. Hunter was always so careful and secretive about his work. He told me only what he thought I needed to know.

"Um . . . there's a Mexican witch's shop he took me to off Hudson Street. She's the one who told him about the woman he's searching for. She might give you the address."

"I'll find her," Bree promised. "But first I'll leave a note here in case he comes back."

"I'm going to stay here and keep an eye on the house," I told Bree. "If you find Hunter, will you tell him to meet me here?"

"Okay. But call me again in twenty minutes," Bree ordered. "I want to know that you're safe."

I promised I would. Then I sat down on one of the park benches that offered a clear view of the house. It was not a day for sitting outside. The air was damp and bitter cold. Within a few minutes I could hardly feel my feet.

But I could feel the house. Even though I was across the street from it, I could sense powerful magick wrapped around it.

I thought I saw a flicker of movement in one of the upper windows, and a knot of dread lodged itself in the middle of my chest. I wished I could go off searching with Bree, I really did. The idea of staying here on my own across from this house that practically oozed evil terrified me—especially knowing that Ciaran might be inside.

I hunkered down in the cold, concentrating on the house. No one came in or out. Nothing more moved in the windows. Even the wisteria branches barely moved in the icy wind. There was a bleak stillness about the house that suddenly made me wonder if I was wrong and the place was completely deserted. Magick can fool most people, I reminded myself. But not me.

I extended my senses to see what sort of magickal

defenses or traps there might be. I picked up resistance at the door, a warding spell of some sort, but it didn't feel very serious. The house wasn't nearly as heavily spelled as Cal and Selene's house had been. I couldn't sense any electronic security systems, either, just the requisite New York combination of heavy-duty locks on the door. Only one of those bolts was actually shut. Strange.

I glanced at my watch. It was nearly three o'clock. I wondered if Bree was having any luck finding Hunter. Was there some way I could find out what was going on in the house at that very moment? I could search for Killian's aura.

I concentrated, trying to remember what it had been like. A pattern traced itself in my mind's eye so clearly that I could almost hear Killian's voice. And then what I was hearing were cries. I felt the struggle again, the helplessness, the overwhelming sense of terror and despair.

The vision was gone as quickly as it had come, but I knew what it meant. Killian was in the house, captive yet reaching out, crying for help. Maybe he wasn't calling to me specifically, but I had an awful feeling I was the only one who had heard him.

I couldn't wait for Hunter to show up. "Hang on, Killian," I muttered. "I'm coming."

I stood up and immediately began to tremble. Who was I kidding? I was a seventeen-year-old witch with all of two and a half months' experience in my craft. And I was about to go up against a coven of evil Woodbanes and the witch who'd killed Maeve and Angus? Maeve and Angus had been trained in Wicca from the day they were born. If they hadn't been able to stop Ciaran . . . The odds were beyond insane. Ciaran had killed Maeve, his *mùirn beatha dàn*. What would he do to me, her daughter?

Yet I couldn't discount the dreams and visions. I was sure I'd had them for a reason. I could almost hear Hunter reminding me that according to Wicca, nothing is random. Everything has a purpose. I wouldn't have been given those visions if I hadn't been meant do something about them. Even the fact that the school boiler had burst now seemed part of some inevitable plan. I was here in New York City because it was my fate to save Killian.

"Goddess, help me," I murmured. I drew in deep breaths, calming and grounding myself. I had all of Alyce's knowledge and more raw power than most blood witches ever encounter. I was strong, stronger than I'd been three weeks ago when Hunter and I had fought Selene and defeated her. If Ciaran was in that building, didn't I owe it to Maeve to try to stop him once and for all?

I can do this, I told myself. I was meant to do this.

I walked up to the house and stepped onto the first of the three stone steps—and stopped as a feeling of dread snaked around my insides and whispered in my mind, *Turn away. Come no farther. Go back.*

I tried to step onto the second step, but I couldn't. Terror immobilized me, the feeling that taking that one step would seal my doom.

It's a repelling spell, I told myself. It's designed to keep you out. But there's nothing really behind it. I willed the spell to show itself to me. There was a moment of resistance before I saw a glimmering on the winter air. The rune Is—the rune of obstacles, of things frozen and delayed—repeated again and again, like a series of crystalline icicles. I visualized the warmth of fire melting the runes of the warding spell, and within seconds I felt their power weaken.

The spell snapped, and I reached the top step. I found another spell on the door itself. I felt a surge of exhilaration as I realized I knew exactly what to do. It seemed so clear. Either the binding spells weren't all that complicated, or I was stronger than I realized.

This time I drew power up from the earth, from the roots of the wisteria, from the bedrock below. I gathered all the energy poured into the city streets by the myriad inhabitants of New York City. A boisterous, defiant power swelled inside me. I let it build, then flung it at the spell that guarded the door. The spell shattered. The one bolt that had been shut on the other side of the door shot open. And I stepped into the house, nearly surfing on the wave of my own magick.

I stood in a high-ceilinged foyer. The floor was inlaid marble, patterned in black and gray. A staircase led to the upper floors. I sent a witch message to Killian. Where are you? Lead me.

The next instant I was flat on my back, hit with a binding spell stronger than anything I'd ever experienced. It forced my arms flat against my sides, clamped my legs together, pressed down on my throat so I couldn't utter a sound, compressed my chest so that I fought for every breath. Oh, Goddess. Maybe I wasn't as strong as I'd thought.

Quickly I cast a spell to loosen all bindings.

It did nothing. My mind reeled in panic.

I tried the spell that had worked so brilliantly just a few minutes ago. I extended my senses out and down, searching for a connection with the ground beneath me. The hollow echo that came back was mystifying. It was as if the earth itself was empty, flat, drained of anything to give. And I was left in a place where waves of dark magick swirled around me.

Alyce, I thought. Surely Alyce knew something that would help. A spell came to me then for bringing light in the midst of darkness. I began to visualize a single white flame, growing brighter, hotter, blazing through all the dark energy, consuming it, purifying the space around me.

I almost blacked out as something that felt like a blade of jagged ice plunged into my stomach. It's an illusion, I told myself, remembering how Selene had attacked me with pain. I willed myself to go beyond it, to keep picturing the flame devouring the darkness.

Another blade drove into my back. "Aaagh!" My own strangled cry panicked me. I felt the icy blade cut through skin, muscle, bone, and the flame in my mind guttered out.

As if to reward me for losing the spell, the pain stopped.

I glanced down at my body. There were no bloody knife wounds. They had been an illusion. But the binding was real. I couldn't move. I glanced around me, searching for the source of the power that was holding me prisoner. There— I felt magick like a dark, oily cloud swirling across the town house's pristine floor. The magick of several witches, working together.

Nausea rose in the back of my throat. I was completely overpowered. What had I done? How could I have been naive and stupid enough to believe I could go up against an entire coven of Woodbanes? The second I'd walked into the house, I'd walked into their trap.

A slight figure in a black robe and a mask walked toward me. The mask showed a jackal's face, carved out of some sort of dark wood and horribly exaggerated, with an enormous snarling mouth. My fear ratcheted up another notch. Other masked figures appeared: an owl, a cougar, a viper, an eagle.

"We've got her," the jackal said, in a voice so perfectly neutral, I couldn't tell if it was male or female.

"Where's Killian?" I demanded. "What have you done with him?"

"Killian?" the witch in the owl mask repeated. The voice was distinctly female. "Killian isn't here."

"But you're going to drain him of his power!" I said stupidly.

A giddy, high-pitched laugh erupted from the jackal's mouth. "Oh, no, we're not."

"We never wanted Killian," the owl said.

"You've been misled," the viper agreed, and all of them burst out laughing. The viper's narrow golden eyes glittered as it stared at me. "You're the one we're going to drain."

12

Ciaran

February 28, 1984

The beginning of spring is a time to sow the seeds of dreams for the coming year. Here in a tiny village called Meshomah Falls, I am a boy again, full of fantasies and dreams, eager to welcome the promise of spring. I found her. Today Maeve and I saw each other for the first time since I left Ballynigel. I knew in that instant that she still loved me. That nothing had changed, that it had all been worth the wait. Goddess, I see the universe every time I gaze into her eyes.

We waited until evening, for she insisted on making some excuse to poor, pathetic Angus. Then she led me out beyond the town, through a narrow band of woods, across a meadow, and up a hill to a field. "No one will see us here," she said.

"Of course not. One of us will work a spell of invisibility," I said.

That was when Maeve told me she'd given up her magick. I couldn't believe it. Ever since she left Ireland, she's led a half life, her senses shut down, a prisoner of her own terror. "You never have to fear again," I told her. Bit by bit I coaxed her open. Oh, the joy that was in her eyes as she let herself sense the seeds in the earth beneath us, the tender green shoots waiting to break the surface. Then she opened herself to the skies, the stars, the pull of the incandescent spring moon, and we gave ourselves to pleasure and to each other.

Goddess, I have finally known true joy. All the pain I have gone through, it was all worth it for this.

—Neimhidh

"You're the one we're going to drain." The words echoed in my ears, and I suddenly saw it all with sick clarity.

My dreams and visions—they had all been premonitions of what was to be my own ordeal in this house. Not Killian's. Somehow the council got that one key detail wrong when they interpreted the dream. The wolf cub on the table wasn't Killian. It was me.

Some rational part of my mind wondered why I'd appeared as a wolf cub, but before I could make sense of it, the jackal said, "You will come with us."

I stared up defiantly. "No."

The figure waved a hand over me, and I was suddenly on my feet, the bindings loosened just enough to allow me to follow like an automaton. Fury at my own traitorous body

swept through me, but I could no more resist the spell to follow than I could break the binding spell.

I followed through a parlor and a dining room, through a
kitchen to another staircase, this one leading down.

We descended the stairs into a cellar. How could I possibly escape? The cellar door would close, and terrible things
would be done to me.

The cellar was lit by a few black candles set in wall
sconces. The owl held out a robe made of a thin, shiny brown
fabric. "Take off your clothes and put this on," she said.

The robe spooked me. I flashed on an old movie where
they burned witches at the stake and made them wear robes
like this for their execution. "What's it for?" I asked.

The witch in the hawk mask drew a sign in the air, and I
doubled over again in agony.

"Do as you're told," the jackal said.

They watched me change, and I felt the dull burn of shame
over my terror as I took off my clothes and put on the robe.
Then I was forced down into a chair, and two more masked figures—a weasel and a jaguar—came into the cellar with a
steaming cup. They forced me to drink its contents. It was
some sort of hideous herb tea—I recognized henbane, valerian,
belladonna, foxglove. The smell was so revolting, I gagged with
every sip.

When I'd drained the last sickening drop, they left me. I
felt the liquid moving through me, slowing my thoughts,
deadening my reflexes. Then my body started to tremble
uncontrollably, and I was hit by a wave of dizziness. If I'd
been able to move from the chair, I'm sure I would have

fallen to the floor. The floor itself seemed to be swaying, the walls spinning. Menacing shadows crawled in the corners of my field of vision.

I took a deep breath, trying to center myself. I whispered a quick spell drawn from my Alyce memory, and after a few moments the hallucinatory shadows receded a little. The dizziness and sluggishness remained, though.

At last I heard footsteps on the stairs. The owl and weasel returned. "He's ready for you now," the owl said.

I had no doubt of who was waiting for me. Ciaran. My mother's *mùirn beatha dàn*, the one she'd loved. The one who had killed her.

The owl waved a hand over me and muttered an incantation. Again I stood and followed with jerky motions. The dizziness didn't pass, but I found I could walk through it.

We walked up to the first floor, through the kitchen, and then up the main staircase to the second floor. I was led into a wood-paneled room lit by candles. A fire glowed in the fireplace. I was shoved into another chair. The two masked witches left and shut the door.

Ciaran stood in front of the fireplace, his back to me. He wore a robe of deep purple silk with black bands on the arms. I fought down a wave of nausea. My mother's murderer.

He turned to face me, and for a disorienting moment the trembling and the nausea vanished. In their place I felt surprise and a massive sense of relief. This wasn't Ciaran. This was the man from the courtyard and the bookstore, the man with whom I'd had such an affinity, the man in whom I'd placed such an immediate trust.

The nausea returned an instant later as I realized just how badly I'd misplaced that trust. Now I could feel the darkness of his power, like a cyclone of roiling blackness.

Ciaran watched me.

"I never asked your name," I said, my voice once again my own.

"But you know it now, don't you?" he asked. His face was harsh in the firelight, his eyes unreadable dark slashes.

"Ciaran," I said quietly.

"And you are Morgan Rowlands," he replied courteously.

Oh, Goddess, how could I have been so blind? "You've been playing with me all along," I said. "You knew who I was even before we met."

"On the contrary," he said. "I only realized you were the one Selene destroyed herself over when we talked in the bookstore."

"H-how—"

"I became curious when I sensed how powerful you were. So when we got to talking about scrying, I decided to find out more about you. My scrying stone is bound to me. Even though you were the one holding it and I was on another floor altogether, it showed me what it showed you. I saw—was it your sister?—coming out of the Widow's Vale Cineplex. The name Widow's Vale rang a bell, and then when you gave me your name, that clinched it. Truthfully," he went on, "I hadn't planned on taking care of you quite so soon, but when you just put yourself in my hands like that, I couldn't pass up the opportunity, could I?"

"The owl at the window last night—?"

"Was spying on you," he confirmed. "But then, we were

already on the alert. We've been watching the Seeker ever since he came to the city. It was easy to discover what his mission was, and after that it was child's play to set the trap, feeding you the clues that would bring you to us. I gave you the vision of Killian in the candle's flame and the vision you had today. I even helped you break the warding spells on this house. My dear, you should have known you don't have that kind of ability. Not at your level." Ciaran regarded me with a rueful smile.

I'd been such a fool. Time and again he'd manipulated me. And I'd never even suspected.

"Tell me." His tone sharpened with the command. "Where's the Seeker now?"

"I don't know."

His dark eyes raked me. How, I wondered, had I ever thought him distinguished and trustworthy? All I saw in him now was the predator, waiting to devour his prey.

Ciaran steepled his fingers. "Perhaps I shouldn't have blocked the messages you tried to send," he murmured, as if thinking aloud. "Perhaps I should have made it easier for him to find you." Then he shook his head. "No, he's clever enough that he'll find you anyway."

I sagged, despairing, as I understood what Ciaran meant. If Hunter did find me, then he would be destroyed along with me.

There was a knock on the door, and the hawk witch entered the room. I watched in disbelief as she handed Maeve's pocket watch to Ciaran. "We found this in the girl's jacket."

Ciaran's face went totally blank for a moment. Then it grew pale and distorted. "Leave!" he snapped at the hawk. Then he whirled on me. "Where did you get this?" he demanded.

"You should know!" I lashed back, glad for the chance to tell the truth. "You gave it to my mother before you murdered her!"

Ciaran stared at me, his eyes wide with undisguised shock. "Your mother?"

And I realized that Selene had never told him who I was. She'd never told him I was Maeve's daughter.

He bolted from the room then. I took it for the last moment of triumph I would ever know. I'd actually shaken the leader of Amyranth. And I'd only have to pay for it with my life.

Exhaustion descended on me like a heavy cloak. I hung my head, let my eyes close, giving in to the drug they'd fed me.

That lying, manipulative wench Selene! She knew this girl was Maeve's daughter and she never told me! What other secrets did she keep from me?

Maeve's daughter! You wouldn't know it from the girl's looks. She doesn't have Maeve's delicate, pretty face, the sprinkling of freckles across her nose, the soft waves of reddish-brown hair. All she has of Maeve is her power. Though there's something about her eyes that's damnably familiar.

How did Maeve and Angus manage to spawn that one without my ever knowing? And how the bloody hell did she find out what happened at the end? Even those who knew Maeve didn't know we were mùirn beatha dàns, and no one, save Maeve and Angus, knew about how the fire started. All witnesses are dead.

Selene couldn't have told her. Selene knew nothing of what was between me and Maeve. Or . . . did she? I've never been sure just what Selene did and didn't know. All of which raises the question: What else is there that Selene didn't tell me about this girl?

My thoughts are heaving like the sea. There's something at the edge of my mind, a disturbing presence on the edge of consciousness. It has a truth to show me.

Damn it. What is it? What is it?

Hunter, putting the silver chains of the *braigh* on David Redstone . . . Mary K., huddled in a corner of Selene's study, confused, frightened, and spelled . . . Cal, absorbing the cloud of darkness that Selene hurled at me . . . His beautiful golden eyes . . .

No! I started out of my stupor, shaking and grieving at the images that kept parading in front of me. For a moment I couldn't imagine where I was. Then memory returned. The house with the vines. The masked witches. Ciaran.

I was now in a much larger room. My head ached, and I felt even dizzier than before. With effort I focused my eyes on the ceiling, on the leaves and vines and ornate plaster molding, all horribly familiar. Black candles flickered from sconces and from an elaborate silver candlestick atop an inlaid ebony cabinet. Black drapes covered the windows. I cast out my senses. They were frighteningly weak, but I could still faintly detect objects of power inside the cabinet—athames, wands, crystals, animal skulls and bones, all emanating dark magick.

I was lying on a large round table, my hands and feet bound to it with spelled ropes. The table was made of some sort of stone, inlaid with patterns in another stone. Garnet, I thought. There were deep grooves in the surface of the table. The panic I'd felt in the visions returned full blown, and for a few useless minutes I struggled against the bonds.

Panic never helps, I told myself. Focus. Find a way out of this. But it was so hard to think through the haze of Amyranth's drugged tea.

I called on the spell that was binding me to reveal itself. I saw the faintest glimmering of something that might have been a rune before it winked out. I tried to summon the spell again. Nothing happened, and I felt another jolt of panic. Breathe, I told myself, just breathe.

But it wasn't easy. What had happened to my precious magick? I couldn't connect with it, couldn't feel it.

It's mine, dammit, I thought furiously. No one—especially not Ciaran—is going to take my magick from me.

Maybe I lost consciousness again. I'm not sure. I never heard a door open or close, never heard footsteps, but suddenly Amyranth surrounded me. Witches in robes and animal masks formed a perfect circle around the table. Jackal, owl, weasel, cougar, eagle, bear, hawk, viper, jaguar, and a wolf. Predators all. The masks seemed distorted, horrible caricatures of the animals they represented, but I could also tell there was something wrong with my eyesight. It was impossible to say how accurate my perceptions were.

My visions and dreams had come together. Even through the haze of the drug, I could appreciate the irony of it all—if we hadn't tried to prevent my dream from coming to pass, none of this would have ever happened. Never try to mess with destiny.

The bear murmured an incantation, and I realized the power-draining ritual was beginning. The others picked up the incantation, turning it into a low, insistent chant. They moved widdershins. The air felt cruel and thick with danger. This was a Wiccan circle of destruction.

And Ciaran was leading it. I couldn't see his face beneath the wolf mask, but I could hear his voice, familiar yet terrifying. Just like the vision. Goddess.

I could feel Amyranth's dark magick flowing around the circle. It crackled like lightning. The air was charged with it. Slowly the strength of their power intensified. I felt an unbearable pressure along every inch of my body. Amyranth was calling up a ravenous darkness.

Irrelevantly, it hit me that Cal had never had a funeral. The council had taken his and Selene's bodies. As far as everyone in Widow's Vale was concerned, Cal and Selene had simply vanished from the earth.

Or maybe it wasn't so irrelevant. That was what was going to happen to me. My family would never know the truth about my disappearance, and it would always torment them.

The circle stopped moving. A thick, black mist clung to its members. "We give thanks," Ciaran said, "for delivering to us a sacrifice whose powers will make us that much stronger."

"How much power does she have?" asked the owl.

Ciaran shrugged. "See for yourself."

The owl held a hand over my stomach. Fine silver needles of light dropped from it. For a second they hovered inches above me, then began to glow red. The owl murmured a syllable, and the burning needles dropped down. I couldn't hold back a scream as they seemed to pierce my skin. Dozens of sharp embers sank into my belly, my arms, my legs. Involuntarily my back arched, and I pulled against the spelled ropes.

"Stop it!" I cried. "Please, stop it!"

"Be quiet!" the owl said harshly.

And then the fiery torture intensified, burned deeper into my body. I imagined my heart shriveling into a blackened lump, my bones crisping. I was wild with pain.

I can't take this, I thought frantically. I'm going to lose my mind.

"That's enough," Ciaran ordered. "You've seen what's in her."

"Strong, very strong. She'll serve well," the owl agreed.

As suddenly as it had started, the pain was gone. I sobbed in relief and hated myself for that weakness.

The wail of a siren came faintly from outside, and a flash of red light shone through the black drapes. The vision again. Oh God, every detail was coming true. I had seen the future. Now I was living it. Amyranth was going to steal my powers, leave me drained, hollowed out—without magick, without a soul, without life.

Ciaran began another chant. One by one the others joined their voices to his. Again the dark energy began to move, gaining power as it traveled through Amyranth's circle. I lay there helpless on the stone table, every muscle in my body clenched tight against the next horrible assault.

I thought of Maeve, my mother, murdered. I thought of Mackenna, my grandmother, killed when the dark wave destroyed Ballynigel. My family had suffered for their magick. Maybe no more was being asked of me than had been asked of them. I had the Riordan strength flowing through my veins. I had ancestral memories and a legacy of incredible power. Surely that meant I had their courage as well.

Give it to us. I felt the darkness clawing at me, trying to find its way into my very marrow.

Amyranth continued the chant. The dark energy shifted, no longer crackling around the circle. Now it hovered over the table, wreathing my body with sparking purple-black light.

Give it to us.

The purple-black light licked at my skin the way flames lick at dry wood. There was no pain, but I felt a crushing weight in my mind, against my chest, in my belly. I gasped for breath and could find none. But I could not let them get my power. Desperately, silently, I sang my summon-power chant.

An di allaigh an di aigh
An di allaigh an di ne ullah
An di ullah be . . .

The words that I knew from ancestral memory were suddenly gone from me. *An di ullah be . . .* I got no further. The chant had been wiped from my mind.

No! I wanted to scream, to sob, but I had no breath. Don't take it! No! Grief consumed me—grief for the magick that was being taken from me. Grief for this precious life that I was about to lose. Grief for Hunter, whom I would never see again.

Ciaran held out a silver athame. A ruby glowed dully on its hilt. He pointed the athame at me, and the dark power coagulated into a spear of searing light.

"You will give us your power," he said.

No, no, no! I was no longer capable of coherent thought. Just—no!

The chanting broke off abruptly at a sound on the other side of the door. A muffled disturbance, a struggle . . . someone using magick against Amyranth's spells.

Hunter! I felt Hunter's presence, his love, his desperate fear for me. And it terrified me more than anything. Was I strong enough still to send a witch message? Hunter, go back, I pleaded. Don't come in here. You can't save me.

The doorknob turned with a click, and Hunter stepped into the room, his eyes wild. He glanced at me quickly as if to reassure himself that I was alive, then turned to Ciaran.

"Let her go," Hunter commanded. His voice shook.

The jackal and the wolf raised their hands, as if to attack Hunter with witch light. Ciaran stopped them.

"No!" he said. "This one is mine. At least for now." He turned back to Hunter, an expression of mild amazement on his face. "The council must be in bad shape, sending a boy to do a Seeker's work. Did they really lead you to believe you could take me on?"

Hunter's hand shot out, and a ball of witch light zoomed toward Ciaran. Ciaran drew a sigil in the air, and the light reversed course and blazed back at Hunter.

Hunter ducked, his face pale, eyes glittering. When he stood again, he looked taller, broader than he had only a moment before. A new aura of power glowed around him. He emanated both youthful strength and ancient authority.

The council. Sky had once told me that when Hunter acted as a Seeker, he had access to the extraordinary powers of the council. It was a dangerous weapon to call on, taxing to the Seeker, reserved only for emergencies. Like this one.

Hunter stepped forward. The silver chains of the *braigh* glimmered in his hands. He intended to bind Ciaran, to bind his magick. But I could sense no fear in Ciaran at all.

"Hunter, don't!" I croaked. "He'll kill you!"

"This is getting tiresome," Ciaran said. He muttered a few syllables, and the *braigh* suddenly dropped from Hunter's hand. I saw him bite back a scream.

Desperately I summoned the source of all my magick. "Maeve and Mackenna of Belwicket," I whispered, "I call on your power. Help me now!"

Nothing happened. No awakening of magick. Nothing. I was sick with disbelief. My mother's and grandmother's magick had failed me.

Ciaran said, "Bind him," and the other members of the coven surrounded Hunter and enclosed him in binding spells. The jackal gave Hunter a savage kick. He went down with a groan.

"Stop it!" I cried. My voice came out as little more than a whisper.

"I'm sorry, Morgan," Hunter said, and the grief in his voice broke my heart. "I've failed you."

"No, you haven't. It's all right, love," I said, trying to comfort him. I couldn't say more. Total, soul-destroying despair overtook me. It was I who had failed him. Hunter and I were both lost now, and all because of my fatal arrogance. Neither one of us was going to get out alive. I'd signed my own death warrant and Hunter's as well.

"Put him somewhere safe," Ciaran ordered. "We'll take care of him later."

The jackal and the weasel dragged Hunter out of the room. A few moments later they returned. The bear picked up the chant again. The ritual was resuming. I didn't care.

The animals circled widdershins. The circle suddenly stopped moving and parted. And Ciaran in his wolf mask stepped to the head of the table. He placed a deliberate hand on either side of my forehead.

"No!" I screamed. I knew what was going to happen. He was going to force *tàth meànma* on me. Even if I hadn't been drugged and weak, I doubted I would have stood a chance against Ciaran. He was the strongest witch I'd ever known. He'd have access to my every memory, thought, and dream. There was nothing I could hide from him.

I tried to sink into the haze that was clouding my mind. I tried to have no thought. I felt Ciaran's power streaming through his hands into me. For a heartbeat I fought him, and then I was hallucinating, reliving my life in flashes from the moment of my birth. Watching and feeling image after image as they flared in bright, almost unnatural colors.

The rush of air, light, and sound as I came through the darkness of the birth canal.

Angus, with his fair hair and bright blue eyes, touching my arm, tentative and sweet.

A day later. Maeve cradling me, gazing into my face with tears running down her cheeks. Saying, "You have your father's eyes."

"Bloody hell!" It was Ciaran swearing.

He broke the connection, and my vision clouded over. Another spell to obscure something they didn't want me to see. I heard footsteps and the sound of a door closing.

The air in the room had changed. Ciaran was gone. And so was Hunter.

13

Truth

February 29, 1984

The light of day dawns . . . and with it love dies.

Maeve woke in my arms. Morning dew glistened on her skin. I pulled a bit of straw from her hair and told her how beautiful she was.

"No, Ciaran!" She scrambled to her feet. "This can't be. I've made my life with Angus, and you have a wife and children—"

"Forget my wife and children. I've left them. And damn Angus!" I cried. "I'm tired of things coming between what we know is meant to be. We are mùirn beatha dàns. We are meant to be together."

But she wouldn't hear of it. She went on and on, scourging herself with guilt. Angus had been so good to her, so patient and kind. How could she hurt him this way? What we were doing was wrong, immoral, a betrayal of the worst kind.

"What about betraying our love?" I asked. "You've been perfectly willing to do that these last three years." I explained that I'd given up my life in Scotland. My family, my coven, they were no longer a part of me. I was here in America prepared to start my life over with her. What more could she want from me?

"I can't live with you and live with myself," she said. She fled the field like a frightened rabbit, she who was once destined to be high priestess of Belwicket.

"Well, I can't watch you live with Angus," I shouted at her fleeing form.

So tell me, Maeve, now that you've chosen a course I can't forgive, what is the value of your life?

—Neimhidh

With Ciaran gone from the room, the owl took over. "The rites must continue," she said.

They started their chanting again. I felt the dark energy building, the summoning of the purple-black light that would take my magick from me. And there was nothing I could do to stop it. I was completely outmatched.

I thought about Hunter. How much I loved him. How he was about to lose his life for me. How he was my *mùirn beatha dàn* and I'd known it all along but had never let myself embrace that truth. And I'd had the nerve to criticize Bree.

A world of regret rose up inside me. Regret for everything I'd done wrong.

I'd never told my parents how much I appreciated them. They'd given me a wonderful home and all their love, and when I'd found out I was adopted, all of that had seemed insignificant. Because of me, Mary K. had been kidnapped. Because of me, Cal was dead. He'd given his life for me and I'd wasted it completely.

Because of me, Hunter was going to die. That was the hardest thing of all.

My mind was spinning. I'd been alive only a little over seventeen years. How had I managed to make such a complete disaster of everything? The purple-black light crackled around me, and I thought, Take my power. Take my life. You're welcome to it.

Well, I'll drink a toast to you, Maeve Riordan. You pulled one over on me from beyond the grave. You were so young and beautiful when you died. I daresay you wouldn't find me attractive now. My own reflection stares back at me from this silver goblet, distorted, gruesome. How did I ever get such a beauty to love me, even for a night? Look at my eyes, two dark muddy slashes unlike anyone else's . . . except this girl's.

What do you think, Maeve? You know me better than most, so answer the question that looms before me: Can I now destroy our daughter?

The purple-black light surrounded the inner circle, holding me fast. The masked Amyranth witches stood in a circle around me, murmuring their chant.

I couldn't even control my own muscles. I tried to cast my senses to see just how much my tormentors were enjoying the show. But by now I was too weak even to do that.

The cougar held up a hand, and with a dull horror I saw that a cat's curved claws were growing from human fingertips. He muttered an incantation. The purple-black light crackled loudly and shot through my chest. I felt it wrap around my heart, squeezing mercilessly.

The magick was ebbing out of me. I felt it leaving. I didn't want to give in to Amyranth, to Ciaran's coven. I didn't want to let go of my magick. But I was so very tired of fighting. I felt the last bit of my resistance float away, and I followed it.

"Morgan, come back!" It was Hunter's voice. A hallucination, I told myself, and slipped back into the fog.

"No! I won't let you go. Not like this."

I forced my eyes open. Hunter stood in the doorway. A new aura of power seemed to flicker around him, his own sapphire light tinged with a purplish glow I'd never seen before.

Was he really there? How had he gotten away from Ciaran? Where was Ciaran? I couldn't imagine that Hunter had single-handedly overcome such evil. It had to be a dream.

"Seeker." The viper advanced on him.

Not a dream. My heart leaped wildly in my chest.

The weasel hurled a ball of blue witch light at Hunter. It found its target, and Hunter gasped in pain.

I struggled to pull myself out of the deadening fog. Hunter. I had to help him. Mentally I began my draw-power chant again. *An di allaigh* . . .

Power stirred inside me, faint as a hummingbird's heartbeat. But there.

In my mind I sang the chant again and again until I felt a

thin, steady stream of magick pouring into me. And then I sent it all to Hunter. *Help him,* I charged it. *Make him stronger. Heal his wounds.*

Hunter blocked a blow from the jackal, then turned and shot me a quick look of gratitude. I love you, Hunter, I thought. You've got to survive this.

Then Hunter chanted a spell in a language I didn't recognize. The fine garnet inlays on the table began to shudder. I watched wide-eyed as their forms rose into the air, glowing with the bloodred light of the gems. They were sigils, I realized. Hunter was calling them up.

The masked witches moved away from him, and I felt their terror. "Impossible," one murmured. "There's no way a Seeker could know how to use those sigils."

How did he do it? I wondered with distant amazement. Could the council really make him that much stronger? He seemed practically invincible.

The witch in the bear mask charged Hunter, but the witch never made it. He let out a sickening scream as he hit one of the glowing red sigils. He crashed to the floor, where the sigil ate at him the way fire ants devour a body.

And then Hunter was at my side, his athame out, its blade slicing through the spelled ropes that bound me. I felt him lift me from the table, murmur, "Thank God you're still alive."

"Hunter, no," I whispered. "Save yourself."

"Shhh," he whispered. "It's all right."

But the fog was washing over me, drawing me under again. And this time I let it take me.

*　　　*　　　*

Time had passed, I don't know how much. There was only Hunter and me, and we were on the sidewalk. He set me on my feet gently. "Do you think you can walk?" he asked.

"Yes," I said, though I was still terribly weak. Then Hunter was pulling me away from the house.

We got as far as the Museum of Natural History, where we both collapsed on the steps. It was dark and cold, and our breath came out in little clouds of vapor.

"Are you all right?" Hunter asked.

"I think so. My power . . . they didn't take it."

"No," he said softly. "You fought off an entire coven of Woodbanes. Thank the Goddess. I was nearly out of my mind with fright for you."

That was when I started to cry, great, gulping sobs that felt like they'd never stop.

Hunter folded me into his arms and held me. For a long time I stayed there in the shelter of his arms, crying until I had no more tears. Even after I stopped crying, I stayed there, listening to the steady sound of his heart, thinking it incredibly precious.

"I must be a mess," I said, finally breaking away to blow my nose. That's when I noticed Hunter's face was as tear-streaked as mine. "Hunter?" I asked uncertainly. "Are you okay?"

He nodded. "I'd better send a message to Sky, let everyone know we're all right." He concentrated for a moment, and I knew the message was being sent. "Here," he said then, taking off his jacket and draping it over my shoulders.

"How did you find me?" I asked. "I called you, but I got no answer. Ciaran was blocking my messages." I shuddered.

"I finally found Ciaran's ex-lover, and she told me where the coven was," Hunter explained.

"What happened to the Amyranth witches?" I asked.

"Still in the house. Recovering, I imagine. I hit them pretty hard, but I don't think I did much permanent damage," Hunter said. "I was more concerned with getting you out alive."

"But they're still there."

"Yes. I've sent a message to the council, but I doubt they'll get there before Amyranth clears out of that house. They'll surface again, though," he added grimly.

A kid came up to us, clutching a fistful of individually wrapped roses. "Hey, mister, want to buy a flower for the lady?" he asked.

Hunter stood up. "Yes, God, yes, I ought to buy her an entire bouquet, but"—he reached into his pocket and pulled out his billfold—"I'll take one. Keep the change."

"Thanks," the boy said, his face lighting up as he realized Hunter had given him a twenty.

"That was generous," I said as the boy ran off and Hunter dropped down beside me again.

He shrugged. "I'm feeling generous and grateful—and phenomenally sorry. So much more than sorry." He handed me the flower. "Morgan, I don't know how to apologize."

"For what? You don't have anything to apologize for," I protested. "I'm the one who charged in there like the Mounties to the rescue."

He gave me that stern Hunter look. "You did, and remind me to give you a hard time for it someday, but the truth is— this was all my fault."

I snuggled closer. "How do you figure that?"

"Isn't it obvious? I should have realized Amyranth wanted you."

"Stop blaming yourself," I told him. I ran my hand along his smooth cheek. He was so dear to me. "It was the council who got it totally wrong. How could they have thought the target was Ciaran's child?"

Hunter didn't say anything.

"I guess I shouldn't blame them," I added grudgingly. "I mean, I did see myself as a wolf cub in the dream. But obviously that didn't mean what we all assumed it meant."

Hunter gazed at me with an expression of pity and grief. "Oh, Morgan," he said. "I thought you already knew."

"Knew what?" Sudden, nameless dread lodged somewhere below my heart, a dark, cold mass.

"The dream meant exactly what we thought. The council didn't get it wrong. The target was Ciaran's child."

"But Killian was never their captive and—"

"Never mind Killian. There's one thing none of us knew," he interrupted, his voice gentle. "Not even Ciaran—until he did *tàth meànma* on you. He saw Maeve holding you as an infant—and he heard what she said about your eyes. Morgan, Angus had blue eyes. Yours are brown . . . like your father's."

"No." I started to shake again as I understood what he was saying. "That can't be. It's impossible. I won't believe—"

Hunter put one hand on the side of my face. "Morgan, you *are* Ciaran's child."

14

Tainted

May 25, 1985

I tried to forget her, I swear it. I returned to Scotland. Had another go with Grania and the little ones, every bit as miserable as the other times. Killian is an interesting one, though. He has more innate power than Kyle and Iona combined. He could be a real find. Still, I can't share a roof with any of them, not when it's Maeve I ache for. She's a craving in my heart, a sickness in my blood. I wake and fall asleep to her memory. I love her as much as I hate her. She is with me every minute.

But the truth is, she remains with Angus, damn him. Time and again I've tried to persuade her to leave the worthless fool. And time and again she refuses.

I wonder sometimes what would be if she gave me a chance, if she saw who it is I've become in these years since she first *rejected me. The heart she would not accept from me, I gave to the darkness. My power has grown beyond what I ever believed possible. I have served the darkness well, and it me. There is nothing on this earth that frightens me and very little that can stand against me. Would the good witch of Belwicket be able to accept that? I must believe that our love would open her to her own true Woodbane nature and that she would revel in it as I do.*

Meanwhile my love for her only grows. It never seems to diminish, no matter how I distract myself. I've tried everything, even stooping to childish tricks. I've left anonymous threatening sigils around their house. I've even hung a dead cat from their porch rail. Goddess, it's sickening, juvenile stuff, but I am a man possessed. What shall I do? What can I do?

—Neimhidh

I don't know how long I sat there on the steps of the museum, trying to wrap my mind around what Hunter had just told me. I was numb, unable to process it. It was too dark, too monstrous. I couldn't let it in.

Ciaran, my true father?

No. No, no, no. It simply couldn't be.

"Listen, love," Hunter said. "I want to tell you about him."

"Please. Don't." I couldn't say anything else. His jacket hung open on my shoulders. I wasn't even feeling the cold anymore.

"No, you need to hear this. It was Ciaran who freed me.

He told me you were his daughter and that I had to save you."

"Why? So he can drain me again?" I said.

Hunter sighed. "You're not listening. Ciaran gave me the spell for calling up the sigils in the table. And he added his power to mine. Don't you know I couldn't have held off all those witches on my own? Neither one of us would have gotten out of there alive without his help. Morgan, whatever he is, whatever he's done, he couldn't kill you. Not his own child."

"It doesn't matter," I replied dully. "He's still evil. A murderer. And I'm his daughter." Robbie had been right about me. I was fundamentally tainted. It was my birthright.

"Morgan—"

I put my finger to Hunter's lips. "Stop. Please. If there's one thing I've learned from all this, it's that you can't change what's fated to be."

Hunter rubbed his temple. "We need to talk about this, but tonight's obviously not the right time."

"We should get out of the city," I said with a shudder. "Before Amyranth regroups. Let's go get everyone. I'll drive back to Widow's Vale tonight."

Hunter gave a hollow laugh. "I'm not even sure you're capable of climbing into a cab, much less driving upstate. No, we'll spend the night in the city. I expect we'll be safe enough. But first thing tomorrow morning we'll get the hell out."

He hailed a cab and helped me into it.

It was late when we got back to the apartment. We rode up in the elevator in silence. It was only when we got out on Bree's floor that I realized I was still wearing that awful brown robe. "How am I going to explain this?" I asked.

Hunter brushed a strand of hair out of my face. "It's after eleven. Maybe they'll all be asleep."

They were. Sky and Raven were in the living room, nestled together on the pullout couch. Raven looked content, peaceful, almost innocent.

I found a note from Bree on the kitchen counter.

M&H—

I'm so glad you're all right! Since my dad is still in Connecticut, Robbie and I are camping out in the master bedroom. You guys can take the guest room.

—B

In tiny print at the bottom she'd added another note: M— You were right about me. How about that?

Hunter was standing at the closed door of the guest room. "Morgan, look," he said softly. On the doorknob Bree had hung a small wreath wound through with white blossoms. Their sweet, heady scent filled the hallway. "Jasmine," Hunter said with a smile. "Wonder where she found it at this time of year?" He took my hand. "Shall we go in?"

I tried to force a smile, but I couldn't.

"Hunter," I began, my voice breaking, "I don't know how to say this, but—I just hurt a lot right now. I need to sleep on my own tonight."

I saw the flash of pain in Hunter's eyes and felt a remote sense of guilt, of regret. Here, at last, was our chance to spend a whole night together. After surviving the disaster at Ciaran's, sleeping together was exactly what should have followed, a natural way to ground ourselves in life again after having come so close to death. An affirmation of our love, a time for comfort. But I couldn't accept it. Not now.

"If that's what you need . . ." Hunter's voice trailed off.

"It is." I reached up and touched his cheek. "Thanks. For everything."

"Anytime," he said.

I walked into the guest room and caught sight of my reflection in the mirror. For the space of several heartbeats I forced myself to study my own face. My cheeks were tear-streaked, my nose slightly swollen. My eyes were puffy and red. And exactly the same shape and color as Ciaran's.

I felt a sick appreciation for the irony of it. After all these years I finally knew who I resembled.

I couldn't look anymore. I needed a shower desperately, but I was too tired. The shower would wait until morning. I stripped off the brown robe. In the morning I'd stuff it down the garbage chute.

I went into the guest room and climbed into bed. I closed my eyes and willed sleep, but an endless tape kept running through my head: Ciaran is my father. Ciaran is my father. Ciaran is my father.

I couldn't doubt it. Not after the connection I'd felt with him. Not after I'd looked in the mirror and seen his eyes staring out from my face.

My father was a murderer, the leader of a Woodbane coven whose purpose was to destroy other covens. He'd killed Maeve and Angus. He was pure evil.

It occurred to me that Killian was my half brother.

All sorts of things began to fall into place. Things that

hadn't quite made sense before. The sense of connection I'd felt with Ciaran—and with Killian. My unusual powers. Not only was I heir to Belwicket's legacy of magick, but to Ciaran's as well. And my own tendency to abuse power definitely came from Ciaran.

Through the wall I heard Hunter curse the couch in the study. Bree had told me that it was lumpy and uncomfortable.

Tears leaked from the corners of my eyes. I loved Hunter in a way I'd never loved anyone. But I couldn't be with him. Not now, knowing what I really was.

An heir to darkness.

15

Broken

June 1985

I am back in Meshomah Falls now so I can put an end to it once and for all. There will be no more fevers, no more senseless cravings. No more pining for a woman who won't have me. I'm choosing my own peace of mind over all else. Giving in to the inevitable.

If she wants Angus so badly, let her have him for eternity. Let them both die. I've found the perfect place for it, an isolated barn on an abandoned farm about five miles from their house. The means will be Maeve's own element, fire. It seems the only fitting thing. A fire to quench the fire that's been burning in my heart since the day I first saw her.

Fire to fire and ashes to ashes. It will soon be done. I've already closed my heart to love. From this day on I give myself wholly to the darkness.

—Neimhidh

We were back in Widow's Vale by noon on Monday. After I dropped everyone off, I finally drove back to my own house. My parents' cars were both gone, and I didn't see any lights on inside. I cast my senses. No one home except Dagda.

I knew I should go in and unpack, hug my kitten, but somehow I wasn't ready. Instead I pulled out of the driveway again and drove to the road that runs along the Hudson River.

I turned in at the marina parking lot. The town has a dock there where small boats tie up in the summer. In the winter it's deserted, just a crescent of stony beach and a rough wooden dock jutting out into the water.

It was terribly cold, but I didn't care. I needed the solitude. The river, an expanse of silver-gray beneath white winter skies, was calm and seemed infinitely peaceful. I walked to the end of the dock. Despite the snows we'd had, the water level was a good six feet below the dock, so I sat on the end and dangled my feet.

This river flows to New York City, I thought. This river connects the two places, rising and falling with the tides of the Atlantic. I'd been feeling relatively safe since returning to Widow's Vale, but the silver-gray waters reminded me that New York and Widow's Vale were linked, part of a whole. What I'd left in the city would always be part of my life.

Like Ciaran. My natural father. I was still struggling with the implications of that revelation. How was I going to use my magick, knowing that half my power came from Ciaran? Just the thought of magick gave me a sick, hollow feeling.

As for love . . . I'd barely been able to stand the car ride back home. It felt like torture to sit next to Hunter, knowing what had to come next.

I had to break up with him. I just hadn't been able to summon the strength that morning.

It all came down to Ciaran. My biological father wasn't good, kind Angus. My father was a man who'd murdered his own *mùirn beatha dàn*. A man who'd sucked the power and the life from who knew how many innocent people. And if he was capable of those crimes, then what crimes was I, his daughter, his own flesh and blood, capable of committing?

I'd already made so many mistakes that cost me and others dearly. I'd had terrible judgment. I'd trusted Cal, Selene, David, and Ciaran. I'd hurt Bree, nearly killed Hunter—twice now—and watched Cal die for me. I'd almost driven Robbie away. I'd caused my parents pain. I'd put Mary K.'s life in terrible danger. Two and a half months of magick and I was a walking minefield.

And all because of what I was. Like father, like daughter. I was poison. Everyone I touched was tainted by me.

I felt a surge of despair as my senses began to tingle. Hunter was nearby. I heard the sound of his beat-up old Honda driving down the winding path to the water. I guessed I couldn't put it off after all.

Moments later Hunter got out of his car. He was wearing a long, straight navy wool coat that made him look formal and grown up. His hair framed his face in a halo of gold. I'd forgotten how sometimes it seemed like he was made of sunlight.

Whereas I was the heir to darkness.

He walked up to me cautiously. "Am I intruding?"

"Sort of," I said honestly. "I came here because I needed time alone."

"Want me to leave?"

I shook my head. I didn't want him to leave. I wanted to run into his arms, hold him, and never let him go.

We stared at each other while I tried to find the words to say the impossible.

"I wanted you to know," he said. "I just got word on Killian. Apparently he thought the owl was sent to spy on him, as we all did. He took off, fearing that Amyranth really was after him. He's still lying low, but I just got word that he's okay."

"Oh," I said dully. "That's good."

Hunter's green eyes studied me. "Killian may be okay," he said slowly. "You, on the other hand, clearly are not."

"You noticed," I said, trying to sound a whole lot cooler than I felt.

"Of course I noticed," he said, looking at me as intensely as ever. "What do you take me for?"

I felt frozen, unable to speak.

He ran a hand through his hair and said in a gentler tone, "Morgan, tell me what I can do. How can I help?"

"I—" My voice died in my throat. I couldn't say it. It hurt too much. "You can't," I got out at last. "No one can."

I thought of what it felt like to lie in Hunter's arms, to laugh with him, to join my power with his. How could I give up any of that? There would never be anyone who felt that right, never anyone I would love that much, ever again. He was my soul mate.

"All right." He shoved his hands into his coat pockets as if to keep himself from touching me. "Maybe you're not ready to talk right now. Can we get together tomorrow night?"

"No!" I said more forcefully than I'd meant to.

"Why not?"

I thought again of how I'd hurt everyone who came near me. How as Ciaran's daughter, I couldn't possibly do anything else.

"I guess I need to get used to it," I said finally.

"Used to what?"

"To what it's going to be like without you." My voice sounded hollow and alien, like it was coming out of someone else's body.

"What?" He let out a sharp, startled bark of laughter. "What are you saying?"

I couldn't look at him. "I have to be on my own. I'm poison, Hunter. I can't help it."

Hunter blew out his breath, a cloud of steam in the icy air. "Don't be ridiculous. Heritage does not equal destiny."

"For me it does. I can't be with you anymore. We have to break up."

There. It was out. I shut my eyes tight against the pain. It was worse than anything I'd experienced at the hands of Amyranth. I felt like I'd just cut out my own heart.

"We have to do what?" Hunter's voice was carefully controlled, as if he were trying to convince himself he'd misheard me.

"I'm breaking up with you," I said more strongly. I opened my eyes, but I still couldn't look at him. I stared at the wooden slats of the dock below my feet and wondered what it would be like to drop through them, sink into the frigid water below. Don't cry, Morgan. You will not cry. I took a deep breath and said the only thing I could think of that would make him go away. "I don't love you anymore."

"Really?" His voice was like ice. "When did that happen?"

"Things—things have changed," I said, trying to keep my voice steady. "I'm sorry. I just don't love you anymore."

Hunter just looked at me. We both knew I was lying.

"Listen." His voice was ragged. "I came here to tell you something else. I never really believed in all this *mùirn beatha dàn* stuff. I thought it was just romantic nonsense. But Morgan, you are my *mùirn beatha dàn*. I realized that when I thought I was going to lose you to Amyranth. I love you—absolutely, totally, forever. Know that."

Oh, God. It hurt so much, the words I'd been waiting for, words that should have made me so happy. And all I could think was: Don't tell me that now. Please. You can't love me.

"Look at me, dammit." Hunter was inches away from me now. "Look at me and tell me you want to break up."

I raised my eyes to his and saw pain and grief and confusion—and love. No one would ever look at me with that much love again. I blinked back tears. "I want to break up."

"Oh, Morgan," he said. Then he took that final step toward me, and somehow our arms were around each other. He held me while I cried, and I could feel both our hearts breaking.

"I love you," he said again, which only made me cry harder.

I don't know how long we stood together like that. When we finally stepped apart, the front of his wool coat was spongy with my tears.

"I have to go now," I told him. "Don't call me." Before either of us could say more, I turned and ran toward Das Boot. The wind rose, howling down the river, echoing our pain. But Hunter's voice managed to carry over it.

"We make our own choices," he called after me.

BOOK EIGHT

SWEEP
CHANGELING

To my inner wolf

All quoted materials in this work were created by the author.
Any resemblance to existing works is accidental.

Changeling

SPEAK
Published by the Penguin Group
Penguin Group (USA) Inc., 345 Hudson Street, New York, New York 10014, U.S.A.
Penguin Group (Canada), 90 Eglinton Avenue East, Suite 700, Toronto, Ontario, Canada M4P 2Y3
(a division of Pearson Penguin Canada Inc.)
Penguin Books Ltd, 80 Strand, London WC2R 0RL, England
Penguin Ireland, 25 St Stephen's Green, Dublin 2, Ireland (a division of Penguin Books Ltd)
Penguin Group (Australia), 250 Camberwell Road, Camberwell, Victoria 3124, Australia
(a division of Pearson Australia Group Pty Ltd)
Penguin Books India Pvt Ltd, 11 Community Centre, Panchsheel Park, New Delhi - 110 017, India
Penguin Group (NZ), 67 Apollo Drive, Rosedale, North Shore 0632, New Zealand
(a division of Pearson New Zealand Ltd)
Penguin Books (South Africa) (Pty) Ltd, 24 Sturdee Avenue, Rosebank, Johannesburg 2196, South Africa

Registered Offices: Penguin Books Ltd, 80 Strand, London WC2R 0RL, England

Published by Puffin Books, a division of Penguin Young Readers Group, 2001
Published by Speak, an imprint of Penguin Group (USA) Inc., 2008
This omnibus edition published by Speak, an imprint of Penguin Group (USA) Inc., 2011

1 3 5 7 9 10 8 6 4 2

Copyright © 2001 17th Street Productions, an Alloy company,
and Gabrielle Charbonnet
All rights reserved

Produced by 17th Street Productions,
an Alloy company
151 West 26th Street
New York, NY 10001

17th Street Productions and associated logos
are trademarks and/or registered trademarks of Alloy, Inc.

Speak ISBN 978-0-14-241023-3
This omnibus ISBN 978-0-14-241955-7

Printed in the United States of America

Except in the United States of America, this book is sold subject to the condition that
it shall not, by way of trade or otherwise, be lent, re-sold, hired out, or otherwise
circulated without the publisher's prior consent in any form of binding or cover
other than that in which it is published and without a similar condition
including this condition being imposed on the subsequent purchaser.

The publisher does not have any control over and does not assume any
responsibility for author or third-party Web sites or their content.

1

Breakthrough

Surely I did not know the meaning of the word godforsaken until I arrived at this place. Barra Head is on the westernmost shore of the highlands of Scotland, and a wilder, more untamed countryside it would be difficult to imagine. Yet, Brother Colin, how exalted I am to be here, how eager to bring the Lord's message to these good people. Tomorrow I shall set forth among the inhabitants, taking to them the joy of the Word of God.

—Brother Sinestus Tor, Cistercian monk, in a letter to his brother Colin, also a monk, September 1767

"Okay, I'm gone," said my sister, Mary K., whirling to run downstairs. We'd just heard the distinctive horn beep of her friend Jaycee's mom's minivan.

"See you," I called after her. Although Mary K. was my little sister, she was fourteen going on twenty-five, and in some ways, like for instance her chest, she looked more mature than I did.

"Honey?" My mom poked her head around my bedroom door. "Please come with us to Eileen and Paula's."

"Oh, no thanks," I said, trying not to sound rude. I loved my aunt Eileen and her girlfriend, Paula, but I couldn't face having to interact with them, smile, eat, pretend everything was normal—when only days ago my entire life had split at the seams.

"She's made seaweed salad," Mom said temptingly.

"Augh!" I crossed my two index fingers to ward off health food, and my mom made a face.

"Okay. Just thought you'd want to have a last family meal," she said in her best guilt-inducing voice.

"Mom, you'll only be gone eleven days. I'll know you for the rest of my life. Plenty of family meals in our future," I said. The next day my parents were leaving on a cruise to the Bahamas, to celebrate their wedding anniversary.

"Mary Grace?" my dad called. Translated that meant "get a move on."

"Okay." Mom looked at me speculatively, and suddenly all the humor in the situation was gone. My parents and I had been through a lot in the past couple of months, and every once in a while the memories came back to bite us.

"Have a good time," I said, turning away. "Say hi to Eileen and Paula."

"Mary Grace?" my dad said again. " 'Bye, Morgan. We won't be late."

Once I heard the front door close, I felt my shoulders sag in relief. Alone at last. Free to be myself, at least for a little while. Free to feel miserable, to lie curled on my bed, to wander the house aimlessly without having to talk to anyone or try to look normal.

Free to be myself. That was a joke. The *me* that was Wiccan. Not only Wiccan, but a blood witch and a Woodbane—

the most infamous of Wicca's Seven Great Clans. The me whose biological father, Ciaran MacEwan, had killed my birth mother, Maeve Riordan. Ciaran was one of the most evil, dangerous, remorseless witches there was, and half of me came from him. So what did that say about me?

I looked at myself in my bedroom mirror. I still looked like me: straight brown hair, brownish hazel eyes, a tiny bit tilted at the corner, strong nose. I was five-six, seventeen years old, and had yet to develop a feminine curve anywhere on my body.

I didn't look like a Rowlands. For sixteen years I had never once thought I wasn't a Rowlands, despite looking different from the rest of my family, despite the huge differences between Mary K. and me. Now we all knew why those differences existed. Because I had been born a Riordan.

I dropped onto my bed, my chest aching. Only days ago I had narrowly escaped death—Ciaran had tried to kill me in Manhattan. At the last minute, when he'd realized that I was his daughter, had Ciaran changed his mind and allowed my then boyfriend, Hunter Niall, to save me. My father was a man who had killed my mother. Who had tried to kill me. Ciaran was evil beyond belief, and that evil was part of me. How could Hunter even pretend not to understand why I had broken up with him?

Oh, Goddess, Hunter, I thought, filled with longing. I loved him, I lusted after him, I admired and trusted and respected him. He was tall, blond, gorgeous, and had a fabulous English accent. He was a powerful, initiated blood witch, half Woodbane, and he was a Seeker for the International Council of Witches. He was my *mùirn beatha dàn*—my soul mate. For most people, that meant they were supposed to be together forever. But I was descended from one of the worst witches in Wiccan history. My very blood was tainted forever. I was poison; I would destroy anything I touched. I couldn't bear to hurt Hunter, couldn't bear even to take the chance that I would. So I had told him I didn't love him anymore. I'd told him to leave me alone.

Which was why I was alone now, having spent the last few days clutching a pillow, aching with loneliness, and sick with misery.

"What can I do?" I asked myself. It was Saturday, and my coven, Kithic, would be meeting as usual for a circle. One of our eight annual sabbats, Imbolc, was coming up soon, and I knew we would be starting to talk about it and preparing to celebrate it. Going to a circle, making the commitment to observe every week, was part of the pattern of Wiccan life. It was part of the turning of the Wheel of the Year, part of learning. I knew I should go.

But I knew I couldn't. Couldn't bear seeing Hunter. Couldn't bear seeing the other people in my circle, having them look at me with sympathy, fear, or distrust.

"*Meow?*"

I looked down at my kitten.

"Dagda," I said, picking him up. "You're turning into a big boy. You have a big meow." I stroked Dagda, feeling his rumbly purr.

If I went to the circle tonight, I would have to see Hunter, feel his eyes on me, hear his voice. Would I be strong enough to face that? I didn't think so.

"I can't go," I told Dagda. "I won't. I'll make a circle here." I got up, feeling that this was a way to keep my commitment to observe the Wiccan circle. Maybe drawing on the power would help my pain. Maybe it would take my mind off Hunter and off my own inherent evil, at least for a little while.

I went to the back of my closet and brought my altar out from under my bathrobe. As far as I knew, my parents hadn't discovered it yet. It was a small footlocker, covered with a violet linen cloth, and I used it in the rites I did at home. It was hidden in the back of my closet, where it wouldn't be noticed by my devoutly Catholic parents. To them, it was bad enough that I practiced Wicca at all, and they would be really, really unhappy if they knew I had all this witch stuff in their house.

I shoved the footlocker into the middle of the room, aligning its four corners with the four points of the compass. (I had figured this out weeks ago and memorized the position it should be in.) On each of the four corners of the footlocker I set the silver ceremonial bowls that had belonged to my birth mother. As always, I looked at them with love and appreciation. I had never known Maeve—I had been only seven months old when Ciaran killed her—but I had her witch's tools, and they meant everything to me.

Into one bowl I put fresh water. In one bowl half full of sand I stuck an incense stick and lit it. The thin gray stream of scented smoke symbolized air. Another bowl held a handful of stones and crystals, to symbolize earth. In the last bowl I lit a thick red candle, for fire. The candle was red for power, for passion, for fire, for me. Fire was my element: I scried with fire; I could summon fire at will.

I quickly shed my clothes and got into my green robe. The silk was thin and embroidered with ancient Celtic signs, runes, sigils of protection and power. Maeve had worn this, leading circles for her coven, Belwicket, back in Ireland. Her mother, Mackenna, had worn it before her. And so on, for generations.

I loved wearing it, knowing I was fulfilling my destiny, feeling a connection with women I had never known. Could Maeve's goodness cancel out Ciaran's evil? Which half would win in me?

As the folds flowed around me, encasing me with their magickal vibrations, I took out my other tools: a ceremonial dagger called an athame and a witch's wand, long, slim, and decorated with lines of silver beaten into the dark, old wood. I was ready.

First I drew a circle on my floor with chalk. With fleeting pride, I noticed that my circle drawing was getting much better. It was now nearly perfect. I stepped in, closed the circle, and knelt before my altar. "Goddess and God, I call on thee," I said softly, looking into my candle's flame. "Your daughter Morgan calls on your goodness and your power. Help me make magick. Help me learn. Show me what I am ready to know." Closing my eyes, I let out all my breath, then slowly drew it in again. Within a minute I was deeply into meditation: I had practiced so much that meditation was like using a muscle. It was there, it was almost immediate, and it was strong.

What am I ready to know? I asked. In my mind a narrow road unspooled before me. Trees and shrubs lined each side, making the road both inviting and secluded. I moved down the road, smoothly and with no sense of pace—as if I were floating above the hard-packed earth. It felt wonderful, exciting. Eagerly I sped forward.

I flew around a curve and then recoiled in sudden horror, a wordless scream coming from my mouth. Before me, blocking my way, was a dying serpent, a black, roiling, two-headed snake. Its flesh was hacked and eaten away; acrid blood stained the roadbed, its bitter, repugnant scent making me cover my nose and mouth. The thing was dying. It curled upon itself in agony, twisting as it lost its breath and felt its blood flow. I backed up slowly, not sure how dangerous it still was, and then from the sky a beautiful, cold, crystalline cage dropped over the thing. With one last shriek of torment the two-headed black serpent lashed its barbed tail and died. The cage shimmered over it gently, seemingly made of air, of music, of gold, of crystal. It was made of magick. I had made it. And my cage had helped kill the serpent.

Gasping, I clawed my way back to consciousness, opening my eyes to find my heart pounding, the scent of the serpent's blood still in my throat. I wanted to gag, the horrible images still behind my eyes. The serpent had been Cal Blaire and Selene Belltower. It didn't take a psychology major to figure that one out. My subconscious was obviously still working through that particular horror. The deaths of Cal, the first boy I had ever loved, and his mother, Selene, a powerful, dark Woodbane witch, were still ever present in my everyday awareness. I gazed at my red candle and shuddered. There was no way I could explore that path any more tonight. Maybe I needed to see it, maybe magick had needed me to see something, learn something, but I couldn't face it. I hoped that with the passage of time, the memory would sink deeper.

I swallowed and watched the scented smoke rise from the incense. Maybe if I had continued down the road of my subconscious, I would have seen myself, in New York City, about to be sacrificed by Ciaran's coven for my own powers.

No thank you. No more of this. The Goddess must have thought I was ready for this, but I didn't *feel* ready.

Once again I gazed at my red candle. My situation was strange: I was an unusually powerful blood witch. Yet because Wicca had discovered me only about three months ago, I was

relatively unschooled in magick. Even as hard as I had been trying to learn, the breadth and depth of a witch's knowledge
ensured that I would be at it my whole life. Another fact was
that I was uninitiated. An uninitiated witch was not in command
of her full powers—in fact, not exactly in command of her powers at all. Which was what everyone kept trying to tell me.

Until now I had loved feeling my powers stretch and grow,
like a plant toward sunlight. The more I made magick, the
stronger my magick seemed and the easier it was to make it
flow. I had believed that my magick would be good, that
I would walk in sunlight even though I was Woodbane.
Belwicket had been a Woodbane coven but had renounced
dark magick centuries ago. But then I had found out Ciaran
was my father, and all of my assumptions had snapped. I was
no longer sure that I would use magick for goodness. No
longer sure that I could stay out of the shadows. Now with
every breath I remembered that I had been born of evil, the
daughter of a murderer. And that it had cost me Hunter.

I have a choice, I thought. I choose to work good magick.

I looked at my altar and concentrated, centering myself and
focusing my energy. Rise, I thought, looking at the silver bowl
holding the incense. "Rise, be light, be light as air. I lift you up
and hold you there." The little rhyme came into my head, and
simultaneously the silver bowl wobbled a bit, then shakily rose
above my altar. It hovered there, weightless, while I stared at
it in shock. Oh God, I thought. Wicca had shown me many
things in the last three months that I never would have
thought possible, but the idea that I had the power to levitate
anything amazed me.

Okay, concentrate, I told myself as the bowl tilted. I concentrated. Almost immediately it steadied.

Next I made the candle rise and kept the two objects floating before me. Could I make it three? Yes. The bowl of water rose gracefully. I was able to keep them steadier now, and the three objects bobbed before me as I turned my attention to the bowl of crystals. This was amazing, intense magick. I could tell none of this skill came from my friend Alyce Fernbrake, who had shared all of her knowledge with me in a powerful ritual called *tàth meànma brach*.

This was mine; this power was me. It was beautiful and good in a way I could never be.

A slight vibration in the floor barely registered with me as I began to levitate the bowl of crystals in the air. More thin, light, striations of sound—distracting me . . . Crap, they were footsteps!

I leaped up, shoved the altar behind my desk, and kicked the silver bowls and candle out of the way. Hoping I hadn't burned the rug, I jumped into bed. I was pulling the covers up when the door to my room opened.

"Morgan?" my mom whispered, peering into my room.

Asleep, I'm asleep, I thought, feeling my eyelids get heavy. My mother gently closed the door, and I heard her walk down the hallway. I waited until I heard the door to her own room close, then I slunk out of bed and tried to clean up soundlessly. This had been so stupid. I had been so full of myself that I hadn't remembered to put up a border spell that would alert me when my parents came home. I hadn't been casting my senses, paying attention to my surroundings.

Gently I shoved my altar back into my closet. I took off the robe and gathered the bowls and tools and hid them with the altar. Tomorrow I would put them where I usually hid them: behind the HVAC vent in the hallway. Pretty full of yourself, aren't you? I thought with disgust as I tried to scrape up the sand with my hands. You just want to make any kind of magick you can, with no thought as to the consequences. That's a Woodbane way to behave.

I cleaned up the circle as best I could, knowing I would have to finish tomorrow. I brushed my teeth and got into my pj's. Then I climbed back into bed and pulled up the covers. All of my misery was back and more. I had missed a coven circle tonight. I was Ciaran's daughter. I didn't have Hunter. If things were this bad when I was only seventeen, what would they be like when I hit thirty?

2

Alone

Brother Colin, I shall not prevaricate to you, who are my flesh and blood as well as a fellow servant of God. I have only begun my work here and shall be content if it takes me until the end of my days to reach the people of Barra Head. But it has been a surprise to discover how the populace resists the Good Word. There is a handful of devout souls, to be sure, but everywhere the old religion pervades. Where I look, I see ancient sigils chipped into rock faces, painted on the crude sod and stone houses: even herb gardens grown in heathen patterns. Surely God has sent me here to save these people, these so called Wodebaynes.

—Brother Sinestus Tor, to his brother Colin, November 1767

Hours later I lay in bed, watching the interplay of shadows on my recently painted bedroom walls. I'd thought I was exhausted, but sleep hadn't come. Now I let my senses float out into the house. Mary K., separated from me by a bathroom, was deeply asleep. She'd come home shortly after my parents had, completely excited by the prospect of eleven days at her friend Jaycee's house: an uninterrupted slumber party. Her three suitcases were already packed and by the front door.

My parents, too, were asleep: my mother lightly, fitfully, my dad more deeply. They were nervous about the trip, about being away from us.

I turned on my side. Tonight I'd made objects levitate. It had been amazing and even a little frightening. If I weren't so distraught, it would have been joyful, beautiful. Well, that was Wicca: light and dark at the same time and part of the same thing. Day turning into night. Beauty and ugliness, good and bad. The rose and the thorn.

Morgan. As the voice echoed inside my head, I blinked, sending my senses out more strongly. Oh my God, Hunter was right outside the front door. It was one-thirty in the morning. I had two thoughts: I can't face him. And: I hope he doesn't wake my parents.

Morgan. I bit my lip and got of bed, knowing I had no choice. Despite my unhappiness, my traitorous heart skipped a beat in anticipation of seeing Hunter. Very quietly I pushed my feet into my bear claw slippers and padded downstairs. I put on my parka and opened the front door as silently as I could.

He stood there, his fine, fair hair glinting with winter moonlight. His face was in darkness, but I saw the hard line of his jaw, the sculpted curve of his cheekbone. It had been only a few days, but I longed for him with a physical ache.

"Hi," I said, looking away from him. My hair was unbrushed, and my face felt tired and drawn.

"You missed a circle," he said evenly, tilting his head back to see me. The cold January air made his words come out like a dragon's breath. "Why?"

Experienced witches can lie and deceive each other fairly

successfully. But if I lied to Hunter, he would know it. "I didn't want to see you." I tried to sound strong, but I'm sure my body language was screaming anguish.

"Why?" His expression didn't change, but I could sense the hurt and anger I had caused him. "Am I *repellent* now?"

I shook my head. "Of course not," I said. "But I wanted more time alone since we just broke up."

"Part of Wicca is making the commitment to observe the turning of the Wheel," Hunter said. "The weekly circle is just as important as your personal life."

Count to ten before you speak, I reminded myself. He made it sound like I had missed the circle because I had a zit. But he had seen how upset and shocked and freaked out I had been after what had happened in New York—after finding out that my father wasn't gentle Angus Bramson, the man who had loved and lived with my mother for several years, but Ciaran MacEwan, the evil and destructive witch who had eventually killed her. Hunter had seen for himself how ruthless Ciaran was, so much a pure Woodbane, dedicated to acquiring power at any cost. With a father like that, did I have a chance of turning out okay? I was pure Woodbane myself. Was it just a matter of time before I was lured by dark magick? And how could I stand to see the look on Hunter's face if and when I finally went bad? His horror and disillusionment?

"I know the circle is important," I said stiffly. "But I wanted some time alone."

"I guess it's a matter of priorities," he said in a tone he knew infuriated me.

Knowing that he was trying to goad me didn't stop me from reacting as if he had thrown a match onto a puddle of gasoline.

"My priorities are to keep you and everyone else in Kithic

away from a potentially evil influence!" I hissed into the night air.

"Funny how you can decide what's best for us all." Hunter, of all people, knew exactly how to get to me. "You'd do well to remember just how little training you have. Perhaps we can make our own decisions about who we want to associate with. Who we want to make magick with."

I looked at Hunter, trying to control my anger. I knew that he was angry with me for missing the circle, but it was infuriating that he could ignore what had happened between us so easily—that my being a powerful witch meant I wasn't allowed to have human emotions. I had spent the last few days in complete misery; how could I just go back to the circles like nothing had happened to me?

"Plus there's the fact that I don't love you," I said finally, praying for this conversation to end. "That had something to do with it."

Hunter's green eyes were shaded gray by the pale light. But they seemed to look right through my eyes into my psyche, into the innermost me. He knew I was lying.

"We should be together." His words sounded like they cost him.

"We *can't*." My throat felt thick.

He looked up at the heavy white clouds scudding across the night sky. "You should come to circles. If not with Kithic, then with another coven."

My heart hurt. I wanted so much to tell him about my levitating experience. But it was better for him if I didn't. If I didn't share myself with him at all. Suddenly exhausted, I turned to the front door.

"Good night, Hunter."

"So you say."

His voice rang in my ears as I slipped into the house.

"Morning!" Mary K. sang, unnaturally perky as usual. All of the Rowlandses were morning people, wide awake with the sunrise and ready to go long before my natural biorhythms had kicked me into a vertical position. Before Mary K. and I knew I was adopted, it had been a family joke that I stood out so much. No one mentioned it anymore.

"Morning, honey," my mom said briefly, then turned to me. "Morgan, Dad and I are still concerned about you staying in the house alone. But I understand that if you stayed at Eileen and Paula's, you would have a longer commute to and from school."

"Much longer," I said. "Like forty-five minutes."

"Not that it would kill you to get up earlier," Mom went on. "But your father and I have discussed it, and we trust you to stay here because we know that you would never want to let us down or make us feel that trust was misplaced."

"Uh-huh," I said. Behind Mom, Mary K. watched us with interest.

"But to be on the safe side," Mom went on, "I've jotted down a few house rules. I'd like you to read them and make sure you understand everything."

My eyes went wide as she handed me a sheet of notepaper. I took it from her and slowly read it while Mary K. hovered, barely disguising her curiosity.

It was about the behavior they expected me to display while they were out of town. Display? I thought. As if I would be doing everything out on the front lawn. I read further. It basically said no boys in the house, I couldn't miss school, I had to do my homework, call Aunt Eileen every day and check in, I couldn't have parties. . . .

My response was crucial here—I was awake enough to recognize that.

"Well, it looks like you covered everything," I began.

My dad came in then and headed for the coffeemaker. He glanced over at us and made the strategic decision to take his coffee into the living room.

"I mean, it seems fair," I told her. "Pretty much common sense."

"So all this seems okay?" Mom asked.

"Well, sure," I said. "I mean, I wouldn't be having parties, anyway."

"Or boys in the house? Hunter?"

I tried not to wince. "We broke up, remember?"

"Oh, honey, I'm sorry for mentioning it," Mom said, looking concerned. "Will you be all right alone?"

"Of course I will, Mom. I'm fine."

She hesitated, but I waved her off, plastering a cheerful smile on my face. After Mom went upstairs, I sat with my tea while Mary K. perched on a chair across from me, her big brown eyes asking for details. "What were all those rules about?"

"Oh, about being straight and narrow while they were gone, like a saint."

"Really? So no orgies?"

I groaned. "So funny."

She giggled. "I can't believe they gave you a list of rules. It's not like you're Bree."

Bree Warren had been my best friend for eleven years, until Cal Blaire had moved to Widow's Vale. When she first laid eyes on Cal, she knew that she wanted him, but he wanted me, and Bree did not take it well. The story got more complicated from there. She and Cal slept together before Cal became my boyfriend, and Cal tried to kill me when I refused to practice dark magick with his mother's coven. It had all come to a close one horrible night in his mother's library, when both Cal and his mother, Selene, were killed as she tried to steal my powers. Bree and I had been trying to forge a new friendship, but we were moving slowly.

Mary K. was referring to the fact that Bree's parents were divorced, and she lived with her dad. Mr. Warren was a lawyer with tons of money and not much time for Bree. She often stayed by herself in their big house for weeks at a time, which gave her a lot of opportunity to experiment. Bree wasn't really wild, but she was rich and unsupervised.

"No, I'm not Bree," I agreed.

"Are you going to follow the rules or blow them off?"

My sister's sweet expression and innocent demeanor always made me forget that she was very shrewd for a fourteen-year-old.

"Ugh." I put my head down on the table. "They make me feel like I'm ten years old."

Mary K. giggled and put down her mug. "It'll be good for you, Saint Morgan," she said, standing up. "Like penance."

"Good-bye, honey," my mom said an hour later. "Be careful. And if you need anything, call Eileen."

"Sure," I said. "Don't worry."

"I will worry," she said, looking into my eyes. "That's what mothers do."

All at once I got that awful feeling in my throat that signaled I was about to cry. I reached over and hugged the only mother I had ever known, and she hugged me back.

"I love you," I said, feeling embarrassed and sad. I realized just how much I would miss them while they were away.

"I love you, too, honey." Then she turned and got into Dad's car, and Mary K. waved at me from the backseat. I waved back and watched the car until it went around the corner and I couldn't see it anymore. Then I realized I was freezing, standing out here, and went into the house that would be mine alone for the next eleven days.

It was extremely quiet inside. Casting my senses, I picked up only Dagda, sleeping deeply as usual. The refrigerator hummed in the kitchen; the grandfather clock my dad had built from a kit ticked loudly. With irrational panic, I suddenly felt like every ax murderer in the area was pricking up his ears, knowing he should home in on this address right away.

"Stop it," I told myself in disgust, plopping down in front of the TV.

When the doorbell rang half an hour later, I jumped a foot in the air. I hadn't perceived anyone coming up the walk, and that realization made my heart kick into overdrive.

I cast my senses strongly as I crept over to peer through the peephole. I sensed a blood witch right before I saw the small, red-haired woman on the front porch. A witch, but no one I knew. I didn't feel any danger, but I might not, if she was powerful enough.

I opened the door. A strong witch who wanted to come into the house could probably do it despite the ward-evil and boundary spells I had set all around the house.

"Hello, Morgan," she said. Her eyes were a light, warm brown, like caramel. "My name is Eoife McNabb. I'm a subelder of the council. I want to talk to you about Ciaran MacEwan. Your father."

3
Challenge

Winter has set upon us, Brother Colin, and it is a raw one, compared to Weymouth's mildness. It does not freeze, nor yet snow, but it is cold with a wetness that chills one's bones to the marrow. Brother Colin, I have not wavered in my devotion to these people and my blessed calling of spreading God's Word. But I tell you, the people of Barra Head have a deep suspicion of me, the other brothers (we are five), and even our blessed Father Benedict, who is as holy a man as I have known. Heads turn away as we walk through the village, dogs bark, children run and hide. Today I found a marking drawn on the abbey door. It was a star encircled. The sight of this devil's mark made my blood run cold.

—Brother Sinestus Tor, to Colin, January 1768

I stood in my doorway a moment, blinking stupidly at Eoife McNabb. I felt like she'd just somehow sucked all the air out of my lungs.

At last I realized I was being rude. "Um—do you want to come in?" I asked.

"Yes, thank you." She stepped in and looked around our hallway and living room with interest. From what I could pick up, she was worried, a little tense, and unsure about coming here. I guess she felt me scanning her senses because she blinked and looked at me more closely.

"Um, sit down, Eva," I said, waving a hand at the couch. "Do you want something to drink? Some tea?" Since she had (I thought) a Scottish accent, I figured tea was a safe bet.

"It's Eoife," she corrected me. "*E-o-i-f-e*. Tea would be lovely, thanks."

"Eef-uh?"

She gave a slight smile. "Close enough." She stepped into the living room and took off her heavy wool coat. Underneath she was dressed in black pants and a pink turtleneck that clashed amazingly with her carrot-colored hair. Her image stayed with me as I went into the kitchen to put the kettle on. She had no freckles to go with that hair. Her face was smooth and unlined, but she gave the impression of being older than she looked. In her forties, maybe? It was impossible to tell.

I brought the tray out a few minutes later. Eoife waited until we had our cups in front of us, and then she looked at me, as if I were an exhibit she'd heard a lot about and was finally seeing. I looked back at her.

"How do you know me?" I asked.

She took a sip of her tea. "There are very few council members who don't know about you," she said. "Of course we'd been watching Selene Belltower for years, and anyone who came into contact with her. From the very beginning, the council has found you extremely interesting. Then recently we learned that you were the daughter of Ciaran MacEwan and Maeve Riordan. As you can imagine, that heightened our interest."

I could feel my eyes widening. "You mean the council has been spying on me?"

For a moment Eoife looked almost uncomfortable, but the expression passed so quickly that I wasn't sure if I had imagined it or not.

"No, not spying," she said, in her melodic Scottish accent. "But surely you of all people understand that there are dark forces out there. The council tries to protect all witches: especially those who practice only bright magick, who understand the dangers of the dark."

Then where were you when I was in danger of having my power sucked out in New York? I thought angrily.

"We know, of course, what happened to you in New York," Eoife said, and I wondered if she was aware of my thoughts. It was incredibly irritating. "It was appalling," she went on quietly. "It must have been horrific for you. Someday the council would like to hear the whole story—not just what Hunter knows."

A cold fist gripped my heart. Hunter. Of course. He was a Seeker for the council. What had he told them? He knew more about me than anyone else. I felt sick.

I took a sip of tea, trying to calm down. It didn't have the life-affirming jolt that Diet Coke had, but I was getting used to it. It was a very witchy drink.

"Okay, so Hunter's been reporting on me." I tried to sound casual. "Fine. But why, exactly, are you so interested in me now?" Three months ago I would have been too insecure and intimidated to be this direct. Almost being killed more than once had put insecurity into perspective.

"Hunter is your loyal friend," Eoife said. "And we're interested in you for several reasons. First, because you've impressed several of our contacts with your remarkable power. Some of the things you're apparently capable of are simply unfathomable, coming from an uninitiated witch who's been studying only three months. Second, because you're the daughter of two extremely powerful witches—a daughter we didn't know either of them had. Bradhadair was the strongest witch Belwicket had seen in generations."

Bradhadair had been Maeve's coven name. It meant "Fire Starter."

"We know about Ciaran's other children, of course," Eoife went on. "To tell you the truth, none of them has caused waves of excitement."

Ciaran had three children with his estranged wife, back in Scotland. I had met one of them, Killian, in New York. My half brother. Ciaran and Maeve had been lovers, and I was the illegitimate result. Ciaran hadn't even known I existed until a few days ago.

"The council needs you to find Ciaran."

Eoife dropped this bomb right after I had taken a sip of tea, and I almost spit it out all over her. I gulped and swallowed, trying not to cough.

"What?" I asked.

"Do you know what a dark wave is?" Eoife asked.

"It's . . . devastation," I said. "I read about it in my mother's Book of Shadows. A dark wave can kill people, level houses, destroy whole villages, whole covens."

"You have Maeve of Belwicket's Book of Shadows?" Eoife's eyes practically gleamed.

"Yes," I said quietly, feeling a little resentful of her excitement. "But it's private."

She sat back and looked at me. "You're very . . . interesting," she said, as if speaking to herself. "Very interesting." Then she remembered where we were in the conversation. "Yes. In essence, a dark wave is destruction. Utter destruction. Belwicket was obliterated by one. Until recently, no one knew Maeve and Angus had survived."

Angus Bramson had been Maeve's lover also. They had known each other since childhood and had lived together after they had fled to America. But Angus wasn't her *mùirn beatha dàn*. Maeve loved him, but she never felt the connection to him that she did to Ciaran. Maeve had never married Angus, and he wasn't my father. But he had died by Maeve's side in a barn in upstate New York. Ciaran had locked them in the barn and set it on fire.

"Belwicket isn't the only coven that has been decimated by a dark wave," Eoife went on. She took a picture out of her black leather briefcase. "This was Riverwarry," she said, handing me the photograph. It was a black-and-white shot of a charming village. I couldn't tell if it was Irish, English, Scottish, or Welsh.

"This is Riverwarry now," she went on, handing me another photograph.

My heart filled with sadness as I saw what had happened to Riverwarry. It looked like a bomb had gone off right in the center of the village. Only rubble remained: bits of wall, shiny, melted lumps of glass that had once been windows, blackened remains of trees and shrubs. I was afraid to look too closely— in Maeve's BOS, she had described how she had seen the body of her cat among the ruins and her mother's hand beneath a crumpled wall.

"There are many others," Eoife said, gesturing to a stack of photographs in her briefcase. "Chip Munding, Betts' Field, the

MacDougals, Knifewind, Crossbrig, Hollysberry, Incdunning. Among others."

"Why were these covens destroyed?"

"Because they had knowledge and power," Eoife said simply. "They had books, spells, tools, charts, or maps that Amyranth wanted. Amyranth gathers knowledge at any price. As you know, they are willing to steal power from witches outside their coven to make themselves stronger. We call them old Woodbanes because they conform more closely to the traditional Woodbane tenets: knowledge is power, and power above all."

Of course she knew I was Woodbane. Belwicket had been a coven of "new" Woodbanes, those who had renounced dark magick and sworn to make only good and positive magick. Ciaran was one of the old Woodbanes. Yet he and Maeve had slept together and made me, a Woodbane who had one foot in darkness and one foot in light.

"These pictures are awful. But what do they have to do with me?" I asked.

"We've recently received information that Amyranth is planning on calling another dark wave," Eoife said. She tucked the photographs back into her briefcase. "Here, in Widow's Vale. They plan to wipe out the Starlocket coven."

My mouth dropped open. Whatever I had expected, it wasn't this. Starlocket had once been Selene Belltower's coven. When Selene had fled Widow's Vale, her most loyal Woodbane followers had disappeared with her. But not all of Starlocket had been Woodbane or dark Woodbanes. The members who had been from the other great clans—Leapvaughn, Brightendale, Vikroth, Rowanwand, Burnhide, or Wyndenkell—and also those who were not blood witches had continued on under the leadership of my friend Alyce Fernbrake. Alyce owned Practical Magick, a store in the next town over that specialized in Wiccan necessities. Ever since I first discovered my powers, Alyce had been a kind adviser, and after our *tàth meànma brach*, in which we shared each other's knowledge and experiences, I felt a special closeness to her.

Now my birth father and his coven were planning to plunder Starlocket for its books, tools, spells, star charts—anything they could find. Not only that. I knew from bitter firsthand experience that Amyranth could actually steal people's magick, their power and their knowledge, in a dark ritual. Unfortunately, the person didn't usually live through it. That was what had almost happened to me in New York before Ciaran had helped Hunter stop the ritual.

"How do you know about this?" I asked faintly.

"We had an agent who infiltrated the San Francisco cell of Amyranth. It was in the last message she sent us," Eoife said. "Right before she died."

I was startled. "Died?"

"She was killed," said Eoife sadly. "Found drowned in the bay, with the Amyranth sigil burned into her skin."

"Oh, Goddess." My brain began piecing together ideas. "But if she was killed because of passing on that message, then surely Amyranth knows the council is onto them. Surely they'll change their plans," I said.

"We thought of that. But it's not necessarily true. After all," Eoife went on, her voice turning bitter, "even though we have agents inside some cells, we've been singularly ineffectual in finding out anything about most of Amyranth—especially the New York one. And even having this bit of information doesn't really help us. Alyce and some of the other Starlocket members have been having disturbing visions. Some of their spells have gone terribly awry. They have bad dreams. It all feels like a noose closing around their necks."

"But why can't the council help? Isn't it made up of some of the strongest witches alive?"

Eoife looked at me with anger. "Yes. But we're not gods or goddesses. Simply knowing about a dark wave doesn't help us stop it. Frankly, we have no idea how to stop it."

"So what can I do?" I asked carefully.

My guest took a deep breath, trying to control her emotions. Her fingers trembled almost imperceptibly as she sipped tea that by now must be cold.

"We want you to help us stop the dark wave," she said.

My world went white in an instant. Jagged images of what had almost happened to me in New York crashed into my mind, and my breath went shallow. With tunnel vision I stared at Eoife, sure that horror and panic were written on my face.

"Eoife," I breathed. "I'm seventeen years old. I'm not initiated. I don't see how I can help with *anything*."

"We know about your situation. But you have a great deal of power." She tried to keep defeat out of her voice but didn't succeed. "And you're our only hope."

"Why?"

She looked at me. "You're Ciaran's daughter. His daughter by the woman he loved. And you're very, very powerful. He would be intensely attracted to that. You could get close to him."

"And *then* what?" I was trying not to sound hysterical. Inside my thoughts were running around like a chicken with its head cut off.

"We need information," Eoife said. "We have strong evidence that Amyranth is planning a strike on Starlocket during its Imbolc celebration. There's a possibility we could stop them if you could learn something—anything—of the spell they plan to use to call the dark wave. Knowing even a few of these words would help us fight it. If Ciaran were to make you his confidante, you might be able to get us this information."

I looked at Eoife in disbelief. "And what if he tries to *kill* me?"

"He's your father," she said. "He didn't let his coven kill you in New York."

I crossed my arms over my chest and sighed. "Okay. Get close to Ciaran. Discover what I can of the dark-wave spell. God, this is so surreal."

Eoife gave me a level glance. "There's more."

"Why am I not surprised?" I muttered.

Eoife shifted in her chair. "If you planted a watch sigil on him, it would help us track his movements. We'd have a better chance of knowing where he was."

"How am I supposed to plant a watch sigil on him? He's a thousand times stronger than me!" I was frightened now and running out of patience with this crazy conversation. What this woman was suggesting could easily get me killed.

"We don't believe he's a thousand times stronger than you," Eoife said, but her gaze dropped from mine. "Anyway, we would teach you how to do it. We would cover you with deception spells, with protection, with every weapon we have. With luck, you could even attend an Amyranth circle. Any information you pick up there would be useful. The more we know about them, the more chance we have of being able to dismantle their coven, remove their power, scatter them so they could never again call on a dark wave to obliterate a clan, to pillage their knowledge, to destroy their homes. With your help, we can save Starlocket. Without your help, they are surely lost."

"The witches in Amyranth would recognize me," I pointed out.

"But now they know you're Ciaran's daughter," Eoife said. "They would believe you'd want to be close to him."

This was all just too incredible, too absurd. "You must have someone more qualified," I said.

"We don't, Morgan," Eoife said. "The San Francisco cell of Amyranth is the only one we've been able to get any information from—and that was ultimately unsuccessful. It's only because we're so desperate, so without options, that we even considered asking you to take this risk. Amyranth has been gaining power for the last thirty years, and we've made hardly any progress in fighting them. But now we have you, the daughter of one of the main leaders. Ciaran is incredibly powerful, incredibly charismatic. Anyone would believe you would want to be closer to him."

"What about you?" I asked. "I'm Ciaran's daughter, after all. Do you believe I'd want to be closer to him? Do *you* believe I might actually turn to the darkness?"

The older witch gazed at me steadily. "It's true that great witches have fallen before this. But many have resisted, too, Morgan."

But which will I be? I thought desperately. "Oh, God," I said, standing up and lifting my hair off my neck. I walked around the living room, stretching, not really seeing anything. I realized it was chilly and knelt before the fireplace to make a small tepee of kindling. I looked around for matches, but didn't see any. I thought, *Fire,* and a tiny spark of flame leaped into existence, catching the dry sticks of fatwood, chewing them eagerly. When the kindling was well on its way, I added two small logs, then stood up and brushed off my hands.

"I didn't believe them when they said you could kindle fire," Eoife said. Once again her gaze fixed on me, measuring me, examining me.

I shrugged self-consciously. "I like fire."

"One of my teachers studied with her teacher for more than three years to learn how to kindle fire," Eoife said.

Startled, I glanced at her. "How can you even teach it? It's just there."

"No, my dear," she said, softening for the first time since she'd come in. "It isn't. Not usually."

I sat down again and twisted my fingers together. Get close to Ciaran. The idea made my stomach clench. He was my blood father, and he was the epitome of evil, guilty of hundreds of horrible crimes: unaccountable devastation. He was the very image of everything bad that Woodbanes had ever been accused of. He had killed my mother and tried to kill me. Yet . . .

Yet, before I had known who he was, I had felt a strange connection to him, a sort of bond or kinship. I could tell he was very powerful, and I wanted him to teach me what he knew. Then so many things had happened, and I was still sorting out the pieces. Now Eoife wanted me to pretend to have a relationship with him in order to give the council information. Information that would lead to his being stripped of his powers, certainly. I'd watched Hunter perform the spells that wrested a witch's magick from him, and I still shuddered at the memory. I had heard that most witches who had their magick taken away never really recovered. They lived a kind of half life—more of a pale gray existence than a real life. Eoife and the council wanted to do that to Ciaran, and they wanted me to help them.

"I won't lie to you," Eoife said. "This will be very hard,

perhaps impossible, and very dangerous. You'll be tempted by darkness, as we all are at times. How well you resist it is up to you. You probably know what is likely to happen to you if you are found out, if you fail." She looked down at her hands in her lap. "But if you succeed—you will have saved not only Starlocket, but all the covens and clans after them, the ones who will in the future be targeted for a dark wave. And . . . you would have more power."

I looked at Eoife. "Magickal power?"

"Perhaps, though that isn't what I meant. I meant the power that comes from doing something profoundly good and selfless, the power that comes from putting good out into the world. Remember, what you send out is thrice returned."

"Does Hunter know about this? What you're asking?"

"Yes. He's against it. But this decision is yours."

"What makes you so sure Ciaran will trust me?" I asked.

"We're not," Eoife admitted. "But you're our only hope."

I paced the room. I noticed it was dark outside—hours had passed since Eoife had come. My parents might be boarding their cruise ship by now.

What if I failed? Not only would Alyce and the rest of Starlocket die, but I would be forever corrupted. If I wasn't strong enough to resist Ciaran, I would become as evil as he was. On the other hand, where was I now? I had lost Hunter, I was afraid to make magick with my coven. . . . What did I have left to lose? How strong was I? Think, think.

Eoife waited patiently, just as her teacher who was trying to kindle fire must have waited patiently for three years, trying to learn it. I wasn't patient. I didn't have the inner calm that most witches had, the inner compass that allowed them to stay on track, stay focused yet completely connected with the world. I didn't know if I would ever have it.

Could I do good?

Oh, Goddess, help me.

I don't know how much time passed. Finally I turned to look at Eoife, so small and still, like a garden statue.

"I'll do it," I said.

4

Danger

Brother Colin, my hand shakes as I write this. I have told all to Father Benedict, and he is praying on the matter now. Tonight after matins I found I could not sleep and determined to walk in the chill air along the cliffs in the hopes that healthy exercise would help me to rest.

I set out at a brisk pace, giving thanks for my sturdy wool cloak. After a time I spied the glow of a cheerful fire. Thinking it was a lone shepherd, I hastened to join him and share in the warmth before heading back to the abbey. Coming quite close, I saw this was no lone shepherd, but a group of people. Women from Barra Head, each soul bare to the sky, danced in pagan nudity around the fire, wailing some unearthly song.

Horror overwhelmed me, and after but a few moments I dashed away from the evil place. I immediately found Father Benedict and confessed what I had seen. What do you make of this, Brother Colin? I had assumed that Wodebayne was simply a clan name, but now I wonder if they are some darker, heathen sect. Please send me your earliest counsel, for I am most distraught.

—Brother Sinestus Tor, March 1768

To my surprise, Eoife McNabb didn't jump up and down in joy at my announcement. She looked very solemn and then nodded slowly. "I was hoping you would say that."

I released a deep breath and tried to relax. "So what now?"

"Well, you'll need to go to New York at once," she said.

"What? I can't." I shook my head. "My folks are out of town, and I have to house-sit and cat-sit and go to school every day, or they'll kill me."

Eoife blinked once, and we looked at each other. Realizing the ridiculousness of my situation, I began to laugh nervously. After a moment of surprise, Eoife smiled.

"All right," she said, shrugging. "I know that you're unusually young to have so much power. But remember, we're talking about the destruction of countless innocent witches. There has to be a way for you to help us and still keep your grades up and feed your cat."

As if he'd been called, Dagda prowled into the room and fixed his green eyes on Eoife. He walked toward her, sniffed her delicately, then presented his triangular head for petting.

"You're a beauty," Eoife murmured while he purred. Finally he purred so hard, he fell over on his side, and she tickled his gray tummy.

"You must stay in Widow's Vale," she said, thinking aloud.

"Yeah."

"Right. Let's see. You met your half brother Killian in New York, yes?"

"Yes." I nodded.

"Does he know you're his sister?"

"I don't think so. By the time I found out, he had disappeared. I haven't seen him since then."

"We're speculating that he was supposed to take part in Amyranth's ritual," Eoife explained. "Ciaran would like one, any one, of his children to be a worthy successor. If that was Killian's test but he left town instead, Ciaran would be furious with him."

"He didn't strike me as a coven leader," I said. "He seemed more like just a party guy to me."

"Killian isn't power hungry, like Ciaran," Eoife said. "But he does seem to be amoral—he does what he wants but for the pleasure of it, not to gain anything. I'm thinking—maybe the way to get to Ciaran is through Killian. We could get Killian to come here somehow. He'd come out of curiosity, if nothing else. Once Killian is here, explain your relationship to him. Then ask him to have Ciaran come here so you can get to know him better, as his daughter."

A chill went down my spine, despite the cheerful warmth of the fire. It was horrible—the name Ciaran brought such conflicting images and feelings: the understanding, compelling man at the bookstore and then the terrifying, powerful Woodbane witch who had wanted to take my magick by force. He terrified me in a way that nothing else did, and . . . he was my father. I wanted to know him. And how would I hold out for one second against his power if he really wanted me to join him in Amyranth? I would have no chance.

"You have until Imbolc," she said, interrupting my thoughts. Imbolc was February 2. Less than two weeks. Two weeks from now, what would I be? Alive? Dead? Evil? I felt like throwing up.

"A few more things," Eoife said, sounding businesslike. She poured herself more hot water from the teapot and once again steeped the tea leaves. Their smooth, complex, smoky fragrance rose through the air. "One, you'll be functioning as a council agent and as such will check in with your council mentor, who is me. We can set up a contact schedule. If I'm not available, Hunter will take your reports."

Great, I thought, already feeling the pain that seeing him would bring. Somehow I didn't think that Eoife would care that we were broken up.

"Second, we'll be teaching you the spells you need to help you through this. It goes without saying that learning them perfectly is imperative."

No kidding, I thought. Crap. What had I gotten myself into?

Her face softened, and I wondered again if she was in tune with my thoughts. "This could be worse than what happened in New York, but I wouldn't ask you to do it if I thought the mission was hopeless. I—and the rest of the council—truly feel that you can do this."

I digested this. "Okay. So now I call Killian?"

"Do you have his phone number?" She looked surprised.

"No," I said, confused. "I thought you meant, you know, a witch message."

Her face was carefully blank. "You can send messages? With your mind?"

Why didn't I just get "Zoo Exhibit" tattooed on my forehead? "Uh-huh."

Eoife swallowed. "I thought Hunter was exaggerating," she

said quietly. "An uninitiated witch—kindling fire. Sending witch messages. Calling on the ancient lines of power. Even putting a holding spell on Hunter. I couldn't believe it was true, though Hunter has never been inaccurate before. I came here expecting to leave in disappointment. Expecting to go back to the council and tell them we had no hope."

"Then why did you even go through this?" I asked. "Telling me you'd teach me the spells, that you'd help me. That I was your only hope. Why do it if you really thought I wouldn't be able to help you?"

"I was doing as I was instructed," she replied with dignity. "Believe me, I far prefer this reality to what I was afraid I would find. Now I think it's time to call Killian."

"Okay," I said. Killian, I thought, sending it toward him. Killian. Come to Widow's Vale. For long minutes we sat silently. I wondered how far away Killian was and if that made any difference. But then I felt his response.

I took a minute to breathe and orient myself. When I stood, I felt creaky, like I had been there for hours. "Okay," I told Eoife. "I think he's going to come."

"Very good," said Eoife. "Morgan, I'm going to teach you the watch sigil in case things start to move quickly and you have the opportunity to mark Ciaran before we meet again."

I nodded and watched Eoife carefully as she drew the sigil in the air.

"The symbol itself is not complicated," she continued. "What will be difficult is getting close enough to Ciaran to place it on him without his detection. Practice the sigil so that you'll be ready when the opportunity presents itself."

Slowly I began to mirror Eoife's motions in the air. "All

right," I said finally. "I think I've got it. I'll keep practicing when you leave."

Eoife nodded. "Excellent." She reached for her briefcase and stood, glancing around to make sure she hadn't forgotten anything. "I'm glad to have met you, Morgan Riordan," she said formally, holding out her hand to shake.

"Rowlands," I said, frowning. "That's my last name."

Her eyebrows drew together. "Oh, of course. I'm going to report back to the council about the nature of our plan and that you've sent Killian a message. I'll check in with you soon to set up a time for you to start learning spells."

"Okay." I walked her to the front door, feeling a deep sense of foreboding. After what happened in New York, I had hoped to lie low for a while, to have everything be calm and quiet. Now I was signed up to enter the lion's den. And I might not make it out alive.

"You know you're more than welcome to come stay," said Aunt Eileen an hour later.

I had called her to check in, though my parents hadn't been gone even a whole day yet. I had needed some normalcy after the surreal visit with Eoife McNabb. "Oh, no, I'll be fine," I said. "I'm just going to go to school, do homework, eat, and sleep." Oh, and try to trap one of the world's most dangerous Woodbanes. That, too.

"Okay," she said. "But promise you'll call us anytime, day or night, if you need anything or want to talk or feel worried. All right?"

"Okey dokey," I said, trying to sound cheerful.

As soon as I hung up, I felt my senses start to tingle. I

opened the front door and saw Hunter at the end of our dark walkway, heading for the house. He looked up, saw me, and didn't smile.

Just seeing him made me want to cry. This was the one person who could comfort me, who would understand, who would be on my side. Yet I couldn't be with him, couldn't turn to him for support or love. I knew that it was better to hurt him now than crush him later—what if I turned on him down the road? After seeing what Ciaran had been willing to do to me, I could only imagine the pain I could cause Hunter if and when my evil Woodbane nature showed itself. As painful as this separation was, surely it was better than the pain of knowing I had attacked him from the darkness.

Typically, he didn't say hello. He just leaned against the house while I rubbed my shoulders to keep warm. It was another bitter night. He waited until I met his eyes, then launched in.

"I can't believe you've decided to go along with this ridiculous, far-fetched plan!" he began, his English accent more pronounced than usual. "Do you have any idea how dangerous it's going to be? Do you have any idea what you're up against? This isn't one of our circles! This is life or death!"

"I know," I said quietly. "I was there in New York, remember?"

"Exactly! So how can you even consider going along with this? It's not your responsibility."

I just looked at him. In the dim yellow glare of the front porch light he looked gorgeous, as usual, and angry, which also seemed fairly common these days. But I had also seen him laughing, his head thrown back; I had seen his face flushed with desire; I had seen the look in his eyes before he kissed me. My chest felt fluttery as I thought about it, and I rubbed my arms again, grateful for the distraction of the cold.

"Have you heard anything more about your parents?" I asked. In New York, Hunter had made the decision to begin looking for them. I knew that the loss of his mother and father was a huge event in his life, and it hurt me to see him unable to find them.

Hunter's angry expression softened slightly. He looked away. "No," he said. "Nothing. You're changing the subject. I don't want to talk about it." He looked me in the eye briefly. "These last few days haven't been a lark for me, either, Morgan."

I nodded, unable to speak. God, I hated not being in his life like I had been. I wanted to comfort him, to tell him it would be okay, but now I was the person who was causing part of his pain.

"It's cold," he said unnecessarily. "Why are we out here? Let's go in." He moved toward the door, but I held up my hand.

"No," I said.

"Why?" His perfect brows arched over eyes as green as sea glass. All I wanted was for him to hold me and comfort me and tell me everything was going to be all right.

"Remember, I told you about my folks going on a cruise? They left today."

"Where's Mary K.?"

"Jaycee's."

His face took on a speculative expression, and I braced myself.

"You're saying you're alone in the house," he said.

"Yes."

"That cruise was for . . . eleven days?"

"Yes." I sighed.

"So you're alone in the house. All by yourself."

"Yes." I couldn't look at him—his voice had softened, and the anger was gone. Oh, Goddess, he was so attractive to me. Everything in me responded to everything in him.

"So let's go in." He sounded much calmer than when he had arrived.

I almost whimpered from wanting him. If he came in the house, if we were alone together, how could I keep my hands off him? How could I stop him from putting his hands on me? I wouldn't want to. And what would that do? Making out wouldn't change anything: not my heritage, not my fears, not the possibility that I was going to end up more Ciaran's daughter than Maeve's.

"No, that's not a good idea."

"Got some other guy in there, have you?" His tone was light, but I felt tension coming off him like heat.

"No," I said, looking at my feet. "Look, I just don't want to be alone with you, okay?"

"Then how about my house? We wouldn't be alone there." Hunter lived with his cousin, Sky Eventide.

I gave him my long-suffering look. "I don't think so. We broke up, remember?"

"We should talk about that," he said, frowning. "Speaking of bad ideas."

Tell me about it, I thought. I wanted to be with Hunter more than anything. But I knew—and I had to make myself remember—how terrible it would be to hurt him later. I shook my head to clear it, trying to get back to the subject at hand. "We should talk about your trying to control the decisions I make."

Hunter frowned as he seemed to remember why he had come. "I'm not trying to control your decisions," he said. "I'm trying to help you not make irresponsible ones."

"You think I'm irresponsible?"

"You know I don't. I think you made this decision without having all the facts. Like about exactly how dangerous Ciaran and Amyranth can be. How many deaths they're responsible for. How much power and knowledge they have at their disposal. Pitted against you, a seventeen-year-old uninitiated witch who's been studying Wicca for a grand total of three months."

I knew all that, but hearing him state it so baldly made me cringe. "Yes, I know," I said. "I still think I need to try." I need to know if I'm good or bad, I added to myself. I need to know who my father is, what my heritage is. I need to know that I can choose good. If I don't know these things, we can never be together.

"I don't want you to get hurt," he said, his voice sounding frayed. "It's not your job to save the world."

"I'm not trying to save the world," I said. "Just my little part of it. I mean, today it's Starlocket—and Alyce, remember? Tomorrow it's us. Don't you see that?"

Hunter looked around, thinking, deciding on another plan of approach. He was well acquainted with how stubborn I could be, and I could see him weighing his chances of getting through and changing my mind.

He pushed himself off the house and stood before me. "Tell me the instant you hear from Killian," he said.

I tried not to show my surprise. "Okay."

"I don't like this."

"I know."

"I hate this."

"I know."

"Right. So call me."

"I will." After he left, I went back inside, shivering with cold. I sat down in front of the fire and rested my head against the couch. I would have given a lot to have Hunter with me right then. I sighed, wondering if love was always this hard.

5

Connection

I am glad to hear your cough is better, Brother.

As I recounted, the siege (I can only call it thus) has continued against the abbey. Our poor milk cow has gone dry, our kitchen garden has withered, and the mice are keeping our one cat constantly at work. Our daily offices are ever more sparsely attended.

It is the villagers, the Wodebaynes. I know this, though I have not seen it. We are now obliged to buy milk and cheese from a neighbouring farm. Various illnesses have beset us; we cannot shake colds, agues, fevers, etc. It is a desperate time, and I will resort to desperate measures.

—Brother Sinestus, to Colin, May 1768

On Monday morning I saw my sister heading toward our school, followed by some of the Mary K. fan club. I waved at her.

"Mary K.!"

She trotted over, her shiny hair bouncing. I was glad to see her looking more like herself. She'd had a horrible autumn.

Twice I'd stopped her boyfriend, Bakker Blackburn, from practically raping her. After the second time I'd told my parents, who lowered the boom on Mary K. I also told Bakker he'd regret being born if he ever looked at my sister again. I knew we weren't supposed to use magick to harm, but I was absolutely ready to put some serious hurt on Bakker if he hurt Mary K.

But now Mary K. looked happy.

"Hey!" she said.

"Hi," I said, rubbing my eyes. I'd gotten about three hours sleep total. All the little creaks and groans and windows shaking in the wind that I'd never noticed before had been magnified tremendously and made it impossible for me to sleep deeply. "Everything okay?"

"Yep! How about you?"

"Fine. Okay, um, yell if you need anything."

"Sure—thanks." She headed back to the gaggle of freshman friends who were waiting for her. Among them I was surprised to see Alisa Soto, who seemed to be a friend of Jaycee's. Alisa was a sophomore who'd transferred to Widow's Vale High around Christmas, but I had actually hardly seen her at school until today. I knew her because she was in my coven, Kithic—the youngest member. She was one of the people recruited by Bree when Bree had formed a new coven to rival mine and Cal's. When Cal was gone, our two covens had combined to form Kithic, and we were now led by Hunter and Sky.

Most of my coven went to my school: Bree Warren and Robbie Gurevitch, my two best childhood friends, who had recently become a couple; Raven Meltzer, local bad girl and resident goth, who happened to be dating Hunter's cousin, Sky Eventide; Jenna Ruiz; Matt Adler; Ethan Sharp; and Sharon

Goodfine. The last two were a couple, and Jenna and Matt had once been a couple, too, but had broken up.

I was dreading seeing my friends. I didn't know if any of them, aside from Bree and Robbie, knew about me and Hunter. I hadn't wanted to see them Saturday, and I still didn't want to see them. But I had no choice.

All of them, except for Alisa, were sitting, as usual, on the back stairs that led to the school's basement. "Morgan," Robbie greeted me. During our New York trip Robbie had come down on me about my casual misuse of magick. We had made up, but things weren't totally normal yet.

"Hey." My nod included everyone. I popped the top on the Diet Coke I'd bought on my way to school and took a deep slurp. Act casual.

"So how's the bachelorette pad?" Bree asked with a smile.

"Fine. My folks went on a cruise, so I've got the place to myself," I explained to the others. For an instant I thought of Hunter saying, "Let's go in," and my heart contracted.

"Party at Morgan's house," Jenna said, laughing; then her laugh turned into a cough. Bree patted her on the back and looked at me. This cold, damp weather made Jenna's asthma worse.

"No, no party," I said, starting to wake up as the caffeine coursed through my veins. "I can't face the cleanup job after." Plus Mom would have a cow, I thought.

They laughed, and Bree wrapped her arm around Robbie's knee. He looked cautiously pleased. He was crazy about Bree, she seemed to care about him, and they'd been trying to hash out some kind of relationship for a while now. During our trip to New York, they seemed to have made some degree of progress.

"Sky missed you at Saturday's circle," said Sharon. Her black hair swung in a thick curtain just past her shoulders. It was still a little odd to see her all cozy with Ethan, who had been one of the school's biggest potheads until he'd found Wicca. Now he was clean and sober and in love with Sharon.

Raven snorted. "Sky takes everything too seriously." Raven and Sky had been sort of a couple for the last few weeks, but Raven's wandering eye had gotten her into trouble more than once.

Jenna coughed again, and I winced at the sound of her rattly indrawn breath. She looked at me hopefully. I had helped her before, but now I knew that even that kind of magick was forbidden to uninitiated witches. But how could I not help a friend? It seemed so harmless. I hesitated just a minute, then scooted closer to Jenna. She sat up straighter, already anticipating being able to breathe freely again.

I closed my eyes and sank quickly into a deep meditation. I focused on a healing white light and imagined myself grabbing a ribbon of this light out of the air. Then, opening my eyes, I brought my hand to Jenna's back and pressed my palm flat against her thin amethyst sweater. I breathed out, willing the light into Jenna, letting it flow into her lungs, feeling her constricted airways relaxing and opening, all her thirsty cells soaking up oxygen. After just a minute I took my hand away.

"Thanks, Morgan," Jenna said, breathing deeply. "That works so much better than my inhaler."

"You could also wear an amber bead on a silver chain around your neck," Matt surprised us by saying. Seven heads swiveled to look at him. Since he'd cheated on Jenna with Raven, he'd been very quiet and kept a low profile. He always came to circles, always completed the assignments Hunter gave us, but he never participated beyond what was required.

He looked embarrassed by the attention. "I've been doing some reading," he mumbled. "Amber is good for breathing. So's silver."

Jenna looked at him solemnly, at the boy she'd loved for four years until he'd betrayed her. She gave a little nod, and then the morning bell rang. Time to get to class.

I sucked down the last of my Diet Coke and pitched the can into a recycling bin. Our group split up, and Bree and I headed toward our eleventh-grade homeroom. I wished I could tell her about Eoife McNabb and Ciaran and Hunter and everything I was facing. But though I hadn't been officially sworn to secrecy, I knew there was too much at stake to tell anyone who wasn't involved. Not even Bree or Robbie.

"Have you been doing any readings lately?" I asked. Bree had been studying the tarot.

"Uh-huh." Gracefully she swung her black leather backpack onto her other shoulder. Bree was gorgeous. That was the first—and sometimes the only—thing anyone noticed about her. She was taller than me, slender, with a perfect figure. No zit ever dared to mar her skin, her eyes were large, coffee colored, and expressive, and she'd been born with a gift for choosing perfect clothes and makeup. Next to her I usually looked like I ought to have a tool belt strapped to my waist.

"Alyce helped me find another book at Practical Magick that has variant readings of some of the cards. It's so interesting, the whole history of the cards and what they've meant according to what time period they were being read in. It's the first thing in Wicca that I feel I can really relate to."

"That's great," I said. Bree wasn't a blood witch, so while Wicca and magick flowed so naturally to me, it didn't always make it to her. I was glad she'd found something that felt meaningful.

It was hard to go to classes all day, being taught subjects like calc and American history, when I was wondering if my friends were going to be killed by a dark wave soon. It made it difficult to concentrate or to take what the teacher was saying seriously. I tried to keep myself mentally in my classes, but I floated through the day, my mind on other things.

I caught up with Bree on the way to the parking lot after the last bell.

"Your dad out of town again?"

"As usual. I think it's the same woman, in Connecticut. So this makes a record for him—two months with the same person." Since her mother had run off with a younger man when Bree was twelve, Mr. Warren really hadn't had a serious relationship.

"How do you feel about it?" I asked. We pushed through the heavy doors, feeling the force of the cold wind smack us in the face.

"I don't know," said Bree. "I don't think it would affect my life that much. Unless, God forbid, she took an interest in me." She pretended to shudder, and I couldn't help laughing—the first time in days.

"Oi, Morgan," said a voice, and a chill hit me that had nothing to do with the weather. Killian, my half brother, was sitting on a stone bench at the edge of the school property. Our eyes met, and he grinned at me, his attractive, somewhat feral grin. "You rang? It was you, right?"

Bree glanced at me, and I realized she didn't know I had called Killian here. I had told her about my experiences in

New York: that Ciaran was my father, Killian my half brother, and why that meant I had to break up with Hunter. Bree had been incredibly supportive over the last few days, but I knew Killian's presence must have been a shock to her. Hell, it was a shock to me. Somehow I'd thought I would have more time to prepare. With him here, the wheels had to be set in motion, and I felt afraid.

I drew in a deep breath. "Hey, Killian," I said. "I was hoping to talk to you again."

"At your disposal." He spread his arms wide. His English accent was adorable. I hadn't seen him since I'd learned we were half siblings, and now I stared at him, trying to see some resemblance.

"Killian!" called Raven.

I groaned inwardly as she hurried over to us. In New York she had flirted with Killian hard and heavy and in front of Sky, who had not been amused. Somehow I hadn't factored Raven into the scheme of things when I had agreed to be part of Eoife's plan.

"Hey, baby!" she said enthusiastically, leaning down to kiss him on both cheeks. Killian looked happy to see another of his many admirers, and he pulled her down to sit next to him.

"I was nearby, thought I'd drop in," said Killian, giving me a glance. He knew that I was a blood witch and that the others weren't, and he seemed to be gauging what to say. Amusement lit his eyes.

"I'm so glad you did," purred Raven. "I thought we'd never see you again."

"Yet here I am," he said magnanimously. He smiled at her, and though I felt exasperated—Go away, Raven—I also couldn't help being amused, even a little proud. Killian was definitely fun to be around—but even more, I felt a sort of kinship to him. I understood his humor, and his party-guy act didn't bother me like it did so many of the others. Maybe that's what blood ties really felt like.

"And here you are," he said to Bree, checking her out in a way that was so outrageous, it was funny. She gave him a skeptical smile, then turned away.

"I'm starving," she said, turning her gaze to me. "Want to go get something to eat?"

I bit my lip. Now that Killian was here, it was time to bond with him—time to gain his trust, ask about Ciaran, and hopefully get Ciaran out here. "Um, actually . . . Killian and I need to catch up."

Bree looked surprised. "Oh." She glanced over at Killian, who seemed absorbed with Raven, and then whispered to me, "Is everything okay?"

"Yes," I said. "I'm sorry, Bree. I just need some time to talk to Killian."

Bree nodded slowly. "You'll be all right alone with him?" she whispered.

I nodded quickly and circled my thumb and forefinger in the "okay" sign.

Bree nodded again, but her eyes still shone with concern. "All right," she said, loud enough for Killian and Raven to hear. "Well, I'm going to head home. See you guys."

"Oh, yes, you certainly will." Killian turned and grinned suggestively, and Bree smiled in a sort of confused way as she headed off.

"Well, I'm up for anything, as always," Killian said, standing up and turning to me so that Raven's leg was pushed to the side. "Though I should mention that I'm rather famished myself."

"I know a diner we could go to."

"Perfect!" Killian flashed his trademark grin and turned to Raven. "How about you, love? Care to join us?"

"I can't," Raven said, frowning. "Mom's suing Dad again and I have to meet with the lawyers." She rolled her eyes. "They are such losers."

"Oh, too bad," I said, relieved, as Killian and I headed for Das Boot. I wasn't sure if she meant the lawyers or her parents—probably both—and I didn't care. Killian waved behind him as we walked off.

"Cool car," he said as he climbed in, putting his arm across the back of the bench seat. "I love huge American cars. Gas-guzzlers." He smiled. "What year?"

"Nineteen seventy-one," I said, pulling out into the street and heading toward the highway. Despite having called him, I was still rattled by Killian's presence, and the weight of my mission pressed in on my chest, making me feel like I had drunk a couple of double espressos. "Listen, Killian," I added quickly, "do you know who I am?" Might as well plunge right in.

"Sure. The witch from New York. With the friends, at the club." He slouched comfortably against the seat, unconcerned that he was in a car with a virtual stranger going to a place he didn't know, in a town he had just shown up in. He seemed like a leaf, a colorful autumn leaf, tossed about by the wind and content to go where it took him.

I took a deep breath. "Ciaran MacEwan is your father."

He straightened a tiny bit, and I felt tension entering his body. He took a longer look at me, and I felt him cast his senses toward me, trying to figure out if I was friend or foe. I blocked his scan easily, not letting him in, and saw him straighten more.

"Yeah," he answered warily. "You knew that. So?"

My throat constricted as I turned onto the access road to Highway 9. Somehow I just couldn't get the words out, and suddenly the diner was there in front of us. I pulled in and parked, and we didn't speak again until we had ordered.

The waitress brought our drinks. We sat across from each other in the back booth of the fifties-retro diner. Killian took the paper off his straw, stuck it in his chocolate milk shake, and sipped—all without taking his eyes off me. I watched him, unable to decide what my next move should be.

"So, what do you want with Ciaran? Is your Seeker boyfriend looking for him?" Killian finally said lightly, but his face didn't match his voice.

I fought to hide my surprise at his question. "The Seeker is not my boyfriend," I said, looking him in the eye. "I found out Ciaran MacEwan is my father, too."

Killian sat back as if he'd been slapped. His eyes open wide, he scanned me again, looking at my hair, my eyes, my face.

"I realized it in New York," I explained awkwardly. "I didn't know until then. But—Ciaran and my mother had an affair, and my mother had me." And they were mùirn beatha dàns, soul mates, and then Ciaran killed her. And a short while ago he tried to kill me. I wondered if Killian had any idea what had happened to me in New York. I figured the odds were against it—he had told me that he and Ciaran weren't all that close.

Appearing out of nowhere, the waitress clanked our plates onto the table in front of us. Killian and I both jumped. After she left, he continued to look at me, stroking his chin.

"What was her name?" he asked finally. "Your mother."

"Maeve Riordan, of Belwicket."

I might as well have said Joan of Arc or Queen Elizabeth considering his reaction. He stared at me as if I'd suddenly grown two heads.

"I know that name," he said faintly. Then, seeming to come back to himself, he shook his head and looked down at his hamburger. "American hamburgers." He sighed happily. "I'm so sick of mad cow disease." He picked it up with both hands and took a big bite, closing his eyes in pleasure.

Now what? How did I get from here to having him tell me everything about Ciaran and getting Ciaran to come to Widow's Vale? Somehow I had to find a way. Every day, every hour counted. At this very minute Alyce was at Practical Magick, feeling a heavy mantle of doom lowering over her head.

"How did you find out about Ciaran?" Killian asked after a minute, taking another bite. Apparently discovering he had a half sister hadn't dulled his appetite.

"I've read Maeve's Book of Shadows," I said. "She talks about Ciaran in it. Then in New York, I sort of—got in trouble. Ciaran helped me get out of it. And we figured out how we knew each other . . . that he was my father. I—I have his eyes."

"Yes, you do," Killian said, studying my face.

"Anyway," I went on. "He helped me, and he's my biological father. I didn't get a chance to really talk to him in New York or even thank him." I shrugged and glanced up to find Killian looking at me intently, and I felt a surprising strength coming from him.

"But you weren't raised by Maeve," Killian said quietly. "You couldn't have been. How did you come to be here, in Widow's Vale?"

"Maeve put me up for adoption," I explained. "My family,

the Rowlandses, adopted me. They're the only parents I've ever known. I have a sister, but not a blood sister, of course. I mean, when I realized who Ciaran was and that you were his son, I realized that I had an actual half brother . . . by blood." Mary K., please forgive me.

Killian blinked, as if this notion were just occurring to him. He focused on his food, working his way through his burger and shake with steady intent.

As the minutes went by, I felt more and more anxious. What if Killian hated me, the flesh-and-blood evidence of his father betraying his mother? At last he looked up, his plate completely clean. He smiled.

"Well! A little sister," he said cheerfully. "Brilliant. I always hated being the baby." He stood and leaned across the table to kiss me on the cheek. "Welcome to the family." He made a rueful face. "Such as it is. Now. What do they have for pudding here?"

I watched as Killian devoured a slab of chocolate silk pie, and the new silence felt awkward. I studied Killian, trying to think, trying to prod my addled brain into motion. I needed information from him. That was why he was here. I needed to know everything he could tell me.

"Was Ciaran a . . . good father?" I asked.

"Not particularly," Killian said, sitting sideways on his bench and putting his feet up. "He wasn't around a lot, you know. He and Mum hate each other. He used to come around a couple of times a year, and he would test us kids and find us all wanting and blame my mother, and she'd cry, and then he'd take off."

"That isn't how I pictured it at all," I said. "I thought, he's your real father. He would teach you. He would show you magick. I thought you were so lucky to have him around."

"Nope." Killian seemed unconcerned, but I could tell it was a facade. "What about you? How's your dad?"

"Great," I said. "He's really brilliant—does all sorts of research and design and experiments. But then he'll leave his glasses in the fridge, and forget to put gas in his car, so it runs out, and you'll ask him to get something and find him an hour later, reading in his office."

Killian laughed. "But he's nice?"

"Really nice. He loves me a lot."

"There you go, then." Killian rubbed his hands together and looked up, as if to say, Shall we go?

"It must be difficult for you," I said quickly, trying to keep this conversation going. "I mean . . . I hope you're not upset with me. For bringing you here. For springing all this stuff on you so quickly."

Killian looked surprised for a moment, and then he seemed to regard me differently. He gave a rueful smile. "Well, love, it's not as though my family life has been *The Cosby Show*. Finding out that I have a little sister. . ." He seemed to take me in, and at that moment I felt a sense of connection to him, like this wasn't just an awkward conversation between strangers. I sensed in him that—kinship, I guess—that sprang from this less-than-ideal connection by blood. ". . . well, there are worse ways to spend a Monday afternoon."

I smiled in response, and immediately started to feel guilty about using Killian to get through to Ciaran. It saddened me to think that he was a real person, my real half brother, with feelings, and I was really getting to know him only as part of a spy maneuver. The fate of Starlocket was a pretty good motivation, but I was beginning to feel that I liked Killian and that I might enjoy getting to know him even if Ciaran weren't involved.

"So do you and Ciaran ever . . . see each other?"

Killian made a face as though he tasted something sour and took a last sip of chocolate shake. "No." He shifted, and I realized all at once that he was incredibly uncomfortable with this conversation and wanted to flee. "I'm beat, sis," he said as I kicked myself mentally for not changing the subject earlier. "It was lovely speaking with you. I'll see you around."

"But—" I watched helplessly as Killian left some money on the table and walked briskly out the door. "Killian! Wait!" I threw some money down on top of Killian's, grabbed my stuff, and ran out the door behind him. How would he get home? We were too far from anything to walk. Widow's Vale wasn't exactly a place where you could just hail a taxi.

But I didn't see Killian in the parking lot, and a quick scan of the highway found no pedestrians, no cars headed in either direction. In fact, I realized, I hadn't heard a car go by in the last five minutes or so. I looked back at the parking lot, moving closer to study the woods on the perimeter of the lot. There were no footprints anywhere; the ground looked untouched by human feet. Frustrated, I leaned against Das Boot and took a last look around. Where had he *gone*? Had he actually used magick just to get away from me?

Finally, after a few more minutes trying to make sense of it, I climbed into Das Boot, checking my watch. Five o'clock. Barely twenty-four hours after accepting Eoife's mission, and I was already feeling pretty certain that I had just ruined the council's plan.

*　　*　　*

Eoife was staying at Hunter and Sky's, and Hunter answered the phone when I called. The sound of his voice made my heart flutter inside my chest, but I ruthlessly pushed down the pain. "Hunter? I need to talk to Eoife."

"What's wrong?" Hunter's voice was warm with concern. Oh, Goddess, I thought, I can't talk to you about how I've already ruined everything.

"Um—Killian's here. But he kind of . . . got away."

"Got *away*?" Some of the warmth leached out of his voice, and I sucked in my breath to prepare for his disappointment.

"Well—"

"Listen, Eoife just walked in." Hunter cut me off. "I'll put her on."

Before I could react, Hunter was gone from the line and I heard Eoife's voice. "Morgan? Is there a problem?"

"Well," I began, "Killian came, and we were talking, but he took off before I could talk to him about calling Ciaran. And then he sort of . . . disappeared, and now I don't know where he is or when I'll see him again."

"Morgan, calm down. It's not a disaster." Eoife's sensible voice, if not exactly warm, still calmed my nerves a bit. "Listen, I was just heading out to attend a Starlocket circle. Would you like to meet me there?"

Starlocket? Oh, no. How could I face Alyce and all of the innocent members of Starlocket when I might have just thrown away their one chance for survival?

"I don't know, Eoife. I mean . . . maybe this mission isn't for me. Maybe you should find someone who's better equipped—"

"Morgan," Eoife interrupted me, "I think you're overreacting. Come with me to the circle—it will calm you down. And we can talk a bit about how to approach Killian from now on."

I sighed. It *would* calm me to attend a circle, especially since I'd skipped Kithic's this week. And Alyce was always a warm and comforting presence—I could only hope that no harm would come to her anytime soon. "All right," I said finally. "Where is it?"

Starlocket was meeting at a cozy, cedar-shingled house on the outskirts of town. When I rang the doorbell, the door was answered by a tall, formidable woman who looked to be in her late thirties. She had long, dark brown hair that reached all the way down to her butt, and she wore a brilliant robe of purple silk. "Hello," she greeted me.

"Hi," I said. "I'm Morgan Rowlands. I'm a friend of Alyce and Eoife's."

"It's nice to meet you, Morgan." The woman regarded me calmly. "Welcome to my home. I'm Suzanna Mearis." Suzanna stepped back from the doorway and gestured into a small living room. "The circle will be held in here. Eoife hasn't arrived yet."

I thanked Suzanna and headed past her into the warm, golden-hued room. Nature-themed oil paintings adorned the walls in shades of green, gold, orange, and red. A rust-colored velvet couch sat before a brick fireplace, and candles burned on every available surface. Several members of the coven were sitting on the couch, chatting, and I noticed Alyce standing by a window, looking out into the night. I walked over to her. "Alyce?" I said softly. She turned and hugged me tightly without a word.

"Morgan," she whispered finally. "I'm so happy you've come."

"It's good to be here." Seeing Alyce made me realize how much I'd missed my friend and confidante, and I had to fight back tears.

Alyce's eyes met mine, and I could see her concern shining there. Her voice dropped. "I know that you had a difficult time in New York."

A difficult time, I thought. Difficult was right. One blessing of this new assignment was that it kept my mind off just how much my life had changed in the last week. I nodded, not feeling up to talking about it just now, even to Alyce.

"Morgan?" I felt a hand on my shoulder and turned to find Eoife in a green linen robe. "We should talk."

I nodded and followed Eoife to a private corner of the room, after saying good-bye to Alyce, and promising we'd get together as soon as possible.

"Listen," Eoife began, "Killian isn't going to open up to you right away. What we've asked you to do is get close to him, and that's going to take more than just one meeting. Given what we know about Killian's upbringing, I can imagine that he doesn't trust people too easily. If you were able to make contact and tell him who you are, you should consider this first meeting successful."

She had a point, I realized, but I hadn't counted on my half brother disappearing into the blue. "But how can I be sure there'll be a next meeting?" I asked. "I have no idea where Killian went or how he got there. And he's not answering my witch messages."

Eoife put her hand on my shoulder. "Morgan, remember: Killian is your half brother. He may not want to share everything with you right away, but we believe that he will feel a connection to you and that he will want to meet with you again. You just have to give him time."

I sighed. I didn't have time. Starlocket didn't have time. "What if I scried for him?" I asked hopefully. "I've always had good luck scrying with fire. I could find out where Ciaran is, what he's up to—"

"Absolutely not," Eoife said instantly. "What's most important right now is to keep Ciaran and Killian's trust. You don't want to scare them off with a lot of questions at once or by letting them know that you're watching them. Once Killian gets to know you, the subject of Ciaran will inevitably come up. But for now, as hard as it is, you just have to be patient."

I nodded reluctantly. "I understand," I said quietly. "I'm just . . . scared." I looked over to where the coven was gathering. I couldn't bear knowing that I'd failed to save them.

"Being afraid is natural, Morgan." Eoife followed my gaze to the coven members. "But you mustn't allow that fear to drive Killian away."

An hour later I no longer felt afraid. Joined with Eoife and the members of Starlocket, I swirled ecstatically in our circle, feeling my magick course through me in a way that made me feel powerful, unstoppable. The fire in the fireplace glowed orange and blue, and I was a part of that fire: fire was my partner, and together we were capable of anything. I would see Killian again, I felt sure. The power in me could not be contained. I would help Starlocket any way I could.

Then, suddenly, everything changed. There were other voices in the room, voices that didn't belong to any of the members of Starlocket. They were lower, harsher, inhuman. Slowly they began to get louder, until they were almost shouting. They were chanting words I didn't recognize, but the mere sound of them made my skin crawl. The voices built to a crescendo, and suddenly the fire sputtered and was gone. The circle stopped moving. Through my haze of magick I saw somebody falling to the floor. A sudden shock of fear ran through me, like ice water pumping through my heart.

I dropped to my knees and closed my eyes, and I could feel the magick running out of my body. I remembered the first few times I felt my magick, before I understood what it was. The feeling was overwhelming, and sometimes the power of it made me sick. I wondered if somehow I had lost control again. Slowly, painfully, I opened my eyes.

Before me on the floor lay Suzanna Mearis. Alyce was bent over her.

"Someone help me carry her to her room," Alyce commanded. Her face was drawn. Suddenly she looked haggard.

I felt a welling of fear. "What happened?" I asked. "What's wrong with her?"

Eoife was the one who answered me. "A *taibhs* came," she said in a hushed voice. "More than one, I'd say. Dark spirits. They broke through all our protections and attacked the circle. Suzanna took the brunt of the attack. We were able to banish them, but . . ."

"Is she okay?" I asked in a near whisper. "Will she be okay?"

Eoife's face was somber. "I hope so, Morgan. But I just don't know."

6

Forbidden Magick

There is a villager here named Nuala. Without the abbot's per-
mission I asked to meet with her, as she was one of the few
Wodebaynes who would meet my eyes.

I asked her frankly what deviltry was at work here. She said no
deviltry at all since there was no devil. I cried out that that was
heresy and that if she had no fear of the eternal fires of hell, how
could she hope to join our Lord in heaven? Brother Colin, she
laughed and said there was no heaven, either. As I gaped in horror,
she leaned close so I could smell heather and smoke in her hair. She
said, "I'll fill your cow's udder if you kiss me."

I turned and ran. Surely, Brother Colin, this Nuala Riordan is
the devil's own agent.

—Brother Sinestus Tor, to Colin, May 1768

By the time I left Suzanna Mearis's house that night, she was
still unconscious, and Alyce had finally made the decision to

call an ambulance. Whatever had happened to Suzanna, she wasn't waking up. We could only pray that the doctors at the local hospital might be able to offer some help.

I spent the rest of the night wide awake in my bed, terrified by every little sound I heard. Tuesday was another meaning-less day: moving through classes, lunch, classes, without any of it registering. It was endless and foggy, clouded by my worries for Suzanna and the possibility of more dark presences to come, not to mention my misery over Hunter and the deep dread I had of failing Starlocket. Eleven days, I kept thinking miserably. I had eleven days before all of Starlocket was hit by something even stronger than what had happened to Suzanna.

When the final bell rang, I shuffled out with the other students, lost in thought.

"Hey, sis." My head snapped up at the voice.

"Killian!" I couldn't believe he had come back after yesterday. As I walked toward the stone bench, I felt a renewed sense of purpose: today I would get useful information out of him. Yes, I liked him. But I had to save Starlocket. And my time was running out.

An hour later I was sitting at a huge table in a local chain restaurant, feeling more relaxed than I had in days. We were a huge party, with emphasis on the word *party*. While I had been talking to Killian at school, he had managed to charm all the other Widow's Vale High members of Kithic, including Alisa Soto, who had never joined us on the basement steps before. Now we were sitting at four tables pushed together, eating potato skins, fried mozzarella sticks, popcorn shrimp—every kind of appetizer on the menu.

Killian was the center of attention—right now he was in

the middle of a story about magick gone wrong—"Oh, Goddess, and there I was in that field, with a flipping angry bull, and me in my robe and nothing else. . . ."

Bree was laughing, leaning against Robbie. She hadn't been impressed with Killian in New York, but she seemed to have accepted him now that she knew he was my half brother. Anyway, I was glad that Bree hadn't been attracted to Killian. In the past, she had always gone after whoever she wanted and had always gotten him—except Cal. But she was definitely not flirting with Killian, and she had deliberately sat next to Robbie at the table. True, Robbie was better-looking than Killian. But then, Robbie was better-looking than most guys.

Raven was another matter. If Sky could see her with Killian's hands all over her, well, it could get pretty ugly. With any luck, Sky wouldn't find out.

"Pass the salt, please," Matt said. He had been smiling and chuckling tonight for the first time in months.

"Cheers," Killian said, and looked at the saltshaker. It began to slide quickly down the tables, hopping over the cracks between them, and stopped in front of Matt. After a moment of surprise I gave in to the fun and giggled at this casual show of magick. Everyone else laughed and seemed to admire Killian's power, and he basked in the attention like a sunflower.

"Too much," Jenna laughed, her face flushed and pretty. Matt's dark eyes met hers, and she looked away.

"What do you think, sis?" Killian asked me. "Do you think it's too much?" His smile was wide, his face open, but I sensed a challenge there. Was this a test?

I shook my head. "No. But *this* might be too much." Remembering what I had done on Saturday, I concentrated on the saltshaker. Light as air, I thought, and then the shaker rose slowly off the table. Everyone went quiet in surprise. Quickly I lowered the shaker, feeling my face color with self-consciousness. Everyone was staring at me, and I felt Alisa's huge dark eyes on me, as if she was afraid. I shouldn't have done that, I realized. It was too much, especially for a public place. Why did I feel like I had to impress Killian?

"I didn't know you were initiated," Killian said.

"I'm not. I just—" I shrugged.

Robbie was looking at me. I couldn't meet his gaze, I knew what I'd see there: the lack of trust I'd seen in his eyes in New York.

Bree was staring at me, too. "You *move* things?" she demanded. "You *levitate* things?"

"Uh, just recently," I said, feeling guilty. Hunter would so kill me if he had seen that. Speaking of Hunter, I realized that I should probably tell him where I was. After what had happened last night, the seriousness of our situation seemed much more real.

"Why did you call Morgan 'sis'?" Matt asked. My stomach fell. I didn't know if I was ready to deal with Kithic knowing that we were half siblings.

Killian grinned broadly and stretched his arm across the back of my chair. "Oh, you know—Morgan and I, we're kindred spirits."

Startled, I caught Killian's eye, and he winked.

"You and *Morgan?*" Robbie looked at me questioningly, and when I shrugged, he gave me one of his skeptical half smiles. "Whatever you say. . . ."

"Can I borrow your phone? I was supposed to call Eileen," I asked Bree. She took out her tiny red cell phone and handed it to me. I got up and moved ten feet away.

I punched in Hunter's phone number from memory. Crap! His phone was busy. Get call waiting, I thought. I'd have to try him again later.

"Hey, I know what," Killian was saying as I returned to the table. "I found a pub over in Nortonville. What say we adjourn there?" Nortonville was a slightly bigger town about twenty minutes away.

"Ooh, yeah," said Raven at once.

"I'm up for it," Bree said, glancing at her watch. It wasn't eight yet. She looked at Robbie, and he nodded at her.

In the end everyone but Alisa, who asked to be dropped off at home, claiming that she needed to cram for a geometry test, piled into three cars and drove over to Nortonville. I was in front, with Matt's white pickup and Breezy, Bree's BMW, behind me. Jenna, Ethan, and Sharon were laughing in the backseat of my car. Next to me, Killian was humming cheerfully and keeping time by hitting his knee with his palm.

My brain was already in the pub, trying to plan a way to get closer to Killian. If Killian started drinking, maybe he would let something slip. Maybe then it would be easier to talk to him about Ciaran, ask him to get Ciaran to come to Widow's Vale. Tonight was the night to get him to open up. Eoife had made sense last night, but right now Suzanna Mearis lay in a coma. Every time I thought of Imbolc and the remaining members that could be hurt before then, I felt sick. Time was all too short.

"Turn down this road," Killian directed.

"Oh, this is old Highway 60," I realized. "We're not quite in Nortonville. We come down this road to get to the mall."

Killian shrugged. "Up there." He pointed. "There it is."

When Killian had said "pub," I had pictured a publike restaurant, maybe with an Olde English theme. But this was an actual bar. It was called the Twilite, and it looked like a converted Dairy Queen with its windows painted over and red lightbulbs blinking out front.

The three cars parked, and we gathered in the cold night air.

"So, Killian," said Jenna. "How do we plan to get in? We're all underage."

"Not a problem," Killian said lightly. "Leave it to me."

From the corner of my eye, I saw Sharon and Ethan having a whispered conference. In the end Sharon sighed, and they joined us by the bar's door. It was a Tuesday, so there were only a few other cars in the lot. The battered pink door opened, and a big guy leaned out to look at us.

"Yeah?"

Here's where we get bounced, I thought, but Killian looked at the guy and said quietly, "There are nine of us."

The man frowned and glanced at us. Killian waited patiently, and when the bouncer looked back at Killian, he seemed confused for a moment. "Right, nine," he said finally, as if from a distance.

Killian smiled broadly, clapped the bouncer on the back, and strode into the bar. The rest of us followed him like baby ducks. Inside it was dark and smelled like spilled beer and sawdust and fried food. With my magesight I could see clearly at once, but Bree and Robbie hesitated next to me. I touched Bree's arm lightly, and she followed me deeper into the Twilite.

"And another Jell-O shot for me and my friend!" Killian called loudly.

The waitress smiled and nodded and headed to the bar. It was ten-thirty, and the Twilite had picked up a lot.

"This place isn't so bad," Bree said loudly into my ear.

Music was streaming from the old-fashioned jukebox that Killian kept feeding with quarters. By now we were all used to the noise and the dim light and the flickering of a TV that was mounted high in one corner. There were two pool tables in an alcove in back, and a group of townies was playing and getting progressively louder.

I nodded in agreement. "It looks like a dive from outside." This felt similar to being with Killian in that club in New York, except this place was smaller, much less cool, and much less crowded. And of course, this place wasn't packed with blood witches. And Hunter and I were no longer together. . . . Oh, Goddess, don't go down that road, I told myself. Still, the festive air that surrounded my half brother had caught up to us in the Twilite, and once again we were all laughing until our faces hurt, even me. The fact that most of us were drinking, underage or not, wasn't hurting.

"Hey, are you all right?" Bree spoke into my ear again, struggling to be heard over the music but still be quiet enough so the whole pub wouldn't hear. "I know it must be hard for you, being out but not having Hunter anymore."

I nodded. I was grateful for Bree's concern, but this didn't seem like the time or place to talk about it. "It's hard," I agreed. "Thanks for asking. I'm okay, though."

"If you ever need to talk . . ." Robbie came up behind Bree and kissed her cheek. She giggled, and suddenly I felt very single. Bree gave me one last concerned look, and I smiled to show her I was okay.

"Sip?" Bree asked Robbie, holding out her screwdriver.

He shook his head, half smiling. "No—some of us have to be able to drive." Bree was being extremely friendly to him, pressing close and talking in his ear. I looked around the table, feeling like everyone here was my good friend, that we could all trust each other and that we could celebrate Wicca together. Not having Hunter with me, being a single girl among all the couples—I missed what I'd had with Hunter more than I could say. But still, having a group of friends I loved helped ease the pain inside me, just a little.

Jenna, on her third beer, giggled and leaned against Sharon, who wasn't drinking at all. She looked like she wasn't having as good a time as the rest of us. Ethan wasn't drinking, either, but he'd been getting twitchier and twitchier, and I wondered if they'd had a fight. To keep everyone else company, I had ordered a whiskey sour, which was what my mom usually drank. It hadn't been too bad, and I had ordered another. Killian and Raven had downed so many Jell-O shots that I had lost count. Now seemed a good time to talk to him. Smiling at him, I edged closer.

"Killian, I wanted to ask you—" I began.

"I love this song!" Killian shouted as the jukebox started another number. "Come on!" Clambering out of our booth, he grabbed Bree's hand, who grabbed Robbie's hand, who grabbed my hand, and then we were all dancing together on the tiny dance floor with sawdust slipping under our feet. And my opportunity was lost.

I've never been a big partyer, and I hate dancing in public. The thing about whiskey sours, though, is they make you mind that kind of stuff less. Back at the table, Sharon and Ethan were actually bickering. When Ethan grabbed a beer off the waitress's tray, Sharon's face set like cement, and she grabbed her purse. I saw her ask Matt to take her home, and he agreed, shooting Ethan a glance.

"Do you want me to come with you?" Jenna said, and though

I couldn't hear the words physically, I heard them in my mind. Sharon shrugged, looking upset, and Jenna got her coat and followed Sharon and Matt. Ethan was sucking down his beer, watching Sharon angrily, but he didn't stop her from leaving. In moments he had finished the first beer and started on another.

"What was that about?" I asked Robbie. He and I had edged away from the crowd and were now leaning against a back wall that felt sticky. I felt hot and out of breath, and a third whiskey sour felt fabulous going down my throat.

"Ethan had stopped drinking," Robbie told me, not looking happy. "I don't think it was a great idea for him to come here."

"Oh, crap," I said, my head feeling light.

Robbie shrugged. At the table, Ethan's second beer was empty. He signaled for another, but the waitress tapped her watch.

"Good," I said, setting my empty glass on top of the jukebox. "It's closing time. They'll cut him off, and we can go home." I staggered a bit when I pushed myself off the wall, and that seemed amusing. It took forever for us to get our coats and scarves and hats and gloves and pay our check, which was a truly stunning amount. Bree put it on her credit card, and we all promised to pay her back.

The shock of the night air took my breath away. "Oh, it's beautiful out," I said, gesturing to the wide expanse of sky. The night seemed darker than usual, the stars brighter. But looking up made me lose my balance, and I would have fallen over if I hadn't crashed into Killian.

Laughing, he held me up until I was steady, and I blinked at him as the realization slowly came to me: I was wasted.

Robbie was loading Bree and Ethan into Breezy, and they were both feeling no pain. Raven was plastering herself up against Killian, kissing him good-bye, and he wasn't resisting.

"Take me home," she said softly, holding his face between her hands. I rolled my eyes and started pawing through my fanny pack for my keys. Do not go home with her, I thought. Sky will kill you. And I need to talk to you alone. With a sudden pang, I wished Hunter were here. He would know what to do. He would help me. I would feel so much better.

"Raven, come on with us," Robbie said. My hero. "You live close to Ethan, and I can drop you off. Morgan takes another exit."

"I want to go home with you," Raven told Killian. She pressed her hips against him and smiled. "And you want me to."

He laughed and disengaged himself easily. "Not tonight, Raven. I'll take a rain check."

For a moment Raven couldn't decide whether to be angry or to pout, but in the end she was too drunk for either and fell backward into the backseat of Bree's car. Robbie sighed and slammed the door shut. Bree's fine dark hair was pressed against her window, and I saw her eyes were closed. With a wave good-bye, Robbie started Breezy and drove off.

"Fun people, your friends," said Killian. His words came out with puffs of condensation.

I looked at him for a moment until I understood the actual words. "Uh-huh," I said stupidly.

Killian grinned with delight and brushed my damp hair off my neck. "Little sister, are you tipsy?"

"I'm a mess," I said, feeling like my tongue needed to lie down and rest. Then two more synapses fired. "Oh, crap!" I said. "We're both drunk. Who's going to drive? We'll have to call a taxi."

"Oh, love, you're so concerned with what's right and

wrong," Killian said soothingly. "It'll be fine. You know these roads. This car's a tank. No worries."

I was so drunk that I almost believed him. Then I shook my head, which felt loose and floppy. "No. We can't drive drunk," I slurred. "That—*that* would be bad."

His dark eyes glittered in the night.

I'm related to him, I thought in a daze. We share the same blood. I have a brother.

Slowly Killian reached out again and spread his hand on the side of my head, pushing his fingers beneath my hair. Smiling down at me, he whispered some words in Gaelic that I didn't know but somehow understood the meaning of. I started to feel strange and closed my eyes. When he quit speaking, I waited till he had moved his hand, then opened my eyes. I felt stone-cold sober.

I looked around. I felt completely normal. I could walk, talk, and think. Killian saw the comprehension on my face and laughed again, his white teeth gleaming against his lips.

"Okay, I can drive," I said.

We got into Das Boot, my brain clicking away efficiently. I was sober; Killian was plastered. And I was going to find out where he was staying. There were possibilities here. I might get some information from him after all.

I drove slowly back down old Highway 60. Killian was leaning against his door, his head against the window. Eyes closed, he was singing under his breath.

"How did you get home last night?" I asked. "I ran after you to offer you a ride home, but you were already gone. How'd you do it?"

Killian was looking out the window, not at me, but I could

still sense his mischievous smile. "Oh, didn't you see, love?" he asked. "I had my portable broomstick in my pocket."

All right, I thought. I took that as something that I shouldn't press further. Let's try a new tactic.

"Where am I taking you now? Where are you staying?"

"Oh, ah . . ." Killian peered out the window, as if trying to figure it out himself. "I don't really know the names of the roads here. I'll just have to tell you where to turn. You stay on this road for a while."

Okay. "You and Ciaran don't seem that much alike," I said, keeping my eyes on the road.

He blinked sleepily, giving me a sweet smile. I could see how he would be popular anywhere he went. He was fun, undemanding, flexible, and not at all mean-spirited.

"No," he agreed. "We're not."

"Is that because he just wasn't around that much when you were little?"

Killian thought. "Maybe. Partly. But it's the whole nature-and-nurture thing. Even if he'd been around all the time, signing my school mark report, I'd probably still be pretty different from him."

"Why?" Note to self: Do not become a lawyer. Your interrogation skills suck.

He shrugged. "Don't know." He sat up in his seat. "Take a left here."

So he wasn't Mr. Introspection. Okay. New tactic. "What are your brother and sister like?"

"They're different from him, too. I don't know." Killian looked out the window into the dark woods on his side of the car. There was no moon tonight; the sky was laden with heavy clouds that seemed almost to touch the treetops. "It's just—Da is very ambitious, you know? He married Mum so he could lead her mother's coven. He just wants power, no matter what. It's more important than family or . . ." His voice trailed off, and I wondered if he thought he'd said too much. He still seemed very drunk—his words were thick and seemed to take a lot of thought.

"Is your mom like that, too?"

Killian gave a short bark of a laugh. "Goddess, no. Which is why Da inherited her coven, not her. She should be really strong, it's in her blood, but she just pisses it all away, you know? Ma's a housewife, a princess, really. Always complaining about her lot in life. I think she loved Da, but he loved her inheritance. Plus she was pregnant with my older brother when they got married."

This picture of Ciaran's life seemed so different than what I'd imagined, reading the romantic, agonized entries in Maeve's BOS.

"Anyway—if he loved your ma, then maybe that explains why he couldn't stand any of us." There was a bewildered hurt in his voice that I didn't think would have been there without all the Jell-O shots.

"I'm sorry, Killian," I said, and meant it. In his own way, he was another of Ciaran's victims. Did everyone Ciaran touched pay a price for it? Did I have the same effect?

"Yeah, well." Killian gave a smile. "I don't lose sleep over it. But I don't want you to think you're inheriting Mr. and Mrs. Lovely. Our family's kind of different." He gave what seemed like a bitter chuckle and leaned his head against the window again.

"But they're still your family," I said. "They're yours. They belong to you and you to them. That's something." I wasn't aware of the tense catch in my throat until the final word and didn't turn around when I felt my half brother's eyes on me.

"Stop here a minute," he said.

"Here?" I looked out at the deserted road. We were in the middle of the woods; I couldn't see any houses anywhere. Why did he want me to stop?

"Right here." I stopped the car, and Killian leaned over and kissed me on the cheek. It was very gentle and grape-flavored. "Now you belong to us, too, little sister."

To avoid bursting into unexpected tears, I opened my door and got out, standing next to Das Boot in the dark night. Killian got out also, clumsily hanging on to the car door to avoid falling down. He started laughing at himself, and I smiled.

"Look, sis," he said, gesturing at the sky. He looked at me with mischief glittering in his eyes. "Repeat after me: *grenlach altair dan, buren nitha sentac.*" Watching his face, I repeated the words, imitating his pronunciation as best I could. They sounded much better with his accent, but when he went on, I followed, feeling the thin coil of magick awakening within me. What were we doing?

He was watching the sky, and I was, too, not knowing what to look for. Then Killian waved his right hand in a smooth, sweeping gesture, oddly graceful, and I saw the heavy clouds overhead parting reluctantly to reveal the clear, star-speckled sky behind them. My mouth went slack as I realized what he had done.

"Now you." He tapped my hand, and disbelieving, I moved it in a gentle circle before me. The clouds above moved at my command, and with a broader movement I pushed the huge billows aside. All was clear above us. Weather magick was forbidden; it was considered an assault on nature and could have far-reaching, devastating effects. So I had just worked forbidden magick. And I had loved it.

My heart was pounding with excitement, and I looked at Killian, my eyes wide and shining. He laughed at my expression.

"Don't say I never gave you anything," he said. "I gave you the stars. Good night, little sister."

He started to walk away, weaving slightly down the dark road.

"Good night? Where are you going?" I yelled. "This is the middle of nowhere!"

He turned and gave me a mock-severe look. "Everyplace is somewhere. I want to walk from here." He turned and began to walk away again.

"But—" I stared at him, feeling something close to panic. "Killian! Wait!"

He turned again from the woods and looked at me. I took a deep breath. "I want to see Ciaran again. Can you ask him to come here, to see me?" There. It was out. I had said it.

For a moment Killian was silent, then his faint laughter floated to me just as a glowing sliver of moon appeared in the clouds' clearing. "I'll think about it," he called back. Then he was gone, into the nothingness, and I was left alone in the cold, wondering whether I had actually succeeded in my mission— or whether Killian was just playing with me the same way he played with the clouds.

7

Witch Fire

Brother Thomas's wound continues to fester. He is near delirium, and I fear he will lose the leg. Brother Colin, I must set this letter aside; Father Benedict has motioned to me. I will finish later.

The Lord works in mysterious ways. Father Benedict came to me in all gravity and voiced his concern about Brother Thomas. He commanded me to go seek help from a village granny-wife. I asked if that was not like asking for help from the devil, to which he replied that God judges what is good or evil, not man.

In the village no granny-wife would see me, but Nuala Riordan came with me and is still with Brother Thomas. I tremble in fear for our very souls: she is chanting devil's words over him, fixing him foul teas, applying seaweed poultices to his wound. To my mind it would be better if he died rather than have the devil heal him.

—Brother Sinestus Tor, to Colin, June 1768

I pulled into our dark driveway and felt Das Boot's big engine stop with a tremble. What a night. It had been incredible. Now I had to go in and steel myself to call Eoife, to tell her I had asked Killian to call Ciaran.

I was almost to my front door, keys in hand, when suddenly every bit of alcohol I had drunk flooded back into my brain with a whoosh. I staggered on the walk, dumbfounded. Oh my God. Killian's spell had worn off—what if it had worn off while I was driving? Now I was completely polluted again.

Inside the house, I dumped my stuff on the floor and literally crawled upstairs to my room. How much had I drunk? More than I ever had in my life. My stomach felt iffy, and I began to regret downing those whiskey sours.

Ten minutes later I lay in my bed with the spins, wanting to cry. The room was rocking back and forth as if I were on a ship, my stomach felt extremely fragile, and I had to get up to go to school in about six hours.

A moment after that I realized that the dull, heavy pounding I felt in my head was really someone banging on my front door. Jesus, who could that be? I tried to focus my senses to cast them but couldn't concentrate. I was all over the place and starting to panic. Then I heard the front door open—had I locked it?—and footsteps thudding up the stairs.

"Morgan!" Hunter yelled, right before he opened the door to my room. I looked at him stupidly while he stormed over to loom above me in my bed. "Where the hell have you been? I sent you a witch message, I've been calling your house. Do you think this is a game? Do you think—"

"I tried to call you earlier!" I said, my voice sounding thick. "Your phone was busy!" Then, with a sickening rush, my stomach gave notice that it was about to rebel. I stared at Hunter in horror, then lunged toward the bathroom I shared with Mary K. I just barely made it to the toilet before everything I had eaten and drunk that evening came back up.

Throwing up is the most disgusting thing I can think of. I flushed the toilet after the first time, but then I vomited again and again, my stomach muscles heaving. I felt the little blood vessels around my eyes burst and wanted to cry but couldn't yet.

The only thing worse than barfing your guts up is doing it in front of someone you love desperately and are no longer with. I didn't hear him follow me, but my face crumpled with sobs when I felt Hunter's strong, gentle hands carefully lifting back my long hair. He twisted it away from my face while I was sick, and then when I sagged against the porcelain, he stepped away just long enough to wet a washcloth with cold water. He stroked it over my face as I sat mortified, humiliated tears filling my eyes.

"Oh, God," I muttered in misery.

"Can you stand up?" His anger had dissipated. I nodded, and Hunter helped me over to the sink, where I brushed my teeth three times, feeling shaky and hollow. He wet the washcloth again, gently pressing it against my face and the back of my neck under my hair. It felt incredible.

Feeling completely defeated and beyond any hope of redeeming myself, I shuffled back to my room and collapsed on my bed. That was when I realized I was wearing only the Wonder Woman undies Bree had given me months ago as a joke and my dad's threadbare MIT sweatshirt. Hunter was rooting through my dresser and finally found a long-sleeved rugby shirt that had seen too many washes. Businesslike, he came over, stripped off my sweatshirt, then popped the rugby shirt over my head, helping my arms find the sleeves.

Then he left my bedroom, and I slid sideways in my cool, comfortable bed, knowing my humiliation was now complete. Hunter and I had made out seriously before, and we'd put our hands under each other's shirts, but he'd never seen me practically naked until now. Now he had seen me in nothing but my Wonder Woman undies.

Hunter came back into my room, holding a cold can of ginger ale. He poured it into a glass and helped me sit up again so I could sip it. It was nirvana. "Thank you." My voice sounded harsh, scraped.

"So, you've been drinking a bit," he said unnecessarily, taking the glass from me and putting it on my bedside table.

I moaned pathetically, burying my face in my pillow. I still felt wretched but much, much better since my stomach had gotten rid of some of the poison in my system. The spins were gone, and the awful queasiness.

"Liquor dulls your senses," Hunter said mildly, stroking his hand down my hair, across my shoulder, down my side. I pulled the covers up past my waist. "It makes your magick go awry if you don't compensate for it. That's why most witches just have a little ceremonial wine, at most. . . ."

I started weeping, and he shut up. He didn't have to tell me this—I didn't want to drink again in my whole life. "I was with Killian tonight. He told me why Ciaran inherited his mother's coven and not her, but I didn't get anything else. But I did ask him to ask Ciaran to come here." Then I burst into tears, holding my pillow, feeling like I was releasing days' worth of tension, fear, and worry. Hunter sat close to me, his hand on my neck, smoothing my hair. He didn't say shhh or anything to make me stop crying but just waited while I got it out.

Finally I slowed down to shudders and hiccups. I gazed up

at him through tear-blurred eyes, thinking how incredible he looked, how attractive and appealing and sexy and magickal, thinking about how wonderful and caring and thoughtful he had been tonight. My heart was breaking all over again. And here I was, having just been horribly sick in front of him, having him see me in my joke underwear and nothing else, and knowing that I looked like a total bowser when I cried. It was too much to bear, and I closed my eyes against the onslaught of emotional anguish that rushed over me.

"Tell me more about tonight, love," he said gently, leaning over me.

Slowly I reported everything that Killian and I had talked about. It seemed extremely thin. I was a failure. I talked about going to the bar tonight, and everyone drinking, and Ethan falling off the wagon. I confessed to Killian's working weather magick but not that I had done it also.

"Then right before he left me, I asked him to call Ciaran. He said he'd think about it."

"You did well," Hunter said. He looked at me and seemed about to say something but then decided against it. Instead he stroked my hair and down my back. I realized I was completely exhausted, hollowed out, wrung out, numb.

"Go to sleep," Hunter whispered.

"Mmm-hmm," I murmured, my eyes already closing.

"By the way," he said from the door, "nice knickers."

Then he was gone, and despite how horrible I felt at the moment, I was smiling because I had seen his face, just for a little while.

The next afternoon Killian was waiting for me, the faithful spaniel, on his usual stone bench. It was odd—my heart was glad to see his smile. I was really beginning to like Killian. He was completely irresponsible and a bad influence, but nice. I immediately wanted to ask him about Ciaran—I was down to ten days now and Ciaran was nowhere in sight—but then I remembered Eoife's pep talk from the Starlocket circle. How pushy could I be without turning him off or making him suspicious? I decided to play it by ear.

He rubbed his hands together when he saw me walking toward him, Robbie and Bree in back of me. "What's up for tonight?"

"Anything that doesn't involve alcohol," I said. I thought briefly about my vow to study tonight but then figured that saving Starlocket mattered more than memorizing a list of presidents. Anyway, there would be plenty of time to study after Imbolc.

Killian threw back his head and laughed. "We have to get you up to speed," he said.

Even in our hungover state, we all gravitated toward the good time that Killian seemed to promise, and half an hour later we were sprawled in Bree's family room. I tried to sit next to Killian, determined to find out if he had passed my message on to Ciaran.

We were all making fun of Bree's awful CD of French pop music when the doorbell rang. When Bree came back to the family room she was followed by Sky Eventide, Alisa Soto, and Simon Bakehouse, who was also in Kithic. Jenna and Simon had recently started going out. Sky looked at Raven, who was leaning toward Killian, offering him a bite of a mini powdered doughnut.

Killian looked up at the newcomers and gave them a welcoming smile, licking powdered sugar off his lips. Bree, always the good hostess, introduced him. Simon smiled politely.

"I remember Sky," Killian said in a silky voice, smiling into her eyes. Sky narrowed hers at him so they looked like slits of obsidian. She was dressed in formfitting black clothes, which made her moonlight-pale hair stand out in stark contrast. She turned to look at Raven, who had a bored expression on her face.

Simon sat next to Jenna, putting his hand on her knee as she smiled up at him. Across the room Matt looked like he'd just bitten a lemon. Alisa seemed uncomfortable and awkward and very young. She perched on the edge of the couch, and I wondered why she had come. This wasn't an official circle, after all.

"Well!" said Bree, artificially brightly. "Who needs something to drink? I have seltzer, juice, sodas, or I could make coffee or tea."

"How about a drop of whiskey?" Killian asked.

Only someone who knew Bree as well as I did could tell that she was disconcerted by his open request. "Sorry," she said. "The liquor cabinet's locked."

Killian laughed. "Lock or no lock—it doesn't matter to a witch."

Bree wasn't so easy to influence. "Sorry," she said again, with a touch more warning in her voice.

My glance flicked to Ethan, who looked relieved. Sharon reached up and rubbed the back of his neck under his long curls. He gave her a little smile, and she kissed him. I felt a renewed sense of warmth for both of them.

Only Bree was so irrevocably cool that she could say she didn't want to drink and not look like a Girl Scout. For the millionth time in my life, I admired her easy self-confidence.

We talked. We listened to music. We laughed at Killian's stories and told some of our own. Bree lit incense and candles when the sun went down. Her family room became a dimly lit, exotic, magickal place. Around dinnertime we ordered pizza and the people who needed to call their parents did. I checked in with Eileen to let her know where I'd be.

It was eight o'clock when I remembered again my intention to hit the books tonight. Today in school Mr. Alban had reminded us of an English composition that was due soon. My grades were slipping a little this semester—I had to get it together. I looked over at Killian, who seemed to be enjoying playing Sky and Raven off each other.

I sidled over to him and touched his shoulder. He leaned toward me, smiling, and I put my face close to his to speak privately. He slanted his head toward mine, and I felt so duplicitous, like a user.

"I was wondering if you had contacted our father yet," I said bluntly.

His dark eyes met mine, and I noticed for the first time that they tilted up at the corners ever so slightly, like mine. "Not yet," he said softly so only I could hear. "You're more eager to see him than I am."

I didn't know what to make of this and was still pondering my next step when Killian got up to get another can of soda. Damnation.

The clock was ticking even now, but still, I decided that pushing Killian was a bad idea. As Eoife had cautioned, I didn't want to make him suspicious of my motives—he was already cagey enough. Reluctantly I got to my feet. "Gotta go," I said, trying to remember where I had put my coat.

"No, no, little sister," Killian protested. "The night is young yet, and so are we." He laughed, and I felt my body tense in frustration.

"I better go study," I said, feeling like a failure again. At least my schoolwork was something I could control. There was no chance of ending up at a pub on the edge of town with my history book.

"Stay, love," Killian said coaxingly, and suddenly his voice was like a velvet ribbon wrapping around my wrists, keeping me there. Maybe my studying could wait. "Stay, and I'll show you some special magick."

Well, *that* was something worth checking out, at least. I sat back down.

He grinned in delight and gestured to the others. "Sit in a circle."

When we were in a circle, Killian again rubbed his hands together, as if he were a stage performer. Sky, sitting next to him, looked as if she would rather be eating glass. Killian cupped his hands and blew on them (I was sure that was just for effect) and then tossed a little ball of blue, crackly witch fire at Sky. Startled, she caught it in her cupped hands, and it transformed into a ball of glowing, pinkish light.

"Pass it!" Killian urged her.

With a little shrug Sky passed it to Robbie, next to her. Robbie looked fascinated, his face bright and a little scared, holding it in his hands. When Killian waved toward him, Robbie passed it to Bree, next to him. And around it went, this glowing ball of light. When it was my turn, I thought it felt like an electrified pom-pom. When it got back to Killian, he bounced it in one hand and looked at us.

"Now add to it," he said, once again tossing it lightly to Sky. She held the light for a moment, concentrating. It glowed a bit bigger and brighter, and she passed it to Robbie. Robbie did the same, with less perceptible results. Of this group only

Killian, Sky, and I were blood witches. When we passed the light, it grew obviously bigger and brighter. When the others passed it, any change was less visible, but at the end of each circle round, the cumulative effect was definitely noticeable. And it became more sensitive to the increasing energy—after the fifth round Alisa passed it, and it jumped in size and brightness as it passed from her hands. She giggled nervously.

It was kind of a juvenile game, like hot potato, but it was also a beautiful, electric thing: making magick out of thin air. I could feel the magickal energy increasing, crackling around us, as if it were another presence in the room. Again and again we infused the light with our individual energies, watching as it changed color and brightness, depending on who held it. I felt filled with light, with energy, with magick, and it was exciting and satisfying in a way that nothing else could ever be.

The next time it landed in Killian's hands, he held it and then suddenly shot it straight at me. "Do something!" he commanded.

Without a moment to think, I opened my heart and my mind. I caught the witch fire lightly in my hands and spun it toward the ceiling, shaping it into a long blue stream of fire. Feeling magick flowing through me, surrounding me, I let the energy do what it wanted to, and I opened my hand out flat to release it. It bounced against the ceiling and then shattered like crystal, raining down on us in prickly, multicolored sparks.

"Oh my God," Jenna breathed, her eyes reflecting the pinpricks of light.

Flowers, I thought, and in the next instant the shower of sparks had changed into a gentle rain of real, petal-soft flowers, brushing gently against our faces. Tulips, daisies, poppies, anemones, all in summer-bright colors, landing as light as butterflies all around us. I smiled with pleasure at the beauty I had wrought. *Witch, witch,* I thought, claiming the title as my own.

Then I looked up. My friends' faces were a mixture of disbelief, amazement, and a little bit of fear, from Alisa. Even Robbie, who had been so concerned about my abuse of magick in New York, wore an expression of amazement and joy. Killian was smiling big at me, a familial smile that made me feel more connected to him. Sky was watching me with solemn silence, and I realized—too late, as always—that I had just committed another Wiccan faux pas or worse. Inwardly I groaned. There were so many rules! Things that felt so natural were bound and regulated.

My next thought was that I was supposed to get up extra early tomorrow to meet with Eoife before school. Hunter had relayed my report on last night's meeting, but I was supposed to check in with her in person.

I sighed and got to my feet.

8

Longing

Brother Colin, I have doubts that I have not been able to confess to good Father Benedict. My brother, I fear I am possessed by evil spirits. Since the night of Brother Thomas's healing, Nuala Riordan has haunted my waking moments and my dreams. Only during prayer does she not intrude upon my poor mind. I have mortified my flesh, I have prostrated myself before God, I have spent days and nights in prayer until I am half feverish.

My brother, if you have any hope for my immortal soul, please remember me in your prayers.

—Brother Sinestus Tor, to Colin, July 1768

When the alarm went off at six-thirty on Thursday morning, I felt like I was trapped in an unending nightmare. I pawed at the clock until the hideous noise stopped. Almost forty minutes later I awoke again, wondering if it was time to get up for school. Then I sat bolt upright. Eoife!

I threw some food at Dagda, scrambled into jeans and a

sweatshirt, quickly braided my hair, and was out of the house in less than twenty minutes. I was already late. My heart was pounding as I drove to Hunter's house, and not even the pinkish morning light soothed me. My life was out of control. Last night I'd gotten home after eleven. I had taken out my textbooks, then stared at them uncomprehendingly as my bed beckoned. Five minutes later I was asleep, with Dagda kneading the comforter next to me.

So for the last four days I hadn't done any homework, hadn't gotten enough sleep, hadn't gotten Ciaran to Widow's Vale. I was late for my meeting with Eoife, I wasn't checking in with her often enough, I'd made illegal magick. . . . What the hell was I doing?

I pulled up fast in front of the somewhat shabby little house that Hunter and Sky shared. The back deck that Cal had sabotaged had been rebuilt. There was an ugly ligustrum hedge in front that had been ignored for so many years that it was just a gnarled collection of half-leaved branches. My breath coming out in little puffs of smoke, I trotted up the walkway and rang their doorbell.

As I did, it occurred to me that I was at my ex-boyfriend's house at seven-thirty in the morning, looking like total hell. True, I had broken up with him, and for very good reasons, but that didn't mean I had to make him glad about it when he saw me by looking like a wreck.

Eoife opened the door, her small face solemn as she looked at me, and I wondered if Sky had mentioned the sparks-and-flowers incident of the night before.

"Sorry I'm late," I said. Without thinking I cast my senses through the house and discovered that Sky was asleep upstairs but Hunter wasn't in the house. Good. A reprieve.

"Do you always do that?" Eoife said as I followed her into the kitchen in back.

"Do what?" I took off my coat as Eoife poured boiling water into a waiting teapot.

"Cast your senses." She brought the teapot to the table, and smoky plumes of fragrance swirled above us. I inhaled deeply, enjoying the scent.

"Um . . ." I tried to think. "Yes, I guess so. I don't really think about it. But if I feel like I need to know what's going on, who's around, that kind of thing, then yeah, I guess I usually cast my senses."

She poured tea into two delicate cups with saucers. "Who taught you how to do that?"

"No one. It just came to me." I circled my left hand over my tea, widdershins, and thought, Cool the fire. Now the tea was the perfect temperature, and I took a long sip. Ahhh.

Frowning, not angrily but as if perplexed, Eoife looked at me from across the table. "You cooled your tea."

"Uh-huh. It's great. Thanks for making it." Another big swallow, hoping this tea had caffeine in it. I couldn't tell.

"Morgan—" Eoife began, but then shook her head. "Never mind."

I took a packet of Pop-Tarts out of my backpack and opened it. They're better toasted but perfectly edible cold if necessary. I offered one to Eoife and thought I detected a faint shudder as she refused.

Holding her teacup with both hands, Eoife said, "I'm sorry to tell you, Morgan, that Suzanna Mearis is still in a coma."

I looked at Eoife, and sudden guilt crashed down on me. The truth was, I had barely thought of Suzanna in the last couple of days. I had been there to see her fall, I had witnessed the *taibhs*, I knew that her coven was destined for destruction, yet I had spent the last two days partying and abusing my power. What kind of a witch was I? "Has anything else happened?"

"Not as of this morning, thank the Goddess." She put down her cup and gazed at me. "Has Killian spoken to Ciaran?"

"Not yet," I admitted. "He said I'm more eager to see Ciaran than he is. I guess Ciaran's angry at him, and Killian wants to delay having to deal with it." I looked up at Eoife's chestnut-colored eyes, remembering again Suzanna's warm house and serene expression. "I feel like I should press harder," I admitted. "I know that you said not to make Killian suspicious, but Imbolc is getting closer and closer. Maybe if I told Killian I was desperate to meet my father again . . ."

I felt tension tightening Eoife's slight body. "No, Morgan," she said, leaning over the table. Her eyes burned in her porcelain face. "We have to tread cautiously. I know that this is difficult, but we mustn't destroy the mission by acting in haste."

I nodded slowly and looked deep into my teacup. "Okay," I murmured. "I'll keep working. Ciaran will come here, and I'll get information out of him."

Eoife sat back in her chair, her eyes still on me. "I'm sorry," she said again. "You make it easy to forget that you're young and uninitiated."

"I can do this," I said firmly, pushing aside my tea. Looking vaguely sympathetic, Eoife nodded back at me, and I picked up my coat and left.

School seemed more surreal than usual that morning since I had just come from a meeting with Eoife. I felt schizophrenic: high school student by day, undercover ICOW agent by night. In first period I had barely sat down when my American history teacher, Mr. Powell, pulled out an ominous sheaf of papers.

"As I mentioned last Friday," he said, starting to hand them out, "this is a test on what we've learned since the winter holidays."

I stared at him in horror, then mentally said every bad word I could think of. Tara Williams handed the pile of papers back to me, and I numbly took one and passed the rest to Jeff Goldstein. Just this morning I had worried about my life being out of control. Here was the proof. My grades had been slipping, and in three months I had gone from being a straight-A student to a straight-B student with maybe even a couple of Cs, which my parents were going to freak about. Now I was about to get a big, fat F on this test.

Unless . . .

Unless. I thought about Killian, about his charm, his skill, the easy comfort with which he did things. Life had not come pleasantly for my half brother, but he'd gone a long way to making it easier and more fun. What would he do in this situation?

I looked up at Mr. Powell. All it would take was a simple spell that would make Mr. Powell forget he'd intended to give us this test. Or to think this one was the wrong test, and he'd bring another tomorrow. Or to think we were supposed to have the test next week.

I bit my lip. What was I thinking? This was exactly what Hunter always talked about: making the wrong decision, making the decision that benefits only yourself, making the decision that doesn't take other people into account. He always said that was why the council had introduced regulations and guidelines back in the early 1800s. Because it's so easy to make the wrong small decision. And once you do, it's even easier to make the wrong big decision. And then, boom. You're part of the darkness.

I made choices every day, all day long. I needed to be more aware of all of them, needed to consciously try to make the right decision, a decision for good. I resigned myself to the fact that the only thing I would get right on this test was my own name.

When Killian wasn't waiting for me after school, I felt relief as well as disappointment. I could try sending him a witch message, I knew—but maybe that would make him suspicious. After all, we had seen each other almost every day this week. Would I seem too clingy if I called him today, too?

"Want to come hang out?" Bree asked as I walked toward Das Boot. "Robbie and I are going to my house for a while."

"Thanks," I said. "But I've been letting a lot of things slide. I better get home and crank."

"Okay. See you later."

I started my car and turned the heater up. I wondered where Bree and Robbie were in their relationship and how it was going. Although I had been seeing all my friends every day this week, I felt oddly disconnected from them. Being with Killian had meant only fun and magick. Unfortunately for my mission, it hadn't meant really talking to one another, sharing our feelings, or feeling closer.

Okay. Now I was all touchy-feely. This was getting me nowhere. I had to focus: concentrate on getting Killian to call Ciaran, getting closer to both of them, saving Starlocket. There wasn't any time to think about my own problems. And probably, I thought as my heart sank into my stomach, that was a good thing.

When I got home, I cleaned the kitchen, loaded the dishwasher for the first time since my parents had left, fed Dagda and cleaned his litter box, and called Aunt Eileen.

"Yep, everything's fine," I told her, trying to sound like that was true. "No—no coed sleepovers. At least not yet. Ha-ha." After we hung up, I headed upstairs to my room and determinedly sat down at my desk. I would study for a while, then send a witch message to Killian, asking him about Ciaran.

I started with American history, reviewing chapters and making notes. I hoped that I could undo some of the damage of today's test with extra credit. Dagda came and settled himself on my desk right under the heat of the lamp.

"You have it good," I told him. "No school, no parents, no choices between good and evil. No history tests."

Ugh. If only I could simply do a *tàth meànma brach* with Mr. Powell and just absorb all his knowledge. Then I could ace this class.

A couple of hours later I ate an apple with peanut butter for dinner and got ready to send a witch message to Killian. I was just calming my thoughts to do it when my senses tingled: Hunter was coming up the walk. I still seemed to be able to pick up on his vibrations more easily than I could almost anyone else's.

It occurred to me that the last time I saw him, I'd been throwing up my guts. So I felt really lovely and feminine, waiting for him to come to the door. At least this time my face was clean.

"Hi," I said as he stepped onto the porch.

"Hi." His green eyes swept me from head to foot. "How are you feeling?"

"Fine. Thanks for your help the other night," I said, not looking at him.

"You're welcome," he said, just as coolly. "I'm here to receive your report. Can we go inside?"

What report? I wondered. I'd given my report to Eoife this morning. Had he not heard it from her? Or was there some other reason he wanted to come over? Puzzled, I frowned at him for a second before realizing he'd asked me a question.

"No, you're not supposed to be in the house. Here, let's sit in Das Boot," I said, digging in my pocket for the keys. It was frigid inside my car, and the vinyl seats didn't help any. But I blasted the heater, and a few minutes later we were comfortable.

"You met with Eoife this morning?" he asked, taking off his gloves and shoving them in his pocket.

"Yes. Is Suzanna Mearis still in a coma?"

He shook his head. "They did healing spells all day, and she woke up a little while ago."

I sighed in relief. "Thank the Goddess."

"Yes." Hunter nodded somberly, then turned his green eyes back to mine. "So tell me about Killian."

I shrugged. "I saw him yesterday at Bree's. Practically everyone from Kithic was there. I asked him if he had contacted Ciaran, and he said he hadn't. Didn't Eoife tell you this?"

Hunter frowned, and I got it: he was here because he had an excuse to be here, with me. Oh, Hunter, I thought longingly.

"Anyway," I said, looking at my hands, "I was about to send him a witch message, asking to get together."

"He's unbelievably slippery," Hunter said, almost to himself.

"Excuse me?"

"He gets out of everything, like an eel," Hunter went on. "He got out of New York before the ritual, he got off scot-free the night you were sick. He careens through life, having a good time and not worrying about anyone else."

"I think that's a little harsh," I said. "Killian's—incredibly fun. He's irresponsible, but I don't think he's hurtful. There's no reason to think he's deliberately keeping Ciaran from meeting me."

Hunter looked at me, and all at once I remembered other times sitting in my car, with our hands all over each other and our mouths joined fiercely. I swallowed and looked away.

"Give up the mission," Hunter said quietly.

"No. I'm getting it done."

"I don't think anyone can do it. It's too dangerous. I think Starlocket needs to disband and get out of town."

"Why don't they?" I asked.

He sighed. "Covens never do. When they're in danger, they stay together, no matter what. A coven never splits up if they can help it. Almost never." He paused, and I knew he was thinking about his parents. "Most covens feel they're less at risk if they stay together—the dark wave can't divide and conquer them."

Thinking about what Starlocket was facing, I once again felt the fear that I was sickeningly inadequate for this job. But somehow Hunter thinking that, too, was enough to make me go forward.

"We still have nine days. This could still work," I said.

Hunter shook his head, looking out the car window at the darkness. "Want to go have something to eat?" he surprised me by saying.

"I already ate. I've been studying all afternoon, trying to get caught up."

"Deities? Correspondences? Basic forms of spellcraft?"

"Uh, American history. For school."

Hunter nodded and looked away, and I felt that once again

I had disappointed him somehow. Sometimes it seemed like everything I did was wrong.

"I flunked a test today, so I'm trying to catch up." Hoping to make Hunter smile, I said, "I'm so tempted to do a *tàth meànma* on my teacher so I wouldn't have to study the rest of the year."

His eyes flicked to me. "Morgan. Doing a *tàth meànma* with a regular human would likely leave that person a drooling vegetable."

"I was just kid—"

"Rules about things like that exist for a reason," he went on. "Witches have been using magick for thousands of years. Witches far more experienced than you have created these guidelines to benefit everyone. They saw what could happen if magick was unchecked."

"I was just *kidding*," I said stiffly. Sometimes Hunter seemed so inflexible and humorless. He wasn't, I knew, but he definitely seemed that way sometimes.

"Things are very clear for you, aren't they?" I asked almost wistfully. "Decisions seem clear, the right path is in front of you, you don't have to agonize over what's right or wrong."

He was silent for a few minutes. I cracked a window so we wouldn't die of carbon monoxide poisoning. "Is that how I seem to you?" he asked softly, his words barely reaching me.

I nodded.

"It isn't true." His words were like velvety leaves, falling between us in the darkness. "Sometimes nothing is clear. Sometimes there is no right path, no correct decision. Sometimes I absolutely want what I shouldn't have and do what I shouldn't do. Sometimes I want to reach out, grab power from the air, and bend everything around me to my will." He gave a slight smile as I reacted to his words. "So far I haven't," he said more lightly. "Most of the time I do all right. But not always, and not without a struggle."

I'd never known this about him, and of course it made me fall even more in love with him than I already had. He had vulnerabilities. He wasn't perfect. Oh, Goddess, I wanted him so much.

"That's what magick is," he said. "Many choices, through your lifetime. How you make them determines who you are. And who you are determines how you make them."

Wicca is full of pithy sayings like that. I was tempted to write them all down in a book and watch it become a bestseller. *Chicken Soup for the Witch's Soul.*

But I knew what he meant. I got it. I rubbed my hands down my jeans. "I'll go call Killian."

"All right. Be careful. Call me if you need me. Don't do anything that feels unsafe."

I smiled wanly. "Yes, Dad."

In a move so fast I didn't see it, Hunter was across the seat, his arm around my back, holding me against him, hard. As I gasped in surprise, he slanted his mouth across mine and kissed me with a hunger and an urgency that rocked me to the core. Yes, yes, yes. Just as suddenly he pulled back, leaving me wide-eyed and breathing fast and awash in a desire so strong, I didn't know what to do with it.

"I'm not your dad," he said, looking at me. Then he opened his door and got out. Agape, I watched him head to his own car, his long wool coat billowing around his legs like a cape. I was shaking, and my arms felt empty because he wasn't in them.

9

True Name

I am sorry for the delay in answering your last two letters. I have been ill. The summer grass sickness felled our community, and we have lost both Brother Sean and Brother Paul Marcus, God have mercy on their souls.

Myself, I owe my sad life to Nuala, who nursed me back from death not once but several times. In a babe's weak voice I bid that pawn of the devil to be gone. She laughed, her voice like a mountain stream. Surely you'll not think me evil, said she. Truly, we in Belwicket do more good than you, holed up in your abbey of gloom.

Through my delirium I insisted she did the devil's work. She bent close to me, so that her black hair fell across my chest. In a whisper she told me, "We do no work but that which should be done. My ancestors were gathering knowledge while your people were still fighting the Crusades."

I felt as if I were drowning. Today my head is clearer, and I do not know whether that interview took place. Remember me in your prayers, Brother Colin, I beg you.

—Brother Sinestus Tor, to Colin, August 1768

In American history I got a forty-seven on my test. I had never flunked a test before in my life, and my stomach clenched in a knot of embarrassment.

"Morgan, can you see me after class, please?" said Mr. Powell.

I nodded, my face flushing.

After class I waited until the other kids had left. Mr. Powell looked up at me, his wide gray eyes thoughtful behind gold-wire glasses. "What happened with this test?" he jumped in with no preamble.

"I forgot about it," I admitted.

He looked perplexed. "But even if you forgot, you should have known enough to squeak by with a D. This test shows that you've learned virtually nothing since the winter holidays. I don't get it."

I was so hating this. "I just . . . I've just had a lot going on."

Once again he waited. I'd always liked Mr. Powell, even though I couldn't stand American history. I felt he always tried to make it interesting.

"Morgan, I'll be frank with you." I hate it when teachers say that. "You've always been an excellent student. But the other teachers and I have noticed a significant drop in your grades this past quarter." He paused, as if waiting for me to explain. I didn't know what to say. "Morgan, I've heard . . . rumors."

I blinked. "Rumors? About what?"

"About Wicca. Students having witchcraft circles, performing rites." He looked as uncomfortable as I felt. How in the world had he heard about that? Then I remembered the kids who had come to one or two of Cal's first circles. They'd left—it wasn't for them. I guessed they'd been talking about it.

"Do you know anything about it?" he pressed.

I felt like he was asking if I had ever been a member of the

Communist Party, if I was gay, if I was Jewish. "Um, well, I practice Wicca." Morgan takes a stand.

Mr. Powell looked nonplussed for a moment, then tapped his fingers on his desk, thinking. Finally he said, "Is this interfering in your schoolwork?"

"Yes," I almost whispered. Far from being surreal, I was smack-dab in the middle of harsh reality. I was going to flunk my junior year if I didn't get my act together.

"What are you going to do about it?" he asked.

"Study more?"

"Will that be enough?"

"Do extra credit?" I offered hopefully.

"Let me think about it." He shut his notebook, no longer seeming approachable.

"I'm sorry," I said, and he looked back at me.

"Morgan, you're only seventeen. You're extremely bright. You could do anything you want with your life. Don't screw up this young." He turned and walked out of the room, as if he was personally hurt by my poor grade. I felt awful. I was being slowly crushed by pressure from all sides. I just had to get through and do the best I could do. The problem was, that probably wouldn't be good enough. For anyone.

"Morgan!" Killian was waiting for me on his usual bench. But as I started toward him, I heard Mary K.'s voice behind me. My heart clutched suddenly—I didn't want them to meet. Quickly I turned my back to Killian and went to meet my sister.

"I didn't see you this morning." She grinned. "Let me guess. You're having a hard time getting up in the morning."

"You know me too well. How are things at Jaycee's?"

My sister's face clouded. "It's fine," she said unconvincingly.

"Jaycee's got a new friend—you know her. Alisa Soto. And a new boyfriend—Michael Pulaski."

I wasn't sure, but I thought Michael was a sophomore. "She sounds busy."

"Yeah." Mary K. shook her head. "I guess I'm not really used to sharing Jaycee. And Alisa's into Wicca, and I don't want Jaycee to get into it." This said with an apologetic glance. I knew she hated my involvement with Wicca. "And it's hard to watch her being all happy and lovey-dovey with Michael after—"

"Hmmm," I said. "Yeah. I can see how that would bother you. Are you going to tell Jaycee how you feel about these things?"

"No. It wouldn't do any good, and it'd just make me look weird and clingy. Anyway. We're going to the mall tonight 'cause it's Friday. Alisa isn't going, and Michael has hockey practice."

"Good. You and Jaycee have a good time, then. And call me tomorrow, okay? Since I won't see you at school."

She nodded. "Okay. Thanks." She gave me one of her quick, sweet smiles, and I felt a rush of love for her. My sister.

After Mary K. had rejoined her friends, I walked over to Killian. Raven was practically in his lap. I wondered meanly how she avoided getting pneumonia, showing as much skin as she did. As I walked up, other members of Kithic drifted toward us.

"Hey!" Killian greeted me. "I found something I wanted to show you all. Do we have enough cars?"

And just that easily we were all swept into the Killian tide. Fifteen minutes later I realized we were almost to the old Methodist cemetery where our original coven, Cirrus, had first made magick. Where Cal and Hunter had had a showdown and I had put a holding spell on Hunter that he was probably still pissed about. What had Killian found here?

"We've been here before," Matt told him as we gathered at the edge of the property.

"You have? Then you know about the power sink?" Killian looked disappointed.

"What power sink?" I asked, and he perked up and began to lead us through the overgrown brush to the actual graveyard.

"You know about power leys?" he asked. At our blank faces, he went on. "All around the earth, like strings wrapped around a ball, there are ancient lines of power that were created when the world was made. If a witch stands on one, works magick on one, their magick will be enhanced, more powerful. Anytime two or more of these leys intersect, the inherent power is even greater. Right in this cemetery is a huge power sink, probably five or more lines crossed together."

It was somehow demoralizing that my party-guy, irresponsible, devil-may-care half brother was so much more knowledgeable than I was. Then we were standing in front of the stone sarcophagus that Cirrus had used as an altar on Samhain. The marker read Jacob Henry Moore, 1845–1871.

"Right here!" Killian said enthusiastically. "This is an incredible power sink."

Bree met my eyes, and the other Kithic members were quiet. Cal had brought us here several times. Obviously he'd been aware it was a power sink and had used it to his advantage. And none of us had known.

It occurred to me that of course Hunter knew about it also. He must have felt it when he was here with Cal. The power sink might even be the reason my holding spells had worked so well when I'd used them to stop Hunter and Cal from fighting. But Hunter hadn't told me.

"Is a power sink important?" Bree asked.

"Oh, yes," said Killian. "It's like turbocharging your magick—for both good and bad. I mean, sometimes magick shouldn't be turbocharged. Know what I mean?"

"No," Robbie said.

"I mean, some spells need to be gentle and shallow," Killian explained.

While he was talking, I felt paranoia creeping into my veins. Quickly I cast my senses out strongly, sweeping the area for any kind of danger, anything out of the ordinary. Killian looked at me, his brows knit together, but I didn't stop until I was sure there was nothing unusual going on. Then I met his gaze calmly, and he cocked his head to the side.

"Watch this," he said, and held out his left arm. He wore a thick suede glove on his hand and pulled the heavy wool tweed of his coat over his wrist. Then he opened his mouth and began to sing into the setting afternoon light. It was an odd, unholy song, in a voice nothing like his own. It sounded inhuman but also frighteningly, hauntingly beautiful. The notes rose and fell and waxed and waned, and all the time my half brother, Ciaran's son, watched the sky. I realized he was repeating the song over again, and we all started watching the sky also.

Slowly, in the deepening twilight, I became aware of a large bird wheeling above us, dropping down toward us in reluctant spirals of grace.

"Uh-oh," Ethan breathed, and Sharon moved closer to him.

I could now see that the bird was a large red-tailed hawk, big enough to pick up a small dog in its talons. It dipped and swayed above us, descending ever slower as if being reeled in on a kite string.

"What are you doing?" I whispered.

"I know its true name," Killian said. "It can't resist me."

We all stepped back as the large, powerful predator dropped the last eight feet, wings beating, to land on Killian's arm. I couldn't breathe. This wasn't a zoo bird, wings clipped so it couldn't fly. This was a raw piece of nature, a killing machine, with eyes the color of liquid gold and a beak designed for ripping open rabbits' stomachs like silk. Its talons gripped Killian's coat sleeve, but if it hurt, he didn't show it.

"So beautiful," Jenna whispered, looking mesmerized.

The bird was clearly nervous and afraid, not comprehending why it was here, so against its will, against its nature. I could smell the fear coming off it, an acrid fragrance overlaid by anger and humiliation.

"That is one fine bird," Ethan said in awe.

"Incredible," said Bree.

"Let it go," I said with clenched teeth. "Let it go now."

Killian looked at me in surprise—the killjoy—then spoke some words. Instantly, as if released from a prison, the hawk took off. Its powerful wings beat the air with a sound like a helicopter's rotors. Within seconds it was a dark speck in the sky, leaving us behind.

"Well," Killian began.

"It hated being here," I said impatiently. "It hated it. It was afraid."

Killian looked intrigued. "How do you know?"

"I felt it!" I said. "Just like you must have."

"How did you do that?" Raven asked, interrupting us.

Killian turned to her, as if he had forgotten his audience. "I know its true name. The song I sang was its true name, the name that it was born with. Everything has a true name that's irrevocable and individual and unmistakable. If you know something's true name, you have power over it."

"Is a true name like a coven name?" Matt asked.

Shaking his head, Killian said, "No. No one can give something else its true name. It's part of the thing or the person, like eye color or skin color or the size of your hands. You're born with it, you die with it."

"Do you have a true name?" Raven asked.

He laughed, showing the smooth column of his neck. "Of course. Everything has one, every person, every rock, every tree, every fish or bird or mammal. Crystals, metals—anything natural. They all have a true name. And if you know it, you own them."

I watched Killian intently. Own them? There was a difference between owning a living being versus a crystal or even a plant. I wondered what my true name was. A chill went down my spine as I considered what might happen if somebody else were to know it. If there was one thing I had learned over the past few months, it was that there were plenty of people out there who would love to be able to own me and my power.

"Does anyone else know your true name?" Robbie asked Killian. "Like your parents?"

"Oh, Goddess, no!" Killian looked appalled at the thought. "It gives someone power over you if they know your true name."

"You don't want your parents to know?" Robbie asked.

"And give them power over me? Never. I'd rather be dead." All his humor was gone, and his face was closed and set. He glanced at the empty, darkening sky. "It's getting late. We'd better go."

As we walked back to the cars, I thought about what Killian had just done. It had been beautiful—beautiful, painful magick. He had forced a living thing to act against its nature, and he had done it lightly, capriciously, and solely to impress. He had broken about a hundred council rules with this one stunt. If every witch were like this, it would be a disaster. I began to comprehend the role the council played in the order of witches.

I was almost to Das Boot when Killian took my arm gently. He leaned close to whisper in my ear: "Speaking of parents . . . I heard from Da. He's coming to see us."

10

Blood Ties

Brother Colin, my battles are usually of the spirit, but today I had one of the flesh. On the road home from Atherton to Barra Head, I saw three roadside bandits set upon Nuala Riordan.

I commanded them to unhand her, and two of them immediately set upon me. God forgive me, Brother Colin, but it was as if I were a lad once more, wrestling with you and Derwin. You'll remember that I always trounced you both at wrestling, and I trounced both those sorry louts today. As for the third, he fell into some sort of fit; with no warning he fell to the ground, writhing in pain. At last he fainted, and Nuala and I left with all haste.

Thanks be to God, she was unharmed. When I suggested that perhaps she should not leave the village without her husband, she looked at me oddly. Then boldly she told me she had no husband, nor a lover, either.

My cheeks burned at her frankness, Brother Colin, I admit it. Then, *as softly as a dove's wing, she said my name—Sinestus—and it was as if her very voice were weaving a spell around me. I left her as quickly as I could, for to speak truth, I feared the temptation of sin.*

It is time for vespers, Brother Colin, and then Brother Edmond is taking the post. I must finish this letter another time.

—Brother Sinestus Tor, to Colin, September 1768

"Well, I'm still fine," I told Aunt Eileen the next day. So far. I checked her name off my list of phone calls.

"Are you sure?" she asked. "Why don't you come spend the weekend here?"

"Oh, that's okay," I said. "I'm just going to stay home and study. I need to pull up some grades."

"You? Pull them up to what? What's past an A?"

I laughed nervously. We chatted a few more minutes, then hung up.

Next I called Mary K. at Jaycee's. It turned out that Jaycee's parents were taking the girls skiing for the weekend. I felt relief. I'd spent most of the night lying awake, dreading Ciaran's arrival. I wanted Mary K. away from here—I didn't want her associated with whatever happened between me and my blood father. I told her to be careful and to not break her leg and asked if she needed money, which she didn't. She was a chronic babysitter and consequently as rich as Midas.

"Take care," I told her. "Use your good manners."

She laughed at my Mom imitation.

Next on my phone list was Hunter. "I haven't heard from Killian yet," I reported. "I don't know when Ciaran's coming in."

"All right. Listen, I just got a cell phone. Write down this number."

I did.

"Now I need you to come to my house. Eoife's here, and we need to talk about plans and also teach you some spells you'll need to deal with Ciaran."

I sighed. So much for hitting the books today. "Okay," I said. "I'll be there soon."

"Try to hurry."

"All right." We said our good-byes, and I went to take a shower.

Hunter let me in half an hour later. When I saw Eoife perched on the couch in the living room, my mood darkened. She looked paler, more fragile than the last time I had seen her, as if she were carrying a heavier weight. She gave me a faint smile.

"So you were successful," she told me.

"Well, Killian says he's coming. We'll have to see if he does or not," I said.

"He'll come," said Hunter, already pouring tea. "Now, tell us again everything Killian has told you."

I did. I drank my tea, feeling its warmth slide down my throat, soothing me from the inside out. I told them about Killian finding the power sink at the cemetery and met Hunter's eyes. His expression betrayed nothing. I told them any snippets of conversation I had remembered, anything he had mentioned about his family. I felt disloyal to Killian, doing this, yet that had been the plan. That was what I had signed up for.

"Anything else?" Hunter said, his eyes on me.

I thought about the hawk spell and closed my mind to Hunter. I didn't even know why, except I didn't want to get

Killian in trouble. He didn't seem evil to me—just irresponsible. I wondered if he even understood the abuses that knowing something's true name might lead to. When I looked up, Eoife's eyes seemed to look right through me, and I prayed I didn't blush. I wasn't fooling either one of them. Was I already failing the inherent test in all this, my choosing good over evil not just sometimes, but every time? I felt so inadequate.

Hunter expelled his breath and sat back in his chair. He ran long fingers through his short blond hair, and to me it seemed like he only became more attractive every time I saw him. The bastard.

"Right," said Eoife, sitting up straighter. "So let's talk about Starlocket. Suzanna Mearis has come out of her coma but has paralysis on her left side. They're continuing to work healing spells but since they don't know exactly what spell Amyranth used against her, they haven't been successful. In the meantime smaller things continue to happen: Rina O'Fallon's car lost its steering, and she had an accident. Someone's cat was found dead of no apparent cause. Someone's winter garden wilted overnight in its cold frame."

I digested this silently.

"The noose is closing," Hunter murmured.

"Why can't they disband?" I asked, wanting it clarified.

"It's traditional not to, in times of trouble," Eoife said, her eyes sad. "The bond between coven members is considered unbreakable. Only in very rare, extraordinary circumstances do members separate during dangerous times." Her glance flicked toward Hunter, and I remembered again that his parents had fled along with the rest of their coven before it was destroyed by a dark wave. I wondered what that extraordinary circumstance had been, but Hunter's face gave no clue.

I felt that if I were in Starlocket, I'd be in Tennessee by now.

"They're determined to fight evil in all its forms," Eoife added. "But I did tell them that we're still working to infiltrate Amyranth, and they were much cheered by this news."

I looked at her blankly, then gulped when I realized that their only hope was me. If something happened to Alyce and Starlocket because I wasn't strong enough, good enough, how could I ever live with myself? Assuming I survived.

"Anyway," said Hunter briskly, "we need to teach you some sigils of concealment and more wards of protection."

"Yes," Eoife began, but then we were distracted by Sky's angry voice coming from the kitchen.

"Dammit, that's not what I meant, and you know it!" she was practically shouting.

"Who's here?" I asked. I hadn't picked up on anyone else's presence.

Hunter shook his head. "No one. She must be on the phone."

"Anyway, Morgan," Eoife went on, "one of the first things I want to teach you is a simple concealment spell. It doesn't lit- erally make you invisible, of course, but most people, animals, and even witches won't notice you're there."

I nodded. "Like a you-see-me-not spell."

Eoife looked startled. "You do this already?"

"Um, only occasionally," I answered, wondering if I had just stepped on more Wiccan toes. "You know, if I don't . . . uh, want to be seen."

Eoife shot Hunter a glance, and he sort of threw up his hands, as if I were an unhousebroken dog he'd tried his best with.

"Raven, I'm talking about last night!" Sky interrupted us loudly.

We all felt embarrassed to be hearing this conversation. Then Eoife shook her head and focused again.

"This spell should get you into and out of most situations," she said. "If Ciaran knows you quite well, if he's familiar with your vibrations and your aura, he may be able to pick up on it, but not right away."

"He knows some of that, if not all," I said, thinking back to New York. He'd tried to steal my magick, so yeah, he probably knew my aura.

"We'll have to do the best we can," Eoife said. "Ciaran is quite adept at knowing one intimately, only to use that knowledge to destroy. He enjoys destruction in and of itself, which is why he's so dangerous. He enjoys the act itself, not just the dividends. He is the opposite of a creator."

I hated hearing this about Ciaran but knew immediately it was true. What had happened in his life to make him that way? How much of his legacy had he passed on to me, to Killian, to his other children? Knowing he was evil the way I did, how could I still remember our odd connection with longing? What did that say about me?

Eoife moved to sit cross-legged in front of the fire crackling in Hunter's fireplace. Gesturing to me to sit across from her, she said, "We'll bolster this with other spells of protection and attack. With your inherent strength, I feel it will work. If you learn it perfectly."

Sitting across from Eoife on the floor, I tried to clear my mind and relax my breathing. I could still hear Sky in the kitchen, her voice rising and falling in anger. I tried to block it out. Hunter stayed where he was, in his chair, but I felt his eyes on me unwaveringly.

"We'll start with the words," said Eoife, starting to murmur them.

Leaning closer, I let my mind expand to envelop the softly spoken words. I loved spellcraft. There were so many different kinds: ones using crystals, oils, incenses, herbs. Ones using only words, ones combining words and gestures, ones made only within a circle and some you could make anywhere. This one had three parts: words, runes written in the air, and the casting of a glamor.

Ten minutes later I had the words and runes down pat and felt confident I would remember them. The casting of a glamor I would have to work on. It was odd, but unlike school learning, which could sometimes go in me like a stone sinking in water, never to be seen again—magick seemed quite different. I had never forgotten a spell. Once learned, it seemed part of the fabric of my being, another colored thread that made up the complete Morgan.

I almost jumped when Sky raised her voice again.

"No!" she shouted. "That's not what I'm saying. You're twisting my words."

I really didn't want to hear any more and had stood up to ask if we could go work in the circle room, when Sky stalked out of the kitchen, her black eyes shooting sparks of anger. She saw us sitting there, and her gaze lasered in on me.

"He's your brother," she said acidly. "You brought him here. He's a total bastard, and Raven's thick enough not to see it. But she should know better—after all, he's Woodbane." This last was spit at me, and I felt the blood drain from my face as she grabbed her black leather jacket and slammed out of the house. Outside I heard the roar of Sky's car as she peeled out, brakes squealing.

It was true: I had brought Killian here, and Raven was making a fool of herself over him, with his enthusiastic help. But I had brought him here at the council's wishes and for the greater good. I sat there feeling mortified, not knowing what to say. Hunter looked tight-lipped and withdrawn, but Eoife was calm as she arranged the tea things on their tray.

"This is all part of life, my dear," she said in her soft Scottish accent. "Even pain and embarrassment are part of it."

With a heavy sigh Hunter reached over and patted my knee. "Sky's just really angry. Not every Woodbane is evil," he said. "Your mother wasn't. Belwicket wasn't. I'm half Woodbane. There are many, many good Woodbanes out there."

"But not Killian, right?" I asked somberly. "And not Ciaran."

Neither Hunter nor Eoife spoke, and silently I reached for my coat and let myself out of that house. Once again my heritage was catching up to me.

11

Shades of Gray

I thank you for trying to intercede on my behalf, but it has been decided, Brother Colin. I have been remanded to the abbey at Habenstadt, in Prussia. I expected such action to be taken against me once I confessed my many sinful thoughts to Father Benedict. And how can I question the fairness, the wisdom of such a judgment? There, away from the source of my temptation, among the contemplatives, perhaps God will show me a path through my tortured mind. As for Nuala, she has disappeared. I pray that God watches over her.

—Brother Sinestus Tor, to Colin, April 1769

That night, at Bree's house, Raven didn't show for the circle. I'd arrived on time, and I was wearing cargo pants and a soft, thin sweater. After I'd gotten home from Hunter's, I'd felt depressed and confused, so I had cleaned the kitchen, done some laundry, scooped Dagda's box, and promised myself to try not to look so scruffy all the time.

After Bree opened the door, the first person I saw was Sky. I was still stinging from her Woodbane comment, but at the same time, I knew she was in love with Raven and getting burned and was not in a good frame of mind.

"I think we're all here," Hunter said. His voice sounded both rough and melodious, and for no good reason I suddenly remembered how his voice sounded in my ear, talking to me when we were making out, hearing his breath coming hard and fast because of what we were doing. I felt myself blush and turned away from him, taking a long time to dump my coat on the pile in the hallway.

"Let's go into the den," Bree said. "It's more comfy in there."

"Actually," Hunter said, "I checked it out and it's full of electronics and furniture. Do you have someplace more bare?"

Which is how we ended up sitting in a chalk circle on the flagstones at one end of her enclosed pool. Above us we could see the stars, wavering and dim through the glass enclosure. The furniture had been stacked and covered; the water was still and dark. The vibrations were very different here, surrounded by water and stone and glass.

"While we wait to see if Raven's coming," said Hunter, "let's go around the circle and get a quick rundown of what you've been up to, what you've been studying, any questions you have, and so on. We should be preparing for Imbolc, also. It's a time to think about new beginnings." He nodded to Matt, who was sitting on his right.

Matt was starting to look more like himself after weeks and weeks of looking both odd and somewhat disheveled. Tonight he was wearing a dark red shirt and black cords, and his thick black hair was neatly cut and brushed smoothly back. "I'm okay. I've been doing some general studying of correspondences—especially how to work with crystals."

"Good," said Hunter. "Next?"

Thalia sat up straighter. I didn't know Thalia all that well; like Alisa, she had been part of the original Kithic coven, led by Sky, before they had absorbed the six of us who had been in the Cirrus coven, originally led by Cal. "I've been crazed with a science project. Other than that I've been reading a book about candle-burning rituals. It's really interesting."

"I'm still doing a lot with the tarot," said Bree. "I'm really loving it. Every time I do a reading, it's like a therapy session. I have to sit and really think about what the cards said and how it applies to my life."

Robbie was next. "My dad lost his job. Again. Mom's threatening to kick him out. Again. He'll get another job, Mom will get off his back, everything will be back to normal. Again. It's a little stressful, but I'm used to it. In terms of Wicca, I've been reading Ellis Hindworth's *Basic History of the White Art*."

"That's a good book," said Hunter. "I hope things quiet down for you at home."

Sharon, Ethan, and Jenna all checked in. Simon Bakehouse, between Jenna and me, said he'd been studying Celtic deities.

I thought about how ironic it was that Amyranth was planning to destroy Starlocket at Imbolc, which is supposed to be a time of rebirth. It seemed especially horrible. I felt a twinge of panic at the weight of my responsiblity. When it was my turn to speak, I cleared my throat. "I've been studying a bunch of different stuff—history and spells and the basics of spellcraft. I'm having a hard time in school. And my parents are against Wicca."

Alisa Soto was next. Most of us were seventeen and eighteen, and so she, at fifteen, seemed very young. "My dad is against Wicca, too. He thinks it's some kind of weird cult. I don't get it. Two of my aunts practice Santeria, so he should accept alternative religions. I've been reading a biography about a woman who discovered Wicca and what it meant to her."

Last was Sky. She didn't look at any of us, and her voice was low and steady, almost expressionless. "I've been studying the medicinal uses of herbs. I'm thinking about going back to England for a while."

I looked at her in surprise, wondering if she wanted to leave because of how Raven was acting. Sky and I had never been close, but we had forged a mutually respectful relationship, and I would miss her if she left.

"Okay," said Hunter. He didn't look surprised. I figured that this must be something he and Sky had already discussed. Turning back to the circle, he held a hand out to each side. "I guess we can assume Raven's not coming, so let's stand up, join hands, close our eyes, and concentrate. Relax everything, release any pent-up energy, focus on your breathing, and open up to receive magick."

Now the twelve of us stood in a circle. Hunter and Bree had lit many candles, and they surrounded us, flickering with our movements. I was beneath stars, next to water, standing on stone, in a circle of magick, and I felt that quick, ecstatic fluttering in my chest that told me my body was open to receive what the Goddess wanted to give me.

Slowly we moved deasil around our central candle. Hunter started a basic power chant, one we'd used before. Our voices wove together like ribbons, like warm and cold ocean currents sliding into one. Our faces were lit by candles, by joy, by fellowship, by an unexpected yet required trust of each other. Our feet flew across the flagstones, our energy rose, and the magick came down and surrounded us, lifting our hearts, filling us with peace and excitement, making our hair crackle with static. During this time my worries about Ciaran, my dangerous mission, my fears all melted away. This was pure white magick, and it seemed a million miles away from the darkness and destruction that Ciaran represented.

I could have stayed in the circle all night, whirling, feeling the magick, feeling beautiful and strong and whole and safe. But gently, gently, Hunter brought it down, slowed our steps, smoothed the energy, and then we sank gently onto the stones again, our knees touching, our hands linked, our faces flushed and expectant.

"Everyone take a moment, close your eyes, and think of what you'll turn your energy toward," Hunter said softly. "What do you need help with, what are you ready to know, what are you able to give? Open your heart and let the answer come, and when you're finished, look up again."

My head drooped, and my eyes fluttered shut. There was a strong, pulsing cord of white magick inside me, there for the taking, there for me to use as I would. The answer came to me almost immediately. *Let me save Starlocket. Let me protect Alyce from harm.*

I straightened and opened my eyes to see Hunter looking at me intently. He blinked when I met his gaze and looked away. What had I seen in his eyes?

When everyone had looked up, we dropped our hands, and Hunter began the lesson.

"I want to talk about light and dark," he said, his English accent seeming elegant and precise. "Light and dark are, of course, two sides of the same coin. They make up everything we know in life. This concept has been more readily described as the principle of yin and yang. Light and dark are two halves of a whole. One cannot exist without the other. And, more important, they are connected by infinite shades of gray."

Uh-oh. I was starting to see where this was going. I'd had similar conversations with Cal and with David Redstone. The whole point of this light/dark concept is that it isn't always crystal clear what belongs on which side. Making a choice for good isn't always easy or even identifiable.

"For example," Hunter went on, "a microbe can kill—like botulinum toxin. But the same thing, in a tiny amount, can be healing. A knife can be used to save a life or to take it. Love can be the most joyous gift or a strangling prison."

So true, I thought, thinking of what I'd lost with Hunter. I also couldn't help flicking my eyes toward Sky. Her face was composed, she was looking at the ground, but at Hunter's words a delicate pink blush bloomed on her pale cheeks.

"The sun itself is necessary for life," Hunter said, "but it can also burn crops, make people die of thirst, sear our skin until blisters form. A fire, too, can bring life, make our food healthy, help protect us—but it can also be a raging avenger, consuming everything in its path, taking life indiscriminately, and leaving behind nothing but ash."

I swallowed, a mosaic of fire images dancing in front of me. Fire and I had a love/hate relationship. Fire and I had been close allies until Cal had tried to kill me with fire . . . and fire had been Ciaran's weapon against my mother.

"Light and dark," Hunter said. "Two halves of a whole. Everything we do, say, feel, express—it all has two sides. Which side to promote is a decision we each make every day, many times a day."

I felt like Hunter was speaking directly to me. The differences between light and dark, good and evil were simply blurred for me sometimes. Almost every experienced witch I had ever spoken to had confessed the same thing. The horrible thing was, the more you learned, the less clear it was. Which was why an unshakable inner compass of morality was so necessary. Which was what Hunter was trying so hard to help me develop.

I sighed.

After the circle Bree pulled out some sodas, seltzer, and munchies, and we fell on them. I often craved something sweet after making magick, and now I eagerly downed some chocolate-chip zucchini bread.

"This is delicious," Jenna said, taking a slice of the bread. "Did you make this, Bree?"

Bree laughed. "Please. I don't know how to work an oven. Robbie made it."

I avoided talking to either Hunter or Sky, and when people started going home, I nipped out the door to my car. I was exhausted and wanted to digest tonight's magick. I didn't want to talk or think about light and dark anymore. I wanted to go home and fall into bed. For the first time since my parents had left, I wished they were home, waiting for me. It wasn't that I hadn't missed them so far—but I hadn't felt a need for them. Tonight I knew I would have been comforted by their presence in the house.

As I pulled into my dark driveway, I wondered where Raven had been tonight. Had she blown off Sky because of their fight, or had she and Killian gotten together?

My chest felt heavy and my hands were cold as I went into the house. In my room I got ready for bed. With Dagda snuggled next to me, purring, I lay in the dark for a long time, thinking. Killian couldn't be trusted, not really. And Ciaran was getting closer with every breath.

It was a long time before I slept.

12

Ciaran

Thank you, Brother Colin, for your kind words and also the gift of wine you sent. I have added it to the abbey's cellar, and Father Josef was most appreciative. Thanks be to God, I am well, though still troubled by confusing visions and dreams. My knowledge of the Prussian language is expanding greatly, and I am in awe of the abbey's library of precious and holy books. They have amassed a glorious storehouse of religious works, and I believe they are most selective about with whom they share this wealth.

Here, living, working, and praying in silence, I feel that I am free from my troubles of the past.

—Brother Sinestus Tor, to Colin, April 1770

When I awoke on Sunday, I lay in bed until my head seemed clear. I wondered what my parents were doing and if they had church services on cruise ships. Surely they did. I wondered if Mary K. had found a Catholic church near their ski resort. Since I had discovered Wicca, my sister had thrown herself into Catholicism with a vengeance.

"Maybe I'll go to church," I said out loud.

Dagda sat on the kitchen table, where he was so not allowed, and washed a front paw. He looked at me with his solemn gray kitty face, his big green eyes. "I just feel like it," I told him, then went upstairs to get dressed.

My family has been going to St. Mary's all my life. It's like attending a family reunion. I had to talk to five people before I even sat down.

The thing about Catholicism is that it can be comforting. It provides a structure to live your life within. In Wicca everything is wide open: choices about good and bad, ideas about how to live your life, ideas about how you celebrate Wicca and all its facets. Nothing is really, truly set in stone. Which was why individual knowledge is so important, because each witch has to determine all these things for herself. The way I saw Wicca, it was more based on the individual's choices and beliefs and less based on a set of rules. However, along with freedom comes responsibility and the increased possibility of completely screwing up.

Today, as I sat and knelt and stood automatically, reciting words and singing hymns, I was able to see some of the things that Wicca and Catholicism shared. They both had days of observation, reflection, and celebration, according to the year's cycle. Some Wiccan Sabbats and Catholic Holy Days of Obligation coincided—noticeably Easter, which occurs at the same time in both religions, except we called it Ostara in Wicca. Both holidays celebrate rebirth and use the same symbols: lambs, rabbits, lilies, eggs.

Both religions used external tools and symbols: sacred cups, incense, prayer/meditation, robes, candles, music, flowers.

To me it offered a continuity that helped me make the transition from one to the other. I hadn't completely given up being a Catholic—I didn't truly see how I ever could. But more and more my soul was turning to Wicca. It seemed a path I couldn't go backward on.

The choir filed out, singing, their voices raised in one of my favorite hymns. Father Thomas, his censer swinging, walked past, followed by the cross and Father Bailey. When it was my pew's turn to leave, I fell in line. I felt pleased and calmed and was glad I'd be able to tell my parents I'd attended services today. The rest of the day stretched before me, open, and I began to think about what I should do.

I was almost to the doors when my gaze fell lightly on someone sitting in the last pew, waiting for his turn to exit. Then my heart stopped, and my breathing snagged in my throat. Ciaran. My father.

He saw me recognize him. Standing, he followed me as I left the church, passing through the tall, heavily carved wooden doors. My heart kicked into gear again and thumped almost painfully in my chest. This was my mother's soul mate: the one person meant for her to love and to love her. And they had loved each other desperately. But he'd already been married; Maeve wouldn't be with him, and so he had killed her.

Killed her. A cold knife of fear slashed through my belly. Ciaran could have killed me, too—hungry for my power, wanting to use it to strengthen Amyranth. I was entirely convinced that I was going to die at his hands until he had realized who I was and allowed Hunter to set me free and transport me to safety. Now we were going to meet again. What to expect? Should I be afraid now? How could we ever have a normal conversation?

Outside the church the sunlight hurt my eyes, and the

daylight seemed harsh after the dim church. I smiled and nodded good-bye to several people, then took a left and walked
around the side of the church to a small, winter-dead garden.
Ciaran followed a few steps behind. When we were apart
from everyone else, I turned back to him. My eyes drank him
in, trying to see the person who had almost killed me in New
York—and then had helped to save my life. Our eyes were
similar; his hair was darker and flecked with silver. He was
handsome and barely more than forty.

"My son contacted me," he said in his lilting accent, that
deep, melodious voice that entered my bloodstream like
maple syrup. "He said that he was here with you. I thought
perhaps he had called me at your request."

"Yes," I said, trying to project courage. "He did. I met
Killian in New York. I realized he and I were half siblings. I
don't have any other siblings except your other children—not
by blood." Mary K., please forgive me again. "I asked him to call
you. I decided I wanted to know you because you're my biological father." All this was true, more or less. Very subtly I
shut down my mind so he couldn't get in and projected an air
of innocence and frankness.

His eyes on me were as sharp as snakes' fangs. "Yes," he said
after a moment. "You're the daughter I didn't know about. My
youngest. Maeve's daughter. Your coloring is more like mine,
but your mouth is hers, the texture of your skin, your height
and slenderness. Why didn't she tell me about you, I wonder?"

"Because she was scared of you," I said, trying to control
the anger that was seeping into my voice. "You'd threatened
her. You were married and couldn't be with her." *You killed her.*
"She wanted to protect me."

Ciaran looked around. "Is there someplace we could go?"
I thought for a moment. "Yes."

The Clover Teapot had opened winter before last, on a little side street off Main. It was the closest thing we had to an English-style tea shop, and it seemed appropriate. Also, it was public and safe. I still wasn't sure what to expect from Ciaran. When we had ordered and sat at a small table by the front window, I felt his keen eyes on me again.

"Have you seen Killian?" I asked, playing with the handle of my teacup.

"Not yet. I will soon. I wanted to see you first."

We sat there, looking at each other, and I felt him cast his senses toward me. I shut him out gently, and his eyes widened almost in amusement.

"How long have you known you're a witch?" he asked.

"Four months, a little less."

"You're not initiated." It was a statement.

"No." I shook my head.

"Goddess," he said, and took a sip of his tea. "You know your powers are unusual."

"That's what they tell me."

"Who is your teacher? The Seeker?"

"Well, not really formally. It's hard because I also have regular school. And my parents don't feel comfortable with the whole Wicca thing," I surprised myself by saying. Ciaran was easy to confide in. I had to be on guard against that. Was he already spelling me, trying to get inside my mind?

"I can't believe any child of mine has to be concerned about such banalities," he said.

I sat there, trying not to look stupid. Despite having known about his coming, I felt ridiculously unprepared to deal with him, to have a conversation with him. How could I have a normal conversation with the man who had killed my mother, had tried to kill me? Only my sense of obligation to Starlocket and my affection for Alyce kept me from giving in to fear and getting the hell out of there. Did he already know I was working for the council? He knew Hunter and I were—had been—going out. Was he just playing with me before he struck me down?

"You should have grown up surrounded by gifted teachers who would have helped you develop your natural powers," he went on. "You should have grown up among the moors and rocks and winds of Scotland. You'd be unmatchable." He looked regretful. "You should have grown up with me and with Maeve." A spasm of pain crossed his face.

He was unbelievable. He had been *married*, had seduced my mother, then followed her to America and *killed* her because she wouldn't be with him. And Amyranth had no doubt been responsible for Belwicket's destruction! And now he was all upset because we hadn't been a happy little family. I looked down at my tea, numb with disbelief.

"I've asked people about you," he went on, and I almost choked on my lemon Danish. "I've found out surprisingly little. Just that Cal Blaire sniffed you out, revealed you to yourself, and then he and Selene tried to seize your power." His eyes were steady on my face. "And you resisted them. Did you help kill them?"

Blood drained from my face, and I felt almost faint for a moment. My anger fled. I had intended to control this interview, to lead him where I needed him to go, to get information out of him. What a naive plan that had been. "Yes," I whispered, looking out the lace-curtained window to the street outside. "I didn't mean to. But I had to stop them. They wanted to kill me."

"Just like you tried to stop me in Manhattan," he said. "Would you have killed me if you could? When you were on the table, knowing your powers were about to be taken from you—if you could have stopped it by killing me, would you?"

What kind of question was that? Would I kill him to save myself, when he had killed my mother, when I had never known him as a father? "Yes," I said, resenting his easy manner. "I would have killed you."

Ciaran looked at me. "Yes," he said. "I think you would. You're strong. Strong not only in your powers, but in yourself. There isn't anything weak about you. You're strong enough to do what needs to be done."

If he had been anyone else, I would have blurted how often I felt afraid, weak, incapable, inadequate. But we weren't really having a father-daughter chat. I needed him to give himself up to me.

"Do you still want to kill me, Morgan?" he asked, and the pull of his question felt like a tide, drawing me out to sea.

Resist, I thought. How to answer? "I don't know," I said finally. "I know I can't."

"That's an honest answer," he said. "It's all right. You must do what you can to protect not only yourself, but your beliefs, your way of life, your heritage. Your birthright. And it's amazing how often others want to impinge on these things."

I nodded.

He looked at me speculatively, as if wondering if I were genuine. I tried to relax, but I couldn't. My palms were sweating, and I rubbed them against my skirt. This was Ciaran, and as much as I wanted to take him apart and throw away the pieces, there was a part of me that still wanted to run into his arms. *Father.* How sick was that?

"Have you met witches who think badly about Woodbanes?" he asked.

"Yes."

"How does that make you feel?" He poured more hot water into his cup and dipped in the mesh ball filled with tea leaves again.

"Angry," I said. "Embarrassed. Frustrated."

"Yes. Any witch who can trace his or her heritage back to one of the Seven Great Clans has been given a gift. It's wrong to be ashamed of being Woodbane or to deny your heritage."

"If only I knew more about it," I said, leaning forward. "I know I'm Woodbane. I know Maeve was from Belwicket, and they were a certain kind of Woodbane. I know you're Woodbane, and you're different. Your coven in New York was totally different from the covens I've seen. I read things in books, and it's like everyone blames the Woodbanes for everything. I hate it." I spoke more vehemently than I had intended to, and when Ciaran smiled at me, I was startled by how it pleased me.

"Yes," he said, looking at me. "I hate it, too." He shook his head, watching me. "I'm proud of you, my youngest, unknown daughter. I'm proud of your power, your sensibility, and your intelligence. I deeply regret that I didn't see you grow up, but I'm glad I have the opportunity to know you now." He took a sip of his tea while I tried to get a handle on my emotions. "But do I know you?" he murmured, almost to himself. "I think I don't."

My breath stopped as I wondered what he meant, if he was about to accuse me of trying to trap him. What could he do here, in the tea shop?

"But I want to change that," he said.

That night I found out that if you lie with your head flat on the open page of a textbook, you don't necessarily absorb knowledge any faster than if you read the words. God, it was impossible to concentrate on this stuff! What the hell difference did it make which general did what in the Revolutionary War? None of this made any difference in my life whatsoever. All it did was prove I could memorize, and so what?

The phone startled me from my history-induced coma, and I could tell immediately it wasn't Hunter. Eoife? I had already called to tell her about my tea with Ciaran, so it seemed unlikely that she would call again so soon. Killian? Oh, God, could I handle another marathon Killian party?

"Morgan?" The voice on the other end greeted me before I could even say hello, and it took me a second to place it.

"Ciaran?"

"Right. Listen, Killian and I are having dinner at a place called Pepperino's. Would you like to join us?"

My head felt foggy from too much studying. I tried to make sense of Ciaran's invitation. Dinner with my murderous father and unpredictable, charming half brother? Could I think of a better way to spend my Sunday night? "Sure, I'd love to. I'll be right there."

Pepperino's is an upscale Italian restaurant in downtown Widow's Vale. It has tuxedoed waiters, white tablecloths, and candles, and the food is incredible. My parents went there sometimes for a birthday or an anniversary. It was almost empty since it was late Sunday night, and the maître d' led me to Ciaran's table.

"Morgan, welcome," said Ciaran, standing up. He shot Killian a glance, and Killian also stood up. I smiled at them both and sat down.

"We've just ordered," said Ciaran. "Tell me what you'd like. The waiter says the calamari ravioli is superb."

"Oh, no thanks," I said. "I already ate. Maybe just some tea?"

When the waiter came, Ciaran ordered me a cup of darjeeling and a slice of mocha cheesecake. I watched him, thinking how incredibly different he was from the father I had grown up with—my real dad. My real dad is sweet, vague, and slow to anger. My mom usually takes care of the money, the insurance, anything complicated. Ciaran seemed like he was always in charge, always knew the answer, could always come through. It would have been quite different, growing up with him. Not better, I knew, though we did seem to have a connection. Just different.

Ciaran and Killian were drinking wine that was a deep, dark purple-red. I detected the scent of crushed grapes and oranges and some kind of spice I couldn't identify. My mouth watered, and I wished I could have some, but I had sworn never to drink again for the rest of my life. I could almost taste the full, heavy flavor.

The waiter brought their appetizers and my cheesecake at the same time, and we all began to eat. How could I make this meeting work for me? I needed information. Thinking about this, I took a bite of cheesecake and smothered a moan. It was incredibly rich, incredibly dense, with notes of sour cream riddled with streams of sweet, smooth coffee and dark chocolate. It was the most perfect thing I had ever eaten, and I took tiny bites to make it last longer.

"Tell me about growing up here," said Ciaran. "In America, not knowing your heritage."

I hesitated. I needed to share enough to make him feel that I trusted him, yet also protect myself from giving him any knowledge he could use against me. Then it occurred to me that he was so powerful, he could use *anything* against me and my being on guard was a waste of time.

"When I was growing up, I didn't know I was adopted. So I believed my heritage was Irish, all the way through. Catholic. All my relatives are, all the people at my church. I was just one more."

"Did you feel like you belonged?" Ciaran had a way of cutting to the heart of a matter, slicing through smoke and details to get at the very core of meaning.

"No," I said softly, and took a sip of the tea. It was light and delicate. I took another sip.

"You wouldn't have fit in any better in my village," Killian broke in. His face looked rough and handsome in the dim light of the restaurant, his hair shot through with gold and wine-colored strands. He didn't have Ciaran's grace or sophistication or palpable power, but he was friendly and charming. "It was a whole town of village idiots."

I was startled into laughter, and he went on. "There wasn't a normal person among us. Every single soul was some odd character that other people had to watch out for. Old Sven Thorgard was a Vikroth who had settled in our town, Goddess knows why. The only magick he worked was on goats. Healing goats, finding goats, making goats fertile, increasing goats' milk."

"Really?" I laughed nervously. As hard as Killian was trying to entertain us, Ciaran was still watching us both with a suspicious, dark expression. I wondered whether that was his response to Killian or just evidence that he was actually planning to do away with the both of us.

"Really," Killian said. "Goddess, he was weird. And Tacy Humbert—"

At the mention of that name, Ciaran broke into a smile and shook his head. He drank some wine and poured a tiny drop more in Killian's glass. I relaxed a bit.

"Tacy Humbert was love starved," Killian said in a loud whisper. "I mean starved. And she wasn't bad-looking. But she was such a shrew that no one would take her out more than once. So she'd put love spells on the poor sap."

Ciaran chuckled. "Her aim wasn't perfect."

"Perfect!" Killian exclaimed. "Goddess, Da, do you remember the time she zapped old Floss? I had that dog climbing all over me for a week!"

We all laughed, but I thought I detected a warning glance exchanged between Ciaran and Killian. I wondered what Ciaran's problem was. I loved hearing about the very different life Killian had lived in Scotland. "Here, top us up, Da," Killian said, holding out his wineglass.

With narrowed eyes Ciaran filled it half full, then put the bottle on the other side of the table. Killian gave Ciaran a challenging look, but being ignored, he sighed and drained his glass.

"Were there many Woodbanes in your village?" I asked.

Killian nodded, his mouth full. He swallowed and said, "Mostly Woodbanes. A couple of others. People on the outside of the village or who had married into families. My ma's family has been there longer than folks can remember, and they're Woodbanes back to the beginning."

At the mention of Killian's mother, a shadow passed over

Ciaran's face. He toyed with the last of his salad and didn't look at Killian.

"It must have been nice, being surrounded by people like you. Feeling like you fit in, like you belong," I said. "All celebrating the same holidays." Like Imbolc.

"It is nice to have an all-Woodbane community," Ciaran put in smoothly. "Particularly because of the commonly held view that most witches have about us. If it were up to them, we would be broken up and disbanded."

"What do you mean?" I asked.

"I mean, Woodbanes are like any other cultural or ethnic group who has been forcibly dispersed. The Romany in Europe. The Native Indians here. The Aborigines in Australia. These were intact cultures that other cultures found threatening and so were killed, separated, dispersed, exiled. Within the Wiccan culture, Woodbanes have been cast in that role. The other clans fear us and so must destroy us."

"How do you fight that?" I asked.

"Any way I can," he said. "I protect myself and my own. I've joined with other Woodbanes who feel the same way."

"Amyranth," I said.

"Yes." His gaze rested on me for a moment.

"Tell me about them," I said, trying to sound casual. "What's it like to have an all-Woodbane coven?"

"It's powerful," said Ciaran. "It makes us feel less vulnerable. Like American pioneers, circling their wagons at night to keep intruders out."

"I see." I nodded, I hoped not too enthusiastically. Maybe this was my chance, I realized. Ciaran was opening up. Talking about our Woodbane heritage seemed to animate him, to make him less suspicious. I remembered the sigil and thought if I could just touch his arm, in a loving, daughterly gesture, I might be able to quickly trace the sigil on his sleeve. . . .

"I'm glad to hear you say that," I said confidently, shifting my chair closer. "Woodbanes are persecuted, so it's only natural that we'd try to protect ourselves, right?" I smiled, and Ciaran only regarded me curiously. It was impossible to read that expression. Did he trust me? Trying to keep my hand from shaking, I lifted it from my lap. I will touch his hand and say thank you, I thought. Thank you for telling me that I shouldn't be ashamed of my heritage. I reached out to touch him. "Th—"

"Excuse me for a moment," Ciaran broke in, rising. He headed toward the back of the restaurant, and Killian and I were left alone. I was stunned. I moved my hand back to my lap. What was he doing? Had I been too obvious? Was he calling Amyranth to get help in capturing me again?

Ciaran had left his suit jacket folded over the back of his chair, and my eyes lit on it. If I could put the watch sigil on his jacket . . . But Killian's bright gaze stopped me.

"Do you have plans for Imbolc?" I asked quickly.

Killian shrugged, giving me an almost amused expression. Had he seen what I was thinking? "I'll hook up with a coven somewhere. I love Imbolc. Maybe I could sit in with Kithic."

"Maybe," I said evasively, wondering what Hunter's plans were for our celebration.

Ciaran was back in a few minutes and paid the check. I didn't sense any anger in his demeanor. He put on his jacket, and I regretted not tracing the sigil on it. What to do now? Should I press him for information? Goddess, I was bad at this.

"Morgan, can you come to the house where Killian's staying?" Ciaran asked as we left Pepperino's. "It's the house of a friend who's currently out of the country. She's been kind enough to let him stay there."

As I looked at Ciaran, trying to remain calm, terror gripped at my insides and refused to let go. This was the perfect opportunity to learn more about their plans and to plant the watch sigil. Yet the thought of actually being with Ciaran and Killian was beyond terrifying. What if he'd seen what I'd been trying? What if he was leading me back to the house to punish me for it?

"I got a glimpse of your remarkable powers in New York," he continued. "I'd like to see how much you know and teach you some of what I know. I'm impressed with your gifts, your strength, your bravery."

My glance flicked to Killian, who was carefully blank-faced.

He could kill me, I thought with a sick certainty. He could finish the job he was planning to do in New York. I tried hard to fight my fear—wasn't this what I'd been praying for all those party nights with Killian?—but my terror was too strong. I could only think about getting out of there.

I was hopeless. As a secret agent, I was a fraud.

"Gosh, I really can't," I said lamely, hoping I didn't sound as terrified as I felt. "It's late, and I've, um, got school tomorrow." I tried to produce a convincing yawn. "Can I take a rain check?"

"Of course," said Ciaran smoothly. "Another time. You have my number."

Another time. I gulped and nodded. "Thanks for dessert."

13

Comfort

Brother Colin, I am sure you will be most distraught to learn that I have received a letter from her. The abbot of course reads my post, and I cannot imagine he would let a missive from her pass, so perhaps the letter was spelled. (Do not think this to be my insensate fear—I am quite certain that the villagers of Barra Head had powers beyond what I as a mortal can comprehend.)

Naturally once I realized who it was from, I turned it over to Father Edmond and have since been praying in the chapel. But I could not stop myself from reading it, Brother Colin.

She wrote that she has been living in Ireland, in a hamlet called Ballynigel, and that she was delivered of a girl child at summer's end last year. The child, she says, is sturdy and bright.

I shall pray to God to forgive her sins, as I pray for forgiveness of mine.

She intends to return to Barra Head. I do not know why she

continues to torment me. I do not know what to think and fear a return of the brain fever that so weakened me two years ago.

Pray for me, Brother Colin, as I do for you.

—Brother Sinestus Tor, to Colin, October 1770

"All right, class," said Mr. Alban. "Before we start on 'The Nun's Tale,' I'd like you all to hand in your compositions. Make sure your name is on them."

I stared at my English teacher in horror as my classmates began to bustle purposefully, pulling out their compositions. Oh, no! Not again! I knew about this damn composition! I'd picked out my topic and done some preliminary research! But it wasn't due until . . . I quickly checked my homework log. Until today, Monday.

I almost broke a pencil in frustration as everyone around me handed up their papers and I had nothing to hand in. I was seriously screwing up. I had zero excuse except that my life seemed to be about more important things lately—like life or death. Not Chaucer, not compositions, not trig homework. But actual life, the life I would be leading from now on. I had five days until Imbolc.

The rest of the day passed in a drone. When the final bell rang, I went outside and collapsed on the Killian-less stone bench, feeling very depressed. I was confused; it was hard to focus; I felt like a horse was standing on my chest. I couldn't even summon the mental or physical energy to go home and meditate, which usually pulled all my pieces together.

"You look beat," Bree said, sitting next to me.

I groaned and dropped my head into my hands.

"Well, Robbie and I are going to Practical Magick," she said. "Want to come?"

"I can't," I said. "I should go home and study." Actually, I would have loved to have gone, but it seemed likely that Ciaran was keeping tabs on me. I didn't want him to have a chance to suspect I was working with Alyce on anything. There was only a handful of days before Imbolc. I felt the clock ticking even as I sat there.

As the Kithic members drifted off, I felt sad and alone. My miserable failure last night weighed heavily on my conscience. If I had had the guts to go with Ciaran, who knows—I might be done with the mission by now. I had spent the entire day kicking myself, yet the memory of my terror was so real. I understood why I had refused to go; I just wished that somehow I could conquer my fear.

Across the parking lot my sister waved at me as she and Alisa got into Jaycee's mom's minivan. I'd talked to her this morning—she'd had a great time skiing.

I missed Hunter with a physical pain. If only he could be right by my side during this whole mission. I knew I had to see Ciaran and Killian again. I had to find out the exact time of the dark wave and possibly some of the spell words. I had to try to put a watch sigil on Ciaran. Part of me actually wanted to see them again, despite my mistrusting them and my deep-seated fear of Ciaran. They drew me to them because we were related by blood. Oh, Goddess. What to do?

The honk of a car's horn made me jump. Hunter's Honda glided to a halt next to me, and the passenger door opened.

"Come," he said.

I got in.

*   *   *

We didn't speak. Hunter drove us to his house, and I followed him up the steps and inside. Neither Sky nor Eoife was there, and I was grateful. In the kitchen Hunter still didn't speak but starting frying bacon and scrambling eggs. It occurred to me how hungry I was.

"Thanks," I said as he put a plate in front of me. "I didn't even know I was hungry."

"You don't eat enough," he said, and I wondered if I should take offense. I decided I would rather eat than argue, so I let it go.

"So," he said. "Tell me what's going on."

Once I opened my mouth, everything poured out. "Everything is so difficult. I mean, I like Killian. I don't think he's a bad guy. But I'm spying on him and using him. I think that Ciaran mistrusts me, but he also seems to—to care about me. And I'm completely terrified of him and of what he tried to do to me, what he did to my mother, what he's done to others. But I wonder how this is going to end. I mean, I'm going to betray both of them. What will they do to me?"

Hunter nodded. "If you weren't feeling these things, I'd be bloody worried. I don't have any answers for you—except that the ward-evil spells you know are more powerful than any you've worked before. And the council—and I—are going to protect you with our lives. You aren't alone in this, even if you feel that way. We're always with you."

"Are you following me around?"

"You're not alone," he repeated wryly. "You're one of us, and we protect our own." He cleaned his plate, then said, "I know Ciaran is incredibly charismatic. He's not just a regular witch. From the time he was a child, he showed exceptional powers. He was lucky enough to be trained well, early on. But it's not only his powers. He's one of those witches who seems to have an innate ability to connect with others, to know them intimately, to evoke special feelings in them. In humans this kind of person, if they're good, ends up a Mother Teresa or Gandhi. If they're bad, you get a Stalin or an Ivan the Terrible. In Wicca you get a Feargus the Bright or a Meriwether the Good. Or, on the other side, a Ciaran MacEwan."

Great. My biological father was the Wiccan equivalent of Hitler.

"The thing is," Hunter went on, "all of those people were very charismatic. They have to be to influence others, to make others want to follow them, to listen to them. You're confused and maybe scared about your feelings for Ciaran. It's perfectly natural to have those feelings. You're related by blood; you want to know your father. But because of who he is and what he's done, you're going to have to betray him. It's an impossible situation and one that I didn't want you to take on, for just these reasons."

Hearing him imply he didn't think I could handle it made me want to insist I could. Which might have been why he said it. "It's not just that," I said. "It's other stuff. I mean, I like the way he talks about Woodbanes. Everyone else hates Woodbanes. I'm sick of it. I can't help who I am. It's a relief to be around someone who doesn't feel that way."

"I know. Even being half Woodbane, I catch that some-times." Hunter cleared our places and ran the water in the sink. "A lot of that is old-fashioned prejudice from people who just don't know better. But covens like Amyranth do tend to set us back hundreds of years. Here's a group of pure Woodbanes who feel justified to murder and pillage other covens simply because they're not Woodbane. One coven like them can ruin things for the rest of us for a long, long time."

He was talking about the awful things Ciaran had done, and the thought of all the people he had killed made me shiver. My father was a murderer. I was right to be scared to be alone with him. In the end, Hunter hadn't made me feel better—but I didn't know if that had been his intention in the first place. He drove me back to school, to my waiting car, as silent as he had been on the ride to his house.

"Morgan," he said as I started to get out. I looked at him, at the glitter of his green eyes in the dim glow of the dashboard lights. "It's not too late to change your mind. No one would think worse of you."

His concern made my heart constrict painfully. "It is too late," I said bleakly, grabbing my backpack. "I would think worse of me. And if you're honest, you'll admit that you would, too."

He said nothing as I swung out of the car and headed for Das Boot.

14

Father

Brother Colin, you would hardly recognize me. I have lost almost three stone since last autumn. I can neither eat nor sleep. I have given up on myself; I am lost. God has chosen that I should pay for my sins on earth as well as in the burning fires to come.

—Brother Sinestus Tor, to Colin, February 1771

On Tuesday morning when I got in Das Boot to go to school, I found a book on the front seat. I was sure I had locked the car the night before. I'm the only person with a key. With a sense of foreboding, I climbed into the driver's seat and picked up the book. It was large and bound in tattered, weather-beaten black leather. On its cover, stamped in gold that was now almost completely flaked off, was the title: *An Historical View of Wodebayne Life.*

I turned the book this way and that and flipped through crumbling pages the color of sand. There was no note, nothing to say where this had come from or why. I closed my eyes for a moment and spread my right hand out flat on the cover. A thousand impressions came to me: people who had held the book, sold it, stolen it, hidden it, treasured it, left it on their shelf. The most distinct impression, no more than a fluttery butterfly-soft trembling, came from Ciaran. I opened my eyes. He had left this book for me. Why? Would having this book spell me somehow? Was it a no-strings gift or a devious trap? I had no clue.

At school I joined Kithic on the basement steps. Alisa was there, which was unusual, so I made a point to say hi.

I didn't mention the book, which I had just barely squeezed into my backpack, but sat down as Raven informed us all that she and Sky had broken up.

"It just wasn't working, you know?" she said, popping her gum in an ungothlike manner. "She couldn't accept me for who I am. She wanted me to be as dull and serious as she is."

"I'm sorry, Raven," I said, and I was. Raven had seemed a little softer, a little bit more happy, when she and Sky had first gotten together. Now she seemed so much more like her old self: cold, calculating, uncaring. I wondered if my bringing Killian to town had been the thing to finish off their relationship or whether it would have crumbled on its own. I couldn't decide.

"Yeah, well, don't be," she said, shrugging. "I'm glad to be out of it." She almost sounded sincere. But when I cast out lightly with my witch senses, I felt a surprising level of pain, sadness, confusion.

I waited for someone to mention Killian or to ask Raven pointed questions about him, but to my relief, no one did. I was pretty sure Killian had a lot to do with this breakup, whether or not he realized it or cared.

When the bell rang, I lugged my backpack to homeroom, feeling the book calling to me to read it. In English class I had a chance to and opened it up under my desk. It was written in old-fashioned language and had no copyright date or publishing info. The type was hard to read, which made it slow going. But after the first page I was hooked. It was fascinating. As far as I could tell, it was a nonfiction account of a monk's life, back in the 1770s. He had been sent to a far-off village to bring God to the pagans. I could barely take my eyes away from the pages and wondered why Ciaran had wanted me to read it.

I managed to escape detection through the whole class, and when the bell rang, I sneaked it back into my backpack and went up to Mr. Alban.

"Morgan," he said. "I seem to be missing your composition. Did you forget to turn it in?"

"No," I admitted, embarrassed. "I'm sorry, Mr. Alban—I spaced it. But I wanted to ask if I could do a makeup paper—maybe six pages long instead of four? I could turn it in next Monday."

He looked at me thoughtfully. "Ordinarily I would say no," he said. "You had plenty of time to do this paper, and every other student managed to turn it in on time. But this is unusual for you—you've always been a good student. I tell you what—turn in six pages, double spaced, on Monday, and we'll see."

"Oh, thanks, Mr. Alban," I said, relieved. "I absolutely will turn it in. I promise."

"Okay. See that you do."

I trotted off to calculus, already planning my outline.

*　　　*　　　*

Morgan. The power sink.

I looked up, though I knew I wouldn't see Ciaran.

"Morgan?" asked Bree. "What is it? You were in the middle of telling me about Mr. Alban."

"Oh, nothing." I shook my head. "Yeah, so he's letting me do a makeup paper. It's going to be cool, and this time I won't forget."

I sent a message back. *Tea shop?*

Fine, Ciaran responded.

"I said, do you want to go to the mall tonight?" Bree repeated patiently. "We could grab something to eat, shop, get home early."

"That sounds good," I said. "But I can't. Homework."

"Okay. Some other time." Bree walked toward her car, her fine dark hair being whipped by the wind.

On the way to the Clover Teapot, I tried to concentrate on my mission. Four days remained. It was still possible. I needed to get more information out of Ciaran. I needed to plant the watch sigil on him. I'll do it, I promised myself. Today is the day. I will accomplish my mission.

When I got there, Ciaran was already sitting at one of the smaller tables. I ordered and sat down, once again looking at him closely, seeing myself in him, seeing the possibilities of who or what I could have been or might still be. If I had grown up with him as my teacher, my father, would I now be evil? Would I care? Would I have almost unlimited powers? Would it matter?

I felt him looking at me as I took a sip of Red Zinger tea, holding the paper cup to warm my fingers. I needed a good opening. "Is it true that kids in Killian's village don't have to go to school?"

"Not to a government school," he said. "The village parents get home-schooling certificates. As long as the children can pass the standard tests . . ." He shrugged. "They can read and write and do sums. It's just that all the indoctrination, the governmental oppression, the skewed view of history—they don't get that."

"How much did you teach Killian, and Kyle, and Iona?" Killian had told me the names of his siblings. My other half brother, my half sister.

A troubled look clouded Ciaran's face, and he looked out the window into the thin, pale winter sunlight. "Is there somewhere else we could talk? More private? I had mentioned the power sink. . . ."

"I have an idea," I said. I stood up and gathered my cup of tea and a scone in a napkin. "I could show you our park." I acted like his agreement was a given. I couldn't go to the power sink, knowing that any magick he worked there would be dangerously enhanced. But if I were driving, if I chose the place—though really, these were only superficial reassurances. Ciaran was so strong that there wasn't much I could do to protect myself from him except work the ward-evil spells Eoife had taught me and hope for the best. But I was almost glad to be spending time with him. When we were apart, I was both scared and intensely curious about him. When I was actually with him, my fears danced around the periphery of my consciousness, and mostly I just soaked up his presence.

"Lead on," he said, and fifteen minutes later I parked Das Boot next to a Ford Explorer at the entrance to our state park.

We sat and drank our tea and ate our scones in silence. It wasn't an uncomfortable silence. But I had noticed that most witches were more peaceful to be around than most regular people. It was as if witches recognized the value of silence—they didn't see a lack of noise as a vacuum that needed to be filled.

"So how much did you teach Killian, Kyle, and Iona?" I repeated.

"Not very much, I'm afraid," was his quiet reply. "I wasn't a good father, Morgan, not to them, not by any stretch of the imagination."

"Why?"

He grimaced. "I didn't love their mother. I was tricked into marrying her because my mother, Eloise, and Grania's mother, Greer MacMuredach, wanted to unite our covens. I was just eighteen, and Grania got pregnant, and they promised me leadership over the new, very powerful coven. I would inherit all their knowledge, my mother's and Grania's."

I knew he was lying about being tricked into marrying Grania, but I played along. "Why would you inherit and not Grania? I thought lines were usually matriarchal."

"They usually are. But by the time Grania was eighteen and had been initiated and all the rest, it was clear that she lacked the ambition, the focus, to lead a coven. She wasn't really interested." His words were tight with derision, and I felt sorry for Grania. "But I was amazingly powerful. I could make the coven something new and stronger and better."

"So you married her. But she was pregnant. She didn't get pregnant by herself," I pointed out primly.

Ciaran's body tightened with surprise, and he looked at me as if trying to look through my eyes to something farther in. Then he threw back his head and laughed, an open, rolling laugh that filled my car and seemed to make the darkening twilight brighter.

I waited with raised eyebrows.

"Maeve said the exact same thing," he said. Saying her name, he grew more solemn. "She said the same thing, and she was right. As you are. My only excuse is that I was an eighteen-year-old fool. Which is not much of an excuse and not one that I've ever accepted from Killian. So I have a double standard."

His frankness was disarming, and I tried to picture him as a teenager. A very powerful Woodbane teenager. I had to lead him back to my question about Imbolc.

"Then I met Maeve," he went on, and his voice took on a richer timbre, as if even remembering his love made his throat ache with sadness. "I knew almost instantly that she was the one I should be with. And she knew it about me. Her eyes, the wave of her hair, her laugh, the shape of her hands—everything about her was designed to delight me. We were drawn to each other like . . . magnets." He looked at his own hands, fair-skinned, strong, and capable. The hands that had set my mother on fire.

I desperately wanted to hear more, more about her, about them, about what had gone so terribly wrong. But I struggled to keep my focus on Starlocket. I had to put other needs before my own.

"Imbolc is coming up," I said. "Are you going to celebrate with Amyranth? Is Amyranth the coven you inherited from Greer?"

The inside of my car became very still. We kept our gazes on each other, each of us measuring, waiting, judging.

Then Ciaran said, "Amyranth is part of the coven I inherited from Greer. Not entirely—not everyone from Liathach wanted to join. And Woodbanes from other covens have joined us. But for the most part, those are people I grew up with, who I'm related to, who I can trust with more than my life." His words were soft, his voice like warmed honey. "We share blood going back thousands of years," he went on. "We're intensely loyal to each other."

"Like the Mafia?" I said.

Again he laughed.

Still, I found his description oddly compelling. The idea of being among people who were completely accepting and supportive, who only wanted to help you grow and increase your powers, whom you could trust implicitly, no matter what—it would be amazing. That picture of a Woodbane clan was too painful to think about—I could almost taste my own longing for it, and it terrified me to know that I was thinking about Amyranth. The coven that had tried to kill me. The coven that right at this moment was planning to destroy Starlocket. From the inside, I realized, it might not feel evil at all.

No one in my life had ever accepted me exactly the way I was. I didn't fit in as a Rowlands. Within my coven I stood out because I was a strong blood witch, and it had become clear to me that not even Robbie and Bree, my closest friends, could feel entirely comfortable around me anymore. Hunter and Sky and Eoife all seemed to want different things of me, for me to be different somehow, to make different choices.

My glance flicked back to Ciaran. How far could I push this? Was this the time to ask about the dark wave? Surely he suspected I was up to something.

"You're nervous," Ciaran said softly. "Tell me why."

It was dark now, and somehow there in the car I felt safe. "I'm incredibly drawn to that picture of Woodbanes," I told him honestly. "But I hated Selene Belltower and everything she stood for. She tried to kill me, and I know she had murdered others. I don't want to be like that."

He waved his hand in dismissal. "Selene was an overambitious, overconfident climber—in no way did she represent what my coven is about."

"What is your coven about?" I asked clearly. "I saw what you were doing in New York. What was that? Is there some larger plan?"

Ciaran sat back against the passenger door. His eyes on me were bright in the darkness, his powerful hands still on the wool of his coat. Slowly, slowly, his lips parted in a smile, and I saw his white teeth and his eyes crinkling.

"You are very interesting, Morgan," he said quietly. "You are a wild, untamed thing with the power of a river about to over-flow its banks. Are you afraid of me?"

I looked at him, this man who had helped create me, and answered truthfully, "Yes and no."

"Yes and no," he repeated, watching me. "I think more no than yes. Yet you have every reason to be terribly afraid of me. I almost took your life."

"You almost took my magick—my soul—which is much worse than taking a life," I retorted. "But you didn't because you're my father."

"Morgan, Morgan," he said. "I find you very . . . gratifying. My other children are afraid of me. They don't ask me hard questions, they don't stand up to me. But you . . . are some-thing different. It's the difference between a child born of Gra-nia and a child born of Maeve."

Frankly, I was feeling kind of sorry for all of us, his children.

"You alone I see as being able to appreciate my coven," he went on. "You alone I feel would understand. There's some-thing being planned—"

I caught my breath silently, willing him to continue. He

stopped and looked out the window, as if he hadn't intended to say so much. "I really should be getting back," he said absently.

I squelched my disappointment and frustration. It would be too easy for him to pick up on them. Without a word I started my car and backed out of the parking space. We drove back through the night, toward town. I tried not to even think about what he'd almost said, what we'd talked about. There would be time enough for that later.

I drove Ciaran back to where he said Killian was staying. The house was nowhere near the deserted road where Killian had had me drop him off. He must have been out—the house was dark.

"Good-bye for now," he said. "But not for long, I hope. Please call me soon."

I nodded and leaned closer. In a low voice I said, "Father, I want to do what you do. I want to work how you work. I want you to show me."

He shut the door, his face flushed with emotion at the word *father*. I drove off without looking back and cried the whole way home. I had called him Father. I hated myself.

15

Persecution

Brother Colin, by now you will have heard of my latest travail. Why God has chosen this fate for me, I do not know. All I can do is submit to His will.

I arrived in Barra Head ten days ago. Father Benedict had changed hardly at all and welcomed me most lovingly, which brought tears to my eyes. The abbey had changed for the better, with glass windowpanes, a pigsty, and two milk cows. The brothers (there are now eight) were planning the solemn celebration of Easter, our Lord's rising, with the handful of villagers who share their worship.

Between matins and land, I left my cell and headed for the village in the darkness. I do not know what my thoughts were on that sole, dark walk, but with no warning I was knocked to the ground and a sleek black wolf was ripping at my cowl, tearing at my shoulder. With God's grace I held off its attack for a moment, and what I saw in those few moments before I fainted can only be part of my insanity, I *fear. When the moon struck this creature's eyes, I saw Nuala, looking out at me. Poor Brother Colin, how you must pity me in my madness!*

Now I am in hospital. I envy you, my brother, for having been spared this hellish existence. As soon as I am able to travel, I am being sent to the hospice in Baden.

—Brother Sinestus Tor, to Colin, March 1771

"So this was a good day," Bree said. She propped one booted foot up on the stone bench next to me. "It's not snowing, it's almost forty degrees, and I missed both trig and chemistry because of that fake fire alarm. Not bad for a Wednesday."

"Do we know who did the fire alarm?" I asked.

"I heard it was Chris Holly," Robbie said, coming up behind us. Chris was an ex-boyfriend of Bree's and a typical Bree castoff: good-looking in a jock kind of way, with the IQ of your basic garden toad.

"Oh, jeez," Bree groaned.

Robbie grinned. "Word is that he didn't study for his English test and panicked. Unfortunately, he was observed pulling the handle."

I shook my head. "What a loser."

A muffled ringing sound overlaced their laughter.

"Your purse is ringing," Robbie told Bree, who was already taking out her phone. She said hello, hang on a minute, then handed the phone to me, mouthing, "Killian."

"Little sister!" came his cheerful voice. "I haven't seen you in days! How are you?"

"I'm fine," I said, smiling at the sound of his voice. "What have you been doing?"

"This and that," he said lightly, and I mentally groaned,

wondering what mischief he'd been causing. "Want to get together tonight? Maybe all the gang?"

"Yeah, let's get together," I said, walking a few paces away from my friends. "But can it be just you and me? I want some time to hang out and talk."

"Sure," said Killian. "Alone's fine, too. Let's meet at that coffee place in that row of shops you took me to. We can decide what to do from there."

"Great," I said. "I'll see you there at eight tonight." I hung up and gave Bree back her phone.

"Okay, I'm gone." Robbie kissed Bree on the cheek and took off, not noticing how virtually every female around turned to look at him.

Bree watched him till he got into his red Volkswagen Beetle. "You do good work," she said, referring to the fact that Robbie had once been incredibly unattractive and now looked like a god, thanks to a little spell I had done. It had had unintended effects. Another lesson for me.

"How are things with you two?" I asked.

"Up and down," she said, clearly not wanting to talk about it. "What about you? How are you doing with your parents out of town, broken up with Hunter, and with a bunch of new relatives you hadn't known about?"

For a long moment I looked at Bree. Until four months ago I had known her as well as myself. But now we each had big secrets, unshared things between us. And I couldn't share this with her—about my mission, about my imminent betrayal of Killian and Ciaran, about my fear of being inevitably pulled toward dark magick.

"It's been up and down," I said, and she smiled.

"Yeah. Well, see you later. Call if you want to get together."

"I will," I said.

At eight o'clock I walked through the door of the coffee place that Killian and I had agreed to. I ordered a decaf latte and a napoleon.

An hour later I was royally pissed and rehearsing how I would blast him when he finally did drag his ass through the door. Except that I wouldn't be here to blast him because I was going home. I stomped outside to Das Boot and opened my door, only to see Raven's battered black Peugeot pulling up next to my car.

"Where's your friend Killian?" she said through her open window.

"He's somewhere being an hour late to meet me," I snarled.

Her eyes narrowed. "What do you mean? He was meeting me."

"*Au contraire*," I said. "We had an eight o'clock date."

"Well, princess," she said. "Your time is up. I've got him at nine. See ya."

I frowned. This was too strange. Why would Killian stand me up? What if he had messed up somehow, pissed someone off—had Ciaran done something to him? Or allowed someone else to do something to him?

I looked at Raven. "Will you do me a favor? Will you follow me to the house where he's staying?"

She frowned. "Why? He's supposed to meet me here, not at his place."

I gestured to the empty parking lot. "Do you see him?

Besides, if he's on his way, we'll pass him and you can turn around. I just have a funny feeling about this."

Furrowing her brows, Raven gazed around the empty parking lot one last time. "All right," she said finally. "But if we pass him, we turn around and you go home."

"Deal." I climbed into Das Boot and headed out.

This was one of those times when I should have slowed down, thought things through, asked myself questions like, Is this smart? Am I likely to be killed or maimed doing this? Should I have some sort of backup plan? Any plan at all?

I screeched to a halt in front of the house where I knew Killian was staying. No cars were in the driveway, but the house was ablaze with lights, and even from out on the sidewalk I could hear music blasting. Raven and I looked at each other.

I rang the doorbell four times, but no one answered. Picturing Killian lying in a pool of blood, I used a little unlocking spell that Hunter had taught me and opened the door. The scent of incense drifted toward us. The house wasn't large, but it was old, and even I could tell it was beautifully decorated. A hundred candles of every color were burning in the living room. There was an open bottle of scotch on the coffee table and a couple of used tumblers.

Raven frowned, and I followed her glance. At the entrance of the hall leading to the back a black leather jacket lay on the floor. We walked over to it: a clue. My eyebrows rose. This jacket was Sky's—I recognized the silver pentacle hanging from her zipper. Together Raven and I, the unlikely duo, looked farther down the hall. I recognized Sky's black boots on the floor.

"What the hell?" Raven muttered, stalking forward.

Right next to Sky's boots was a man's belt. I thought I remembered Killian wearing it but wasn't sure. As if we were two puppets drawn on strings, Raven and I went forward. We came to a door that was slightly ajar. I heard the murmur of voices, and then good sense at last kicked in and I decided to get the hell out of here. Whatever Killian was doing, he was fine.

But Raven, not coming to this same conclusion, punched the door open with her fist. I knew it must have hurt, but not as much as the scene before us. Sky was sitting on the bed, and Killian was standing at the foot. They looked up in surprise when the door burst open, saw us, and started laughing. Killian was wearing only a pair of black pants. Sky was in a camisole and her underwear. My mouth dropped open in naive shock. Ridiculously, I remembered Hunter saying he didn't think Sky was actually gay—she just liked who she liked. Apparently right now she was liking Killian.

"Hi," Sky said, and laughed so hard, she almost fell sideways. She was drunk! I couldn't believe it. Killian, however, seemed a little more together.

"Little sister!" he said, and hiccupped, which made him laugh more. "Oops. I forgot our date, didn't I?" All around the room I could detect the faint traces of tingling magick, in the air, on the bed, on the floor. Goddess only knew what they'd been doing.

"And ours, too, you bastard!" Raven screeched, launching herself at Killian. He was unprepared and so went down heavily under her fury. She smacked the side of his face as hard as she could, and I winced as his head snapped to the side.

"Ow, ow," he said, but he was still laughing weakly.

"Oh, stawp, stawp," Sky was saying ineffectually in her

slurred English accent. Leaving Raven and Killian rolling grace-
lessly on the floor, I went in search of a phone. Once I found
it, I called Hunter.

"Come get Sky. She's smashed," I said, and gave him the
address.

When I got back to the room, Raven was shrieking at Sky,
Killian was on the floor, watching the scene with fascination,
and Sky was starting to yell awful things back at Raven, personal things about their relationship that made my ears burn.

"Hold it!" I yelled, waving my arms. "Hold it!"

Surprisingly, the three stopped to look at me. I snatched up
Sky's black leather pants and what I hoped was her shirt. Lean-
ing over the bed, I grabbed her arm, hard. "You come with me,"
I said firmly, and she actually did, practically falling off the bed.

I dragged her out into the hall and down to the bathroom,
where I shoved her roughly into her clothes. As soon as her
arms were in the correct sleeves, I heard Hunter slam through
the front door, shouting for Sky.

I produced her, handing him her boots and jacket.

At that moment the other two Stooges emerged from the
bedroom. Raven's face was still contorted with fury, and Killian
was starting to look a little less cheerful. Sky laughed when she
saw him, and as Hunter began hauling her toward the front
door, she yelled, "Go for it, Raven! He's a great kisser!"

I dropped my head into my hands. I was completely disgusted
with all of them. Was everyone going completely insane? Looking at Raven and Killian with disdain, I left the house and went
to see if I could help Hunter pour Sky into his car.

He was buckling her in. She looked tired and wasted but
not unhappy. He turned to me, his face furious. "Are you happy
with your charming brother now?"

My mouth dropped open. "I don't—"

"When is he going to learn to consider others?" he shouted. "Does he think it's a game, making magick in there, in this situation? Does he think it's funny to do this to Sky?"

I stood there, shocked, as he swung into the driver's seat and slammed the door. I knew he was upset about Sky, but I felt like he was blaming me for Killian's behavior. And I was the most blameless person in this ugly scene!

Futile tears of rage started coursing down my cheeks as Hunter peeled off into the night. I had given up the person I loved most just to prevent him from being tainted by my potential inherent evil, and here I was being blamed for my blood ties, even when I had nothing to do with their actions. I was risking my life to try to save Starlocket, and he thought I was cooking up party games with those three idiots.

Still crying, I was starting to cross the street to get to Das Boot when a car honked in my face and almost gave me a heart attack. I leaped back onto the curb in time to see a pimply-faced kid race past me in a souped-up muscle car. I watched him speed off, and as he did, he shot me the bird.

My mouth dropped open for the ninth time that evening. Without having one second to think, I raised my hand in a quick gesture and muttered just five little words. Instantly the kid's car locked up and he started skidding out of control, spinning sideways and heading right for the crash rail in front of a steep ditch. I was shocked.

"*Nul ra, nul ra!*" I said fast, and with another second the kid had gained control of his car and come to a stop. After a moment he started the engine and continued down the road at a slower pace.

I sat down weak-kneed on the curb. What had I done? I

had almost killed a stranger because I was upset at Hunter. I was unbelievable. Just last month I'd been involved in two deaths. What was wrong with me, apart from being Ciaran's daughter? Was this how my descent into evil would begin? After looking both ways I crossed the street and sat in my car. I cried for a long time, too upset to drive, and then I heard a voice, Ciaran's voice, saying, Power sink.

16

Shape-Shifter

I received your letter yesterday, and I thank you most gratefully. To answer your question, this hospice is not at all like a prison; as long as we stay on the grounds, we are allowed much freedom. There is no one here who is dangerous to himself or to another, though we are all tormented. I thank God that Father's estate can subsidize my stay here. They have allowed me to wear my monk's habit, and I am grateful.

I do not want to answer your other questions. Forgive me, Brother, but I cannot think on it.

—Simon (Brother Sinestus) Tor, to Colin, July 1771

The old Methodist cemetery was dark and cold, and a frigid wind whipped through the scrub pines and unshaped cedars that surrounded it. I strode forward, casting my senses strongly, and felt Ciaran waiting for me.

"Thank you for coming," he said in that soothing, accented voice. With no warning I burst into tears again, embarrassed to do it in front of him, and then his arms enfolded me; I was pressed against the rough tweed of his coat, and he was stroking my hair.

"Morgan, Morgan," he murmured. "Tell me everything. Let me help."

I actually couldn't remember the last time Dad had held me when I cried—I was too cool for that. I cried alone, in my room, quietly. Ciaran's embrace seemed so welcoming, so comforting.

"It's everything," I choked out. "It's being Woodbane and Catholic, it's having witch friends and nonwitch friends. It's Killian and Sky and Raven. Cal and Selene died, and I was so relieved, but I actually still miss Cal sometimes. Or the Cal I thought I knew." More sobs racked me, but still Ciaran held me, letting me lean on him. "And my folks are so nice and I feel like scum because I want to know my birth father!" I sobbed and wiped my nose on the back of my glove. "And I wish I had known Maeve, known her in person, but I *can't* because *you* killed her, you *bastard*!" My fist flew out quickly and slammed Ciaran in his chest. He swayed backward a bit, but I'd been too close to put much into the punch. I swung again, but he caught my wrist in a grip like a *braigh* and stilled me.

"I'm so sorry, Morgan," he said, his voice sounding torn. "I'm tortured about Maeve's death every day of my life. She was the best and the worst thing that ever happened to me, and not a day goes by that I don't feel pain and anguish over what happened. The only good thing about her being gone is that she can no longer feel pain; she's no longer vulnerable and can no longer be hurt."

I leaned backward into a tall tombstone and buried my face in my hands. "This is all too hard," I cried. "It's too much. I can't do it. I can't bear it." In that second all that felt absolutely true.

"No," Ciaran said, holding my wrists gently. "Yours is not an easy path. Your life feels hard and difficult now, and I can promise you it will only become harder and more difficult."

I made an indistinct sound of despair, and his voice went on, slipping into me like a fog.

"But you're wrong in thinking you can't do it, can't bear it," he said. "You absolutely can. You are Maeve's daughter and my daughter. You have our strength in you. You are capable of things beyond your imagination."

I kept crying, the tension of the past week spilling out of me into the dark night. Tonight's awful scene, all my conflicting emotions, were being dissolved in a salty wave of tears.

"Morgan," Ciaran said, brushing my hair out of my face. "I cherish you. You're my link to the only woman I've ever truly loved. I see Maeve in your face. And of my four children, you are the most like me—I see myself in you in a way I don't with the others. I want to trust you. I want you to trust me."

A chill shook me, and Ciaran rubbed my arms. Slowly my crying subsided, and I wiped my eyes and nose. "What happens now?" I asked him. "Are you going to disappear from my life, like you did with your other kids?" I saw Ciaran wince but went on. "Or will you be with me more, teach me more, let me know you?"

How much was true and how much manipulation to fulfill my mission? Goddess help me, I no longer knew. He hesitated, and a slow shivering made me tremble from head to toe.

At last he said, "You're young, Morgan. You're still gathering information. You don't need to make any life decisions today, tonight."

Gathering information? Chills ran up and down my spine. What did he mean by that? How much did he know?

I nodded slowly, unable to look in his eyes.

"What I would like you to do," he said, "to have, is a more complete understanding of what being Woodbane can mean—the joy, the power, the beauty of its purity, the ecstasy of its potential."

I looked up then, hazel eyes meeting hazel eyes. "What do you mean?"

"I would like to share something with you, my youngest daughter," he said. "You, who are so close to my heart and so far from my life. I sense in you something strong and pure and fearless, something powerful yet tender, and I want to show you what that could be. But I need your trust."

I was scared now and also unbelievably drawn to what he was saying. There was a taste in my mouth, and I licked my lips, then realized it wasn't actually a taste so much as a longing: a longing for what Ciaran was talking about.

"I don't understand." The words came out in a near whisper. "Is this about—"

"I'm talking about shape-shifting," he said quietly. "Assuming another being's physical form in order to achieve a heightened awareness of one's own psyche."

Suddenly I realized where he was going with this. I tried not to gape. I had heard about witches shape-shifting before—in fact, I knew that the members of Amyranth shape-shifted—but I understood that it was generally forbidden, considered dark magick. Of course, that wouldn't stop Ciaran.

"You're kidding, right?" I asked.

"No. Morgan, you have so much to learn about your own persona. You must trust me—there is no better way to know yourself than looking through another being's eyes."

"Shape-shifting? Like a hawk? Or a cat?" He couldn't be serious. Where was he going with this?

"Not necessarily a hawk or a cat," he explained. "No witch can change themselves or someone else into a being that does not resonate with the one to be changed. For example, if you feel an affinity for horses, want to know what it would feel like to race across the plains, then it's fairly easy to shift into that. But if you feel no affinity for the animal, have nothing of that creature in you, then it can't be done. Which is why witches don't usually shift into most reptiles or fish."

Oh, Goddess, he seemed serious. I tried to stall. "Can all witches do this?"

"No. Not even very many. But I can, and I think you can, too." He looked deeply into my eyes until I felt that the two of us made up the entire universe. "What do I feel like to you?" he whispered. "What do you feel like?"

An image came to me, an animal. I hesitated to say it. It was the animal that had come to me in terrifying dreams in New York—the animal that represented Ciaran and all of his children, me included. I was so scared about what might happen right here, right now, that it was beyond comprehension. But if I couldn't understand it, then I couldn't really feel it. "A wolf," I said. "Both of us."

His smile was like the moon coming out from behind a bank of clouds. "Yes," he breathed. "Yes. Say these words, Morgan: *Annial nath rac, aernan sil, loch mairn, loch hollen, sil beitha . . .*"

Mindlessly, wondering if I were being spelled by Ciaran but no longer caring, I repeated the ancient, frightening words. Before my eyes Ciaran began to change, but it was hard to say how—were his teeth sharper, longer? His hands curling into claws? Did I see a new, feral wildness in his eyes?

His voice was growing softer and softer, and I cast my senses out to hear the words so I could repeat them. Then I heard something that wasn't a word. It was . . . a sound and a shape and a color and a sigil, all at once. It was impossible to describe. No. It was Ciaran's true name, the name of his essence. I don't know how I recognized it . . . it was instinctive. I had learned Ciaran's true name, I thought hazily. That meant . . .

In the next second I gasped and bent double, racked with a searing, unexpected pain. I stared down at my hands. They were changing. I was changing. I was shape-shifting into a wolf. Oh, God, help me.

I cried out, but my voice was already not my own. I dropped to my hands and knees, feeling the soft loam beneath me, barely aware of Ciaran changing, slipping out of his clothes, revealing a thick black-and-silver coat. His intelligent hazel eyes looked at me from a wolf's face. I tried to scream in horror and pain, but my voice was strangled and broken. My body was in a rack, being forced to bend and curl in unnatural ways, as if every bone was being stretched or compressed or twisted in some incomprehensible nightmare. Helplessly whimpering, I closed my eyes and fell on my side, unable to fight or resist this overwhelming process. When Ciaran nuzzled me, I reluctantly opened my eyes again, and when I got up, it was on all fours. I was a wolf.

My fur was thick and russet-colored. I looked down and saw four straight, strong paws tipped with sharp, non-retractable claws. I looked at Ciaran and recognized him: he was absolutely himself, yet he was a wolf. I felt absolutely myself, but as I began to cautiously examine my internal processes, I felt quite different. Foreign. Like a wolf instead of a person. It was as if my humanness was a rope hammock that had come undone on one end, and I was now watching it unravel. Soon it would be completely gone. I had two thoughts: How would I get it back? And what of my mission?

I stepped closer to Ciaran, my four legs moving smoothly, precisely, with no effort. I felt how strong I was, how powerful—my jaws felt heavy, my legs were roped with lean muscle, and I was breathing easily, although the change had been horribly stressful. Ciaran opened his mouth in a sinister, wolfy grin, as if to say, Isn't this great? I grinned back at him and was awash with a sudden ecstasy, an exhilaration that I was experiencing this. Instinctively I stepped closer to Ciaran and nuzzled his neck, and he returned it.

Then I remembered. The watch sigil. The wolf in me wanted to be running, to be away, to be coursing through the dark night. The last vestige of a human Morgan remembered the watch sigil. I pressed my face against Ciaran's thick neck fur and breathed the words of the spell against him. In a quick, desperate move I traced the sigil against his neck with my wet canine nose.

Ciaran made no response, as if he hadn't noticed, hadn't felt it. I had no idea whether it would "stick," since he was a changed being. Then Ciaran nudged me with his head and, turning, bounded off into the night. Feeling fiercely happy, all thoughts of Morgan and missions and spells gone, I leaped after him. My muscles contracted and expanded effortlessly; it was easy to catch up to him, and we loped along side by side as a million new sensations flooded my animal brain. With my magesight I could always see well in the dark, but now it was as if things were highlighted and outlined for me with infrared.

With each indrawn breath a world of scents, flavors borne on the breeze, added an incredible depth and dimension to my experience. I felt incredibly powerful, agile, and sure-footed. It was wonderful, beyond wonderful, exciting beyond description.

When Ciaran looked back, I opened my mouth and showed him my pointy teeth. He had given me the gift of a lifetime, I knew. We ran for miles through the woods, leaving the cemetery behind, following scents, feeling the crisp air ruffling through our fur. I ran happily in Ciaran's paw prints, trying to soak up as much of this sensation as possible. I didn't know if it would ever happen again, and I wanted to relish every second.

I hadn't even begun to tire when Ciaran cantered to a halt and sniffed the air. Eagerly I stood next to him, shoulder to shoulder, and lifted my head. My eyes widened, and I looked at him, seeing the knowledge in his eyes. I smelled it too. Prey.

17

The Choice

Colin, I write to you in fevered hysteria. I learned only hours ago that Nuala is to be burned at the stake, in Barra Head. I can see that at last her devil's work has caught up to her, but the sentence! As Father Benedict himself said, God is to judge good and evil, not man! Cannot her soul yet be saved? Can no one bring her to the Lord's joy? It can be done only if she is alive—surely they must see that, Colin!

I have been insane with worry since receiving this news (news that I am sure I was not meant to know). My brain cannot comprehend her fate at the stake. And what of the child? I beg you, send to Barra Head and inquire. I know not the child's name, nor can I verify whether or not it still lives. But try, for my poor sake.

I will await the next post with all anxiety.

—Simon Tor, to Colin, October 1771

Prey. Oh, God, I was hit by a hunger so strong, it almost overwhelmed me. It was a blood lust, an animal's need to kill or be killed, hunt or be hunted. I was a predator—an efficient, predestined killer—and the idea of prey made my stomach tighten in anticipation. I licked my lips and inhaled deeply, drawing the delicious scent into my lungs. It was almost familiar, a wonderful, maddening smell that I had to follow or die trying.

Without waiting for my father, I set off after the prey, my feet moving swiftly and silently over the detritus of the forest floor. Prey, prey, I thought. My prey. The scent swept through these woods, here touching a tree trunk, here brushed against leaves on the ground, here on the holly bushes with their shiny, prickly leaves. Sometimes the trail doubled back on itself, and I circled trees in frustration until I found the one thread that was a fraction newer, a fraction stronger. Then I was off again, moving like a wraith through the darkness, filtering out a thousand other scents: tree, loam, mold, bird, insect, deer, rabbit. But I focused only on the one scent, that one tantalizing smell that made my mouth ache in longing.

I was barely aware of the other wolf, the black-and-silver one trotting behind me; I couldn't hear his breathing, and his paws made almost no sound.

Here I took a sharp right, and at once the scent became closer, stronger. I almost howled in excitement. *Soon. Close. Mine.* The next second I froze: there it was! The scent was washing over me now, the air woven through with it. It was close. With every breath I inhaled the promise of the joy of victory over a lesser being. It was beyond hunger, beyond desire, beyond want. My mouth was wet; my eyes were piercing the night. I scanned the woods all around me as the other wolf came to a silent stop next to me. Tree by tree by tree by bush by bush . . . It was close. It was within range.

There! There, forty feet away. My moving target, my

destination, my fate. It was heading away from me, leaving an obvious trail for me to follow. I smiled. Without having to think, my muscles gathered and exploded, launching me into the night. The distance between us closed rapidly. I felt an intense, palpable hunger, a need to bring my prey down, to sink my sharp white teeth into its flesh, to taste its fresh, hot, salty blood. I whimpered with want and raced ahead.

With one more leap I would bring it down. My weight would knock it to the ground; it would be scared, confused; I would rip into its throat and not let go. . . . The prey turned and saw me rocketing toward it. Then it was on the move, charging away from me, running in zigzags, ducking below branches, crashing through the underbrush with as much noise as a tree falling heavily to the ground.

I chased after it, following the traces of its warm footprints, its scent, now laced with fear, that it left in its wake. My breath came rapidly, my lean sides pumping oxygen efficiently through my blood, my incredibly strong heart pushing fresh blood through my veins.

I was glad my prey was putting up a chase—it shouldn't be too easy. I felt the other wolf behind me, and I sensed that he was enjoying this as much as I was. I detected a familiarity in his movements: he had done this before. Hunted before. Killed before.

A streak of crackly blue light flew through the trees and almost hit my head. I ducked instinctively, and it exploded on a pine next to me. The scent of charred bark and sticky-sweet sap hit my nostrils. Another ball of blue light came at me, and once again I dodged, almost feeling annoyance. I hunkered down, kept my head low, and concentrated on following my prey.

A strong scent of deer crossed my path, and it would have

made me swerve if I had been after any other animal. The air seemed full of delicious scents: deer, rabbit, turkey—but I ignored them, as I ignored the false, confusing trails that told me my prey had taken another path. I was unstoppable, undistractable. I had one purpose. I knew what I wanted, and I wanted it more than I'd ever wanted anything in my whole life.

The other wolf moved away from me, splitting off from my path and heading farther on. I realized he was going to come at our quarry from the left side, while I would chase it from the right. Together we would corner it, and then I alone would bring it down; I alone would get the spoils of victory.

Within a minute we had succeeded: there was a sharp rock outcropping here, and my prey was trapped against it. It flattened itself against the wall, as if that would help. The other wolf moved in, but I growled at him to stay back. This life belonged to me. I could hear it panting, gasping to get air into its puny lungs. The smell of fear covered it and made me wrinkle my nose. Its heart was hammering within its weak chest, and the thought of the blood pumping through that heart made me step closer, baring my teeth.

This was what I wanted more than anything. I had to bring it down, had to kill it, had to taste it. It was created solely to be my victim. The fur on my back stood up in a bristly line with excitement. Hunkering down, a low growl coming from my throat, I began to creep toward it. My eyes never left it, my muscles were poised to leap at any second if it should try to run. Its pale green eyes were wide with fear, and I wanted to grin.

Should I leap on it and drag it down, face-first? Should I launch myself toward it from the side? How much could I play with it before it died? No, better to make a clean, quick kill. It was the wolf's way. Ever so slowly I advanced, feeling a delicious thrill flooding my being. Nothing was better than this sensation, this victory over weakness. Nothing could compare.

I glanced up and found that my prey was staring at me, right at my eyes. I frowned. That wasn't what prey did. Prey cowered, prey hid, prey made it fun. Prey didn't stare at its hunter. I took another step closer, and its gaze caught mine, unwavering. It was *infuriating*. I pulled my lips back to show it my deadly fangs; I growled deeply from within my chest, knowing that the vibrations of the rumble would strike terror into it. Closer and closer I went, becoming more enraged by the second by its boldness.

Then my prey whispered, "Morgan?"

I froze, one paw in midair. I blinked. That sound was very familiar. Behind me the other wolf stiffened, then moved closer, barely rustling the leaves on the ground. I turned my head a fraction and growled a warning to him: Stay back. This is my kill.

"Morgan?" My victim was still panting hard, sweating, pressed against the rocks. It looked deeply into my eyes, and with surprise I found it almost painful. I desperately wanted it to turn away, to quit staring at me. As soon as it dropped its gaze, I would leap on it, tearing out its throat, feeling its lifeblood soaking into my fur. Look away, I commanded it silently. Look away. Play your role, as I play mine.

It wouldn't look away. "Oh, Morgan," it said. With its next breath it straightened up, away from the rock, and my muscles tensed. Unbelievably I felt it relaxing, calming its fear. It raised its paws and unwrapped some covering from around its neck. My eyes opened wider—it had bared its throat for me! I could see pale, smooth skin where before there had been only some thick, wrinkly thing. "Your choice, Morgan," it said, and waited.

Again I blinked, trying to process this situation in my wolf brain. This wasn't making sense. This prey was talking to me, it was saying my name. My name? My name? I thought—I felt only like Me. But like a trickle of water slowly eating through rock, a realization got through to me. My name was Morgan. My name was Morgan?

Oh, Goddess, my name was Morgan! I was a girl, not a wolf, not a wolf! Only a girl. And my prey was *Hunter*, and I loved him, and right now I wanted to kill him and taste his blood more than anything in the world.

What was happening?

"Your choice, Morgan," Hunter said again.

My choice. What kind of choice? I had hunted him down; the right of the kill was mine. Could I choose not to kill him? Abruptly I sat down, my haunches folding neatly under me, brushy tail swishing out of the way.

My choice. I would choose what? To kill or not to kill? Oh, Goddess, was the choice between good and evil? Between power or guilt? Light or darkness? Oh, God, did this mean I couldn't kill this prey? I wanted it, I wanted it, I needed it, I had to have it.

Behind me the other wolf growled: Do something. Kill it, or I will.

Oh, God, oh, God, oh, Goddess, help me. Oh, God, I choose good, I thought, almost weeping with regret at the blood I wouldn't spill, the life I couldn't take. I threw back my head and howled, a strangled, smothered howl of pain and longing and a desire to kill.

And as soon as I thought, I choose good, my exhilarating wolfness began to slip away from me, like a tide away from a shore. This too I regretted: I wanted to be a wolf forever. How diminishing to go back to being a mere girl, a pathetic human; how pitiful, how humiliating! I lowered myself onto my front paws, wanting to weep but unable to: wolves can't cry.

The other wolf—Ciaran, it came to me—trotted forward suddenly with an irate snarl. Hunter tensed against the rock, and I leaped to my feet, thinking, No! No! I saw Ciaran's powerful muscles gather and knew he would be on Hunter in an instant. Quickly in my mind I thought his true name, the name that was his very essence, the name that was a sound, a shape, a thought, a song, a sigil, a color all at once.

Ciaran dropped in midleap like a stone. He turned to me, wolfish eyes wide with astonishment, awe, and even fear. No, I thought. You may not have Hunter.

Things began happening too quickly to comprehend. I began to change back into a human, and it was painful and I cried out. Ciaran, still a wolf, melted into the shadows of the woods like a fog, as if he had never existed. Then Eoife and many other witches I didn't know burst into the clearing, shouting spells and weaving magick everywhere.

"He went there!" Hunter shouted, pointing in the direction that Ciaran had gone. I lay curled on the ground, still mostly wolf, trying not to retch, knowing in my heart that they would never catch Ciaran, that my father had already escaped. But the weight of their magick and the strength of their spells amazed me—I didn't want to be anywhere near them. It was a weight, pressing on me, binding Woodbanes, chasing Ciaran, and the magick made me feel ill.

Vaguely I felt Hunter wrap me in something warm and pick me up, and then the pain of his every step was so much that I passed out and sank into a delicious darkness where there was no pain, no consciousness.

*   *   *

I don't know when I awoke, but when I did, I was stretched across Hunter's lap, wrapped in his overcoat. My eyes fluttered, and I whispered again, "I choose good."

"I know, love," Hunter whispered back.

I saw my naked feet sticking out from his coat; they were freezing. I felt impossibly pale and weak and wormlike after the glorious strength and beauty of wolfdom. I began to cry, thinking again, I choose good, I choose good, just in case it hadn't taken the first time. Hunter held me and stroked his hands over my bare human skin. He murmured gentle healing spells that helped take away the nausea and pain and fear. But not the regret. Not the anguish. Not the loss.

18

Imbolc

Diary of Benedict, Cistercian Abbot, December 1771

Today we held the sad burial and consecration of one of our sons. Brother Sinestus Tor was brought from Baden and laid to rest in the abbey's churchyard. His mother assured me he had received the last sacraments, but the brothers and I performed extra rites of purity and forgiveness. I cannot think that gentle Sinestus, so bright and full of hope, became an agent of the devil, but there are facts of this matter that trouble me greatly, though I shall take them with me to my own grave, God willing. How is it that the boy died at the exact moment of the exact day that the witch Nuala Riordan was burned at the stake? They were hundreds of miles apart and had no earthly communication. And what of the mark found on the boy's shoulder? His mother made no mention of it; I wonder, did she see his body or no? But the scars there cannot be explained unless he were burned. Burned with a star encircled on his shoulder.

I pray we have done the right thing by allowing him to rest in consecrated ground. May God have mercy on us all.

—B.

"Drink this," said Hunter, folding my stiff fingers around a warm mug. I took a tentative sip, then coughed, gagging on its foulness.

"Agh," I said weakly. "This is awful."

"I know. Drink it, anyway. It will help."

I did, taking small sips and grimacing after each one. If this tonic was magickal, why couldn't he have spelled it so it didn't taste like crap?

I was huddled in front of the fireplace at Hunter's house. He had given me some of Sky's clothes to wear since mine were back at the cemetery.

The fire crackled and spit in front of me, but I avoided looking at the flames. I couldn't bear anything else tonight—no revelations, no lessons, no visions, no scrying. Although I had a blanket wrapped around me, I shivered uncontrollably and felt that the fire put out hardly any heat.

I didn't understand anything.

"Is Sky here?" I thought to ask.

Hunter nodded. "Upstairs, sleeping off her drink. Tomorrow morning she'll probably feel worse than you do now."

"I find that hard to believe." Every muscle and bone and nerve and tendon and cartilage in my body ached as if it had been torn. Even my hair and my fingernails hurt. I dreaded having to get up to walk, and driving seemed completely impossible. Creakily, like an old woman, I raised the mug to my lips and drank again.

"Why were you out there?" My words came out as a croak.

Hunter looked at me somberly. "I was looking for you. I got a message from Ciaran that you were in danger."

Ciaran. I don't know why I was surprised. "How did you know where I was? How did Eoife show up at the last minute?"

"We scried," said Hunter. "Ciaran had blocked himself from us, but you hadn't. Ciaran wanted us to look for you. He wanted to plant me in your path while you were shape-shifting. He was testing you."

I shuddered again at the thought of what I had almost done to Hunter. Then, considering Hunter's words, I frowned. "I did block myself. I was covered with protective spells, spells that wouldn't let anyone find me without my will."

For a moment Hunter looked uncomfortable, and I thought, Oh my God, he's lying to me.

"You have a watch sigil on you," he said, and blew out a breath, as though glad I finally knew.

"Excuse me?" I almost dropped my mug.

"You have a watch sigil on you." He looked embarrassed. "Since Eoife taught you the ward-evil spells. During one of those she put a watch sigil on you."

I stared at him.

"We needed to know where you were, who you were with. You're inexperienced, love, and that makes you a target. Any dark witch who knew that would be dangerous to you. There was nothing about this mission that was safe."

If we'd been having this conversation before Eoife had come to town, I would have been furious. As it was, after all I'd been through, all I knew, all I felt was a vague sense of grat-itude. I sighed and murmured, "Take it off now."

"I will," Hunter promised.

I stared into the bottom of my dark mug. "I feel like such a failure. I haven't learned anything about the time of the dark wave, or the spell, or anything. I've sentenced Alyce and Starlocket to death." My eyes stung, and I knew tears would come later.

"No, Morgan," Hunter said, rubbing my knee through the blanket. "You got Killian here, and Ciaran. They know we're here and that we're on high alert. And you have to remember, you did incredibly well just to not have been killed."

"Oh, God." I groaned and shook my head. "At least I planted the watch sigil on him."

"What? You did?" Hunter looked incredulous. "When?"

"Right as we were turning, shifting. I breathed it into his fur and traced the sigil on his neck. Actually, that was probably useless, too. Once he changes back—"

"It will still be on him," Hunter said, his face breaking into a huge grin. "Oh, Goddess, Morgan! The council is going to be ecstatic to hear it. That's the best news I've had in a long time." He leaned and kissed my cheek and my forehead. "Morgan, I think your mission was a smashing success. You planted the watch sigil on Ciaran, and we're both still alive, unhurt. . . ." Hunter took my free hand and kissed it, looking at me encouragingly. I didn't know how to respond.

The truth was, his joy didn't affect me that much. I had planted a betraying sigil on my biological father. And he had given me such a gift. . . . For a moment I remembered running through the woods on all fours, and I closed my eyes.

And then I remembered . . . I had learned his true name. Ciaran's true name. Something that could give me complete power over my father, one of the darkest witches the world had ever known. The thought of using it against him made my stomach clench. For now, I thought, I would guard this as my secret. I wouldn't tell the council—wouldn't even tell Hunter. If it became necessary, I could use it. But I didn't want to give anyone else the power to destroy my natural father. I couldn't.

"He wanted you to kill me," Hunter said softly, as though he was reading my mind. He wrapped his arms around me, and I felt his warmth seeping through the blanket. "If you had killed me, it would have been one less Seeker—and you'd have lost your *mùirn beatha dàn*. It would have bound you to him in a way that love alone never could."

I shuddered at the thought of losing Hunter. "I was starting to care for him," I admitted.

"I know," said Hunter. "How could you not? He's your birth father. And I believe that his feelings for you were sincere also. Despite everything, I believe that's true."

Then I began to cry again, tears leaking silently out of my eyes and running hotly down my cheeks. I didn't have the energy to sob, and it would have hurt too much, anyway.

"I have you," Hunter said, holding me close. "I have you. You're safe. It's all right. Everything's going to be all right."

"There's no way anything will ever be all right again," I said shakily, and he began kissing the tears away from my cheeks.

"That's not true," he said.

I looked into his green eyes, the eyes that had stared me down when I was a wolf. And I knew then: I knew in my heart that I was good.

"I love you so much," I said.

He gave a half smile and leaned closer, blotting out my vision of the fire. He's going to kiss me, I thought, but by then his lips were already against mine. Tentatively at first, then with increasing pressure as I responded. Gradually I felt light growing all around us, bathing us in a silvery white glow. I reached one arm up to curl it around his neck, and then we had our arms around each other. We kissed deeply and more deeply, trying to fuse ourselves together after being apart too long. Then suddenly it was just like the day at Bree's house with Killian: flowers, all different kinds and colors and sizes, showering down upon us, petal soft. I broke away for a moment, gazing around me, and started to laugh. Hunter followed my gaze, looking up at the shower of petals, and his face transformed into a huge smile. He kissed me again, and his body pressed against mine, comforting me to my very soul. I held him to me as tightly as I could, all my muscles screaming in pain as I moved. I didn't care. I was back in Hunter's arms and he was in mine, and everything was going to be all right.

My parents came home the next day, while I was home "sick." I felt their car come up the driveway and quickly ran my hands over my ears, checking to make sure they were still round and naked instead of pointy and furry. Moving gingerly downstairs, I met them at the front door.

"Hi, honey!" Mom said, giving me a big hug. I tried not to moan in pain; every cell in my body still hurt. She glanced at her watch and looked at my face more closely.

"Morgan!" Dad said, struggling through the door with two suitcases. "Are you sick?"

"You look awful," Mom said, putting her hand to my cheek. "Do you have a fever?"

"I think so," I said. "I thought I'd better stay home today. It's the only day I've missed."

"Poor thing," Mom said, and I felt a maternal mantle of

comfort settle around me. "You go get back into bed. I'll bring you some Tylenol and a ginger ale."

I almost wept with happiness. "I'm glad you're home," I choked out, then headed back upstairs to my waiting bed. Ciaran was gone, Killian hadn't been heard from since our father had disappeared, Hunter and I were back together (I thought), and my parents were home. It was a whole new day.

"Today is the feast of lights," said Eoife at our circle two days later. She raised a white candle high. "Today is for new beginnings, for purification, for renewal of spirit, body, hearth, and home. We give blessed thanks to the Goddess for the past year and dedicate ourselves anew to our studies and devotions."

Next to her Alyce Fernbrake ignited her candle from Eoife's, and the two women smiled at each other before Alyce turned and bent to light Suzanna Mearis's candle. Suzanna was now in a wheelchair. Around the circle went the flame, from candle to candle, witch to witch.

"Blessed thanks," we said when the last candle was lit. Then, moving deasil around Hunter and Sky's large circle room, we each sprinkled a small handful of salt on the floor around us. It crunched under our feet. I looked around at the many softly lit faces. It was Saturday night, Imbolc, February 2. For this joyful celebration, one of the four major Wiccan Sabbats, Kithic had joined forces with Starlocket, and there were twenty-six of us purifying ourselves, this room, this year.

After Alyce had led us in a prayer to Brigid—she pronounced it Breed—the goddess of fire, we sat in a large circle. I gazed across at Hunter, thinking about how beautiful he looked in candlelight. He'd pretty much convinced me that after passing the test of choosing good over evil, I was probably safe for him to date. Now every time I looked at him, my heart went all fluttery and I wanted to hold him.

"Blessed be," Hunter said, and we repeated it. "This joyful occasion," he went on, "signifies the beginning of winter's end. The days are becoming longer, the sunlight brighter—it's a time of rebirth."

"Yes," said Eoife. "Many witches choose this time to spring clean their homes, performing purifying rituals and literally making a clean sweep of everything."

"It's also a time for spiritual rebirth," said Alyce, her wise face and blue-violet eyes serene. "I use this holiday to forgive anyone who wronged me in the past and to seek forgiveness from anyone I've wronged. To begin the new Wheel of the Year with a clean slate."

Alisa spoke. "I read there's a ritual where you write down things you wish to be free of in the coming year—flaws, problems, worries—and then you burn the paper."

"We will do that in a little while," Hunter said. "Right now let's stand again and call on the god and the goddess."

We all joined hands.

"May the circles of Starlocket and Kithic always be strong," Hunter said.

"Blessed be," I whispered. The other members murmured their response.

As we began to move widdershins in our circle, Hunter began to chant in a low voice. The chant was unfamiliar to me, but I understood it somehow: it was about new beginnings, casting the darkness behind you and living in light. Gradually Alyce and Sky joined in, and then the words came to me and

I began to chant, too. Energy flowed through my body as we spun around the room. A joy began to fill me that cannot be put into words. We were all alive, safe. I caught Hunter's eye, and he smiled at me. He was mine again. My body filled with warmth and energy, and I smiled back.

On the other side of the circle Alyce's face was turned up in a mask of pure joy. I felt a rush of comfort. Alyce was still with me, and Starlocket was intact. I had helped make it that way. In the time to come, the council would track Ciaran, and if he should ever come for me again, I was ready for him. For the first time in weeks I felt utterly safe and happy.

I stared into the candle flames and felt my power rise.

Later that night, on my front porch, I fished my keys out of my jeans. My shoe tapped something, and I looked down. As soon as I saw the small, lumpy bundle of purple silk, my heart dropped. I whipped my head around, looking for Ciaran. I knew this was from him as surely as I knew I was a witch. I cast my senses out strongly and felt nothing except Dagda on the other side of the front door.

Slowly I knelt and picked it up. It was almost alive with tingling traces of magick. I untied the knot, and the bundle fell open. My mouth opened wordlessly as I stared down at the golden watch. It was the watch I had found in Maeve's old apartment in New York. Ciaran had taken it from me as he had tried to steal my powers. It was the watch that had first made him aware that I must be his daughter.

"Oh, Goddess," I muttered. A fluttering white note caught my eye, and I picked it up. "You should have this," it said.

I stroked the watch, feeling the warmth of the gold, the fineness of the wrought chain. This was truly a family heirloom, something to be kept and handed down for generations.

Unfortunately, it was also from Ciaran, which meant I shouldn't even be holding it. When Cal and I had first gotten together, he'd given me a silver pentacle necklace that I had worn constantly. It had been spelled, of course, and he'd used it to help control me. Goddess only knew what Ciaran had done to this watch: I knew he had given it to me sincerely, out of love, and I knew also that he'd had some ulterior purpose in doing so, that it would somehow be to his advantage. That was Ciaran: light and dark. Like me, like the world, like everything.

I tied it back into its purple silk. I desperately wanted to go inside and sleep, but instead I found myself sliding back behind the wheel of Das Boot. I drove well out of town, at least ten miles, to an old farm I had come to once with Maeve's tools. I walked through the tree buffer that separated the meadow from the highway and stepped into the clearing where Sky Eventide had found me, working magick on my own.

The ground was frozen, of course, but I'd come prepared and said a tiny spell that made digging easy. I dug a hole almost two feet deep and then with bittersweet feelings placed the purple silk bundle at the bottom of it. I filled in the hole. Then I knelt and said all the purifying spells I knew, all the ward-evil ones from Hunter and Eoife and Alyce. I stood up and made my way back to the car, feeling like I would be lucky to make it home without falling asleep at the wheel.

With time the earth's healing purity would work its own magick on the watch, purifying it and removing all traces of spells and evil. It would take a very long time. But one day, I knew, I would reclaim it.

Book Nine

SWEEP
Strife

To the real Erin Murphy

All quoted materials in this work were created by the author.
Any resemblance to existing works is accidental.

Strife

SPEAK
Published by the Penguin Group
Penguin Group (USA) Inc., 345 Hudson Street, New York, New York 10014, U.S.A.
Penguin Group (Canada), 90 Eglinton Avenue East, Suite 700, Toronto, Ontario, Canada M4P 2Y3
(a division of Pearson Penguin Canada Inc.)
Penguin Books Ltd, 80 Strand, London WC2R 0RL, England
Penguin Ireland, 25 St Stephen's Green, Dublin 2, Ireland (a division of Penguin Books Ltd)
Penguin Group (Australia), 250 Camberwell Road, Camberwell, Victoria 3124, Australia
(a division of Pearson Australia Group Pty Ltd)
Penguin Books India Pvt Ltd, 11 Community Centre, Panchsheel Park, New Delhi - 110 017, India
Penguin Group (NZ), 67 Apollo Drive, Rosedale, North Shore 0632, New Zealand
(a division of Pearson New Zealand Ltd)
Penguin Books (South Africa) (Pty) Ltd, 24 Sturdee Avenue, Rosebank, Johannesburg 2196, South Africa

Registered Offices: Penguin Books Ltd, 80 Strand, London WC2R 0RL, England

Published by Puffin Books, a division of Penguin Young Readers Group, 2002
Published by Speak, an imprint of Penguin Group (USA) Inc., 2008
This omnibus edition published by Speak, an imprint of Penguin Group (USA) Inc., 2011

1 3 5 7 9 10 8 6 4 2

Copyright © 2002 17th Street Productions, an Alloy company
All rights reserved

Produced by 17th Street Productions,
an Alloy company
151 West 26th Street
New York, NY 10001

17th Street Productions and associated logos
are trademarks and/or registered trademarks of Alloy, Inc.

Speak ISBN 978-0-14-241024-0
This omnibus ISBN 978-0-14-241955-7

Printed in the United States of America

Except in the United States of America, this book is sold subject to the condition that
it shall not, by way of trade or otherwise, be lent, re-sold, hired out, or otherwise
circulated without the publisher's prior consent in any form of binding or cover
other than that in which it is published and without a similar condition
including this condition being imposed on the subsequent purchaser.

The publisher does not have any control over and does not assume any
responsibility for author or third-party Web sites or their content.

1

The Meeting

August 28, 1971

At the end of the summer the sea always seems to be railing against the thought of another long, fierce New England winter. The waves hurtle themselves against the rocks with blind rage. Fishermen think of August as a terrifying month, but for me, it's the most thrilling. Maybe it's because my family has lived in Gloucester for generations. Or maybe it's because we're Wiccans, and that puts us in greater tune with nature.

It's ironic to think that my family settled so close to Salem—we were very lucky to survive the witch trials. It's strange to think that Wicca could inspire such terror when it's such a gentle, loving, nurturing religion. I guess people are always afraid of power that they don't understand. And Wicca does deal with raw power, although the way my *family practices it, it's never destructive. Both Mom and Dad are very into responsible uses of magick, which they drummed into me before my initiation three years ago. Now they are teaching the same thing to my younger brother, Sam. He won't be initiated for another seven months, but already I can see the energy beginning to spark in him. I know he's going to be a powerful witch. I'm looking forward to his rites, but it's hard not to envy him sometimes. My own power is more fickle, although I like to think that it is growing as I continue to study and practice.*

Every day I pray to the Goddess to make me worthy of my family.

—Sarah Curtis

Calm down, I told myself as I gazed into the bathroom mirror and struggled to pull my long brown hair into a tidy French braid. This is going to be fine. I glanced at my watch. My boyfriend, Hunter Niall, was due any minute. Normally I would have been thrilled to be spending an evening with him, but tonight was no ordinary night. No—tonight was the official meet-the-parents dinner, and I was beginning to feel sick with tension.

I was distracted by a quick tap on the door.

"Come in," I called.

My sister, Mary K., walked into the bathroom. "Is that what you're wearing?" she asked, staring at my faded blue jeans and soft purple fleece shirt.

I looked down at my outfit. "What's wrong with this?"

Mary K. just sighed and marched through the bathroom to the door that led into my bedroom.

"Where are you going?" I asked.

"To find that shirt Aunt Eileen gave you for Christmas," Mary K. said. "I know it'll look great on you, and besides, she and Paula are already downstairs, waiting for us."

"That shirt is practically see-through!" I argued as Mary K. rummaged through my drawers.

"Which is why you'll wear it with this," she countered, holding up a pale pink tank top. Mary K. pulled the sheer, stretchy shirt off a hanger in my closet and handed it and the tank top to me. "At least you're wearing low jeans," she said as I yanked off my fleece. "You've got the body for them."

I pulled on the new outfit and stared at myself in the bathroom mirror. The slate blue shirt did make my dark eyes seem warmer, and the pink tone of the tank made my skin rosy. Once again, I was amazed at my sister's ability to pull together an outfit based on clothes I hardly ever wore.

Just then the doorbell rang. "Showtime!" Mary K. said brightly.

I stifled a groan. For the hundredth time, I wanted to kick myself for letting my parents invite Hunter over for dinner. It had seemed like a good idea when Mom suggested it, but now that the night had arrived, my heart was racing. It didn't help that my mom had decided to make a big event out of it, pulling together an ambitious dinner menu and inviting my aunt Eileen and her girlfriend, Paula, over, too. What if they don't like him? I worried as I stared at my reflection. My parents had met Hunter before but only briefly, in casual settings. Comparatively, this felt more like a college entrance exam.

I could hear the muted sound of greetings in the front hall. Mary K. pulled on her sweater. "Let's go," she said.

I followed her into the hall and down the stairs. Hunter

was in the front alcove, shaking hands with my father and smiling at my aunt and her girlfriend. He was holding a paper cone of roses—they were such a delicate pink that they seemed to glow with their own light, like a bouquet of pearls. I stopped on the steps, and Hunter looked up at me with his steady green gaze. I smiled, and he smiled back, the edges of his brilliant eyes crinkling in a way that was both exciting and familiar.

"Hey, Morgan," my aunt Eileen said with a grin. "That shirt looks great on you." Her back was to Hunter, and she waggled her eyebrows at me, as if to say, "He's cute." I laughed nervously and gave her and Paula a hello hug.

Hunter gave me a quick kiss on the cheek. "You look beautiful," he whispered, and I felt a blush rise to my face.

Mary K. took a delicate sniff. "Is something on fire?" she asked.

My dad looked at me in alarm, his eyes huge behind his glasses.

"I think I'd better go see how Mom is doing," I said quickly. "Shall I put these in some water?" I asked Hunter, taking the roses from him. "They're gorgeous."

"Do you need help?" Hunter asked.

"Oh, no," I said as nonchalantly as I could. "I'm sure everything is under control."

Hunter smiled, and I knew he wasn't fooled for a second.

My dad led everyone into the living room as I hurried into the kitchen. My mom was frantically waving her arms in a desperate attempt to force the smoke pouring from the oven out the open back door.

"Should I do something?" I asked.

"Oh, Morgan!" Relief swept over my mom's face. "Would you put on the fan before the fire alarm goes off? I have to pull this roast out of the oven—I think some of the drippings caught on fire." My mother is a real estate broker and doesn't spend a lot of time in the kitchen. The fact that my parents had both volunteered to cook for Hunter—Dad made his famous black-bottom pie for dessert—was just evidence of how special they wanted this night to be.

I put the roses on the countertop, flipped on the fan, and turned the flame under the carrots on the stove to low as my mom wrestled the roast from the oven and fanned the smoke away from it. She shook her head. "We should have ordered out," she said mournfully, pondering the blackened mess.

I tried not to groan out loud. "Maybe we can make some gravy to cover up the black parts," I suggested.

Mom nodded, straightening her red sweater while I pulled some instant gravy out of the cabinet. "Thank you," she said, giving me a wry smile. "I guess I'd better get out there and say hello to Hunter."

Something in my mother's voice made me look at her. Until that moment, it hadn't occurred to me that my mom might be as nervous about tonight's official meet and greet as I was.

My mom picked up the cone of roses. "These are beautiful," she said. After a moment she added, "Hunter really is nice, isn't he?"

"He really is," I agreed. My mother smiled, and I had the sudden urge to hug her. She and my father knew that Hunter was into Wicca (although they didn't know quite how deeply). For lots of reasons, they were incredibly uncomfortable with the thought that Wicca was a part of my life. But here they were, making an extra effort to get to know Hunter, to be open-minded.

My mom hurried out to say hello to everyone. I made the gravy as Mary K. and my dad came into the kitchen. Dad did his best to carve up the roast. He really had to put his shoulder into it, but eventually he cut it into slices thin enough to be served. I put it on plates and poured gravy over each serving, then added the side dishes, and Mary K. carried the plates to the table. The roast didn't look too terrifying once it was disguised.

By the time I walked into the dining room, everyone was laughing and chatting. Hunter sent me a look that instantly made me feel warm all over, and I headed for my seat between him and Mary K.

"Now that everyone's here," Aunt Eileen said as I slid into the chair across from her, "Paula and I have some news."

"What is it?" I asked.

"We've filed our papers," Paula said with a sheepish grin.

"The adoption agency said that we should get a green light within the next ten weeks," Aunt Eileen added.

"Then you'll get a baby?" Mary K. asked. "That's great!"

I smiled, unsure what to say. I was happy for Paula and Aunt Eileen, but I couldn't help feeling a little weird. After all, I had only found out a few months before that I was adopted. It was a discovery that had led me to realize I was a blood witch, descended from a long line of powerful Wiccan women.

There was a moment of awkward silence, as if everyone was waiting for my response. I looked at my aunt, knowing how much she wanted me to be happy for her. Congratulations," I said finally. "That's—that's great."

"That will be a lucky baby," Hunter said, and Aunt Eileen beamed at him.

Under the table, he reached for my hand and gave it a gentle squeeze.

Turning to my mother, Hunter held up a forkful of roast beef and said, "Mrs. Rowlands, this American smokehouse flavor is unbelievable—it's something we never get in England."

My mother hid her grin behind her napkin. "Thank you," she said.

I concentrated on my food so that I wouldn't look at him and laugh. It was strange to see Hunter acting so confident and natural with my parents. When we were alone together, he tended to be more reserved, even a little intense.

"Mr. Rowlands, Morgan tells me that you're very interested in physics," Hunter went on. "Did you happen to read that article in *Scientific American* about the neutrino collector they're building in Switzerland?"

I could see by Dad's face that this topic of conversation was his idea of heaven. Mom raised her eyebrows at me. On my other side, Mary K. leaned back in her chair to give me a broad wink.

I couldn't believe this night was going so well.

Once we were finished with dinner, Mary K. and I cleared the table and brought out dessert plates. Then I went back into the kitchen to grab the black-bottom pie. Just as I walked in from the dining room, the back door blew open with a bang. I jumped and turned around. Was someone out there? I walked to the door and cast out my senses.

I felt nothing. I took a quick lungful of the crisp night air. It was the middle of February, and in the moonlight the trees loomed black beneath their shrouds of snow. I shivered suddenly. It's just the wind, I told myself as I crossed to the door and grabbed the doorknob. Looking out into the night, I was hit with a sudden image of my old boyfriend, Cal Blaire. His dark, shaggy hair and golden eyes swam in my brain for a dizzying second, and then, just as quickly, the image was gone, leaving me with a dull ache in my chest.

Cal.

For a moment I tried to picture this evening with Cal at the dinner table instead of Hunter, but I couldn't. Cal had introduced me to Wicca, and he had told me that he loved me and that I was special . . . but I had always felt insecure around him. Not that I'm particularly secure to begin with when it comes to guys, but there was something about Cal that made me feel like he was doing me a favor by listening to me.

It had turned out that he only got to know me in the first place because his mother, Selene, wanted to drain me of my magick. She had almost succeeded, but at the end Cal had given his life to stop her. That had left me with a deep well of confusion and sadness. Cal had betrayed me, but in his own way, he had loved me.

"Where's that pie? The natives are getting restless," Mary K. said as she strode into the kitchen. She stopped when she saw my face. "Are you okay?"

I gave my head a quick shake to clear it and shut the outside door. "Sorry." I crossed the kitchen and yanked open the fridge. "I was just off in my own world for a minute. The pie's right here." I handed it to her.

"I think this is going really well, don't you?" Mary K. asked in a low voice as she pulled open the silverware drawer and got out a knife.

"Shockingly well," I agreed. I was grateful that Mary K. was being so supportive. She wasn't exactly a huge fan of Wicca, either, but she really liked Hunter.

My dad's black-bottom pie was a treat, thick with nuts and silky chocolate. Once it was served, conversation slowed as everyone savored each bite.

"I'm stuffed," Aunt Eileen said, once she had finished her pie.

"Everything was delicious," Paula chimed in.

My dad looked around the table. "Coffee in the living room?"

"Hunter?" my mom prompted. "Coffee? Or maybe you'd like some tea?"

"Nothing for me, thanks. I'll help Morgan and Mary K. with the dishes," Hunter said. He started gathering plates. I joined in, torn between awe and embarrassment.

"How am I doing?" Hunter whispered as we walked into the kitchen.

I snorted. "I never knew you were such a ham. Or rather, such a smokehouse-flavored roast beef. I think my parents are just about ready to adopt you."

"Fine with me. Can I share your room?" He gave me a look, and my heartbeat suddenly picked up.

"Eww, Morgan!" Mary K. said from the sink, where she was scraping food into the garbage disposal. "Is this your plate? I can't believe you hid your roast beef under a pile of mashed potatoes!"

"Well, you didn't expect me to eat it, did you?" I countered. "I didn't see you asking for seconds, either."

"I don't like red meat," Mary K. said primly.

"I thought the roast beef was good," Hunter said, looking surprised.

Mary K. and I snickered. "Well, he is British," Mary K. pointed out.

"I thought you were just sucking up to my mom," I told Hunter. "The fact that you were actually sincere is a little scary. Should I worry about you?"

Hunter laughed, and I felt a rush of delight. It was a surprising sound—deep and rich—and one I didn't hear all that often, especially lately. A few weeks ago Hunter and I had gone to New York to investigate Amyranth, a coven of Woodbane witches. The Woodbanes were one of the Seven Great Clans of Wicca—the ancient clans of blood witches. Historically, Woodbanes were dedicated to expanding their own power at any cost.

In a horrible surprise we'd discovered that one of Amyranth's leaders, and the man who killed my birth mother, was actually my birth father, Ciaran MacEwan. Ciaran had almost killed me, too, before he realized I was his daughter. The realization that I had come from someone so totally evil had thrown me into a tailspin, and for a while Hunter and I had broken up. During that time, Ciaran had manipulated me into almost killing him. But now we were back together—ironically, thanks to Ciaran—and Hunter's warm laugh in my family's bright yellow kitchen made all the horrible things we'd been through seem like they'd happened ages ago instead of only weeks.

"All right, Mary K.," I said, "I'll scrape the dishes if you'll clear off the table."

"Deal," she said, wiping her hands on a towel.

"You scrape, I'll stack," Hunter said. Once Mary K. was out of earshot, he gestured after her. "How is she?"

I felt a pang. Twice in the last week Mary K. had woken up screaming from a nightmare about being trapped in a small room. I was worried that these dreams were tied to the night months ago when Selene had kidnapped Mary K. and used her as bait to lure me to her house. Mary K., spelled by Selene, had seemed unaware of the horrible battle Hunter and I had fought with Selene, but I always suspected that at least some part of that evening had penetrated her subconscious. Now I was afraid the suppressed knowledge might be boiling up into her conscious mind.

"She slept fine last night, as far as I know," I told Hunter.

"Morgan, I think you should tell Mary K. the truth."

"I know." I shifted uncomfortably. "You said that yesterday."

Hunter's voice was low but insistent. "She deserves to know what happened that night—partly for her own sanity."

"What happened what night?"

I wheeled and saw Mary K. standing in the doorway. "What night?" she repeated, her eyes huge. "What were you talking about? What haven't you told me?"

Her voice seemed to expand and fill the room, like thick smoke, then slowly fade away, seeping into the walls. I felt the color drain from my face.

"I—we just meant—" I stammered, turning to Hunter for help.

But Mary K. didn't even look at him. She kept her eyes trained on me. "What haven't you told me, Morgan?" she asked again. "It's about the night I was with Cal's mother, the night they both died. Isn't it?"

I didn't answer. The silence hung in the brightly lit kitchen.

Mary K.'s nostrils flared. "You told me that we were never in any danger."

I bit my lip, hesitating. *Tell her,* I could almost hear Hunter saying. A quick glance at him and I realized that he was throwing up a blocking spell so that my parents wouldn't be able to hear the argument we both knew was coming.

I sighed. "We *were* in danger," I admitted finally. "You remember that you were at Selene's house?" I could hear the waver in my own voice.

My sister nodded. A small crease formed between her eyebrows as she struggled with the memory. In addition to Selene's spell, I had thrown up a number of obscuring and look-away spells as Selene attacked me and Hunter with every weapon in her dark arsenal. Mary K., I knew, had seen very little that night and understood even less.

"Selene wanted . . . " I started, but I couldn't force myself to say, "to steal my magick." My family was ignorant of my powers as a witch, and that was the way I wanted to keep it. I decided to start over. "Selene wanted something from me. She wanted it pretty badly, and she threatened me—and you—to get it. She would have carried out her threats, but Hunter and I managed to stop her."

"And . . ." Mary K. swallowed hard. "That's how she— died?"

"Yes." The word was a whisper.

"You *killed* her?" Mary K.'s voice was shrill.

"She was going to kill us." The words flew out of my mouth before I could halt them. "I stopped her."

My sister's face went pale. I couldn't tell whether it was from fear or rage. "Oh my God, Morgan!" she cried. "When the hell were you going to tell me?"

"I don't know," I admitted. "But we're all okay—"

"No, we are not okay!" Mary K. burst out. "We almost died, and you *lied* to me, Morgan! You hid this from me! And you would have gone on doing it!"

"I never lied to you." The words sounded lame even to me.

"No, you just never told me the truth." Her eyes flashed.

"Mary K.—" I reached out to grab her shoulder, but she jerked away from me.

"Don't touch me," she snarled. The words hit me like a slap, and before I could gather my thoughts to respond, my sister had turned and run out of the kitchen. I stared dumbly after her, hearing her feet thud up the stairs.

"Morgan," said a soft voice behind me. Hunter.

I turned to face him, feeling beaten. "I think I'd better go," he said. His face was grim.

I sighed. "I'm sorry."

"Don't be." Hunter reached out and touched the side of my face softly. "I understand. Walk me to the door?"

I nodded. As we walked toward the living room, a burst of laughter floated into the hall. Everyone looked up as we stepped into the room.

"Hunter has to go," I announced.

"Dinner was wonderful," Hunter said warmly. "Thanks so much for having me."

"Anytime," my father said heartily. He shook Hunter's hand and grinned at him.

"It was truly our pleasure," my mom agreed as she gave Hunter a kiss on the cheek. I was blown away. My mom—who never let me or my sister have guys in our rooms—was giving Hunter the seal of approval.

"Great meeting you," Aunt Eileen said. She and Paula gave Hunter a friendly wave from the couch.

We turned and walked into the front hall. "Morgan—don't forget that you've got homework to finish," my mother called after me.

"Don't worry, I won't," I promised, grabbing my jacket from a peg in the hallway. As if I could forget. I had a ton of work to do. With all of the stuff that had been going on lately, I had fallen horrendously behind. If I didn't hand in my extra-credit paper for English the next day, I could practically kiss a passing grade good-bye.

"Listen, Morgan, there's something I have to tell you," Hunter said as we walked out onto the front stoop. His voice turned serious, and he reached behind me to pull the front door closed. "I heard from Eoife just before I came here tonight."

The cold February wind whipped against my face. "Isn't she in London?"

Hunter nodded. "She phoned. She had a message for you."

Eoife McNabb worked for the International Council of

Witches, the same group Hunter worked for. She was the one who had recently asked me to help the organization by contacting my birth father. The council had been looking for Ciaran for a long time, believing that he and his coven, Amyranth, were behind the dark wave, a hideous magickal cloud of destruction that had wiped out countless covens over the years. I'd almost succeeded in trapping Ciaran, but at the last moment he'd managed to slip through all our fingers.

"Have they found Ciaran yet?" I asked.

Hunter shook his head. "Not yet, but the council is working on it. They believe he's somewhere in northern Spain or southern France. Eoife wanted you to know that the watch sigil you placed on him has been enormously helpful."

Hearing this, I felt a rush of contradictory emotions. Ciaran was my birth father, and I'd felt a strange sense of connection to him when we were together. Still, I knew he was a dangerous man, that the council needed to find him . . . and stop him.

"I just wish you had more formal training," Hunter went on. "Especially with Ciaran still at large—"

"I know," I snapped. "I'm a loose cannon. A witch with power as strong as mine has a duty. I need to see the bigger picture. Et cetera. I've heard it all before."

"I don't want anything to happen to you," Hunter whispered.

The cold around me seemed to melt away as he leaned toward me and his lips met mine.

The kiss went on and on, and for a moment I felt a

strange sort of nostalgia, knowing that I couldn't be in this moment forever. Soon I would have to go back to the real world—the world in which I had homework to do and Mary K. was rightfully angry with me. But I pushed that feeling away. Don't think about what will happen when this kiss is over, I told myself.

My heart raced, and I was suddenly aware of the blood coursing through my body. I was aware of every breath of cold air that I drew into my lungs and released into the wintry night in a puff of steam. I could feel the heat that our two bodies were generating at the heart of the frigid darkness. I felt like more than just a person, and the emotions I felt seemed wilder than desire, deeper than love. I felt like I was a force of nature—a storm, something unstoppable. I felt connected to Hunter and the world around me in an intricate and inseparable way, and I knew I was part of something greater than myself.

2

Contact

September 3, 1971

I feel sick. This afternoon Sam showed me a book he had just "discovered." When I saw the cover, I nearly dropped the book in terror. It was a first edition of Harris Stoughton's book, On the Containement of Magick.

I couldn't figure out where he'd found it. My parents haven't told him about their library yet, and even if they had, I doubt they own any books by Harris Stoughton. Sam told me that he'd found the book in the public library and had just taken it. He stole the book. He told me that he thought the book wanted him to have it.

I couldn't believe this was the brother I'd known for his entire life. I asked Sam if he had any idea who Harris Stoughton was, and of course he didn't. I should hope not. I explained that Stoughton was the most notorious witch in New England—that he used dark magick and antiwitch hysteria to wipe out as many non-Woodbane witches as he could. He even killed a couple of our blood relatives, although I didn't tell Sam that. I could tell he felt guilty enough as it was.

I thought that would be the end of it, but when I handed him the book and asked him what he planned to do with it, Sam just said that he wasn't sure. I know my brother. If I try to force him to get rid of it, he'll only want to hold on to it more. Part of me wants to tell our parents about this, but a larger part of me is afraid of how they'll react.

Goddess, grant me wisdom. And grant me courage to live in the house with that evil book.
—Sarah Curtis

The tall redbrick form of Widow's Vale High School rose bleakly against the gray February sky. I tried to shrug off the feeling of gloom that crept over me as I trudged toward the front door. Morning was never my finest hour, and the short winter days didn't help much. Neither did the fact that Mary K. had gotten a ride to school with her friend Susan Wallace instead of with me. She wasn't speaking to me.

"Hey, Morgan!" Jenna Ruiz stopped me as I stepped into the front hall. Her blond hair was swept up into a ponytail, and she was wearing a brown sweater and dark jeans. Her tentative smile made her look young and unsure. It was funny to remember that before I had joined the coven, I had found Jenna slightly intimidating. "Going my way?" she asked, jerking her head toward the stairwell that led down to the basement—our coven's winter hangout.

I tucked a few strands of hair behind one ear. "Where else?" I replied, and we fell into step together.

Jenna pushed open the door to the stairwell. Most of our regular coven crowd had already gathered. My good friend Robbie Gurevitch was sitting on the bottom step, leaning against Bree Warren's knees. Her arms were draped over his shoulders. Ethan Sharp and Sharon Goodfine sat higher up and to the left.

Raven Meltzer stood at the bottom of the stairs, by the banister. She was wearing a red velvet shirt and low-slung black leather pants that showed off the flame tattoo around her navel. It was actually a demure look for Raven. I, on the other hand, could never pull off that look in my wildest dreams. As I studied her, I wondered if Raven had gotten my cosmic share of curves.

The pale winter light that leaked in through the window at the top of the landing cast a faint glow on everyone's faces. I leaned against the wall by the bottom stair, and Bree smiled at me, taking away at least part of the February chill.

"Hey," she said warmly. "How did it go last night?"

"Great," I replied. "Everyone was charming, everyone was charmed."

Sharon took off her baby blue cardigan and slung it over her shoulders. "What are we talking about?" she asked.

"Hunter did the official parental dinner last night," Robbie explained.

"Oh, man," Ethan said. "Cruel and unusual." Sharon dug her elbow into his knee. "Ouch!" he yelped. "I was just saying . . ."

"No, it's true," I agreed. "It was a little tense at first. But everyone was on their best behavior. It went well."

"Not surprising," Robbie said. "Hunter is every parent's dream."

I looked at him, surprised. "How so?" I asked.

Robbie shrugged. "Hunter's responsible, he's generous, he's intelligent. And everyone can see that he's good for you, Morgan."

"Besides, he's a witch," Raven added dryly. "What parent wouldn't be thrilled?"

I ignored Raven's comment, pleased with what Robbie had said. He and I were close friends, but we'd had a fight a while back. He'd thought I was misusing my powers, and he'd had a point. But I was learning to be more responsible. It was good to know that Robbie realized my relationship with Hunter was a big part of that.

"Hey, Morgan," Ethan piped up, "have you heard anything from Killian?"

Killian was Ciaran's son and my half brother. I had gotten to know him slightly over the past few weeks, but after he'd come up to visit me in Widow's Vale and behaved really badly, he'd pretty much dropped out of sight.

"No," I said, feeling a twinge of regret. Killian was irresponsible, reckless, possibly even dangerous—but I really liked him. And I liked having a big brother. "I don't know where he is. Back in New York, probably."

I heard the door open and looked up to see Alisa Soto, one of the newer members of our coven. She was a sophomore with thick golden brown hair and dark eyes that were so large, she appeared almost owlish. "Hi, everyone," she said shyly. She looked at me uncertainly. "Hey, Morgan."

"Hi," I replied, pleased to see her. She was younger than the rest of us and usually hung out with the other under-classmen before school. I guessed that her appearance meant she was finally—after weeks—starting to relax around us.

Sharon gave Alisa a bright smile and patted the space beside her. Alisa walked down to sit next to Sharon, mur-muring hello to Bree and Robbie along the way.

Robbie glanced at his watch. "I've got to get to the library," he said. Bree released him reluctantly. "I've got to grab these last ten minutes to study before Spanish."

"I'll come with you," Bree said quickly.

An odd look flickered across Robbie's face, but just as soon as it had come, it was gone. "Great," he said. "Let's go. Later, guys." He waved and headed up the stairs.

Bree reached out and squeezed my arm. "We'll talk at lunch, okay? I want to hear all the details."

"Sure," I said. I watched, puzzled, as she turned and trot-ted after Robbie. It struck me as odd that Bree wanted to go with Robbie instead of hanging out with the rest of us. It wasn't really Bree's style to seek out extra study time.

"So Morgan, did you study for the test?" Jenna asked, slip-ping into Robbie's seat.

My stomach dropped. "Test?" I asked.

Jenna bit her lip. "You've got Powell, right?" she asked. "I thought he was giving all of his sections a test on the Civil War today."

It came back to me with sudden vividness and I groaned. "I thought that was *next* Thursday," I said. I was totally screwed.

Jenna touched my arm. "What period do you have history?" she asked.

"Fifth."

"Great—that's not until after lunch," she said reassuringly. "I'll give you my notes on the reading and you can study them then, along with your class notes." She dug in her backpack and pulled out the notes. "Here," she said, handing them over. "Don't worry, it's going to be fine."

I really had no choice but to try to believe her. "Thanks," I said as the first bell rang. I had the feeling it was going to be a very long day.

By the time I slid into my 1971 Plymouth Valiant—affectionately nicknamed Das Boot—my arms were practically shaking with exhaustion. I'd hidden Jenna's notes behind my textbook in every class. Unfortunately, the cramming hadn't helped. I'd wanted to tell Mr. Powell not to bother grading my exam. I knew I'd flunked.

I turned the key in the ignition and smiled as it turned over immediately. Old reliable. Mary K. was at cheerleading practice and had told me she'd catch a ride with one of her friends. It was the only thing she'd said to me all day.

Suddenly I didn't want to go home. I could picture myself all alone in the quiet house. My parents wouldn't be home for hours, and I had no one to talk to about my horrible day. Not that I *wanted* to tell my parents about flunking a test.

I started for Hunter's house. Please be home, I thought, remembering the sense of calm I'd felt with him the night before.

Hunter was standing in the front doorway as I pulled into his driveway, gravel crunching beneath my tires.

"Rough day?" he asked, leaning in to kiss me as I climbed the front steps.

"Horrendous." I wrapped my arms around his neck. His lips tasted like cinnamon tea.

He smiled. "Why don't you come in and tell me about it?"

The warm scent of cinnamon wafted past my nose as we stepped into the worn, comfortable living room. I knew without casting out my senses that Sky, Hunter's cousin, was upstairs.

"Should I say hello?" I asked.

Hunter hesitated. "I think she'll come down if she feels like it. She's been pretty low lately."

I nodded. Sky and Raven had been a couple for a while, but they'd recently broken up—thanks mostly to my half brother Killian. I wasn't sure how Raven felt—it was hard to break through her tough-girl exterior—but I knew Sky was in a lot of pain. I felt a pang of sympathy as I imagined Sky going through a breakup halfway around the world from most of her friends.

I shrugged off my coat. Hunter took it and hung it up next to his in the hall closet. Then he came and pulled me down beside him on the threadbare couch.

"I spoke with Eoife again this morning," he said. "She's concerned about you. She would like for you to learn more about magickal defenses, and so would I."

"What's that?" I asked. "Like, self-defense for witches or something?"

Hunter nodded without humor. "That's exactly what it

is." His green eyes seemed to deepen in color as he added, "Given your history, Morgan, it seems like a good thing for you to study. Also, it's one of the topics covered in the preinitiation rites."

"I thought I would be initiated as a witch a year and a day from the time of my first circle. I didn't realize I had to prepare for it."

"You don't," Hunter said. "That's a simple ceremony. I'm talking about your initiation as a blood witch, which isn't so simple. Once you're initiated into the coven, then you begin preparing for your preapprentice rites, which are a series of magickal power and knowledge tests. They're supposed to screen out blood witches who aren't yet serious enough or in tune with their power enough for apprenticeships." I stifled a groan at the thought of more tests as Hunter went on, "Once you pass those rites, you'll be paired as an apprentice with a blood witch who will guide you until you're ready for the full blood witch initiation."

"How long will that take?"

Hunter shrugged. "It depends," he said. "A few years."

I struggled to hide my disappointment. A few *years*?

"Anyway," Hunter said. "Eoife has found someone who can come here to tutor you in magickal defenses for two weeks. She's going to stay with Sky and me. Her name is Erin Murphy, and she'll be here this weekend."

"Is she good?" I asked.

"The best," he said. In his clipped English accent, the statement seemed to leave no room for doubt. "In the meantime Eoife asked me to show you the basics." He stood up and crossed the room. There was a dinged-up sideboard along the wall leading to the kitchen, and Hunter pulled out a small bronze dish and a piece of chalk. He drew a small circle on the floor on the other side of the coffee table. I stepped inside, and he drew the last piece closed. Then he took a pinch of salt from the dish and sprinkled it around the circle. "With this salt I purify our circle," he said.

We joined hands, closed our eyes, and breathed deeply for a few moments. With every breath I could feel my senses expanding. It was as if I was growing and reaching out, as if the house and everything in it was a living, breathing extension of myself. I felt myself draw power from the breath, and I sensed that Hunter was drawing the same power. Our bodies, joined at the fingertips, had become one, lost in the connection we felt with everything around us, including each other. Then we both dropped hands and found ourselves staring into each other's eyes.

It was as if a window opened, and I could see the true depths of Hunter's emotions—his fierce sense of protection, his trustworthiness, his love for me, and his appreciation for our connection. I also saw harsh and unyielding anger, and I knew that what I was seeing was the rage Hunter felt at what the dark forces had done to his family. Hunter's parents, pursued by the dark wave, had left him at a young age. I saw that Hunter believed they were still alive and that he could help them. I also saw his frustration at not being able to do more, his stubborn belief that if only he tried hard enough, he could put everything right. I saw these things, and I sucked in my breath.

Suddenly the window closed, and he was simply Hunter again.

"The first lesson is in something called *tàth meànma divagnth*," he explained.

"Is that like *tàth meànma brach*?" I asked, recalling the ceremony that I still thought of as the "Wiccan mind meld." *Tàth meànma* was a ritual through which two people could look into each other's minds and share thoughts, memories, beliefs. *Tàth meànma brach* was a sort of turbocharged version of regular *tàth meànma*, in which you exchanged basically everything that was in your brains. Alyce Fernbrake, a blood witch who ran an occult bookstore called Practical Magick, had gone through the ceremony with me.

"Not exactly," Hunter said. "The object of the *divagnth* is to use someone's power and divert it so that it can't hurt you."

"So it's sort of like witch tae kwon do?"

Hunter smiled. Then he grabbed my wrist lightly with his right hand and pointed to the wall with his left. I felt a quick rush through my body, as if I had touched an electric current. A sizzling bolt of blue fire exploded from Hunter's left index finger. It hit the wall and dissolved harmlessly.

I felt dizzy and struggled to suck oxygen into my lungs. "Are you all right?" Hunter asked, placing his hands on my hips.

I took a few deep breaths. "Yeah, but it kind of knocks the wind out of you."

Hunter nodded. "It can be very effective when you're dealing with an enemy." His voice was grim, and as I felt his strong hands on my hips, I realized yet again that Hunter had years of training and knowledge that I could hardly even begin to imagine.

I looked him in the eye. "Teach me," I said.

Hunter spent the better part of an hour showing me different techniques for deflecting power. Although he claimed that these were pretty basic self-defense moves, all of them were completely unknown to me. It was fascinating to realize that—even with all of Alyce's knowledge, which was considerable—there were entire worlds left to learn.

"Excellent work," Hunter said as I used one of his blocks.

Now that the energy wasn't flying around the room, I felt the exhaustion of the day settle on me like a heavy blanket. Hunter touched my hair. "Should I take you home?" he asked.

"No," I said quickly. I definitely didn't want to go home now. "Maybe . . . maybe we could go to a movie?" I suggested.

Sky came down the stairs. She was naturally fair but looked even paler than usual. "Hello, Sky," I said.

"Oh, hello, Morgan," Sky said, looking surprised. "I didn't realize you were here." That struck me as odd. Sky was a powerful blood witch. She should have sensed my presence. But as I looked at her drawn face, it was pretty clear that she was off in her own world. "Am I interrupting?" she asked, glancing from my face to Hunter's.

"I'm just trying to talk Hunter into going to a movie," I said. "There's a—a great new foreign film playing at the Pavilion," I said. Actually, what was playing there was an action adventure I'd been dying to see that I knew Hunter would never go for. But it was made in Hong Kong—that made it foreign, right? "It's still early," I went on, glancing at the clock on the mantel. It was only six-fifteen. "We can grab a slice of pizza before the movie, and I can still be home by ten." I put on my best overeager face and batted my eyelashes.

Hunter laughed and gave in. "All right," he said, holding up his hands.

"Great!" I rushed to the kitchen to use his phone while Sky wandered back upstairs. I punched in the number for my house and listened as it rang a few times and the machine picked up. I left a message explaining that I was going to a movie with Hunter. Considering the way my parents had reacted to him last night, I figured they'd be okay with me spending some quality time with him. At least, until I got my history grade.

Hunter and I grabbed a quick slice at Pino's Pizza, then drove over to the theater. When we walked up to the ticket window, Hunter said, "Two for *Fire Dragons,* please." I gaped at him as he pulled out his wallet. He noticed the look on my face, and the corners of his mouth twitched up into a smile. "What?" he said. "You didn't actually think you had me fooled with that line about going to see a foreign film, did you?"

I laughed and shook my head. The more I felt I knew Hunter, the more capable he was of surprising me.

The wind was blowing my hair around my face, and I pushed it back with both hands as we walked inside. The Pavilion used to be a real theater, the kind where you see plays and stuff, and the interior is decorated with images from Greek myths. I always liked to sit in the front of the balcony because the view is great and hardly anyone likes to sit there but me.

We made a quick stop at the concession stand for a medium popcorn and a Diet Coke for me. When I turned around, I came face-to-face with Bree and Robbie.

"Hey, guys," Robbie said. He pulled a few kernels from the top of my bag of popcorn and stuffed them in his mouth.

"Watch it," I joked. "Do you know how much that popcorn costs?"

"I'll pay you back," Robbie promised, and placed his order for a large popcorn and two sodas.

"And a box of Raisinets," Bree added. I smiled at her.

The blond girl gathered their order and lined everything up on the counter. As she was ringing their total, she said shyly, "Robbie?"

Robbie gave her a blank look. "Yes?"

The girl blushed. "I'm Jessica Watts . . . from Mrs. Carleson's class? Fifth grade? You sat next to me."

"Jessica Watts?" Robbie repeated. He sounded shocked.

I felt my own mouth drop open. Jessica Watts? I thought. As in "Mega Watts"? Bree and I had been in Mrs. Norton's class in the fifth grade, while Robbie was across the hall with Mrs. Carleson. The classes didn't really mix much, but Jessica Watts had been famous at our school. At the age of ten she had already weighed over 150 pounds. She got teased a lot and bullied because of her weight. Now it looked like she had lost thirty pounds—and grown four inches. She looked great.

"Wow, Jessica," Robbie said, "you look *terrific*! I don't know if you remember Bree and Morgan," he went on, waving a hand at us. "They went to Widow's Vale Elementary, too. And this is Hunter Niall," he added.

"Hey," I said.

"Hi," Bree said, checking her watch. "Robbie, the movie's going to start in five minutes."

Robbie looked at her. For a minute I expected him to protest, but instead he just said, "Yeah, okay. We'd better find a seat. Great to see you, Jessica."

Jessica grinned. "See you around."

As we stepped away from the counter, Robbie was still shaking his head. "God, I can't believe how great Jessica looks," he said.

Bree snorted impatiently. "She went on a diet—big deal."

"Bree!" I tossed a kernel of popcorn at her. She batted it away with annoyance.

Robbie gave Bree a look. "I'm not just talking about the weight," he insisted. "Back in fifth grade, Jessica always looked like a dog who was expecting to get kicked. She looks so much more confident now. . . ." His voice trailed off, but I knew what he meant, and he was right.

Bree didn't answer, and I wondered why. She usually had an opinion to voice. I glanced at her sideways and noticed her fiddling with one strand of her dark, perfectly tousled hair. I had known Bree a long time, since we were little kids, and I knew what that gesture meant. She was worried.

But what about? I wondered. It wasn't like Bree to get jealous or possessive. In fact, Bree had a history of never letting any guy get too close. She had left a string of love casualties in her wake. I decided to ask her later what was up. Bree didn't have the world's greatest family life. I wondered whether everything was okay with her.

"Are you two heading up to the balcony?" Bree asked as we neared the foot of the stairs.

"Yup. Want to come?" I teased, knowing what the answer would be. We'd been having the same debate since the seventh grade.

"Forget it," Bree replied. "You know how I feel about that rickety old railing."

"See you guys later, then," Robbie said.

Bree and Robbie walked through the main entrance while Hunter and I headed up the side stairs. I smiled as we walked down the aisle to my favorite seats in the front of the balcony. Looking down on the theater below, I saw that there were quite a few heads in the main part. But the balcony was completely empty. We settled into our seats just as the opening credits began to roll. Hunter put his arm along the back of my seat and I leaned against him, feeling like a corny couple out of the fifties.

"What's this movie about, anyway?" Hunter whispered as the title flashed across the screen in letters of flame.

"A bunch of guys kicking butt," I replied.

"Ah. Lovely." Hunter settled back against his chair.

About twenty minutes into the movie, I began to notice that he seemed uncomfortable. He shifted left, then right, then took his arm away from the back of my seat and gripped the armrest.

"Are you okay?" I whispered. Hunter didn't answer. I turned to look at him and gasped. His face, reflected in the strange shadows of the flickering movie screen, was dead white, and his mouth was opening and closing as if he was trying to speak but couldn't form the words. My heart pounded as Hunter squeezed his eyes shut and sucked in his breath. I grabbed his arm and was nearly crushed by the weight of some unseen force. Wave after wave of emotions flooded over me—despair, agony, longing, regret, fear. Deep fear. The sensations were so strong that I thought they would overwhelm me as they ripped through my body.

Then suddenly the flood of feelings stopped. Hunter sank down listlessly in his seat. It was over.

I flopped back against my chair, exhausted, and listened to the sound of Hunter's breathing—or was it my own? We were both inhaling in ragged gasps.

"What happened?" I whispered.

Hunter was pale, and his chest was still heaving. "It was my father," he said softly.

Cold fingers of dread crept up my spine. "Are you sure?" I asked in a hushed voice. Hunter's father and mother had disappeared when Hunter was a child. In an effort to save themselves and their family, they'd placed their children with relatives and gone into hiding, running from the dark wave. Hunter hadn't heard from them in years . . . until recently, when he'd received a scrying message that he felt certain was from his father. The meaning of the message was still unclear, but Hunter had sent a spelled seedpod down the Hudson River in the hope that he might make contact. But until now there had been no word, and I knew that Hunter feared the worst.

"I'm positive," he replied.

"But—what does it mean?" I asked.

Hunter sat forward, leaning his elbows against his knees. He stayed there a moment, hunched over in that position, as though completely drained. Finally he faced me. "I don't know what it means," he said, "but I'm going to find out."

I exhaled a long breath, trying to release the last of the fear and tension. I looked up at the movie screen. Its flickering images suddenly seemed like nonsense. "Let's get out of here," I whispered.

Hunter was already out of his seat by the time I finished my sentence.

I spent the drive back thinking about Hunter's message, wondering what it could mean. A glance over at Hunter showed me that his jaw was clenched and he was concentrating on the road. I watched the dark, hulking forms of trees flicker past the car windows, and I thought about what it must be like to know that your parents are out there somewhere. To know that they may need your help. And to be unable to give it.

Soon Hunter's battered Honda was gliding to a stop in front of his house. He shifted into neutral and stared straight ahead for a moment. Then wordlessly he swung open his car door and stepped out into the frigid night. I did the same, following him toward Das Boot. I would drive home from here.

Hunter was staring out into the darkness. I didn't feel ready to say good night. "Hunter," I began, but my voice trailed off. I didn't know what to say. I leaned in close and wrapped my arms around him, wishing I could just hold him and make it better.

"I'm going to find them," Hunter said simply. For a moment the words seemed to hang there, coiling around us in the quiet night air. Then he pulled away and turned to me, his green eyes glinting in the dimness with a strange, almost predatory look.

"How?" I asked.

"I'm not sure," Hunter said. "The council was supposed to pursue a few leads, but they haven't had any new information in a long time. They told me not to act, but I think I've waited long enough. The time has come to step in myself."

"But you have no idea where they are!" I protested.

Hunter shrugged. "Not yet," he said. Then his gaze seemed to soften, and he looked into my eyes. He leaned over, and his lips met mine. His kiss was gentle but insistent, and I felt my heart race at his touch. His fingers felt beneath my jacket and traced along my back. I shivered and pulled away from him.

"Hunter," I said, "I know I sound like a goofy movie girl-friend, but will you please just promise that you'll be careful?"

He hesitated before finally shaking his head. "I'll be as careful as I can."

I thought about the dark wave, about what it might take to rescue Hunter's parents. He was right—*careful* wasn't a word that would go very far in helping them. "All right," I said finally, fighting the wave of fear that I felt. It would have to be good enough. "I'll be thinking about you tonight." I gave him one final kiss, then swung open my car door and slid onto the seat.

"Good night, Morgan." Hunter turned, and his form retreated up the walk to his front door. I watched him until he went inside. Then I drove home, alone with my thoughts. I wished I understood what had happened. Memories of the violent emotions I'd felt swirled through my mind until I reached my house.

The hallway was silent when I went inside. I shrugged off my coat and hung it on a peg, then pulled off my boots so that I wouldn't track mud all over the house.

"Hi, Mom," I said, walking into the brightly lit kitchen. She was hunched over a pile of paperwork at the kitchen table. I pulled a glass out of the cabinet.

"Getting in a little late, aren't you?" my mom remarked.

I stopped, confused. We'd left the movie early. "Didn't

you get my message?" I asked. "I was at the Pavilion with Hunter."

"I got your message," my mom replied. "But Morgan, you know it's a school night. Have you finished your homework?"

I hesitated but couldn't lie. "No," I admitted.

My mother heaved an exasperated sigh. "Well, I don't think I need to explain what my problem with that is," she said. Her frown etched deep lines around her mouth, making her look older and tired. "Or do I? I don't know, Morgan, lately I feel like your priorities have shifted."

"That's not true," I protested.

"Isn't it?" my mother asked. She looked even more weary, and there was a catch in her voice as she added, "You never join us at church anymore. I feel like we hardly see you—like you're just disappearing from this family."

I suddenly realized why my mother had been so eager to get to know Hunter. It wasn't just because she wanted to make sure that he was a decent person—it was because she felt like I was slipping away, and she wanted to bring me back. "Mom, I'm sorry," I said, feeling a wave of guilt. "I guess I shouldn't have stayed out late on a school night. I just thought that you and Dad liked Hunter so much, you wouldn't mind. And I don't have a lot of homework tonight. I can still finish."

"Morgan, I don't want to force you to do things you don't want to do." My mom pushed away her paperwork and looked at me. "And I do like Hunter. But I miss you. We all do. I'd like to find a way to make sure that we can spend some time together."

I thought for a moment. "Maybe we could have a regular night to get together," I suggested. "A family night or something."

My mom pursed her lips a moment and folded her arms across her chest, her thinking pose. "Well, maybe we could do something like that once a week."

I nodded, thinking that maybe, if we spent more time together, my parents might realize that it was possible for me to have both them *and* Wicca in my life.

"Okay," my mom said finally. "I'll check with Dad and Mary K., and we'll set up a regular night." She leaned over and kissed me on the forehead. "I'll think of something fun we can do together."

I grabbed an apple from the bowl on the table. "Sounds good. I'm going upstairs to do my problem set. Sorry I was so late," I said. Eyeing her paperwork, I added, "And don't work too hard."

"Mmm." My mom bent over her papers again.

Biting into the apple, I went upstairs and crawled onto my bed with my calculus book. But the minute I got settled on my down comforter, the wave of exhaustion I'd been holding back all day washed over me with full force. I closed my eyes, intending to rest them for just a minute. I didn't wake up until morning.

3

Attack

Okay, Time for another entry in my "Book of Shadows." I feel kind of silly calling This wire-bound notebook by such an imposing-sounding name. "Book of Shadows" is supposed To be for spells and chants and stuff like That—and I don't really know any. Still, both Hunter and Sky Think we should keep one, and everyone else in Kithic seems To do it. So I got one. Which means That I have a special place To share my "wonderful" news.

Dad is marrying Hilary. She's pregnant. And moving in with us in a few weeks.

I Tried really hard To act happy for Dad, but he didn't ask me how I felt about it. So I guess he didn't really want To know.

As I write This, my mother's picture is looking at me from my dresser across The room. I wonder what she would Think of all This. I honestly have no idea—I barely knew her. She died when I was Three. I like To Think That she'd be glad my father is happy with someone new. I like To Think That she was a nicer person Than I am.

Hilary is coming over laTer. I'm glad I won't be around; I'm going To circle. I have To admiT That when Bree first asked if I wanTed To join KiThic, I wasn't so sure That iT was a good idea. But at The very first circle we held hands and Sky TaughT us how To feel each oTher's energy. IT was Truly magickal, The kind of experience you can't puT inTo words. I felT myself opening up like a flower. That's The besT Thing abouT The coven. In a weird way—I don't really undersTand iT myself—iT's almosT like coming home.

Bree jusT called To Tell me she's going To be abouT Ten minuTes laTe To pick me up. She's giving Morgan a ride, Too. I know iT's dumb, buT Morgan makes me uncomforTable. She has magickal powers. Of course, everyone else in The coven Thinks iT's incredibly cool. One Time she made flowers appear ouT of Thin air. I had To look around aT everyone else and Tell myself, "iT's all righT. Nobody else is scared." Then I focused on my breaThing To calm myself.

I know That magick is a part of Wicca, and The smaller spells—using herbs and oils To heal, channeling your energy Toward someThing you wanT To achieve—Those seem beauTiful To me, buT Morgan's magick is differenT. IT feels dangerous, ouT of conTrol. And even her own sisTer is afraid of iT.

But That doesn't mean That I shouldn't drive To circle wiTh Morgan or even That she isn't a nice person. RighT?
—Alisa

"You look gorgeous," I told Bree as I ducked into her BMW, Breezy, on Saturday evening. She wore a soft-looking gray coat over black wool pants and managed to look sleek, sophisticated, and sexy all at once.

"Thanks," Bree said without enthusiasm.

"So," I said, "will Robbie be at the circle?" I actually already knew the answer to this—Robbie and I had chatted for about one second that afternoon before Mrs. Fiorello, my mom's coworker, had beeped in on the other line and I'd had to hand the phone over to my mom. But I was looking for an opening. In fact, I'd asked Bree for a ride especially so I could talk to her.

"Yeah, he'll be there." There was an odd note in her voice. My opening.

"Is everything okay with you guys?" I asked as nonchalantly as I could.

"What do you mean?" Bree's voice was taut, like a piano wire.

"I don't know, you just seem to be . . . not yourself lately." I gripped the door handle, preparing for an attack. Bree could be prickly about personal comments.

She sighed. "Yeah," she said, and her voice trailed off into the darkness. The road hummed beneath us, and for a moment I thought that she wasn't going to say anything else. "I've been feeling—I don't know." Bree shook her head, as if frustrated that the thoughts wouldn't form a cohesive sentence for her. "I guess I've been feeling kind of *possessive*." She laughed. "Pretty weird, huh?"

"For you? Um, yeah," I agreed. "You usually run for the hills when someone acts possessive with you."

"Tell me about it." Bree scowled. "I just can't seem to stop myself. It's just—I've never felt this way about a guy before."

"But that's great," I said. "It means you care."

"Maybe." Bree sounded doubtful. "I've never really let myself get this close to someone before. I guess this is why." Running an impatient hand through her dark hair, she added, "I really hate the way I'm feeling right now, Morgan. I hate the way I'm acting. I don't want to be clingy and needy—but I just don't want to let Robbie out of my sight. I guess I'm just worried that he's going to get bored with me or something. That now that I actually care about someone, he's going to move on."

I reached over and grabbed Bree's hand. Even through our gloves, I could feel her hand radiating heat. "That's not going to happen," I assured her. "Robbie is nuts about you. He's been nuts about you for a long time—and that's not going to change." I pictured Robbie in my mind, remembering how he'd confessed to me his feelings for Bree. "Besides, he'd never want to hurt you."

Bree squeezed my hand. There was a catch in her voice as she said, "I know."

I leaned my head against the cool passenger's-side window. I wanted to say more, but we were almost at Alisa's house, and I didn't want to discuss this in front of her. My breath made a steamy crescent on the side of the window, and I remembered the two of us in elementary school, breathing on the cold glass of the school bus window and writing our names in the steam. That was before Bree's mom moved away to live with her boyfriend in Europe. It was before her older brother, Ty, went off to college and before Bree's corporate-lawyer father began working so hard that she hardly ever saw him anymore. Bree was so beautiful and poised, it was easy to forget that her life was sort of lonely. Until now, she'd always kept the guys she dated at a safe distance. But Robbie was different—they'd been friends before they started going out, and he knew her too well to be satisfied with staying at arm's length. He was chipping away at the wall that surrounded her. I wondered whether it would open her up to caring about people in a new way or whether it might make her crumble.

I briefly considered talking to Robbie about what was going on with Bree but rejected the thought. It was their relationship, after all. Instead I asked her, "Have you spoken to Robbie about this?"

"No," she admitted.

"Maybe you should."

Bree bit her lip and didn't reply. She made a left turn. The silence yawned between us as we pulled up into the circular driveway in front of a small, tidy ranch-style house. Alisa must have been watching for us because a moment later she hurried out the front door.

Bree turned to me. "Okay, I'll talk to him," she said quickly.

Good, I thought. I'd done my good deed for the day.

Alisa said a shy hello, and Bree eased the car back onto the road toward Hunter's house. The car was silent for the rest of the drive. I guess we were all lost in our own thoughts.

Hunter's small living room was already filling up by the time we arrived. The room was lit by the warm glow of candles, and in the soft light the worn furniture seemed comfortable and welcoming. The air was heavy with the scent of mulling spices—Sky must have put a pot of cider on the stove. Robbie stood in the corner, talking to Simon Bakehouse, but the minute we walked in, he flashed Bree an enormous grin and hurried over. I gave Bree an I-told-you-so look, and she smiled as Robbie draped an arm around her shoulders. They melted into the rear of the room.

From his place by the tattered armchair, Hunter waved to me and continued an intense-looking conversation with Sky. Jenna came over and said hello to me, and she and I chatted for a few minutes. "Are you feeling all right?" I asked.

"My asthma's bothering me," she admitted. "I took a shot off my inhaler before I came here, but it hasn't helped much."

I resisted the urge to lay my hands on her back. I'd helped her with her asthma before. But I knew that Hunter and Sky frowned on such practices, and I was trying to show them that I'd turned over a new leaf.

Not everyone had arrived yet, so I headed to the kitchen to help myself to cider. When I pushed open the door, I was surprised to see Alisa sitting alone at the small table, staring off into space. I hesitated a moment, reluctant to barge in on her. But I decided it would look weird to scurry away, so I just plowed ahead.

"Hey," I said, crossing to the stove. Someone had put out some plastic foam cups on the countertop so people could help themselves to the cider. "This smells great—do you want some?"

"Hmm?" Alisa jumped slightly. "Oh—no. Thanks." She tried to smile at me, but she looked tired . . . and something else. Sad, maybe.

I pulled out a chair and sat next to her. I took a slow sip of cider and felt its warmth spread through me, chasing away the February chill. I wondered why Alisa was in here alone. "Is everything okay?" I asked finally. I felt awkward. I really didn't know Alisa that well. Normally I didn't like to pry into people's lives, but there was something about Alisa that made me feel oddly protective, almost like she was a vulnerable younger sister or something.

Surprise flickered over her face. For a moment it seemed like she wanted to tell me what was on her mind. Almost instantly, though, she seemed to think better of it, and her face closed. "I've just had some weird news, that's all," she said. She looked down at the table.

Before I could decide whether to press her for details, the kitchen door swung open to reveal Sky. Her pale skin and fair hair seemed to glow against the midnight blue linen shirt she was wearing. "Morgan, Alisa," she said, "we're getting ready to start."

Stepping into the living room, I saw that Hunter had already drawn a circle on the floor. Alisa and I stepped into it behind Sky. I tried to move toward Hunter but found myself almost directly across the circle from him. Once everyone had settled down, I was surprised to see someone new next to Sky. She looked young and was about five feet tall, with dark red hair and green eyes. Her slim figure made her seem coltish, as if she were about to go through a growth spurt. I wondered who she was.

"Everyone, before we begin, I'd like to introduce our guest," Sky said. "This is Erin Murphy."

Erin Murphy. I knew that name. Erin Murphy was the witch who was coming to teach me magickal defenses. But this couldn't be her! I studied Erin's face more closely and saw faint creases around her mouth and eyes. Maybe she's older than she looks, I thought. Automatically I reached out with my senses and felt her power. She was strong. Really strong.

Erin had been looking at Sky, but her eyes suddenly flicked to me. The steady gaze felt like a hand against my forehead, but after a moment the pressure stopped, and she smiled. I resisted the urge to rub my temples.

"Erin is a healer from Scotland," Sky went on. She didn't say anything to the rest of the coven about the fact that Erin was a magickal defense expert.

Jenna looked hopeful, and I knew that she was thinking about her asthma. From her place next to me, Alisa shuffled uneasily. "A healer?" she repeated.

"You think I'm not old enough to know what I'm doing? I'm forty-seven," Erin said abruptly, turning her sharp eyes on Alisa. I guess she was used to people's confusion about her age. Then her face took on a curious expression as she still looked at Alisa.

Alisa blushed to the roots of her hair. She blinked uncomfortably and brought her hand to her forehead. "I didn't mean—"

"It's quite all right," Erin cut her off in a musical brogue. "If you can believe it, the flight attendant on my flight over asked me if my ma would be meetin' me at the gate." Laughter rippled through the circle, and I felt everyone relax. Erin studied Alisa a moment longer, then smiled. I glanced across the circle at Hunter, and he grinned at me.

"You don't sound Scottish," Matt Adler said.

"I'm an immigrant," Erin said, and something about her

tone made everyone chuckle again. "I'm Irish, living in Scotland. On vacation in America." She looked around the circle, and her eyes landed on me. "Any other questions?" she asked. Her tone was playful but seemed to hold a challenge as well. I had a million questions, but I felt too shy to ask them. I could practically feel the power rolling off this woman.

After a moment Sky took out some salt and began to purify the circle. Raven had managed to maneuver herself so that she was between Sky and Matt, whom she'd fooled around with a few times back in the fall. I wondered how Sky would react.

Sky began placing incense for air, sand for earth, a candle for fire, and a small cup of water at various points on the circle. I could see that the line of her jaw was rigid, although she was making an effort to seem unaffected by Raven's presence. It was actually kind of strange to see the two of them next to each other. Raven had clearly taken more care than usual with her appearance tonight—she was wearing a red velvet peasant blouse that laced up the front and black leather pants. Her dyed black hair cascaded down her back. She looked like a biker-chick version of Lady Guinevere. She was dark and lush, fire to Sky's ice.

Sky set down the last bowl and returned to her place in the circle. Hunter looked up at me. "There's a full moon tonight—very auspicious," he said. "Let's join hands and walk deasil." I was standing between Alisa and Robbie, and I was glad for Robbie's familiar presence as we all began to move clockwise around the room. As the group moved together, I could feel the energy build around me. I remembered the way it used to press in on me when I'd first begun coming to circles, and I was glad that I was now more in control of the magick that surrounded me. Now the power seemed wonderful and exhilarating, without the edge of fear that it used to hold.

"In Wicca we aren't afraid to ask the Goddess for what we need," Sky said. "When you feel it, make a wish. During a full moon it may very well be granted."

Next to me Robbie was the first to speak. "I wish for endurance."

On the other side of him Bree said, "I wish for peace."

Ethan went next. "I wish for strength," he said. He cast a quick look at Sharon, who was standing next to him.

Sharon met his look. "I wish for understanding."

We went around the circle, and everyone said what they wished for. It was kind of interesting. Everyone wished for intangible things.

Finally it was Alisa's turn. "I wish things could stay the way they are," she said quietly. There was a sadness in her voice that tugged at my heart.

I glanced across the circle at Hunter, and my mind flashed back to the kiss we'd shared a few nights ago. That was a moment I'd wanted to preserve perfectly, like a leaf in amber. But things change—that's their nature. I felt a wave of sympathy for Alisa, for her doomed wish. I squeezed her hand.

Hunter gave me a nod, and I knew it was my turn. I racked my brain for something to say, and I suddenly remembered the first circle I'd ever been to. Everyone had named something they wanted to banish. I'd said I wanted to banish limitations. In the weeks that followed, my life had opened up. I'd found Wicca, I'd discovered the truth about my heritage, and my power had started to reveal itself. But now, finally, my world seemed to be settling down, and I was growing comfortable with who I was.

"I wish to learn my limits," I said. I felt Alisa turn toward me, but when I faced her, she had already turned away. I wondered at my own choice of words. In order to learn my limits, I would have to test them. How much further would I have to go?

We continued walking deasil for a moment, then we all stopped and threw our hands up. "That was good," Sky said. Her cheeks were flushed pink, and I knew that she was feeling the same energy I was. "Let's take it down." We all sat on the floor.

"I feel a little dizzy," Alisa whispered as she crossed her legs.

I nodded. We had been moving in the circle for quite a while, building up a lot of energy. I was glad to be sitting, too.

Sky reached out and picked up the cream-colored pillar candle that represented fire. With a gentle breath she extinguished the flame and set the candle in the center of the circle. Smoke curled toward the ceiling as Sky said, "Morgan, please light this."

I frowned. I could only assume that Sky was hoping to demonstrate my magick to Erin, but reluctance swelled in my chest. Most of my friends in the coven had no idea that I could light fires with my mind, and I wasn't really keen on their finding out. I loved my power, but I'd seen the gulf it had created between Robbie and me, and, in another way, between Bree and me. I was something different. I didn't want my friends to fear me.

Hunter looked at me with serious eyes. I could tell that he wanted me to light the candle, too. Erin leaned forward slightly, one eyebrow arched, almost as if she doubted I could do it.

The circle was hushed and still. A feeling of expectancy filled the room.

I faced the candle and quieted my mind. The energy that still curled through the room flowed through me, and in a moment the wick sputtered and burst into flame. A few people gasped. Alisa's eyes flew wide, and she drew her knees toward her chest and leaned away from the candle, as if it were a snake that might bite her.

"Oh my *God,* Morgan," Bree said. She was staring at me.

The candle flame burned steadily, and I looked over it at Hunter. His face was golden in the soft glow.

Suddenly a frigid breeze blew through the room, as if someone had opened a window. The candle flame hissed and went out, then the candle itself toppled over, spilling wax on the carpet. An icy finger of fear tickled my scalp. That was a big candle, I thought. It shouldn't have blown over so easily.

A murmur ran through the room.

"What's happening?" Alisa whispered.

But before I could answer, the lightbulb in the lamp behind Hunter exploded with a loud *pop.* Someone screamed. For a moment I thought it was me, but then I realized it was Alisa. She stared at me in horror.

On the other side of the room the bookcase behind Hunter shuddered, and a book flew off the shelf, hurling itself against the opposite wall. Reflexively I threw up my hands as the entire shelf of books flew after the first one, landing on the wall with thud after vicious thud. The bulbs of the other three lamps exploded in rapid succession, the sound like gun-fire. Hunter stood up and ran to the windows.

"Stop it!" Alisa screamed. "Stop it, Morgan!"

"I can't!" I shouted. I had no idea what was happening or what had caused it.

On Alisa's other side Sharon reached to pull her into a hug, but Alisa fought her off as the room was plunged into darkness. Hunter stepped away from the window, letting the cold moonlight trickle in. Alisa was still screaming. I could see Erin's small form as she stood up and began to chant.

Goddess, we trust in you to protect us,
With this prayer we banish fear.

It was a short chant, and as she said it over and over, Alisa's cries grew more faint until the only noise I heard was a faint sniffling. The rest of us took up the chant. There was strength in the simplicity of the words, and as I said them, I felt their magick working on me. I took deep breaths and imagined a white light growing inside me, and I tried to release the fear that had held me in its grip. After a few min-utes the room felt calm again, although the warm energy from before had disappeared.

There was a light scraping sound, then a small burst of flame as Sky struck a match. Leaning forward, she stood the pillar candle up and lit it. Hunter, who was still standing, took the packet of matches from her and began lighting can-dles all around the room. I looked around the circle at everyone's faces. Robbie's lips were pressed tightly together, and I could feel anger flowing from him. Bree looked at me like she couldn't remember who I was, and Jenna stared at the floor, avoiding my eyes. Matt, Thalia Cutter, and Simon were wide-eyed, silent. Hunter and Sky were impassive, but Raven was gazing at me with what looked like respect. And Erin looked at me like I was a fascinating bug, something slightly revolting but nonetheless interesting.

"I didn't do anything," I said loudly. "That wasn't me."

Alisa shakily got to her feet. Sharon stood and put her arm around Alisa's shoulders. Alisa turned to her and asked, "Will you take me home?" She sounded very young. Sharon nodded, and Alisa turned toward the door. I tried not to feel hurt. I knew Alisa blamed me, but this *wasn't* my fault.

"I'm sorry, you guys," Sharon said. "But I think Alisa—".

"It's all right. Actually, why don't we call it a night?" Hunter said quietly. "We'll talk about this next week, when we've had a chance to sort it out."

"Right." Robbie got to his feet. He didn't look at me.

Bree peered around him. "Morgan—?"

"I'm staying," I said. "Hunter, you can take me home later, right?"

Hunter confirmed with a nod. In a few moments everyone had said their good-byes, and the house was empty except for Hunter, Sky, Erin, and me. The blood witches.

Sky extinguished the candles, and we moved to the kitchen, where Hunter poked around, looking for new light-bulbs.

"Well, that was a very interesting circle," Erin said brightly as she pulled up a chair to the farmhouse table.

I ladled hot cider into four cups and handed them out. "What *happened*?" I asked as I warmed my hands on the sides of my cup.

"I was about to ask you that, my dear," Erin replied. She took a sip of her cider.

"It wasn't me," I said again, feeling resentful.

Erin put down her cup. Leaning forward on one arm, she looked at me closely. "Are you sure?" she asked. I opened my mouth to reply, but Erin held up a hand. "I'm not saying that you caused it on purpose. It might have been an accident." Leaning back in her chair, she added, "It was my understanding that there were only four blood witches here tonight. And only one who hasn't been trained. Or initiated. You."

"It wasn't me," I insisted. "I would have known if I were making something happen. I would have felt power flowing through me." I turned to Hunter. "Right?"

Hunter looked at Erin. "Morgan is extremely powerful," he said. "She may not be initiated, but she has gained a great deal of control over her magick."

Erin shrugged. "Perhaps," she said. I couldn't tell if she was convinced. "All right, then," she went on, turning to Sky, "what else might have caused it?"

Hunter and Sky exchanged glances. "Amyranth?" Sky asked. Hunter nodded, and I felt a tightening in my chest. Amyranth. Ciaran's coven. They had kidnapped me, tried to drain my power. Were they after me again?

Was . . . was Ciaran himself after me? I felt cold at the thought. I was more or less certain that he knew I'd worked with the council to try and trap him. He might want revenge. True, I was his daughter. His flesh and blood. He loved me—I really believed that. Then again, he had loved my mother. And that hadn't stopped him from killing her.

Erin cocked her head and thought for a moment. "There are sigils of protection on this house, I presume?"

"Yes, of course," Hunter said. "But I should redraw them."

Erin stood up. "Do that." She put a gentle hand on my shoulder. "Sky and I will do a few spells to protect Morgan herself."

I looked up at her in surprise, but she just continued to watch Hunter as he grabbed a flashlight and went out the back door. In a few moments we could hear his footsteps crunching through snow as he visited each window and door and retraced the runes of protection on them.

Erin took her chair again, and then she, Sky, and I joined hands around the table. Erin began to chant. Though I didn't understand them, the words sounded beautiful in her lilting voice. The energy flowed between us, and suddenly I felt filled with light, with magick. Serenity flowed around me.

After a few moments Erin let go. Picking up my hand, she traced a sigil on my palm, one I had never seen before.

"This will protect you." Her voice was strong and sure. I looked into her cool, clear eyes. She's a master of magickal defenses, I told myself. I can believe her.

Anyway, what choice did I have?

4

The Vision

The sky is the color of steel today, and the bitter wind has begun to blow from the North. The flags are flying at half-mast, and there seems to be a hush over the town of Gloucester. We heard this morning that the _Lady Marie_ went down in last night's storm.

All five fishermen aboard are believed dead — Captain James Dallman, Tim Flanagan, Arnold Jennings, Jason McGreevy, and Andrew Lewis. The storm came up so suddenly that the men on board weren't even able to radio for help. They sank fifty miles off Eastern Point.

They haven't found the bodies.

Sam has been quiet all day. He knew Andrew Lewis pretty well. We all did, actually — Drew grew up only two blocks from our house. He was two years older *than I am and was a big baseball hero in high school. He always let the little kids play in the neighborhood games and taught them how to field and bat. Sam looked up to him.*

Some people said that Drew should have tried for a career in baseball—he even got a college scholarship to play. But Drew just wanted to be a fisherman like his dad. He didn't want to leave Gloucester.

And now he's gone. Of course, that's the risk you take, being a fisherman. It's a dangerous job. Not even all the magick of Wicca can save you from the full force of a storm.

—Sarah Curtis

"Let me take you home." Hunter stood over me, worry etching fine lines around his mouth. "I've finished with the sigils. There isn't much else we can do tonight."

When I stood, I felt like every muscle in my body was aching. The night's tension had made me stiff.

Erin and Sky were talking together in the living room, and they both seemed subdued as we said good-bye. Still, there was something in Erin's gaze as she looked at me that seemed sharp and wary. I felt like I had spent the evening under a microscope. I was on edge until Hunter and I were safely tucked into his beat-up Honda. He turned the key in the ignition, and we were off.

As we neared a heavily wooded dip in the road, the fog grew thicker and Hunter had to slow the car. My senses snapped to alert. The road revealed itself only a yard at a time, and deer were known to dart out onto the asphalt. It could be very dangerous.

Hunter slowed even further as we headed into a curve that I knew all too well. It was here, almost two months before, that Cal had suddenly reappeared after he and his mother had left Widow's Vale. It had been a dark night like this one, and Cal had been standing right in the middle of the road. At the memory, the hair on the back of my neck began to prickle, and without even realizing it, I cast out my senses.

I felt nothing. I exhaled slowly, trying to calm myself. There's nothing here, I told myself. Focus on your breathing and calm down. Another deep inhale and Hunter was easing around the curve, beginning to accelerate slightly. I felt better.

Just then, Hunter slammed on the brakes and the car swerved sickeningly.

Someone was standing in the middle of the road.

"Cal!" An involuntary cry escaped me.

Goddess, help me, I thought desperately. Hunter muttered curses and fought with the steering wheel. I felt the jarring pressure of the seat belt across my chest as we came to a sudden skidding stop and I was thrown forward in my seat. We were half on, half off the shoulder.

I turned to make sure Hunter was okay and saw that his eyes were huge. He was staring straight ahead, still gripping the steering wheel. In front of us, the figure in the fog had not moved.

I stared at it, my lips moving dumbly for a moment before I realized that it wasn't Cal—at least, not in any incarnation I knew. The figure had a human form, but it was shadowy and indistinct. It looked vaguely female. Who—or what—was it?

I leaned forward to look at it more closely and saw that it seemed to be part of the mist—as if the fog itself were struggling to come to life. For a moment I thought it was an optical illusion, a trick of mist and light, but then the figure actually turned and looked directly at us. Its eyes seemed to see, and it gazed at us mournfully. Sadness gripped me with iron claws. Holding my breath, I didn't dare to look away.

I reached for Hunter's hand and found that it was icy. After a long moment the figure disappeared.

"What was that?" I whispered.

Hunter didn't respond. Instead he merely closed his eyes, and I knew that he was pouring every ounce of concentration he had into casting out his senses. I leaned back against the plush car seat and did the same. Around us, by the side of the road and into the forest, I cast out with my mind. I felt the heartbeats of a brood of young fox kits, frightened by the footstep of a doe nearby. I sensed a small field mouse and the silent swoop of an owl overhead, diving toward its prey in an elegant, deadly arc. I felt the quietness of the trees, their collective silence that had stood sentry and witness, rooted to that spot, in some cases, for over a century.

But there was no human presence in the woods.

A shudder rippled through Hunter, and I knew that he had felt what I had. Nothing.

"Was it—" Thinking again of Cal, I felt my body grow cold. "Do you think it was—a ghost?"

I didn't even know whether such a thing was possible, but Hunter didn't laugh at me. "I don't think so," he said slowly.

Something about his tone of voice made me ask, "Do you think it could be another message from your parents?"

For a moment Hunter was silent. "Yes," he said finally. "It could be. But it could also have been a number of other things." I realized that Hunter was holding back, but I didn't ask him what he was thinking. I could guess. Amyranth. Ciaran.

"I think we should tell Erin about this," he said.

At the mention of her name, a mental image of Erin's appraising glance flashed through my mind, and I felt a small pinprick of impatience. But I immediately pushed the feeling aside. Hunter was right, and I knew it. "When can we meet?" I asked.

"Are you free tomorrow night?" Hunter asked, and I nodded. That was the last thing we said as the car plodded forward at its snail's pace. Wrapped in fog, the night had a sense of unreality, and I was so, so glad to have Hunter sitting next to me—strong and sure, like the trees that loomed in the mist, standing guard over the forest.

The next day dawned clear and chilly, with a pale blue sky dotted with puffy clouds. Last fall's brown, brittle leaves danced by my windowpane on the breeze.

It was such a beautiful day, the incidents of the night before seemed unreal . . . and unlikely. Had everyone really freaked out over a few lightbulbs bursting? That could have been an electrical surge—a problem in the wiring at Hunter's house. And the figure in the fog could have just been an odd mist formation. Clouds took on strange shapes all the time, I reminded myself.

I lay in bed, enjoying the warmth of my flannel sheets and down comforter, listening for the sounds of my parents and sister as they went through their usual Sunday routine of showers and breakfasts. But the house was silent. Rolling over, I glanced at my digital clock. Nine forty-seven!

They hadn't even bothered waking me for church.

I lay back against my pillows, unsure how I felt about that. Wicca was my religion, after all, the religion that felt like home to me, as natural as breathing. And I hadn't been going to church much lately. Still, our church filled me with warm feelings. It held lots of good memories for me, memories of my family and of my community.

Suddenly I felt like the last child to be picked up from a party—neglected and forgotten. I knew the feeling was childish, but I couldn't help it. It wasn't so much that I really wanted to go to church. I just wanted to be *asked*.

Slowly I crept out of bed, moving aside my cat, Dagda's, warm, furry form. He mewed softly, then stretched and rolled onto his back, only to curl up again and doze off. What a life.

After a long, steamy shower I began to feel almost human again. I puttered around the house awhile, reading the paper and microwaving myself a bowl of oatmeal. Desperate to talk to somebody, I called Robbie, but he wasn't home and I didn't leave a message. I didn't know what I wanted to say. Finally I decided to meet my parents for brunch at the Widow's Diner. It was a tradition for my family to eat there after church. This would be a good chance to show my mom that I could spend time with the family and still be involved in Wicca. Besides, I wanted to see them.

Quickly I pulled on a gray cable-knit sweater and my faded jeans. I put on my thickest socks and sank my feet into my heavy brown boots. In just a few minutes I was in Das Boot, tearing up the road on the way to the Widow's Diner.

As I walked into the diner, my stomach squirmed with

nerves. Between Mary K being mad at me and the lecture I'd gotten from my mom, I wasn't sure what to expect. I glanced around and saw that my family was sitting in our usual spot—the booth against the windows. They were all laughing at something someone had said. Across from my mom and dad was the back of Mary K.'s head . . . and someone else, a girl with thick, golden brown hair. I stopped short. Who was that? Then my mom looked up and saw me. She looked surprised and pleased. She waved me over.

Mary K. turned around in her seat. After a moment she flashed me an uncertain smile, and the nervous caterpillars in my stomach quieted. Had she forgiven me? I hoped so. I grinned back and hurried toward them. The other girl still hadn't looked up, so I didn't see until I got to the table that it was Alisa.

"Hi, everyone," I said, sliding into the booth next to Mary K. The Formica tabletop was littered with my family's half-eaten lunch. "Hey, Alisa," I added when she didn't look up from the straw wrapper she was fiddling with on the table. For a moment I wondered what she was doing there. But I knew that she went to our church and that she and Mary K. had gotten pretty tight ever since Mary K.'s best friend, Jaycee, had found a boyfriend. Alisa had been close to Jaycee, too, so I guess that made both Alisa and Mary K. boyfriend refugees.

Alisa gave me a hesitant smile. "Hi," she said. There were dark circles under her eyes and a strange note in her voice that brought back the eerie scene from the night before. Instantly I remembered just how real it had all been. Alisa went back to fiddling with her straw wrapper.

"Have you eaten yet, sweetie?" my mom asked, and my dad twisted in his seat to flag the waitress down.

"Some oatmeal," I replied. "I really just came by to see you guys."

"Only oatmeal? Have a bagel," my mother urged, "or a cup of soup. It's lunchtime—you should have a bite to eat."

I realized that my parents wouldn't be satisfied until I ordered something, so I asked for some wheat toast and chamomile tea. By the time I'd finished ordering, my mom and dad were engrossed in a conversation about some problem she was having with her boss. I turned to say something to Mary K., but now she had her back to me. She was whispering something into Alisa's ear. My heart sank, and I had the strangest feeling. It was almost as if I were invisible. I sat quietly, staring out the window for a few moments, waiting for my tea. Here I was, right in the middle of my family—and missing them more than ever.

I spent the afternoon trying to do all the math homework that I should have done the week before. I actually finished most of it before I drove to Hunter and Sky's place at eight to meet with Erin.

Hunter let me in. Erin and Sky were sitting on the couch as we walked into the living room. The lamps were glowing with new lightbulbs, and the books sat quietly on their shelves. There was no sign of what had happened the night before.

"I've already told Sky and Erin about last night's fog," Hunter said as I pulled off my jacket and kicked off my duck boots. Padding across the room in my thick socks, I curled up into the corner of the large brown velvet armchair that sat to the side of the couch, pulling my legs beneath me.

"You say the shape you saw looked like a woman?" Erin said to Hunter. He nodded.

Erin pursed her lips. "Did she say anything?" she asked me abruptly.

I flushed slightly under her intense gaze. "No. She didn't do anything at all," I said. "She just looked at us a minute and disappeared."

Erin lifted her eyebrows and turned to Hunter for confirmation. He nodded again.

"But there's no doubt in your mind that this was *something*?" Erin asked. "This wasn't just some kind of problem with the weather—a strange-looking patch of mist?"

"It was real enough that I nearly drove the car off the road." Hunter's voice was certain, but I remembered the flash of doubt I'd felt that morning.

Erin sat back and pressed her lips together. She sat perfectly still, and with her pale skin and delicate features, she looked almost like she was made of marble.

"Do you think it was Ciaran?" Sky asked. Her oval face was tense.

"Perhaps," Erin said. Her gaze locked on my face.

The look made my stomach lurch. I felt afraid and defensive at the same time. "Do you think it was *me*?" I demanded.

Erin was unperturbed. "Perhaps," she replied coolly.

I opened my mouth to defend myself, but Erin cut me off. "Morgan, I merely said it was a possibility. You *may* be causing these incidents unconsciously—we simply can't rule it out. But right now, only two things are certain: strange things are happening, and they seem to involve you."

"Or Hunter," I pointed out.

"That's true," Hunter agreed. He quickly described what

had happened in the movie theater a few nights before.

Erin seemed to ponder this a moment. "It seems that someone is trying to get in touch with one of you," she said. "Perhaps it's time we went looking for them."

"Should we scry?" Hunter asked.

"The sooner the better, I should think," Erin said. She disappeared into the kitchen for a moment and returned with a small stone bowl filled with water. I was intrigued by the fact that she chose to scry with water—I'd heard most witches found it unreliable.

We joined hands, and Erin began to chant as we gazed into the water. I'd never heard the words before, and they had an ancient quality that was both beautiful and terrifying. Although I didn't understand exactly what she was saying, I felt certain that Erin was calling on whoever was interfering with us to reveal him- or herself.

The water shimmered, and for a moment it almost seemed to glow silvery pink. The clock on the wall ticked on, but nothing happened. Erin began her low chant again, and this time Sky joined her. Still nothing.

Hunter sat to my left, and after a few moments I felt a shudder run through him. I squeezed his hand. I knew that he thought the strange incidents might have been messages for him from his parents. I knew that he was hoping they were—and that by scrying we would see them. I was struck with the irony of it—Hunter was hoping to see his father, while I was terrified to see my own. Hunter shuddered again. I turned to look at him just as a wave of pain and fear washed over me. It was flowing from him. He groaned and fell backward against the floor, as if he were being held there. Sweat broke out over his face, which had gone deadly white.

"Hunter!" I cried.

Erin leaned over Hunter and peered into his face as I brushed damp golden hair away from his forehead. Sky hurried behind him and put his head in her lap. Hunter moaned and began to say something. I didn't catch the beginning of it, but I heard him murmur something that sounded like, "Troptardeef." Then there was a string of words that made no sense to me.

I dug my fingernails into my palms. Goddess, please help him, I begged silently.

Hunter's body shuddered once more, then he lay still. His breathing was labored and ragged for a moment, then began to slow. Finally he opened his eyes. Looking up at me, he murmured, "What happened?"

I swallowed hard, unsure how to answer.

"Did you see anything?" Erin asked brusquely.

Hunter struggled to his elbows, and Sky helped him sit upright. He rubbed his head, then said, "Shadows. There was a narrow street, with cobblestones. And there was a wall. I . . . I was in a walled city."

"You said something," Erin informed him. "Do you remember what it was?"

Hunter shook his head. "No—I just remember the shadows . . . and the feelings. What did I say?"

"You said, 'It's too late—there's nothing I can do,'" Erin replied. "In French."

Hunter stared at her. "I don't speak French," he said.

Erin didn't reply to that. "Do you know why this happened?" she asked.

"No," Hunter replied. Then he said, "No," again, but his voice was less certain.

Erin leaned toward him. "Do you *think* you know why this happened?"

"I think it may have been one of my parents, trying to contact me," Hunter admitted.

"Hunter." Sky's voice was almost a gasp. "Are you sure?"

"No," he said quickly. "No, I'm not. That's only what I think it was. But it could be anything."

The words settled over me like a cold weight, sinking into my bones. A feeling came over me—it was the same feeling I'd had the night before, when Hunter and I had rounded the bend in the road. It was a deep feeling of dread.

I reached for Hunter's hand and felt slightly better at the familiar warmth of his touch. I was worried for him. But more than that, I was worried about the future. Worried about us. I didn't know what the messages meant . . . but I had a horrible feeling that their power was great enough to tear us apart.

"Morgan, I think we had better begin our lessons as soon as possible," Erin said. "Are you free tomorrow afternoon?"

"Yes, of course. Where should we meet?" I asked. "Here?"

"Actually," Hunter broke in, "Alyce suggested that you hold your lessons in the back room of Practical Magick. She thought it might be a good idea in case you need any books or tools."

I nodded. "That works for me."

"For me as well," Erin said.

Everyone was subdued as we said good night. Sky seemed particularly pensive. As I laced up my heavy boots and pulled on my jacket, I wondered what she was thinking.

"That was frustrating," I said as Hunter walked me to Das Boot.

"I know," he agreed. "I just wish we knew what all of this meant."

I remembered the violence of exploding lightbulbs and kamikaze books. Could Hunter's parents really have been behind those things? It seemed unlikely. I thought of my own father—Ciaran. That sort of violence was more his style.

As if he'd been reading my mind, Hunter said, "Morgan, I heard from Eoife this afternoon. The council has found out Ciaran is definitely in Spain. They're closing in. It's only a matter of time before they have him in custody. Eoife said to tell you they couldn't have done it without you."

Relief swept over me, followed by anger, startling me with its strength. Anger at the council for making me spy on my own father. Anger at Ciaran for all the evil he had done, for the taint he had passed on to me. Anger at myself for the tug of kinship I still felt for him. "Oh, no problem. I'm great at spying on my relatives," I said bitterly. "Just let me know if you need any info on Mary K."

"He's dangerous," Hunter said quietly. "You did right, even though it was hard."

I closed my eyes and tried to let Hunter's voice calm me. I knew my father was dangerous. But when I was with Ciaran, I'd felt a strange connection—something I'd never felt before. Knowing that this man was my real father, that his blood ran in my veins, had given me a visceral sense of belonging. I felt that I knew Ciaran almost better than I knew the members of my adopted family because part of him was in me.

And I knew his true name.

The thought echoed up from the depths of my mind. I knew Ciaran's true name. He'd said it in a forbidden spell he'd used when he was trying to win me to his side.

When you know someone's true name, you can control him.

I had never told Hunter. I could have told him right then. I could have said Ciaran's true name. But I didn't. They already have the sigil, I told myself. Hunter's right; they're going to capture him soon. They don't need his true name.

"If Ciaran is the one sending these messages," Hunter said fiercely, "he will be very, very sorry." His words slashed through the chill air like a blade.

"Do you wish you were there—in Spain, tracking him?" I asked. I had seen Hunter put the *braigh* on Cal once, and once on David Redstone. The spelled silver chain burned witches' skin, raising angry red blisters. I knew that Hunter hadn't enjoyed using it either time. But now I wondered how he would feel putting it on the wrists of the man who'd almost killed both of us more than once.

"My job is to protect you," Hunter said simply. "According to the council, that is my sole responsibility for the moment."

I frowned. "That doesn't answer my question."

"Doesn't it?"

Hunter gazed at the hulking forms of the trees, and I suddenly realized the full weight of what he was saying. He thought he was receiving messages from his parents. And he couldn't do anything about it because he had to stay in Widow's Vale to take care of me. That had to be incredibly frustrating. More. It had to be agonizing.

"Can't you tell the council how important this is to you?" I asked. "If they catch Ciaran, I won't be in danger anymore."

Hunter shook his head, not looking at me. "The council wants me here."

I looked at him, feeling a rush of sympathy. I thought of how very young Hunter had been when his parents had disappeared. I could only imagine how fiercely he wanted them back. "I'm sorry," I whispered.

Hunter didn't speak. He just reached out, took my hand, and brought it briefly to his lips before letting it go.

"I'll help you find them," I said.

"Good," was the last thing he said before retreating up his front walk. He didn't look back as I got in my car and drove away.

5

Forces

Morgan lost it last night. I don't know if she went crazy or if her powers short-circuited or something, but things started flying around the room and exploding, and it scared the holy crap out of me.

Now I don't know what to do. The circle started off really well. I don't know much about Wicca, but there's something about it that feels almost like a tune I only half remember from childhood. The words are long forgotten, but if I try hard enough, I'll remember the melody, and everything will fall into place.

That was the way I felt last night . . . for a while.

Morgan's magick feels like something else. I'm afraid of it in the way I used to be afraid of leaving my closet door open when I was five years old.

I wish she'd just leave the coven. Then Mary K. would feel better and I wouldn't have to be afraid anymore.

—Alisa

Mr. Powell waited until the last five minutes of class to pass back the graded exams.

The class buzzed as he made his way around the room, placing papers facedown on desks. "Well done," he whispered to Claire Kennedy, and, "Great job," to Andy Nasewell. Hope fluttered in my chest. Andy wasn't a great student. Maybe I hadn't done as badly as I thought.

Mr. Powell slapped a paper on my desk. His hand was still a moment as he looked down at me. "See me after class," he said. Crap. I turned the paper over, my heart thumping. At the top there was a big red number. Sixty-three.

The bell rang and everyone streamed out of the classroom, comparing papers and chatting. Quickly I shoved my exam inside my binder and shuffled up to Mr. Powell's desk. I could hardly even look at him.

"Morgan," he said, folding his arms on his desk, "we've spoken about this before. Your grade in this class has dropped significantly since first semester, and I'd hoped to see more improvement." Mr. Powell looked up at me. He was a good teacher—the kind who really seemed to care about his students—and he looked concerned.

"I know I messed up," I replied. "I've just been a little . . . overwhelmed lately."

"This was the second of four major exams for this marking period," Mr. Powell said. "The exams are what determine your final grade."

I did a quick mental calculation. Even if I got a hundred on each of the other two exams, my final average would be a seventy-eight. *Seventy-eight.* That was pretty far from my usual honor roll standards.

"You do realize, Morgan, that junior-year grades are what most colleges look at when they are determining admissions," Mr. Powell went on. "I'm afraid I'm going to have to let your parents know about this."

Oh, no. "Is there anything I can do?" I asked. "Some extra credit or something?"

Mr. Powell thought for a moment. "I don't like to give one person a shot at extra credit without giving the whole class the same chance," he said slowly.

"I'm sure other people would like to bring up their grades," I suggested.

Mr. Powell sighed. "All right," he said. "I'll announce it to the class tomorrow. Write a five- to eight-page paper on any historical subject for a maximum of twenty extra points on the next exam."

I stifled a groan. Twenty points. That didn't sound like much. But when I did the average in my head along with two other perfect exams, I realized I could end up with an eighty-three average for the marking period—a B. It would be tough, but I could do it. "Thanks, Mr. Powell," I said quickly, and turned toward the door.

"Morgan," he called after me.

"Yes?" I paused in the doorway.

He looked at me over the tops of his bifocals. "Make it good," he said.

"Did you talk to Robbie?" I asked Bree as we walked out of English. It was our last class. I hadn't seen her or Robbie all day, except from a distance—neither one of them was at the usual spot in the morning or at lunch, either.

Bree hugged her notebooks to her chest. "No," she admitted. She was wearing a long black leather skirt and a woolly black sweater with a plunging neckline, and it made her look mysterious and a little sad.

I wasn't all that surprised. Bree hated "relationship" talks. "Why not?"

"To be honest, Robbie was pretty freaked out by the circle on Saturday," Bree said. "Yesterday didn't really seem like the best time for a chat, you know?"

"Bree, you need to talk to him," I said.

"I know, I know." Bree hesitated, her dark eyes clouding over. "Actually," she said finally, "I think maybe *you* should talk to Robbie. That scene at the circle scared the crap out of him. God, Morgan, it scared the crap out of everyone. Me too."

"But that wasn't *me*," I insisted. "It scared me, too."

We stood there in the hall for a moment, just staring at each other as students streamed past us. I had no idea what to say. Finally Bree reached out and grabbed my hand. "Look, Morgan. If you say it wasn't you, then I believe it. I'll talk to Robbie for you. But you should know that he's worried about you, and so am I." To my dismay, her eyes filled with tears. Bree wasn't a big weeper. "We're friends, right?"

I swallowed hard. "Right."

"Okay." Bree gave me a watery smile. "I'll talk to him. About both things."

She dropped my hand and turned toward her locker. I trudged to mine, silently cursing these strange things that kept happening. I was as afraid of them as everyone else. Yet everyone thought I was behind them.

Standing in front of my locker, I felt a faint, icy breeze

blow past me. The small hairs at the back of my neck rose. Had anyone else felt it? To my right, I saw Cindy Halpern struggling with her locker combination. Maybe it was just my imagination.

I spun the lock and yanked on my locker door. It swung open with a bang. I jumped back to avoid the avalanche of books and papers that cascaded out.

"God, Morgan," Cindy said, rolling her eyes at the mess, "get a Trapper Keeper."

I ignored her. My instincts were clamoring. It was true that my locker was a royal disaster, but the way my stuff had shot out of it . . . I peered down the hall to see if other strange things were happening, but all I saw was students shoving books into backpacks and pulling on jackets. I cast my senses, but I didn't sense any sort of sinister presence. Frowning, I eyed the mess on the floor. Maybe it really was just the result of a locker that hadn't been cleaned out in a while. I bent and started gathering papers.

"Need some help?" asked a voice behind me.

I glanced up as Alisa crouched and began stacking my books. "This looks like the bottom of my dad's closet," she said. Her voice was heavy, and she seemed tired.

I stopped gathering my papers and looked at her. "Are you okay?" I asked.

Alisa frowned. "Actually, no," she said. "I—I wanted to tell you . . . I'm leaving the coven."

I was so surprised, I sat down on the floor. "You are?" I asked. The image of Bree with tears in her eyes, telling me that Robbie was worried about me, clicked into my brain. "Why?" I asked carefully.

Alisa ran her fingers through her hair, pulling it away from her oval face. "Things are just going too far for me." She looked down at the floor, then up at me. "The magick I've seen lately . . . it scares me. These are powerful forces, Morgan." She leaned toward me until I could see myself reflected in her eyes. "They're dangerous."

I got the feeling that Alisa wanted me to promise that nothing frightening would happen at a circle again. But I couldn't. I didn't have any idea what had caused the strange magick on Saturday—and I certainly didn't have any control over it. "I'm sorry, Alisa," I said finally. "I guess you have to do what's right for you."

Alisa looked at me a moment and then nodded. "Okay. But I just wanted to tell you . . . I have a bad feeling. The magick you've been practicing is bad for everyone. I'm talking about the whole coven," she said in a low voice. "I think you should stop what you're doing. Be careful, Morgan."

"Yeah, Morgan, be careful," said a voice above us. It was Mary K., her book bag slung over one shoulder. I tried to read the expression on my sister's face. Mary K. and I hadn't had a real conversation since the night of Hunter's dinner, but I'd felt that she was softening toward me a bit—and now she was obviously here so I would give her a ride home. I hoped she hadn't overheard anything just now that would freak her out again.

"What does Morgan have to be careful about?" Mary K. asked Alisa.

I waited nervously. Alisa glanced at me, then picked up a pile of my books. "She has to be careful not to get buried in this pile of crap," Alisa said as she slid my books into place on the shelf. "I was just recommending that Morgan wear bright-colored clothing so we can find her if she gets hidden in the next locker paper slide."

I gathered the rest of my papers and scrambled to my feet. "Just a second, Mary K.," I said. "Let me find what I need. I'll be ready to roll in a minute."

"Actually," Mary K. said, "I'm here for Alisa. We're going over to her house to study." She turned to Alisa. "Ready?"

"Sure," Alisa replied. "See you around, Morgan," she said over her shoulder as she turned to walk down the hall.

"See you later," Mary K. added, giving me a small wave. "I called Mom already—I won't be home for dinner." She trotted after Alisa.

"Okay," I said. "See you." Watching their retreating figures, I couldn't help feeling a little stab of jealousy . . . and fear. Sure, Alisa had just covered for me now—but what if later she told Mary K. that the coven was dealing with powerful forces? What if she described what had happened on Saturday night?

Would my sister turn against me even more?

6

Restricted

I tried to talk to Morgan today. I told her that I was uncomfortable with some of the magick being used in Kithic. So, naturally, Morgan said, "Oh, Alisa, thank you so much for telling me. I'm sure that if you're uneasy, others in the coven must be, too. I'll be sure to tone down my freakish witch powers so that we can all enjoy the simple, quiet magick of Wicca together without unleashing dark forces of the underworld over which we have no control."

Yeah, right. Actually, what she said was more like, "Whatever. Too bad for you."

So now I've said that I'm leaving Kithic. There's only one problem. That means I actually have to <u>leave</u> Kithic. There's a nursery rhyme that keeps repeating in my mind. I think my mom must have said it to me when I was little: "No beginning or end to hearth, home, or friend." It's about belonging.

I feel like I belong in Kithic. But Morgan doesn't care.

I wonder if The other people in Kithic have really ThoughT about what Morgan is doing. I mean, her powers <u>are</u> amazing. I guess it's possible ThaT everyone is so wrapped up in The mysTique ThaT They haven'T really boThered To Think abouT what she's doing or where iT mighT lead. Or maybe They have, buT They jusT cover up beTTer Than I do.

iT's noT ThaT I Think Morgan is evil. I jusT don'T Think she realizes how dangerous she is. Maybe I should wriTe a leTTer To The Town paper To warn people ThaT This is happening. iT feels kind of underhanded. BuT This is dangerous sTuff. I feel ThaT people have a righT To know.

I jusT don'T wanT anyone To geT hurT.

—Alisa

The bell over the door at Practical Magick jingled as I walked inside. Closing the door quickly against the cold, I breathed in the warm spicy scent of incense and the familiar smell of old books. Alyce looked up at me from behind the counter, and her face instantly broke into a smile. "Morgan," she said, "you've got a visitor."

There were two other people in the store, browsing through the herbs. "Is she here already?" I whispered as I walked to the counter.

Alyce nodded gravely. "In the back."

I grimaced. That meant I was late. "Thanks." I hurried past the tall wooden bookshelves toward the curtain that separated the rear of the store. I was irked that I couldn't stop to chat with Alyce. Besides being the owner of Practical Magick, she was the leader of the Starlocket coven and a good friend.

We'd been through a lot together these last few months.

"You're late," Erin said coolly as I pulled back the curtain and stepped into the combination storeroom-office.

"So I heard," I replied, sliding into the folding chair across from hers. I hadn't gotten much sleep the night before and wasn't in the best of moods.

Erin's eyes flashed. "Morgan, I am here at the behest of the council. I've traveled a long way to get here," she said. "And I've got less than two weeks to teach you everything I know about magickal defenses."

"Sorry," I mumbled to the table. Okay, so I was late. Was that the world's biggest tragedy? Did she have to treat me like a five-year-old? It was bad enough that the reason I was late was that my English teacher had grabbed me on my way out of school and lectured me for twenty minutes about how I wasn't "working up to potential."

Erin leaned forward, and I felt compelled to look up at her. "There are some members of the council who put a great deal of stock in your powers," she said in a voice that sounded almost like a purr or a growl. "But let me tell you something—those powers will never be anything but a dangerous toy until you learn to control them."

There was half a moment while we stared at each other, and I felt Erin's intensity like heat from a fire.

"Here we are!" said a voice. Suddenly the curtain was pulled back, and Alyce bustled in with a teapot and mugs. She glanced at Erin. "Licorice still your favorite?"

I looked from one to the other. "Do you two know each other already?" I asked.

"Of course," Alyce said. "We've been friends for years."

I tried to hide my surprise. They were friends? But they were such opposites—Erin seemed as hard as steel, while Alyce was about as hard as a featherbed.

"We haven't seen each other in a long time, though," Erin said, smiling at Alyce.

"Too long," Alyce said. "Which reminds me. I've been saving something for you." Pulling a key ring out of her pocket, she crossed to a heavy wooden desk at the back of the room. She opened one of the drawers and pulled out a large gray metal box. Then she chose another key, opened the box, and pulled out something large and flat and wrapped in a piece of dark cloth. When she came closer, I saw that it was a square of black silk. My pulse quickened. Black silk had strong blocking properties—it was often used to wrap magickal objects that might be dangerous. Alyce put the object on the table, then pulled the fabric away from it, revealing an ancient leather-bound book.

"Where did you get this?" Erin whispered. She'd gone pale.

"At a library sale, if you can believe it," Alyce said. "About a year ago. I don't think they had any idea what they were selling."

I read the faded gold lettering on the cover. *On the Containement of Magick,* it said. "Harris Stoughton," I said aloud, looking at the author's name. It sounded vaguely familiar to me.

"A horrible man," Erin said. "A witch who used hysteria to wipe out other witches."

When she said that, I remembered where I'd heard the name before—from some of my reading on the Salem witch trials. I hadn't read anything about his being a witch, though.

"I thought that you should have it," Alyce said to Erin. "I

don't like keeping it here, but I don't want it to fall into the wrong hands, either."

Erin flipped through a few of the pages warily, as if the book were something dangerous, then snapped the cover closed. "It's a rare book." Looking up at Alyce, she added, "Thank you. A book like this can be dangerous, but it can also be useful." Erin faced me. "The first rule of magickal defenses is 'Know your enemy.'"

The bell over the front door jingled, and Alyce went to see to the customers.

Erin pushed herself up from the table and walked over to the curtain. Tracing her fingers around its edges, she muttered a harsh-sounding phrase. "Now no one will be able to hear us," she explained when she saw my confused expression. "Ready?"

I stood up and followed her to the center of the room. We faced each other for a moment. In a flash Erin caught my wrist, and I felt a crackle of electricity ripple through me. But I had been expecting this move. Quickly I threw up a block, as Hunter had taught me. Instead of building, the energy quickly dissipated through my body. Where she held my wrist, I felt the energy die in Erin's hand as well.

Erin stepped back. "That was good," she said simply. "You know the *divagnth*. And you're strong."

Damn straight, I thought, feeling a rush of pride.

Erin took a step away from me. I took in her small form. I stood at least a full head taller than her. I felt great— strangely strong, physically powerful, as if I'd been pumping iron or something. Weird, I thought. But very cool.

"Things are not always as they appear," Erin said. As I

stood wondering what that meant, she suddenly seemed to grow taller. Her mouth elongated, and she smiled, revealing long sharp fangs, each as thick as my finger. I felt my pride evaporate as her shoulders broadened and her green eyes turned darker, glowing with a cruel light.

I shrank away from her as cold panic washed over me like a slap of icy water. With horror, I understood that she was more powerful than I was and that she was evil. Why hadn't I seen it before? She had put up a spell so that no one could hear us, and now she was going to kill me and take my magick.

Erin—or whatever the thing before me truly was—sent out slim wisps of gray smoke. The dark vapor grew thicker and began to fill the room. I felt myself choking.

The creature took a step toward me, and I stumbled away from it. It opened its horrible jaws. "Fight," it said in a voice that was more animal than human. "Fight me."

I racked my brain for a blocking spell, but I couldn't think clearly. My body was pulsing with adrenaline. Did Alyce know that Erin was evil? Did Hunter know? What would happen to them once I was gone and this thing had my magick? I had survived so much in the last few months. Was this really how I would be done in?

The creature leaned toward me as the darkness closed in. I didn't know what to do. Blindly I threw out my hands and sent a white ball of energy at the creature. It was fearsome-looking, brilliant and powerful. I had never called up something like that before, and for a moment I felt a surge of hope. But the creature merely made a flicking gesture with its left arm and easily deflected the ball across the room. It slammed against a metal shelving unit with an enormous crash. Back stock of notebooks flew off the top shelf and rained all over the floor. I could hardly see anything through the black vapor. I cowered against the wall behind me and finally sank to the floor.

The creature reached out a claw and grabbed my shoulder. "Morgan," said a voice through the darkness. It was a lovely, musical voice, and for a moment I couldn't remember where I'd heard it before. "Morgan," it repeated, "are you all right?"

I looked down at the horrifying claw on my shoulder. Slowly it began to shift and change. The thick, muddy gray skin began to lighten, and the cruel claws receded until it was nothing but a small, pale hand almost the size of a child's. I looked up into Erin's clear green gaze. "Are you all right?" she repeated.

The fog around me began to lift, and I sat up. "What happened?"

"Take a deep breath," Erin advised. "Now release it. Do it again," she urged. "Focus on the breath. Now ground yourself."

Leaning forward, I placed my forehead against the cool tile floor. Slowly my head cleared. "You need to learn to control your emotions," Erin said. "Pride and fear can cut you off from your power and leave you vulnerable. I'm sorry," she added as I sat up. "You fooled me with the *divagnth*. I didn't realize you weren't ready for that lesson."

Standing up, Erin reached out her hand and pulled me to my feet. "You're strong, Morgan," she said. "That's your weakness."

I frowned. "That doesn't make sense."

"You have strong native power," Erin explained. "Strong abilities. You just called up white witch fire, no easy task. But you don't have control." She gestured toward the scorched metal shelves and the Books of Shadows that had spilled all over the floor. "That makes you dangerous."

"But you're here to teach me control," I protested.

"Morgan," she said with forced patience, "I understand that you've been in a complicated situation. I don't know all the details, but I do know that you've been forced into a situation in which you've had to begin your education in the middle of things, instead of at the proper beginning."

"What are you saying?" I asked warily.

"I'm saying that you should back up." Erin's voice was brittle. "Take a break from magick that is too advanced for you and focus instead on learning your plants and witch history. I know it's not what you want to hear, but when you're sailing in the wrong direction, sometimes it's faster to go back than it is to keep pushing on until you've gone around the world."

"I feel like you're punishing me," I said bitterly.

"It's for your own safety." Erin's voice was like a door slamming shut, and I knew that there was no use arguing. "And it's not forever, Morgan," she added. "We'll begin again tomorrow, at the library. At three-thirty sharp."

The bell over the door jingled again—the customers leaving—and Alyce poked her head through the curtain. "Is everything okay back here?" she asked. Her eyes fell on the ruined mass of notebooks. "Oh, my."

"We were just about to clean that up," I said quickly. Erin and I walked over to the pile of Books of Shadows and began brushing them off and placing them back on the shelf. Thankfully, most of them were undamaged. Erin told Alyce that she would pay for the ones that were.

"It's my fault," Erin told her, digging in her bag. "Besides, the cost of a few blank Books of Shadows isn't one-tenth of the value of this book." She jerked her head in the direction of *On the Containement of Magick.*

I watched Erin hug Alyce as we said good-bye. Erin was stiff, but her affection seemed real as she tucked the silk-wrapped book under her arm. Then again, she'd seemed pretty real when she'd looked like a hideous monster only half an hour before.

I sensed who was calling a second before the phone rang.

"I'll get it," I called, starting up from the dining room table, where I was doing my homework. But it was already too late.

"Hello?" my mom's voice said from the kitchen. Dad was working late, so she and I were the only ones home. We'd finished dinner about two hours ago, and Mom had been working on her various documents in the kitchen since then.

"Yes, this is she," I heard her say. "Oh, hello. Yes. What? Well—no, she didn't. I see. Mmm-hmm." Even through the door, I could hear the edge of anger dawning in my mom's voice.

I stared down at the books and notebooks spread out before me and tried to focus on the analysis of vectors I was doing for physics, but it was no use.

"Was that out of a hundred points?" I heard my mother ask, and I bit my lip.

After a moment I heard Mom hang up, and the door between the dining room and the kitchen swung open. "Morgan, we need to talk." Her voice was grim.

My stomach churned. I put down my pencil. "Okay."

Sitting down across from me, my mom said, "I just got a phone call from your history teacher, Mr. Powell."

I didn't even bother trying to act surprised. "I know," I said.

"He's concerned about your grade in his class. So am I."

"I know," I said again. Shifting in my seat, I added, "I've already talked to him about doing some extra credit—"

Holding up her hand traffic-cop style, my mom cut me off. "Morgan, I'm not happy about the fact that you failed two tests. But I'm even more unhappy about the fact that you hid it from Dad and me. When were you going to tell us?"

"I thought that if I brought my grade up—"

"But what if you didn't?" my mom interrupted. "Mr. Powell says that these two exams count for fifty percent of your final grade. Were you going to wait until you failed the class to let us know that there was a problem?" She ran her fingers through her russet hair in an I-don't-know-what-to-do-with-you gesture.

"With extra credit, I could still get a B in the class!"

"You could still get an F!" my mom snapped. "Have you even started this extra-credit work?"

I dug through my stack of papers and pulled out the notes I'd already made for my history paper. I didn't realize until after I'd handed them to my mom that I was making a horrible mistake.

"This can't be your history paper." Mom's voice was tense. "What *is* this?"

"We're allowed to write on any subject," I explained weakly.

She simply looked at me for a moment, then slapped the notes down on the table in frustration. "Why do you have to test us? You *know* how Dad and I feel about witchcraft nonsense!"

"The Salem witch trials aren't nonsense," I pointed out, my own temper starting to flare. "They were an important historical event."

"That's not the point. Morgan, your interest in Wicca has grown to the point where it's crowding out almost everything else," my mom said. "I don't want you throwing your future away."

"I'm not!" I cried. "How can you say that?"

"Look," my mother went on. "I don't want to fight about the witch stuff right now. Your grades have to improve, and I don't see that happening. This is your final warning. If those grades don't improve, Dad and I are going to start talking seriously about changing your environment."

What? This had never come up before. "What do you mean?"

"Saint Anne's has a few openings," my mother said. "It's a very good school."

My jaw dropped open. "It's a Catholic school." My voice was harsh. "You'd really send me to a Catholic school?"

"Why not? The average class size is fourteen students, so they would be able to give you a lot of individual attention." She reached out and touched my hair almost pleadingly. "We want to help you, Morgan."

I stared at her. As if yanking me away from all my friends and sticking me into a place where they still believed in corporal punishment would help! The words *I'm not Catholic* sprang to my lips, but I couldn't bring myself to say them. It seemed almost like a declaration of war. It wasn't exactly true, anyway. Catholicism was the religion I was raised with, and I still felt like I *was* a Catholic in many ways. "Please, Mom," I answered instead. "Don't do that. I'll—I'll go to the library every day. I'll bring my grades up, I swear."

"We'll see." My mom pushed my history notes across

the table at me and stood up. "Family night is tomorrow," she said wearily. "At six."

"I'll be there." My voice sounded hollow.

She trudged out of the room. I watched her go, then looked down at my books.

I had a lot of work to do.

"I just don't think I can study with Erin right now," I said to Hunter. I was using the phone in the kitchen, summarizing the conversation I'd had with my mom earlier that evening. My parents and Mary K. had gone to bed, but I—the night owl—would be up for another few hours. "I just can't, can't get sent to Catholic school."

"That would be awful," Hunter agreed quietly.

"But my grades are really in the gutter."

Hunter sighed. "Isn't there any way that you can learn from Erin and still improve your grades?" he asked. "We can try to make sure you have time to finish your schoolwork, too. It's very important that you study with Erin right now. Especially with all the mysterious things that have been happening."

Pushing aside some of my mom's paperwork detritus, I made room for the cup of tea I'd just brewed. I took a sip, debating whether or not to tell Hunter what had happened with Erin earlier that day. "Actually, Erin doesn't even want to teach me magick," I admitted finally. "She just wants me to study witch history and plants."

"Those things are important, too," Hunter replied.

I stared at the receiver a minute, unable to believe he was taking her side. How typical. "Oh, yeah, they'll come in real handy if I'm ever attacked by the dark forces," I said sarcastically.

"I'm here to protect you in case that happens," Hunter reminded me. "And basic knowledge is necessary to learn more advanced magick. Witch history, herbs, runes—all of these things are part of the initiation rites. Erin is right to make sure you know them. Once you're a full apprentice, then you can start learning more magick and more spells. You know more than most initiates already."

I sighed. "It's just hard to see the value in that. I mean, you know the dangers of the dark forces even better than I do. I need to learn about them."

"I know." Hunter's voice was gentle. "But you have to look at the big picture. The sooner you can be initiated as a blood witch, the better. Once you're in total control of your powers, Morgan, you'll be a great asset."

I rolled my eyes. Sometimes Hunter had a real gift for making things sound unromantic. "All right," I said. "I'll figure out a way to do both." We said our good-byes, and I stood up to place the phone in its cradle. When I turned around, I nearly jumped a foot in the air. "God, Mary K.," I said, placing my palm on my chest. "You scared me."

She stood in the doorway in a white nightgown. Beneath the fluorescent kitchen lights, she looked pale and strange.

"What's wrong?" I asked quickly.

"Alisa was right," she said in a low voice.

I swallowed hard, mentally running through the conversation I'd just had with Hunter. How much of it had she overheard? "What are you talking about?" I stalled.

"You *know* what I'm talking about." Mary K.'s whisper had the intensity of a scream. "My God, Morgan—don't try to cover this up with *lies*."

I jammed my hands into the soft pockets of my flannel robe. "Look, Mary K., I don't know what you heard—"

"I want you to leave the coven." The words hung there, ugly and irrefutable, as Mary K. folded her arms across her chest.

"No." I shook my head. "I'm sorry, but—"

"Morgan, don't you get it?" Mary K. interrupted. "This isn't just about you. What about Mom and Dad? They don't have any idea what's really going on! How do you think they'll feel if anything happens to you?" Her voice wavered, and she tucked a strand of hair behind her ear. "How do you think I'll feel if something happens . . . and I never even warned them?"

I stood there wordlessly for a long time. I understood what she was saying . . . but what could I do about it? I couldn't leave the coven now. I had chosen Wicca, and it had chosen me. And even though I wanted to comfort Mary K., I knew I couldn't lie to her. In the end, I just said, "I'm sorry."

Mary K. was still standing in the kitchen when I went up to my room. I lay in my bed, listening for her footsteps, on the stairs for a long, long time. She still hadn't come upstairs by the time I finally fell asleep.

7

Danger

September 22, 1971

Today was Andrew Lewis's funeral. Mother and Father didn't want us to go, but Sam insisted, and in the end our parents had to give in. I don't often have a chance to go to a Catholic church for any reason, and I was surprised at how much I enjoyed the service. Sunlight streamed in the stained-glass windows, and the whole ceremony seemed very ancient and peaceful, even though it was a bit too solemn. I couldn't help comparing it with the circle we'd held the night before at Patience Stamp's house. She's a potter, and her house is very simple but filled with beautiful handmade things. We'd held hands and had felt the magick flow between us, easing the pain we felt at losing our friends to the sea. I felt the same kind of magick in the church—a healing magick that exists between people. In the middle of the service I noticed that tears were streaming down Sam's *cheeks, and I handed him a tissue. I was touched by his sorrow. But later I discovered he was feeling more than simple sorrow.*

After the service Sam walked into my room and sat on the edge of my bed. When I saw that he was holding The Book—the Harris Stoughton book—I was afraid.

Then Sam told me that he'd tried a small spell—a weather spell—because it hadn't rained for so long. He'd just wanted to see if he could call up a little rain, so about ten days ago, when the moon was waxing, he'd tried it. He hadn't known what would happen, he said, so it couldn't really be his fault, could it?

It took about half a minute for this to sink in. When I realized what he was telling me, I could hardly breathe. How could he? How? The storm that killed the crew of the <u>Lady Marie</u> was his fault. I grabbed him by the collar and started to shake him. <u>"What have you done?"</u> I was almost screaming, and Sam started bawling. The Book fell from his lap, and I dove for it. It felt warm in my hand, like something alive, and I wanted to throw it down, but I didn't dare.

I must burn the vile thing before it destroys us all.

—Sarah Curtis

"Morgan!" I knew the voice was Bree's, but I couldn't reply or even turn my head because I was gripping a paper cup of tea in my teeth as my cold fingers fumbled to lock the door of my car. Plumes of steam rose from the hot liquid and combined with my breath, dissipating quickly.

"Here," Bree said as she reached for the paper cup.

I released it gratefully. "Thanks."

"Got a minute?" Bree asked.

"Sure," I said, taking the tea back from her. "What's up?"

"Robbie and I broke up."

I choked on the sip of tea I'd just taken. "What?" I looked at Bree more closely. Her face was ashen, and her eyes were red-rimmed. She wasn't kidding.

Bree glanced at my car. "Can we——?"

"Of course." I put my tea on the roof of the car and unlocked the door. A quick glance at my watch told me that we had ten minutes until the first bell. "What do you mean, you broke up? What happened?" I asked when we were seated inside the car.

"Just what I said. Robbie and I talked last night." Bree gave a small half shrug, lifting only one shoulder. "He said he needed space."

I waited a moment. "And——?" I prompted.

"That's it." Bree gazed straight ahead. The parking lot was filling up as teachers and students hurried to class.

"Bree," I said, "that doesn't necessarily mean that Robbie wants to break up." I didn't *think* it did, anyway. If it did, I was going to have to have a long talk with Robbie.

Bree flashed me an oh-grow-up glance. "Spare me. I know what it means." Raking her fingers through her hair, she added, "Not that it really matters, anyway. I mean, the relationship was getting a little old. I've been thinking about dating other people."

"Bree," I said gently, "it's me. Don't."

She turned toward me, and her facade broke. Her eyes welled up, tears ran down her cheeks, and she looked like the same Bree whose heart was broken by Todd Hall in the seventh grade. "I know. I just—I just needed to say something bitchy."

I opened my mouth. But just then the first-period bell sounded, far away, and Bree opened the car door and stepped out.

"Bree," I called after her, "talk to Robbie!" But she'd already slammed the door and was striding toward the school. I didn't know whether she'd heard me, and I wasn't even sure that it mattered.

"I should be home by six," I said into a pay phone in the lobby of the public library later that day.

"Great," my mom said at the other end of the line. "I was thinking for family night we could play some board games and make hot fudge sundaes."

Even the faint crackle of static on the line couldn't disguise my mom's excitement. I got the feeling that she was trying to make peace after our argument the night before. "Sounds great, Mom," I said, suddenly struck with a pang of guilt. I'd told my mom that I was at the library to study history and science—but I hadn't mentioned it was witch history and magickal botany with Erin. And here she was, planning fun activities for the whole family. I was a terrible daughter. "See you at six."

I hung up, feeling lousy.

"Everything all right?" Erin asked as I plopped down across from her.

I laced my fingers together and rested my chin on them. "Just parental stuff."

Erin peered at me. As usual with her, I felt like I needed

to explain myself. "It's just—they're Catholics. They don't approve of witchcraft. And they're threatening to send me to Catholic school."

Erin nodded gravely. "I wonder what your mother would think of all this."

For a moment I was confused—hadn't we just been talking about my mother? Then I realized that Erin was talking about Maeve, my birth mother. My heart suddenly skipped a beat.

I had never known my birth mother. She was from Ireland and had come to America with her lover, Angus, only after their entire coven was decimated by the dark wave. Coming to America hadn't saved her, though. Ciaran—her other, secret lover—caught up with her and killed her while I was still a baby.

"Did you know her?" I asked Erin. My throat was suddenly dry.

"I met her once, briefly, when she was about fifteen and I was twenty-one," Erin said. "My dearest friend, Mary, married a Belwicket man." Her eyes clouded.

Belwicket was the name of Maeve's coven. "Your friend—did she—"

"Gone," Erin said. "Like everyone else."

We sat together in silence for a moment.

"I can't imagine what it must have been like for you, growing up in a house without magick," she said. Her eyebrows were raised, and her face held a question.

"It wasn't a big deal," I admitted. "I never knew anything else." I paused. The next part was harder to talk about. "Until I met Cal." I looked at Erin, unsure how much of the story she already knew.

Erin nodded. "Sgàth," she said, using Cal's witch name.

The word sounded like a low susurration, the voice of the wind in the trees. She knew who he was. Of course.

"Yes. He taught me about Wicca, and I started learning more on my own. I discovered that I had powers. And then I learned the truth. That my parents weren't my birth parents . . . and that I was Woodbane."

"Morgan," Erin said, leaning toward me. "You haven't had an easy time of it. But that just means you have to be willing to work very hard—harder than most others have to. Are you willing to do that?"

I didn't hesitate. "Yes," I said.

"Good." Erin held up a small slip of paper. "I've checked the computer. The library has a number of fascinating books on witch history. We can start there." She handed the paper to me. On it was a list of five books and their call numbers.

"I'll be right back," I said. As I headed over to the nonfiction section of the library, I passed a familiar auburn head bent over a notebook at a nearby table. Mary K. She had gotten a ride with Susan Wallace both before and after school—clearly avoiding me again. Alisa sat across from her, murmuring in a low voice. Whispering in my sister's ear about my evil powers, no doubt.

A voice in my mind urged me to go and find the books. I knew it was the smart thing to do, but I just couldn't make myself do it. There was something about the way Alisa looked, sitting there—I wanted to get her away from Mary K. Things were tense enough with my family. I didn't want Alisa getting into the middle of it. I crossed the room in a few quick strides and stood next to my sister. "Hey, you guys," I whispered, trying to sound as nonchalant as possible.

Mary K. looked up with a start and placed her hand casually over what she'd been writing. Alisa practically turned green.

"Uh, hi, Morgan," Mary K. said. There was a thin edge in her voice. Was it anger, or fear? I couldn't read her expression.

"What are you guys working on?" I asked.

"Oh," Mary K. said, glancing down at her paper. "Just a writing assignment." She shifted in her seat and glanced over my shoulder. "What are you doing here?"

I lifted my eyebrows. "I'm studying." I tried to get a better look at Mary K.'s notes. There seemed to be a lot of them. "You guys seem to be working pretty hard on this thing," I pressed, trying to make conversation.

Mary K. looked really uncomfortable. I turned to Alisa, who was as still as a stone. "Is it a project for class?" I asked. Alisa didn't respond. She stared down at the library table as if it were the most fascinating piece of wood in the universe.

I couldn't imagine what they'd be hiding from me. "What's going on?" I asked finally.

Mary K. stared helplessly at Alisa.

"Mary K. is helping me write a letter," Alisa said without looking up from the table. Then she raised her head and looked me in the eye. "It's to the town newspaper, and it's about the dangerous witchcraft going on around here."

She's lying. That was my first thought: She's lying—she'd never do that. And Mary K. would never help her. I turned to my sister. "Is this true?" I asked her.

Mary K. didn't reply.

"It was my idea," Alisa said, still looking at me with that defiant gaze.

"Mary K.?" My voice was a whisper. Mary K. wouldn't look at me.

"It was my idea," Alisa repeated.

I folded my arms across my chest. "Have I done something to you?" I asked her.

Alisa looked startled. "What?"

"Have I made you mad or something? Or has someone in Kithic done something wrong?" I struggled to hold my anger in check. Why was she doing this? What did she have to gain? "Because you seem to have turned against us."

"That—that's not true," Alisa insisted feebly.

"Isn't it?" I demanded. "Then what's the point of this letter?"

Alisa's mouth opened and closed. "It's just—it's just—" She groped for words. Finally she shook her head. "Look, forget it. Forget the letter. I'm not sending it."

"That doesn't answer my question," I pressed.

"Morgan," Mary K. said, "she just said that she isn't sending the letter. Isn't that enough?"

"I don't know," I said. I really didn't. I wanted to understand what was going on inside Alisa's head—but clearly she didn't want to let me in.

I looked at Mary K. "I guess I'll see you later."

She gave a quick nod and looked down at her paper again. I didn't say anything to Alisa, just turned and walked toward the stacks, fuming. Everything was skidding out of control lately—school, my family life, even my magick.

Just put it out of your mind, I told myself. You can always talk to Mary K. later. I checked the call numbers of the books Erin had listed and realized they were on one of the top shelves. Grabbing a library ladder, I stepped up to the top rung and began hunting for the first title.

"Legacies of the Great Clans," I murmured to myself. "Legacies of—" My ladder tipped slightly, and I instinctively reached out and grabbed one of the shelves to keep myself from falling. It must be uneven, I thought as I wiggled myself gingerly to feel if the legs were stable. The ladder didn't move.

I didn't have time to think about that, though, because in a moment a book flew off the shelf, hurling itself against the books on the shelf across from it. Where have I seen that before? I wondered dimly as the entire bookcase began to rattle and shake. It gave a heavy groaning creak, and I looked back at it just in time to see it tip toward me.

I didn't even have time to let out a cry—I jumped from the ladder as the bookcase toppled. With a fierce crash, it slammed into the shelf across from it, and books slid off the shelves and thudded to the floor. I landed on the floor in a heap, under the tilted shelf, and felt a sharp pain in my shoulder. Around me there were shouts, then scuffling noises as people ran toward me.

"Are you okay?" The gangly librarian leaned over and helped me to my feet. She stared at the bookcase and the mess of books on the floor. "You could have been hurt!"

Staring at the wreckage, I started to shake. It was true. The bookshelf was massive and loaded with heavy volumes. If it had fallen completely, it could have landed on me. And if it had toppled the shelf across from it, it could have landed on someone else. I shuddered.

A small group of people had gathered nearby, and Erin pushed her way through them to come over to me. "What happened?" Her tone was sharp, her forehead creased with worry.

I cast a sideways glance at the librarian, who was inspecting the shelf gingerly. "It was just like the other day at Hunter's," I whispered. "I saw a book fly off the shelf before the whole thing toppled." Now I was shaking for real. Ciaran, I thought. It had to be him. Who else would—or could—do this? My birth father really was after me. Remembering what he had done to my mother, to her whole coven, I had to fight for breath. If Ciaran really was after me, how could I ever escape him?

I saw the muscles in Erin's jaw start to work. "How are you feeling?" she asked.

I felt my shoulder where I'd landed on it. "I'm okay," I said. "Just bruised."

"No," Erin said. "I mean, are you feeling lightheaded? Dizzy?" She frowned and passed a hand across my forehead. "Do you feel like you need to ground yourself?"

Suddenly I understood what she was saying. "You think *I* did this," I murmured.

Erin looked calmly at me. "Who do you think did it?" she asked.

Fear shot through me like lightning. "Ciaran," I said quickly.

"I don't think so." Erin's voice was certain, and I felt a flash of doubt. Could I have been responsible for this? I didn't think so. I would have felt the magick flowing through me, I reasoned.

"Do you have any idea how you summoned white witch fire when we were working together in Practical Magick?" Erin asked abruptly.

"No," I admitted.

"Morgan?" said a voice behind me. "My God, Morgan— are you okay?" It was Mary K. Alisa was right behind her.

"I'm fine," I said as Mary K. rushed over and gave me a

hug. I winced at the pain in my shoulder but didn't complain.

"What happened?" Mary K. said as she eyed the shelf. I turned and stared back at the wreckage. *Someone could have been hurt,* screamed a voice in my brain. *Someone could have been killed!* "What were you doing, leaning on it or something?"

I shook my head but didn't say anything. Alisa was staring at Erin as if she were some kind of poisonous snake or tarantula. Her eyes darted from Erin to the shelf and finally settled on me. I felt I could almost see her mind working. She knows, I realized. She knows it's another magickal aberration. "Freak accident," Alisa said.

"Yes," Erin agreed. She looked at Alisa more closely. "Don't I know you?" she asked.

"We met last Saturday night," Alisa replied coolly. "At Hunter and Sky's."

Mary K.'s glance went to Erin, and she took an awkward step backward. I could see her putting the pieces together. Saturday night plus Hunter's house equals witchcraft. She looked back at me. "Aren't you here *to study?*" she asked sarcastically. Then she spun and stalked out of the library.

I started to go after her, but Erin held my arm in an iron grip.

"I'm glad you're okay," Alisa said quietly. Then she turned and went back to her table, where she started to gather her things.

I stared after her. "Morgan," Erin said, giving me a gentle shake. I looked at her blankly. "Morgan, we need to have a circle. Right away."

"Circle?" I repeated dumbly.

Erin's face was pale and solemn. "This is becoming very

serious," she said, indicating the fallen shelf. "We can't let it go on any longer."

"What do you mean?" I asked. I was afraid to hear the answer.

"I mean that we have to rein in your power right away," Erin replied. "Once you've learned more—once you're more in control of your magick—then we can do an unbinding spell. But right now, you're dangerous." She took my hand. "I'm sorry, Morgan."

I felt the air rush out of my lungs. *Dangerous.* The word echoed in my mind. "No," I wanted to say, "absolutely not." I thought about the white witch fire I had called up the other day. Erin was right; I had no idea where that power and knowledge had come from. Though it was different—I had felt myself channel the energy. Then I remembered the night the candle went out and the lightbulbs exploded. There could have been a fire. And now this. Mary K. was here, I thought. Mary K. could have been standing underneath that shelf.

My chest was tight. Erin was looking at me expectantly. "Okay," I said at last. "I'll do it."

8

LOSS

September 30, 1971

It's been almost a week since it happened. I prepared the ritual, lit the fire in the cauldron, called upon the Goddess and the God for strength, and prepared to destroy Harris Stoughton's vile book. But I couldn't do it.

It's hard to describe exactly what I was feeling. Fear, yes. And revulsion for the book and its author. But I also felt a strange sense of longing. I suppose it's my Rowanwand blood—the love of and hunger for knowledge that we are known for. At any rate, I simply couldn't destroy the book and take this knowledge—even though it's dark knowledge—out of the world forever. I had to find a safe place for it.

My first thought was to bury it behind the house. Earth can be very powerful—it can purify objects that have been spelled. But I didn't want to run the risk that someone, or even some animal, might dig up the book and find it. Besides, the book itself hasn't been spelled. It's a book of dark spells, and there is no mountain of earth in the world that could purify it.

But I realized that there is a place in my very own house that is ringed with spells of obscurity . . . a secret place that no one but initiated blood witches can find: my parents' library. I decided to put it there for now and to warn them about the book as soon as possible. I hadn't wanted to tell them about it for fear of getting Sam into trouble. Then again, I thought that things had gone far enough.

My parents keep their dark magick titles, of which they have quite a few, on the highest shelf in the library. I had to get a stool to reach it. I stood there for a moment, reading the titles before me. Some of them were fairly chilling, and as I placed the Stoughton book among them, I had a deep sense of foreboding.

At the very moment that I slid the book in among the others, the reading lamp on the table in the corner began to rattle and shake. Then it started to move. Slowly at first, then gaining speed, it slid across the table and crashed to the floor. I squeezed my eyes shut tight. It's an earthquake, I thought, and I wanted to believe it—although whoever heard of an earthquake in Gloucester? Besides, I would have felt the whole room shaking.

Finally I managed to calm my breathing and opened my eyes. Everything was still, including the *books on the top shelf. I left the library as quickly as possible and redrew the sigils in a hurry.*

I was so scared that for a moment I considered doing a circle in my room to calm my nerves. But instead I went up to the widow's walk and let the rhythmic crashing of the waves hypnotize me.

I have to be honest with myself. Lately magick has seemed terrifying instead of wonderful. For now, I think I'll let nature be my religion.

—Sarah Curtis

"We have to go right now," Erin said, checking her watch. "Hunter should be home, and Sky is due back from the record store in twenty minutes. She may even be there by the time we arrive."

I nodded, mute. The incredible unspeaking Morgan. Part of me just couldn't believe that this was actually happening, and another part of me grasped that it was vitally important and had to take place right away. I found myself pulled along by the strength of Erin's will—following her like a stick caught in the current of the river.

Time seemed to slow down and everything around me felt surreal as Erin and I walked to my car. As I slid into my seat and turned the key in the ignition, I noticed that Erin's feet weren't touching the floor of the car. She looked ridiculously small on Das Boot's enormous bench seat, like a doll in an easy chair. Pulling into traffic, I felt hyperaware of the cars around me. Somehow a fly had found its way into my car, and it buzzed loudly against the windshield.

Erin's voice cut into my thoughts. "I won't lie to you,

Morgan," she was saying. "The ceremony isn't going to be easy."

I interrupted her. "I've seen someone stripped of their powers," I said with a shudder, remembering David Redstone.

"It isn't like that," Erin said quickly. "It's unpleasant, but not at all like that. Reining puts limits on your powers, but it doesn't take them away. You'll still be able to do some small things, even some bigger things with the help of another, more powerful witch. And you can be unbound once you've gotten further in your training. Think of the reining as like a muzzle on a dog. Once the dog is taught not to bite, the muzzle can come off."

I gripped the steering wheel. "It sounds horrible," I said.

Erin turned and looked out the window. "It is," she said softly. "But Hunter and Sky and I will be there to make it as comfortable for you as we can."

Hunter. A small spark of hope flared in my chest and brought me back to reality. Hunter knew me—he knew I couldn't possibly be responsible for this. He would convince Erin that my magick didn't need to be reined. He would convince *me.*

He had to.

Sky was just striding up the front walk as we pulled into the driveway. She turned and gave us a little wave, as if she were happy to see us. Then we stepped out of the car and she saw our faces. Her smile vanished. Hunter appeared at the door. I guessed that he'd sensed us pull up.

"What is it?" Sky whispered to me as we walked up the front steps.

I didn't respond. No one said anything as we took off our coats and hats. Hunter went into the kitchen to put on a kettle for tea, and Erin, Sky, and I followed him. As I sat down at their table, I willed myself to relax.

"There's been another incident," Erin announced. "Morgan and I were in the library when books began to fly off the shelves, and the entire bookcase nearly crashed down on her head."

"Morgan?" Sky asked, leaning forward. Hunter turned pale.

"It would now seem that the common denominator for these incidents is Morgan," Erin went on. "I am concerned that if we allow her magick to remain unchecked, we run the risk of someone getting hurt."

"I don't think so." Hunter shook his head. "I'm almost certain that some of these incidents have been messages from my parents. I don't know how I know it, but I feel it's true."

"Did you feel that what happened at the circle on Saturday was a message from your parents?" Erin asked.

I felt my heart beat once. Twice. Three times. "No," Hunter replied.

"And this latest incident in the library wouldn't have been, either," Erin went on. "Hunter," she said in a gentler tone, "it's possible that you are receiving messages from your parents. What happened when we scried and what you described at the movie theater, even the figure in the fog—those things *do* sound like messages. It's also possible that Morgan is causing these telekinetic incidents and that they're entirely unrelated to what you've experienced. You've said yourself that she has very strong powers and that she isn't a very skilled witch . . . yet."

"I don't know." Sky spoke up, surprising me. "Skilled or not, it seems to me that if Morgan was doing this, she'd feel it."

I felt so grateful to her that I almost leaped up and hugged her.

"Who, then?" Erin demanded.

"Ciaran," Hunter suggested.

Erin scoffed. "Hunter, you know as well as I do that proximity is important for telekinesis, even for a witch as strong as Ciaran. He has to be near her. He wouldn't be able to control books in a library in Widow's Vale when he's in Spain—it's impossible."

"Well, you were at both Saturday's circle and at the library, Erin," I snapped. "And those have been the only two telekinetic incidents so far."

Erin cocked an eyebrow. "Have they?" she demanded.

My mind whirled, and I felt sick as I remembered my books leaping from my locker and scattering all over the floor. "Maybe not," I admitted.

Sky raised her eyebrows, and Erin leaned back in her chair. Hunter dug his hands into the pockets of his black corduroys. I told them briefly about my locker.

I expected Hunter to ask why I hadn't told him about this before. But he didn't. He just turned and gazed out the window for a long time.

It was Sky who broke the silence. "So—what should we do?" she asked.

"I think Morgan's power needs to be reined." Erin looked from Hunter to Sky. "Now. This evening."

Sky looked at Hunter.

"That ritual isn't to be done lightly," he said to the window.

"Are you willing to risk it?" Erin demanded. "Someone could have been killed today. *Morgan* could have been killed."

Hunter turned and looked at me. His eyes were full of pain. Tell her, I wanted to shout. Tell her that it isn't me! But what he said was, "I'm sorry, Morgan."

There was a long creak as Sky pushed her chair away from the table. "I've got some white clothes upstairs," she said. "Come, Morgan."

I couldn't believe this was happening—that Hunter was letting this happen. I blinked fast, trying to clear my eyes of bitter tears. I wanted to scream, to shout, but what could I say? I tried to imagine how I would feel if I refused to let my powers be reined and then something horrible happened, but it was too awful to think about.

It's only temporary, I told myself as I followed Sky upstairs to her room. I tried really hard to believe it.

When I came downstairs, wearing Sky's white tunic and pants, Hunter had already drawn a circle. At its center was a large, heavy-looking stone basin, filled with water. Thick, pungent incense saturated the air. It was a kind I'd never smelled before, and it had a dark, earthy quality that reminded me of caves and dense forests. The sun had sunk quickly, and the only light in the room came from a few flickering candles.

I stepped inside the circle, and Hunter drew it closed. Each of us stood by one of the four corners—Hunter by earth, Sky by air, Erin by water, and I by fire.

In a low voice Erin began to chant. The words were Gaelic, strange and ancient-sounding.

Acarach ban-dia
Acarach dia

Do cumhachd, do aofrom
Séol lamh
Bann treòir

The water in the basin began to shimmer and glow. For a moment it looked like a pool of liquid gold. Then a light flared from the center of it—small yet brilliant, like a lump of coal that burned as bright as the sun. I couldn't look directly at it. After a moment the coal sent up a column of light bright enough to bathe the entire room in dazzling whiteness. The column was shot through with glowing sparks, specks of silver confetti.

I felt a similar spark rise in my chest—a brilliant light was growing within me. I felt wonderfully, powerfully alive. My heart leaped, and I wanted to shout, "It's beautiful!" but in the next moment something happened that made my skin turn cold.

Ugly black smoke began to pour from the bottom of the basin. It was thick and heavy and rolled along the floor. It had gone no more than two feet in all directions from the basin when it slowly began to rise. But it didn't rise the way normal smoke does, floating on the air through the room. Instead it rose like bars, or long wicked fingers, around the light. It rose until it reached the ceiling, then closed around the light like a dark clutching claw.

My lungs felt tight. I struggled for air. The brilliant light within me was dimming, held in the clutches of the horrible blackness. I fell to my knees.

Hunter, Sky, and Erin began chanting. After a moment the pain in my chest receded and I could breathe, although I felt very sick. The black fingers pulled the brilliant column of light down, slowly, into the bowl, until it was nothing but a swirling pool of gray streaked with flashes of light, like a tiny dark sky full of lightning. The chanting stopped, and I knew that Hunter, Sky, and Erin had done their best to help me. Still, my head was throbbing, and I had to choke down the bile that rose in my throat.

For a moment the room was completely still.

"Morgan." Hunter strode over to me and tried to help me to my feet.

I shook him off. "I'm fine."

A hurt look crossed his face, but I didn't apologize. I stood up, my knees nearly buckling.

"Morgan, you should eat something," Erin suggested.

The thought of food repulsed me. Besides, I was dying to get out of there. Right now I couldn't look at any of them—not even Hunter. "I'll eat at home," I said weakly. I checked my watch and nearly gasped. Seven-thirty! Oh my God—family night was supposed to start at six! I remembered how excited my mother had been earlier that day, and a new wave of nausea rolled through me. I couldn't believe I'd just let my mom down in order to participate in this horrible ceremony. "I have to go," I said, and took a staggering step toward the stairs. Sky swooped toward me, but I held up my hand. "I'm fine," I insisted. "Let me do this."

I gritted my teeth and somehow managed to make it upstairs and change into my normal clothes. By the time I came back downstairs, I was feeling a bit clearer, although the headache was exquisitely painful.

"I'll drive you," Hunter offered, but I shook my head.

"I've got Das Boot," I snapped. "Don't worry, I'll make it home fine."

I turned to leave, but Hunter said, "Morgan." The pain in his voice made me turn around, and I forced myself to face him. Hunter looked pale and worried, and I realized suddenly that he really hadn't wanted to do this any more than I had.

"Call me later" was all he said. He put his hand on my shoulder.

"Okay," I said, but our gazes remained locked for a moment longer. His green eyes communicated a world of thoughts and feelings. He loved me. He was afraid for me. He didn't want anything to happen to me.

I held that look in my heart the entire drive home. It was the only thing that made me feel even a little bit better.

"Where have you been?" my mother demanded the minute I walked in the door. No "Hello," no "Are you all right?" She was sitting on the couch with her arms folded across her chest. The headache threatened to split my skull in two.

I put my fingers to my left temple and rubbed it. "I'm sorry—" I began.

"Not good enough," my mom snapped. "What is going on, Morgan?"

I didn't know how to answer her. I just stood there, a lump in the living room.

My mom threw her hands up. "What am I supposed to do?" she asked. "What? You knew that family night was important to me—yet not only did you blow it off, you didn't even phone to tell me you weren't coming." She pushed herself off the couch and faced me. "Tell me how to get through to you, Morgan," she said. "What's left?"

I didn't know what to tell her. There was no way I could make her understand what had happened tonight, and I didn't really even *want* her to know. The accident at the library, the reining of my powers—it was too scary for me to deal with, never mind my mom. "I don't know," I mumbled.

"Well, that makes two of us." My mom sighed, then said, "I'm sorry, but I just can't take much more of this. I've tried reaching out to you; now I'm going to try punishing you. You're grounded."

I opened my mouth to protest but thought better of it. She was right.

"Okay," I said.

"I mean it, Morgan," she went on. "No phone, no television, no going out—nothing but schoolwork for the next two weeks."

I closed my eyes. I still felt thoroughly awful. "Okay."

"Look at me," my mom said, so I opened my eyes. "I love you," she said. Her voice wasn't sentimental—she was just stating a fact. "And I don't understand what's going on. But whatever it is, I'm not going to let it take my daughter away from me, is that clear?"

I nodded. "Yeah," I said. There was a beat of silence.

"I'm finished," my mom said finally. "For now."

I turned to go upstairs but stopped suddenly. "Mom?"

"Yes?" She sounded tired.

"I really am sorry," I said. The words hung there a moment, but she didn't reply. I trudged toward the stairs. Every muscle in my body—every fiber—ached. My head was pounding, and my heart was heavy. I pictured Hunter in my mind, tried to visualize the look he had given me just before I left. Only this time, instead of making me feel better, it made me feel worse. I wanted to call him. I needed to hear his voice. But now it was impossible—I was grounded.

I lay on my bed, and the pain in my head dulled a little. I wondered about the limits of my magick now that I was reined. Erin had said that I would still be able to do some small spells. Could I send him a witch message? I wondered. I decided to give it a try. *Hunter,* I thought, *Hunter. I need you.*

I felt echoing emptiness inside me and knew it wasn't working. But I tried again, anyway. And again. And again. Even though there was no reply, I didn't give up. I couldn't.

I didn't know what else to do.

9

Fear

I passed Bree in The hall Today. I said hello, but she didn't hear me.

At least, I _Think_ she didn't hear me. She looked kind of preoccupied, but maybe That was just an act so That she could pretend not To notice me. I'm sure Morgan Told her about me quitting Kithic.

I haven't even missed a circle yet, but already There are so many Things I miss about The coven. I miss The energy I felt from being part of The circle. I miss The feeling when a circle goes well and you feel like There's a greater power in The room with you. Like everyone's energy has combined and formed This force That's more powerful Than The sum of its parts. I miss feeling like I have a family.

Well, whatever—who cares? I'm not in The coven anymore. What They do is Their own problem. I'm not going

To Try To warn anyone about anything—I'm staying out of
it. I did my best. From now on, this is just a journal, not
a Book of Shadows. And I'm just a high school sophomore,
not a witch in Training.

I would have made a Terrible witch, anyway. I don't
have the stomach for it.

   —Alisa

"Morgan, what is that?" Jenna asked, peering at the bowl
of steaming hot something I'd gotten from the cafeteria. It
was lunch period the next day, and I was sitting with Sharon,
Raven, Jenna, Matt, Bree, Robbie, and Ethan. Lately I'd been
spending almost all of my lunch periods in the library in a
desperate attempt to pull my grades up, but today I simply
felt too sick to concentrate on anything. I looked around at
the familiar faces. If my grades didn't improve, I might be eating lunch at an entirely different school soon.

"Chili," I said. "I think."

"Isn't that the same stuff they served Monday?" Matt asked.

I gave him a wry half smile, but Bree let out a silky laugh.
Matt grinned at her. Jenna glanced up and gave me a wary
look across the table. What was Bree up to?

"You have to give the school credit on their food-
recycling program," Raven said. "No one can bear to eat
it, but no one can bear to let it go to waste."

Robbie was sitting next to me on one side of the table with
Jenna. Sharon and Ethan were on the other, and Matt was at
one of the short ends, sandwiched between Bree and Raven.
He looked like he was in heaven. Bree and Robbie, on the
other hand, hadn't exchanged a single word during lunch, and

now Robbie was staring down at his sandwich as if he thought he could make it disintegrate with the power of his mind.

"So is everybody going to make it this Saturday?" Sharon asked. Kithic was holding its circle at her house.

"I can't go," I said, feeling even gloomier. "I'm grounded."

"Grounded? What did you do?" Ethan asked, pushing curly hair out of his eyes. "Anything good?"

"Unfortunately not."

"Morgan isn't much good at being bad." Bree gave Matt a flirtatious little smile. "Unlike some people."

"Hmmm," Raven said smoothly. "Tell us about that, Bree."

Bree ignored her, still looking at Matt, who was grinning like an idiot. I narrowed my eyes at Bree. What did she think she was doing?

Robbie stood up. "I've gotta head to the library," he said to nobody in particular. "See you guys later." He grabbed his tray and walked off.

I caught Bree's eye and frowned at her. She made a face at me. "I'll be right back," I said, pushing my chair away from the table.

Robbie was halfway down the hall by the time I caught up with him. "Robbie, wait," I said, catching his arm. "What's going on?"

"I don't know." His eyes were filled with anger. "I guess I just didn't feel like sitting around and watching Bree hit on someone else. Call me crazy."

I folded my arms across my chest and cocked an eyebrow. "I thought you guys were broken up."

Robbie looked shocked. I knew it, I thought.

"That's what Bree told me, anyway," I went on. "She said you dumped her."

Robbie's eyes were wide. "What are you talking about?" he demanded.

I shrugged. "Isn't that what happened?"

"No," he insisted. "No way!" He looked confused and worried. "I just told Bree that I thought we needed some space. We've been spending all our time together lately, and . . . well . . . I've gotten these weird vibes from Bree. Like she's feeling kind of . . ."

"Possessive?" I finished for him.

"Yeah." He nodded. "So I tried to talk to her about it. I mean, look, personally I'd love to spend all my time with Bree. But it seemed sort of weird for *her*. Don't forget that I've known Bree a long time."

"As long as I have."

"Exactly," Robbie agreed. "And we both know she gets bored easily with guys, and then she moves on. Right?"

"Mmm." Dead right.

"So I thought I'd be clever and suggest more space," Robbie explained, "and she's been avoiding me ever since. I thought she was just taking me up on my offer." He bit his lip. "God, Morgan, have I totally screwed up?"

"I don't think it's your fault, but the situation is definitely screwed up," I said. "You have to talk to her. Now."

"What should I say?"

"Just tell her that this is all a big misunderstanding, which it is," I said. "Look, Robbie, you and I both know that underneath it all, Bree is actually insecure in a weird way, right?"

"About some things," he admitted.

"About this thing," I said. "This has just gotten blown out of proportion because she actually cares about you. A lot. And she doesn't know how to deal."

Robbie looked dubious. "You think?"

"I know it," I told him. I didn't think it was betraying a confidence to say that much. "So you'll talk to her?" I asked.

"Yeah," he said. He started to turn back toward the lunchroom, but the bell rang. "Damn," he said, checking his watch.

"Do it after school," I said as people began trickling into the hall. "Don't wait."

"Thanks, Morgan." Robbie reached out and drew me into a hug. I felt glad that I'd finally butted in. My head was still throbbing, but it was good to know that I'd done at least one thing right.

I was halfway through my first problem set when the doorbell rang. "Mary K., can you get that?" I shouted. My head was still splitting, even after I'd taken four Advil. Mary K. didn't reply. Not surprising. She was playing the radio at top volume in her room. I had expected her to be at cheerleading practice, but it had been canceled at the last minute. Now she was upstairs "studying" with her new best friend, Alisa. They were in the same French class.

With a sigh, I hauled myself up from the dining room table and trudged to the door, figuring it was probably someone from Greenpeace or another member of the Mary K. fan club. The latter was more likely.

I looked through the peephole and sucked in my breath. Erin! I'd completely forgotten we were supposed to meet to go over what I'd read about witch history. Crap. And now I *had* to answer the door. She was a witch, after all—she knew I was here.

"Hello, Morgan," she said. Her dark red hair was pulled into a braid, and she was carrying a backpack. In blue jeans and a peacoat, she looked more like a Vassar student than a forty-seven-year-old witch.

"Hi," I said, looking nervously behind her. My mom and dad weren't due home for a couple of hours, but I didn't want to take any chances. I wasn't supposed to have any visitors, and I knew that if they caught me with Erin, I was toast.

Erin cocked an eyebrow. "May I come in?" she asked.

"Actually . . . " I said, pulling the door closed behind me. "I've sort of been grounded. For coming home late. I'm not supposed to have any visitors. I'm just supposed to go to school and come home—no TV, no phone, nothing."

"I see." Erin's face was a neutral blank. "And how long is this going to last?"

I grimaced. "Two weeks."

"I see," Erin said again. We stood there, staring at each other for a few moments. She made no move to leave.

I cleared my throat. "So you see, I'm not supposed to have any visitors," I began again. "Um, my parents are actually thinking about sending me to a Catholic school. So I'm trying to pull my grades up. They might change their minds."

"Yes, I can appreciate that," Erin replied. "But the fact is, Morgan, that I'm only going to be here for a short time. Do you take my meaning?"

I wavered. Erin was right. I was having a rough time family-wise, but she'd come all the way from Scotland and so far hadn't had much of a chance to teach me anything. Something always seemed to get in the way. If I didn't let her in today, her entire trip would be pretty much of a wash.

"I brought you some more books," Erin said, pulling off her backpack. "A few from my own collection on Irish witches in the medieval period."

"Well," I said slowly, "I am writing a paper on the persecution of witches."

"Then it's a school project, isn't it?" Erin blinked at me innocently.

That did it. "Come in," I said quickly, leading her into the front hall. "But my sister is home, so we'll have to be careful."

"Oh, don't worry about me. I won't make a peep," Erin promised. Then she cast a quick see-me-not spell so that Mary K. wouldn't see or hear her as she slipped up the stairs. Not that there was much danger of that, considering the volume of the music pulsing from Mary K.'s room.

"Sorry it's such a mess," I said as I brushed a pile of clothes from my bed to the floor. Dagda, my gray kitten, had been sleeping at the foot of the bed. He stretched and mewed a mild complaint. Erin walked over to him and scratched him under the chin.

"He's a cute one," she said as Dagda stretched his neck and purred contentedly.

I smiled. Dagda had grown quite a bit since I'd first gotten him. Now he was looking like a lanky teenager of a cat, with gangly legs and paws that seemed enormous in proportion to the rest of him. Lately he spent all of his time either sleeping or dashing around the house madly—usually in the middle of the night.

Erin dropped her backpack and turned to look at me. "Have you finished *Legacies of the Great Clans*?" she asked.

I groaned. "Not even half of it," I admitted.

Erin studied my face a moment. "How are you feeling?"

"Like crap," I said bluntly. "I've got a headache that I can't get rid of." I ran my thumb along the ridge of my right eye.

"A stabbing pain?" she asked. "Like a knife to the skull?"

That was exactly what it felt like. "Pretty much," I agreed.

"And your breathing is a little tight? Your chest is heavy?" Erin suggested.

I nodded. "Is that normal?" I asked.

"Unfortunately." Erin took my wrist and felt for my pulse. She seemed to think for a moment, then said, "I'm sorry, Morgan. I know this isn't easy for you."

It was strange. I had gotten so used to magick flowing through me that right now I was feeling like a clogged drain—something less than useless. I remembered when I had first met Cal and my magick had begun to reveal itself. I'd felt frightened and off-kilter. Now I just felt . . . hollow.

"Before we begin, I think we should do a little meditation," Erin went on. "It should clear your head and make the pain recede."

I went and dug my altar out of my closet. Erin lit the candle and the incense, and I drew a circle on the floor and turned out the overhead light. It was gray and cloudy outside, so the room was fairly dark. Dagda stalked over to the altar to investigate, sniffed everything, then dashed away at top speed. I opened the door and let him out, then sat on the floor, facing Erin, my back to the bathroom that connected my room with Mary K.'s.

Erin reached out and took my hands in hers. Her fingers were cool and smooth, and the minute we touched, I felt strength and comfort flowing from her. We didn't speak, but soon I felt magick pulsing through the room.

Clear your mind. I heard the words although Erin hadn't spoken. I closed my eyes and tried to reach out. An image flashed in my brain—Erin standing before me in a yellow field, wearing a brilliant blue dress made of a delicate fabric, embroidered with symbols older than any I knew. *Let go of the pain.* Erin reached out to me, and the fabric of her ancient dress rustled in the breeze.

At her touch, the stabbing pain in my forehead dulled a bit. My head was still throbbing, but it was a muted ache. My chest lifted, and I took a deep breath of clean air. I felt infinitely better.

I smiled at her, and she smiled back.

Just then I felt something slam me in the back. I let out a startled cry and heard someone shriek behind me. I opened my eyes to see Erin falling away from me. Everything, the floor, the altar, everything was falling away. Erin's grip tightened on my hands, and my arm muscles tensed as I tried desperately not to let go. For a dizzy moment I expected Erin to shout at me not to let her drop.

"Oh my God!" the person behind me screamed. I turned and saw it was Alisa. Her face was white and covered in a light film of sweat. She looked confused, like she wasn't quite sure where she was. But something about her orientation was wrong. She was standing, supporting herself against the door frame to the bathroom. And I was sitting, yet my face was almost level with hers.

"Oh my God!" she screamed again, her eyes wide with horror. That was when I understood what was happening. *I was levitating.*

My heart clenched in a cold fist of fear. I was going to fall! I flailed with my legs but only succeeded in kicking the bathroom door shut. My hair fell forward over my shoulders. "Don't let go!" I screamed to Erin. "Don't let go of me!" In my panic I pictured myself flattened against the ceiling of my room, crushed by the weight of reverse gravity.

Erin closed her eyes and made a low humming noise at the back of her throat. I felt myself sinking slowly, an inch, then another, toward the floor.

Alisa's face was greenish white. She backed away from me, then ran toward the door that led into the hall. I heard her footsteps thudding on the stairs and saw a gray streak as Dagda dashed after her.

"What's going on?" I heard Mary K. shout. Somewhere in the back of my mind it registered that her music wasn't playing anymore.

I got lower, and lower. . . . Finally I was only a few inches off the floor. All at once I dropped onto my jute rug in a sprawling heap.

I looked up at Erin. "That wasn't me," I said.

"I know," she said. I looked at her closely and realized that she was afraid.

I heard Mary K.'s footsteps on the stairs, then the front door slamming. All at once there was a squeal of tires and a piercing scream.

Mary K.! I scrambled to my feet and nearly flew down the stairs, Erin right behind me. I dashed out onto the muddy front lawn and came to a stop by Mary K., who was standing perfectly still in the middle of the front walk, her hand covering her mouth. Alisa's dark form was retreating down the street—she was running home, I guessed. But that wasn't what Mary K. was looking at. I followed her gaze and saw that she was staring at a car that had stopped in front of our house. The door opened, and a heavyset woman rushed out and peered at something next to her front fender.

At first I thought that she had hit a piece of wood or some garbage in the road. Then I saw the thing move. One gray paw twitched feebly.

Dagda.

My heart clutched. The woman looked up and saw us. "Help!" she cried. Tears began to rain down her cheeks. "Oh God, I'm so sorry! I love cats." She looked at me helplessly. "He just came out of nowhere."

I couldn't speak. I bent mutely over Dagda.

The woman began crying even harder. "I'm so sorry," she said again.

Dagda's eyes opened, then closed again. He was alive! But though there wasn't any blood on him, I could see at a glance that he was badly hurt. I tried to cast my senses, but it was no use. My magick was still reined.

My vision blurred with helpless tears. I turned around and saw Erin behind me. She bent and studied my kitten for a moment. "The injuries are internal," she said. Her voice was low, but I could tell from her expression that Dagda was dying.

I didn't know what to do. I didn't want to move him for fear of causing him more pain. Tears spilled down my cheeks as I looked at him, his fur matted and soaked with gray leftover snow.

I couldn't just let him lie there, die there, in the street. I picked him up, cradling him in my arms.

Mary K. was still frozen to her spot on the front walk. "Morgan," Erin said. She leaned toward Dagda, and I wanted to scream at her to get away from him, to leave him alone, but I couldn't. Her hand hovered hesitantly over Dagda, her face questioning.

Then I remembered. Erin is a healer, I thought. I could feel the movement of Dagda's tiny lungs as he labored to breathe. I started to sob wrenchingly. Could she heal him? Surely he was too far gone, even for a witch's power.

Erin squeezed my shoulder. Once again strength seemed to flow from her into me. "Quiet yourself," she said gently. "Don't let your emotions control you."

I took a deep breath. Then another. Erin's strength flowed through my body. I said nothing as she lowered her hand and touched Dadga's head. She stroked him tenderly, with the force of a butterfly's wings. Closing her eyes, she stood without moving. Time seemed to stand still, and I held my breath. I don't know how long we stood there like that—it might have been five minutes or five hours.

Dagda let out a small mew.

"Oh thank God," the heavyset woman said. "Oh, thank you, Lord! I thought I'd killed him!"

Erin's face was serious. "He's badly hurt," she said, then turned to me. "You should get him to a veterinarian as soon as possible."

"I know a good one," I said, thinking of my aunt's girlfriend, Paula Steen. Her clinic was the closest one I knew of—only about fifteen minutes away. "Thank you," I said, and Erin nodded.

I don't know why, but I turned to the heavyset woman and said, "He's going to be fine."

"Bless you," she replied, which struck me as odd, but sort of sweet and strangely appropriate.

Still cradling Dagda with one arm, I pulled my keys out of

my pocket and turned toward my car. Then I heard a voice call, "Morgan?"

It was Mary K. She looked lost. "Can I come with you?" she asked.

I didn't even have to think. "Let's go," I said.

10

Confrontation

October 3, 1971

I finally worked up the nerve to warn my mother about the book, but she hardly seemed interested, let alone worried. I told her that the powers of Wicca were starting to seem uncontrollable to me—and frightening in a way that they never had before.

Mother didn't like that. She laid down her knife and told me that I was being "ignorant." She made it sound like she thought I was a hysteric—like those people during the witch trials. Another Harris Stoughton.

I told her that I had some good reasons to be freaked out, but she just said that she didn't want to hear it. She said that we were responsible witches and that we had a right to our beliefs.

Just at that very moment—I mean exactly as she said that—the silverware drawer flew out. It just flew right out of the cabinet and landed on the floor with a clatter. Then an icy wind blew through the room and the cabinet doors burst open.

"Get down!" Mother yelled as the plates flew out and hurtled against the wall—crash crash crash!

I screamed and screamed until the cupboard was empty. I screamed until my mother picked herself off the floor and took me by the shoulders. She shook me, but my scream went on and on until I couldn't scream anymore.

Then Mother held me and told me that everything would be all right. But I don't believe her.

There is dark magick in this house. For a while I thought it was the book itself that was responsible, but I know that's impossible. It's just a book. It may be full of evil, but it can't actually make things happen.

I can hardly bear to think it, but I have to. Could Sam have been behind it?

—Sarah Curtis

"May I help you?" the woman behind the desk asked as I rushed into the veterinary clinic. She was middle-aged with dyed blond hair and looked bored.

"I'm here to see Paula," I said in a rush. "Dr. Steen."

"Do you have an appointment?" the receptionist asked.

"No, I—" Just then Mary K. walked in with Dagda in her arms. The woman took one look at Dagda and said, "Come with me."

We followed her down a long white hallway and into a

small room. "Just a minute." The woman hurried out of the room. Barely a minute had passed before Paula walked in.

"Morgan!" She looked surprised and pleased. "Mary K.!" A quick glance at Dagda and her smile evaporated. "What happened?" she asked.

"He was hit by a car," I said as Mary K. laid Dagda gently on the steel table at the center of the room. Dagda struggled to get up but couldn't.

Paula pursed her lips. She palpated Dagda's ribs and stomach gently. Then she touched his left foreleg and frowned. "This needs an X-ray," she said.

"Is he going to be all right?" Mary K. asked nervously.

Paula looked at her and smiled reassuringly. "This is one lucky kitty," she said. "I think his leg is broken. He might have to hobble around on a cast for a while, but all things considered, that's pretty minor."

I exhaled with relief. "That's great news," I said.

"Why don't you guys wait outside while I take the X-ray?" she suggested. "If we do have to put a cast on, we may have to sedate him. It could take a little while."

I threw myself into one of the large, comfortable chairs in the waiting room while Mary K. went outside to the pay phone to let our parents know where we were. I was glad we had come here. I didn't know where the receptionist was, but she was no longer behind her desk. I was alone in the waiting room as the sky outside grew from pink to dusky gray and the shadows disappeared.

What had happened today? I dug a hand into my pocket, remembering the feeling of the door slamming into my back, the fear as I left the ground, Alisa's screams. Thank the

Goddess that Erin was there, I thought. She saw everything. She knows I couldn't have levitated myself. Especially not with my power restrained the way it is.

But then, who did it?

There was a sudden blast of cold air as Mary K. stepped back into the clinic. "I finally reached Mom," she reported. "She said she hopes Dagda's okay and she's glad we thought to go to Paula."

"Thanks, Mary K.," I said.

"I called Alisa, too," Mary K. said, sliding into the seat next to mine. "But her dad said she's too sick to come to the phone." Mary K.'s voice told me that she wasn't exactly sure this story was true. She looked at me sideways. "What happened in there?" she asked. "Why did she run out of our house?"

I sighed. "I'm really not sure." It was the truth. "I'm not sure why she came bursting into my room in the first place."

Mary K. shrugged. "She wasn't feeling great. Maybe she just got confused which door was which."

I thought about Alisa's face, distorted in fear. "She doesn't like me."

"She doesn't know you," Mary K. replied. After a moment she added, "And you don't know her."

Something in her tone of voice made me look at her. "What do you mean?" I asked.

Mary K. sighed. "It's just—Alisa's going through some pretty rough family things right now. She's not . . . not at her best."

I sank back into the chair, wondering what was going on with Alisa. But Mary K. clearly didn't want to tell me, and I didn't want to press her for details. Suddenly I felt guilty for not reaching out to Alisa more. It was obvious that she was troubled and that probably the animosity she felt toward me didn't really have anything to do with me.

Still, at least she had a friend like Mary K. Someone who didn't give up secrets easily. Someone who cared. I gave my sister a sideways look, loving her. I really hoped we could get past the trouble we were having now.

Paula came out with Dagda in her arms. He was wearing a small cast on his foreleg, which stuck out awkwardly from the rest of his limbs. "Here you go," Paula singsonged. "Good as new—or almost. He's a little out of it from the sedation, but that'll wear off by morning."

I rushed over, and Paula handed Dagda to me. He stirred in my arms, and Mary K. scratched him behind the ears. "Thank you so much, Paula," I said. Dagda's breathing was perfectly normal, and he didn't seem to be in any pain. And thank you, Erin, I added silently.

"It's just a fracture. You'll need to come back in two weeks so we can check on his progress," Paula said. "But I think we'll be able to take the cast off then."

We said good-bye, and I handed Dagda to Mary K. so I could drive. On the way home Mary K. asked, "Who was that woman who was at the house today? She was the same one you were at the library with, right?"

I winced. I should have seen this question coming. "She's a tutor."

"And a witch, right?" Mary K. asked.

"Anyone who has been initiated into a coven is a witch," I replied, figuring that a half-truth is better than no truth at all.

Mary K. stroked Dagda. "So—why are you hanging out with her?" Her voice held a distinct note of unease.

"She's teaching me."

"Like, how to put hexes on people and stuff?" Mary K. asked.

"No," I said curtly. Hadn't she learned anything about Wicca from being around me? "Of course not. She's teaching me about the history of Wicca and about herbs."

Mary K. looked dubious. "Herbs?"

"Herbs have a lot of medicinal properties. Some can speed recovery. I mean, there might even be something I could feed Dagda that would make him get better sooner."

"Really?" She sounded intrigued. "I wonder if she could help Alisa. She's been sort of worn out lately."

"Do you want me to ask Erin about it?" I suggested.

"No," Mary K. said quickly. "No, don't."

I didn't press her. Out of the corner of my eye I watched as she rubbed Dagda's belly and he purred sleepily. She had been there when Erin healed Dagda—but how much had she actually understood? I was afraid to find out.

When we got home, Mary K. handed Dagda over to me, and I took him upstairs and settled him comfortably on my bed. He instantly dozed off once I put him down.

"How is he?"

I turned around and saw my mom standing in my doorway. "He's fine," I said, giving Dagda a small pat. Mom came over and gave him a gentle rub on the head. "Paula says the cast can come off in two weeks."

"That's good news." My mom's eyes lingered on Dagda a moment, then she turned to me. "Come downstairs, Morgan. Your father and I want to talk to you."

I felt my throat tighten, but I followed her downstairs to

where my father was sitting on the couch with his serious face on. My mom sat down beside him. I took the armchair across from them—The Accused.

"Morgan, Mary K. told us that you had a visitor today," my mom began. "And that you were with a friend in the library yesterday."

My body went cold. I tried to read my mother's face— did she know that Erin was a witch? I didn't think so.

"You weren't supposed to have any visitors," my mom went on. "You knew the rules, and you broke them."

I wanted to protest, but I knew that would only make things worse. I clamped my lips together and sat on my hands.

"Morgan, your father and I have talked about this a great deal. We want you to be in a supportive environment. We don't want you to throw your future away. You need guidance and a firm hand and—"

Fear gnawed at my stomach like a hungry rat. No. This couldn't be. "What are you saying?" I asked.

"What your mother is saying," my dad put in, "is that we think it would be best if you went to Saint Anne's starting at the beginning of next quarter."

Oh, no, no, no! My stomach fell. "What?" I cried.

My mother's nostrils flared. "Look, we've given you a number of chances to show us that you're turning your grades around, and you've disobeyed us at every step. This started long ago—back when we asked you not to read Wiccan books—"

"So that's it," I broke in, stunned. "You're sending me to a Catholic school to try to convert me!"

"What?" My mom looked shocked.

"Morgan, don't be ridiculous," my father said. "We just want what's best for you."

"And what's best for me is Catholicism and not Wicca, right?" I shot back. "I can't possibly have both in my life."

"You were raised with Catholic values," my mom said hotly. "Those are *our* values."

I stood up and faced them. "Look, I can't help being a witch," I said. My voice shook. "Wicca is in my blood. I couldn't change it even if I wanted to. But that's the point— I *don't* want to. I respect your beliefs. Why can't you live with mine?"

The minute the words were out of my mouth, I wanted to call them back. My father's face went white, and my heart ached, but it was too late. My parents sat on the couch, stone-faced and silent. It was so quiet that I could hear the seconds ticking by on my watch.

Then my mom stood up. "Morgan, we've made this decision already. We want to put you in a positive environment— and we found one that seemed to offer the kind of academic support and discipline we think you need. We want you to value school and excel in it as you have in the past. I'm sorry if that offends you, but it's something else you're going to have to live with." She turned and walked out of the room.

My father stood and faced me. "We love you," he said in a quiet voice. He took off his glasses and pinched the bridge of his nose, and I saw in his eyes that my father was afraid— afraid for me.

We looked at each other a moment, then he turned and followed my mom.

"I love you, too," I said softly to the empty room.

11

Connection

I'm scared. I think I might be going crazy.

Today I was over at Mary K.'s house, and I started to feel sick—kind of dizzy and nauseated. So I went to her bathroom to splash water on my face.

While I was standing at the sink, something weird started to happen. My hearing started to fade, almost as if someone had stuffed wads of cotton in my ears, and then my vision started to narrow, like I was looking through a tube. I thought I was starting to black out, so I sat on the toilet seat and put my head between my knees. After a few minutes I felt a little better, so I got up and splashed a little more water on my face. Then I headed out through the door—only I guess I got the wrong one because I walked into Morgan's room, and there she was doing some bizarre ritual with Erin. That's when things started to get really crazy. I think I started hallucinating because I thought I saw Morgan rise into the air, like some kind of freaky scene from The Exorcist.

Needless To say, I goT ouT of There. BuT I sTill don't know if whaT I saw was real.

And I can't figure ouT whaT would be more frighTening—if iT was, or if iT wasn'T.

—Alisa

It was a dismal morning—gray and chilly—and I kept my head down and my shoulders hunched as I strode toward the quiet school building. The bell had rung ten minutes ago. Mary K. had always made sure that I was up by seven-thirty, but now that she was barely speaking to me, I didn't have any more wake-up insurance. Today I was late beyond all redemption, thanks to the fact that I'd overslept by forty-five minutes. I was still feeling headachy and ill, and the weather made me feel even worse. The absence of my magick was so overpowering that it was almost like a presence. I couldn't wait to get inside the warm school and distract myself with academics for a while. Or maybe I could catch a few winks in English class. Since I'd be attending Saint Anne's soon, I could afford to catch a nap here and there while I could.

Morgan.

I spun around. Who's calling me? I thought. But of course, my magick was still reined. Apparently I could still receive a witch message—I just couldn't send one. I turned back and scanned the front of the building.

At first I didn't see him. I had to look very closely before I noticed Hunter standing beside the large oak tree that grew to the far right of the building.

"How are you?" he asked as I walked up to him. His navy blue cap was pulled down over his hair, and the wind had made his cheeks pink. "You look tired."

"I'm okay," I said. "Listen, Hunter, I know I said I'd call you the other day—"

"Morgan, it's fine," he interrupted me. "I knew you wouldn't be able to send a witch message, and Erin explained that you were grounded. She told me a few other things, too." Hunter reached out and pulled me into his arms. "I'm so glad you're all right," he whispered into my hair.

I relaxed against his chest, loving the warmth of his touch. I felt him kiss the top of my head, making my scalp tingle, and then pull me tighter. It'll be all right, I thought. Even if I get sent to Saint Anne's, I'll still have Hunter.

After another moment he pulled away. "There's been some news," he said.

I felt my stomach tighten. "Your father?" I breathed.

Hunter smiled wryly. "No," he said. "Yours. Apparently Ciaran has been very active since his arrival in Madrid. That sigil you placed on him shows that he's visited a few of the top people on the council's watch list. Of course, there isn't any concrete proof—yet—that he has been the one behind the attacks against you. But one of the people he visited is Lenore Ammett, a witch known to have very strong telekinetic powers, who is suspected of abusing them." He paused, watching as the meaning of his words sank in. He nodded slightly and went on. "If she's helping him, he may have found a way to get around the proximity problem. Based on what we know, Ciaran looks to be the guilty party. Erin thinks so. The council thinks so." Hunter's jaw set into a firm line. "And *I* think so."

The words were both comforting and unsettling. Of course I wanted Ciaran to be stopped. But then again . . . he was my father.

"So how are they going to stop him?" I asked.

"With our help," Hunter replied.

"Ours?" I repeated faintly.

Hunter nodded. "All of ours. Morgan, I know you're grounded, but this situation has become very grave. Erin has found a spell that she thinks can help us. It's a deflection spell—when it is used against a witch, any magick that he works will come back to him threefold."

I frowned. "Isn't that just the threefold law?" I asked.

"No." Wind ruffled an errant strand of Hunter's pale hair, and I brushed it away from his face. "The threefold law is simply a general rule of the magickal universe, like karma, or what goes around comes around, as you Americans say." He grinned. "But the universe can take a long time to set things right."

"But the deflection spell?" I prompted.

"Works immediately." Hunter's green eyes glittered. "And harshly."

"Wait—why doesn't the council just use this all the time to punish anyone who's abusing their powers?" I asked, thinking of Selene, who almost succeeded in killing me—and probably did succeed in killing others—before she was brought to justice.

"The spell has some drawbacks," Hunter admitted slowly.

"Such as?"

Hunter cleared his throat. "Well," he said, "the spell requires a great deal of combined magick to work. And it tends to sap the energy of those who use it. Basically once the spell is finished, everyone in our circle will be the way you are now—possibly worse—"

"Which means that if someone else is behind these

incidents or if someone else, like one of the other Amyranth branches, decides to attack us, we'll be in serious trouble," I finished for him.

"Yes," Hunter said. "But on the positive side, the spell may not sap our energy for that long. We'll probably just feel ill for about a day. Erin is fairly certain—"

"Erin is *fairly* certain?" I repeated. "Erin hasn't done this spell before?"

"No one in the council has," Hunter admitted uncomfortably. "It's strictly forbidden because of the dangers involved. Also because of the source. But Erin has managed to convince the council that this is one time it's worth the risk."

"What source?" I asked. "Where's the spell from?"

"It's from a book by Harris Stoughton," Hunter replied. "Apparently Alyce gave it to Erin the other day."

"I was there," I said faintly, trying to suppress the shudder that had run through my body at the mention of Harris Stoughton's name. I was liking this plan less and less. "You think this is a good idea?"

Hunter shrugged. "We haven't heard much about Amyranth lately. I went to New York City yesterday and did some digging—it seems that none of the other members of that cell could have been behind this. They all seem to be lying low. And if we do use the spell, we'll know right away whether it worked. First, we'll feel the effects. Second, the spell will hit Ciaran hard—probably making him physically ill for at least a few days. That ought to make it easier for one of the Seekers in Spain to apprehend him. This is our chance to help out."

I looked at Hunter, feeling his desire to stop Ciaran

almost like it was my own. I knew that he wanted to bring Ciaran in for my safety, but there was something else behind it as well. Hunter was a Seeker by nature, not just by training. It was what he lived for. It was a side of him that frightened me. It was also part of the reason I loved him.

"What do you need me to do?" I asked.

"Erin wants to hold a circle tonight: you, me, Sky, and Alyce. I know you're grounded, but do you think there's any way you can make it?"

I shook my head. "No. My parents are really upset. They want—" I looked up at the redbrick school building, which contained all of the friends and classmates whom I'd hung out with my entire life. "They want to transfer me to Saint Anne's."

Hunter frowned. "The Catholic school? They decided?"

I nodded. "You know they don't approve of Wicca."

Hunter sighed. "I'll help you get through this."

"They feel like I'm slipping away from them." I shrugged. "I guess I have been, in a way. Anyway, trust me, there's no way I can make it to a circle tonight."

"Right." Hunter looked disappointed, if not surprised. "Well, we really need you, Morgan. So I've brought you this." He reached into his pocket and pulled out a small dark blue stone. A vein of white ran through it, and it reminded me of the night sky lit up by the Milky Way.

"What is it?" I asked, taking the stone from him.

"It's lapis lazuli," Hunter explained. "It facilitates understanding and communication. I've strengthened it with a spell. If you place this stone on your forehead, I ought to be able to send you thoughts and images, and you ought to be able to do the same to me, like a witch message, only better. It will be almost as if you were there at the circle with us. I should be able to channel your energy. Even with your power reined, the spell and my magick ought to allow the two of us to communicate. But once your power has been unreined, you'll be able to participate fully."

My heart skipped about five beats. "You're unreining my power?"

"Of course," Hunter replied. "Erin feels terrible that you were ever reined in the first place. Clearly you had nothing to do with what was happening."

I slipped my arms around his neck and gave him a kiss. "Thank you," I said.

"There's nothing to thank me for."

My lips were still warm where they had touched Hunter's. I wanted to contradict him, but I didn't. Instead, I asked, "Has there been any new word from your parents?"

Hunter pressed his lips together. "No," he replied. "But I haven't given up. I've thought about the clues I've had—a walled city, the fact that I spoke in French. There are a number of walled medieval cities in France. I've asked the council whether I can have leave to go look for my father and mother—"

My heart literally—literally—stopped beating for a moment.

"—but they've refused. They think my evidence isn't strong enough. They won't tell me what research they've done so far, and they won't send someone to France now. But it looks like there might be someone who is willing to search *for* me. Someone who isn't in the council and isn't bound by their rules."

I was so relieved that Hunter wasn't leaving that the ominous note in his voice barely registered in my mind. "Who?" I asked.

"Sky."

"What?" I asked. Sky was going to France? What about Kithic? "How long will she be gone?"

Hunter looked sad. "It's unclear. She's quit her job already. After she's finished in France, she may go back to England," he explained.

"But—but—" I sputtered. Sky and I had never been terribly close. Still, I didn't want her to leave. Hunter reached out and touched the tips of my long hair.

"We'll all miss her," he said. "But she doesn't want to stay here, Morgan. Things have been hard for her." Hunter looked at me, and I knew that he was talking about Sky's breakup with Raven. I knew she had to be excited at the thought of going home to her friends. "Besides," Hunter added, "I need her help."

I nodded. Hunter was right—this was important. I knew that even though he wasn't saying it, Hunter didn't want to send her. He wanted to go himself.

By the time I stepped into the school building, the bell ending first period had already rung. This was actually a good thing. If I had walked inside in the middle of first period, I would have almost certainly been stopped by Assistant Principal Collello, who seemed to think that it was his personal duty to hand out detentions to as many students as possible. But by coming in during the minutes between first and second period, I could just blend in with all the other students and make my way to class.

I pulled off my cap and felt static running through my hair. It was probably standing on end. I decided I'd better make a quick stop at the girls' room to check if I was presentable before wandering into class. I didn't want to look like I was just coming in from outside, after all.

A quick glance in the mirror showed me that the problem was more serious than I'd thought. My hair looked like a fright wig. I raked my fingers through it. It didn't help. I was just concluding that the situation was hopeless when the door swung open and Bree walked in.

"Morgan," she said quickly. "I'm glad you're here. I've been looking everywhere." She leaned gracefully against the sink and swung her backpack from her shoulder, balancing it on the shelf in front of us.

"I was way late." I wet my fingers under the faucet and attempted to comb my hair with them again.

"Do you want a brush?" Bree asked, rummaging around in her leather backpack. She finally pulled out a wide-toothed comb.

"Fantastic," I said, taking it from her. I pulled it through my hair, which began to settle down. Thank goodness.

"Listen, Morgan, I need to talk to you."

Our eyes met in the mirror. "What's going on?" I asked.

"Well, Robbie and I finally talked. He told me that he'd spoken to you and that he thought there had been a big misunderstanding."

"That's great!" I said. "So are you guys back together?"

"Well, yes," Bree admitted. She twirled the ends of her hair. The worried gesture.

I frowned. "So what's wrong?" I asked.

Bree looked at herself in the mirror, then looked back at me. "It's just that—when I thought that Robbie and I were breaking up, I sort of . . ."

My stomach dropped. "What?" I demanded. "What did you do?"

"I sort of . . . fooled around with Matt."

"Oh my God." I wheeled to face her. "Did you—"

"No." Bree folded her arms across her chest. "Absolutely not. Just, you know, kissing."

I couldn't believe this. Matt Adler! My mind flashed back to the day I saw him cheating on Jenna with Raven. I felt ill. "And you didn't tell Robbie?"

"I didn't know how to." Bree's voice was pleading. "I mean, it isn't exactly cheating because I thought we were broken up. It was really just a mistake. One that will *not* happen again. But I got scared that Robbie might not take it that way. So I kept my mouth shut."

I looked at her closely, trying to remain calm. I knew from personal experience with Mary K. that keeping the truth quiet was usually a mistake. "Keeping your mouth shut about this is like lying, Bree," I told her. "It's the same thing."

Bree bit her lip. I knew that wasn't what she'd wanted to hear.

"So you're going to talk to him?" I prompted.

Bree hesitated. "I guess so."

I folded my arms across my chest. "You might want to do it soon—like before Matt tells anyone that he made out with you."

Bree's face went white. "He wouldn't."

I shrugged. "He didn't think you were cheating, either, right? So he has no reason to keep quiet about it. And I'm guessing he'll boast."

That seemed to do it. Bree thought for a moment, then nodded. "Okay," she said finally. "Okay." I handed her the brush, and she stuck it in her bag. "Did you hear about Sky?" she asked.

"Just now."

"I can't believe it," Bree said. "What's Kithic going to be like? I just can't imagine circles without her." She shook her head and sighed.

"Me either."

"I don't know, Morgan," Bree murmured. "Sometimes I feel like everything's falling apart."

I thought of Hunter, my father, my reined power, my family. . . . I considered telling Bree about my parents' wanting to send me to Saint Anne's but decided that could wait. She had enough to worry about. "Yeah," I answered instead. "I know what you mean."

12

Restoration

October 4, 1971

    I can feel the darkness closing in.

    Today, the day after my argument with Mother, I went back to the library and pulled out The Book. I don't know what made me do it—I suppose I thought that it might have some advice on how to stop the same dark magick it unleashed. Which it did. Page after page on binding witches, both in secret and in the open. It even had a section on how to bind one's own magick. But I wasn't sure—I mean, I didn't know for sure that Sam was behind the latest piece of dark magick.

    I decided to look for another option.

    I flipped through the book, skimming it, and finally came across a chapter called "On the Movements of Objectes Through the Aire." Just like the plates and the drawer in the kitchen, I thought, and the lamp in the corner. So I read it. And guess what it said? It said that some witches, when they're in an agitated state of mind, can mentally move objects without realizing it.

So Sam could be behind these events, I realized. He wouldn't have to be into dark magick to be behind them. As long as he is nearby and is familiar with the objects in question, he could move them with his mind. Obviously he's eaten off the plates in the kitchen often enough to be able to picture them. And he was in the house both times.

I went to leave the library. But as I stood there redrawing the sigils of protection and obscurity around the door, I suddenly realized something.

Sam doesn't know about the library.

He won't be shown the library until his initiation. He doesn't even know it exists. So how could he have made the lamp fall over inside it?

In fact, there's only one witch in the house who knows about the library and is in an agitated state of mind. The same person who was present at both events. The one person I would never suspect.

Me.

—Sarah Curtis

"With this salt, I purify my circle." I couldn't wait to be unbound. I sprinkled salt around the large circle I had drawn lightly on the floor of my room. It was midnight, and my family was asleep. Still, I had shoved a chair up against the door leading from my room into the bathroom and a few books up against the main door to my room. I didn't want any more people accidentally barging into my room while I was in the middle of making magick.

I picked up the lapis lazuli from where I had placed it at the center of the circle. The stone felt cool in my hand. The gentle silk of my birth mother's green robe felt smooth against my skin, and even though my power was still reined, these two things made me feel like I was surrounded by good magick.

Lying down in the center of the circle, I placed the smooth stone on my forehead. I wasn't exactly sure what to do, so I decided to try casting out my senses.

I could feel Hunter's presence almost like he was in the room with me. My eyes were filled with fog that slowly began to lift slightly. As I looked around me, I saw that I was no longer in my room. I was in Hunter's living room. Sitting across from me was Alyce. To her right was Sky; to her left was Erin. Sky's lips were moving, but I couldn't hear what she was saying. Soon the others closed their eyes, and I saw their lips moving as well. They were chanting, I guessed. I watched all of this through a thin film of haze, like static from a channel that wasn't coming in clearly. What was this spell they were casting? It looked totally unfamiliar to me.

After a few moments Erin lit a black pillar candle. Then Alyce drew out a long string of thread and burned it over the candle so that it was broken in two. Silver flame licked up the thread, which dissolved into a fine, shimmery powder. Alyce blew on the powder so that it floated through the room, growing into a large cloud of sparkling dust. Soon everyone was covered in it. The powder gave everything it landed on a magickal glow, as if the room were bathed in the rosy light of a sunrise. All the while their lips were moving in the chant. It was eerie, like watching a suspense movie with the sound turned off, but somehow beautiful.

Erin placed her fingers in a bowl of water, then passed her hand over it three times. Quite suddenly the haze began to lift, and I could see everyone clearly. At the same time I realized that for the first time in days, I didn't have a headache. In fact, I felt wonderful, as if I'd just taken a long nap and a hot shower. I noticed that I was very, very hungry. That was when I knew that the ceremony I had just witnessed had restored my magick.

"Hunter," Sky said to me. Her voice was far away, like a voice in a dream. "Hunter, is she with us?"

"Yes," I said to Sky. I had spoken with Hunter's voice, almost as if we were one person, one will. It was then that I fully understood that I was seeing through his eyes—that I was actually *within* Hunter. I wasn't even certain whether the intention to speak had been my own or his. In the next moment I felt a rush of excitement. It was a visceral feeling, almost like lust, and once again I wasn't sure whether the feelings were Hunter's or my own. Suddenly I felt very self-conscious.

"Welcome to the circle, Morgan," Erin said.

There was so much I wanted to say—I wanted everyone to know how grateful I was to have my magick back; I wanted Sky to know that I was sorry she was leaving. But the power of the moment was intense, and it seemed inappropriate to address anything but the grim task at hand. I focused my energy on Hunter's presence. I felt a warm rush of strength and love and somehow knew that Hunter was sending me his emotions. I pulled those feelings around me like a blanket.

Erin pulled the book, still wrapped in its dark shroud, from its place beside her and placed it in her lap. After untying the silk cover, she turned to a page she had marked with a red bookmark. Erin closed her eyes for a moment and seemed to take a deep breath to steady herself. Then she opened her eyes and began to read the spell aloud.

The words were harsh and ugly, half of them written in an ancient language that I didn't understand—one that seemed older than any language I'd heard before. They seemed to force their way out of Erin's throat, as if she could hardly bear to utter them. Alyce's eyes were closed, and she was grimacing as if in pain with every word Erin spoke. Sweat broke out on Sky's forehead, and a bead trickled down the side of her face. Even I felt dizzy and tired, although I couldn't tell whether it was the effect of the spell or the strain of experiencing the circle through Hunter. I felt a current run through me like a bolt of electricity, and I knew it was the power of the circle growing and combining, running through all of us.

I felt a wave of exhaustion—Hunter's, I was almost certain. Alyce's face was flushing pink, then darker red. Her grimace grew wider, and it seemed like she could hardly bear what was happening. Tendrils of her gray hair worked their way loose from her long braid. I noticed this in a moment, a period of time shorter than a heartbeat, then slowly, slowly, the haze began to return. The scene was filling with fog that grew thicker with each passing moment. *What's happening?* I thought frantically, but not fast enough. The words beat back against me as if I was shouting into the wind. I felt certain that they had reached no one—not even Hunter.

I became aware of a sound, a sound very much like the roaring ocean beating against the rocks, then drawing back, then beating once again against the rocks. It was a sound I knew, though it took me a moment to place it.

It was the sound of my breathing.

I opened my eyes and found myself in my own room. I tried to cast out my senses again for Hunter but found that I couldn't. Hunter, Sky, Alyce, and Erin—had their magick been sapped, too? Did that mean the spell had been successful? I had no idea—I hoped so.

I couldn't believe that everything had happened so quickly. I struggled to sit up, and the lapis lazuli fell from my forehead with a thunk against the floor. I picked it up and held it against my lips for a moment.

I felt like hell.

Standing up, I pulled off Maeve's robe and folded it carefully. Then I yanked on a flannel nightgown and crept to the hiding place where I kept all of my mother's tools, behind the HVAC vent, and carefully put the robe back in its place. I set the lapis lazuli on my nightstand. Crawling into bed, I gently lifted Dagda's soft form and placed him at the end of the bed. I stroked his fur, then pulled the covers over me.

Staring into the darkness, I wished I could call Hunter . . . just to hear his voice and to know whether the spell had worked. It seemed cruel to have my magick back—to feel it flowing through me so fiercely for a few moments—and then to have it ripped away again. Still, I knew the magick would return. And I knew that Hunter would, too.

And if there was one thing I had learned how to do lately, it was wait.

I expected to feel better when I woke up the next morning, which is why it was such a rude shock when I still felt horrible. Every muscle ached, and when I tried to sit up, my body actually shook with the effort. Still, I forced myself over to my dresser and pulled on some fresh clothes. I had to go to school today—my history paper was due. I'd spent practically every spare moment, every lunch period and study hall, working on it. Even if it wouldn't help my quest to stay out of Catholic school, I wasn't about to let those precious twenty points of extra credit go without a fight.

I thought I'd never make it to fifth period. But when I walked into history class and placed my paper on Mr. Powell's desk, I felt proud of myself and happy. Even though my parents had never approved of my topic, the paper was good, and I knew it.

After school I came home and fell straight into bed. I didn't wake up until eight o'clock, when my mom appeared in my bedroom with a tray, looking worried. "Are you all right, Morgan?" she asked.

"Fine," I said, my voice thick from sleep. "I just stayed up late last night. I had to hand in my history paper today." Both of these things were true, although unrelated.

My mom nodded. "I made you some soup." She placed the tray on the floor by my bed. "Lean forward."

I obeyed, and she plumped up the pillows behind me. Then she placed the tray on my lap. The soup was minestrone—one of my favorites. "Delicious," I said when I'd had a spoonful.

"I didn't wake you because I figured you needed your rest," my mom said. "Besides, Dad and I like to have a romantic dinner alone sometimes."

"Where's Mary K.?" I asked.

"She's over at Alisa's house." Mom traced a finger over the edge of my afghan. "Apparently Alisa was out sick today. Mary K. went over to give her the Spanish assignment." My mother studied the pattern in the blanket carefully. I knew she was holding something back. Almost as if she felt me looking at her, my mom leaned over and brushed my hair away from my face.

"I really don't feel sick," I assured her. "I was just tired. I feel better already."

I think my mom could tell I was lying, but she didn't press me. Instead, she just stood up. "Leave the tray by your bed when you're finished," she instructed. "I'll come back and get it later."

"Thanks, Mom," I said.

She nodded and closed the door behind her as she left. I had another spoonful of soup and realized that I really did feel better—a little better, anyway. For once my mom and I hadn't argued about grades, or beliefs, or Catholic school. It had seemed, for a moment, almost like we were back to normal.

Almost.

13

Flame

I can't write much—The pen feels like lead in my hand.

This morning I woke up feeling so sick That my sheets were actually hurting me. When Dad Took my Temperature, he flipped out—IT was 103 degrees. He gave me some Tylenol and made me drink some juice, Then Took me To Dr. HawThorne's office. He Took my blood and a STrep culture. BuT he didn'T really have any idea whaT was making me so sick. He seemed worried ThaT my TemperaTure had spiked so quickly buT couldn'T explain iT. He says iT's The flu. DocTors always say iT's The flu.

Mary K. came over for a while, which made me feel a biT beTTer, buT now I'm feeling worse again—feverish and nauseaTed. NoThing seems To help.

I'm scared. I wish I could call someone in KiThic. I miss iT so much ThaT I'm sTarTing To Think I made a misTake by leaving The coven. BuT I guess iT's Too laTe To go back now.

—Alisa

By the time I stumbled downstairs and into the kitchen on Saturday morning, Mary K. was already dressed and stacking the breakfast dishes in the dishwasher.

"Is Alisa there?" Mary K. asked, and I realized she was talking into the cordless as she straightened up and closed the dishwasher. "She is?" There was a long pause. "What's wrong?" An even longer pause. "Oh. Okay." Mary K. reached out and gripped the countertop. "Can she have visitors?" she asked. "Well, thanks, Mr. Soto," she said finally. "Tell her . . . tell her I hope she gets better soon." Mary K.'s eyebrows drew together in a worried frown as she clicked off the phone and placed it on the counter.

I was tempted to sneak away—this was none of my business—but Mary K.'s expression disturbed me. I cleared my throat to let her know I was there, and asked, "Everything okay?"

Mary K. turned to face me. Her eyebrows lifted, and for a moment I thought she was going to yell at me for eavesdropping, but she seemed to change her mind. "Alisa's really sick," she said finally. "She's in the hospital."

"Oh," I said. A feeling of dread squeezed my lungs. "What's wrong?"

Mary K.'s voice shook a little. "Nobody knows. All they know is that it's serious. She's . . . she's not even conscious. Her dad is really freaked out."

"Oh my God, Mary K." I went over to her and hugged her. "That's horrible."

Mary K. started to cry. I didn't say anything. . . . I just rubbed her back the way I used to do when we were children. After a few moments she took a couple of shaky breaths. "It's just scary," she whispered into my shoulder.

"I know," I replied. "But she's in the hospital now. The doctors are there—they'll figure out what's wrong with her." I rubbed her back again. "It's going to be okay." I hoped it was true.

Mary K. pulled away from me. "Morgan," she said, and stopped.

"What?" I asked.

"Morgan, I'm sorry I told Mom and Dad about your friend."

It took a minute for me to figure out who she was talking about. "You mean Erin?" I asked.

"I was just so s-s-scared." Another tear squeezed out of the corner of Mary K.'s eye and trickled down the side of her cheek. I brushed it away.

"I know," I said. "It's okay."

We looked at each other a moment. "I don't want anything to happen," Mary K. said.

"It won't," I assured her.

"How do you know?" she demanded. "I mean—why are you risking it?"

I sighed. "Mary K., magick isn't just horrible, dangerous, dark things. It can also be beautiful and wonderful. It's part of who I am. And I'm"—How could I put it?—"I'm strong. You don't have to worry about me. I can take care of myself." The words were more forceful than I really believed, but saying them actually made me feel better.

They seemed to have the same effect on Mary K. She straightened up and passed her hands over her face, then she tucked her hair behind her ears. "Morgan—would you take me to see Alisa?"

"Of course," I said quickly. I was about to ask whether she

wanted to go right now, but then I remembered. "Oh, crap, I'm grounded. We'll have to ask Mom and Dad if it's okay."

"They're out running errands," Mary K. said, "and visiting hours are only until three."

"Can we go tomorrow?"

Mary K. nodded. "Sure. That would be great." She started to head out of the room, then turned back. "Thanks, Morgan," she said.

I nodded. "No problem."

Mary K. smiled at me, and for a moment she looked just like the sister I knew—the one who loved me, no matter what.

That night I moped around the house for a couple of hours. The house was deserted—Mom and Dad were over at the Berkows' for dinner, and Mary K. had gone over to her friend Susan's house. My parents had given me permission to watch television, but there was nothing decent on any of the channels. My chest ached. I still felt awful from the previous night's spell, but more than that, I was sad about tonight's circle. It would be the last one with Sky, and I was missing it.

What I needed was magick, and if I couldn't go to Sharon's house along with the rest of Kithic, I could at least try to scry by myself. Maybe some of my power had returned.

Up in my room, the match hissed and flared as I lit my pillar candle. I breathed deeply and stared into the flame. I could feel the rays of warmth radiating off the candle. The heat sank into me, driving away the cold draft in my room. As my breathing grew more regular, I felt calm . . . and after a while, happy. I looked into the depths of the small blaze. The graduated colors, the blue, orange, and yellow, of the fire seemed to swirl together and grow. They flared and changed color, first to red, then purple, then violet, then green. The green fire twirled slowly, like an eddy in the ocean, and I realized that the fire was showing me something and bent closer.

In the depths of the green flame I saw a figure—Hunter. He was waving at me, but it wasn't a wave that beckoned me closer. It was more like a farewell. My heart quickened, but the image faded. I was left only with the swirling green flame, the color of Hunter's eyes. Slowly it faded to violet, then purple, then red . . . and in a moment it was an ordinary candle flame again.

What did it mean? Was it a portent—an image of the future? Or was it a picture of something that *might* come to pass but might not? I didn't know. I was afraid to know.

Although I tried to comfort myself with the certain knowledge that my power was back, I couldn't stop the feeling of dread that squeezed my lungs in its grip, making it difficult to breathe. Hunter and I had been through so much together, and I'd been so happy that he was near me, safe.

I had a horrible feeling that everything was about to change.

I took a long hot shower and put on a clean nightgown. Dagda hobbled into my room and sniffed at a pile of books in the corner. I patted my bed, and he leaped up onto it, purring as I stroked him. It was late—almost midnight—and I was about to click off the lamp by the side of my bed when my eye fell on a flash of midnight blue on my nightstand.

It was the piece of lapis lazuli. I picked it up and rubbed it.

I could call Hunter, I realized. If my magick was back, then his must be, too.

I lay back on my bed and placed the lapis on my forehead, closing my eyes and forming a mental image of Hunter. *I am here,* I thought. *Hunter, I am here.*

Morgan.

It was both a voice and not a voice—almost like my own thought, yet somehow separate—and I knew that it was Hunter.

I miss you, I thought.

Yes, he replied. *I feel the same.*

I couldn't exactly see anything—just the same sort of grainy darkness that I always saw when I closed my eyes. But after a few moments the darkness seemed to grow lighter. It continued to pale until it was almost the same purple-gray as twilight—or as the sky before the sun rises.

Kithic? I thought. *How was the circle?*

Melancholy. Hunter's word reverberated through my mind. *Sky is sad to be leaving tomorrow, although she doesn't say so. And of course, Alisa has left us. Everyone was gloomy. You should be glad that you weren't there.*

I wish I had been there. As it is, I won't get to say good-bye.

Hunter's thoughts were gentle. *Sky understands.*

The darkness before my eyes grew even lighter—pinkish, like the inside of a conch shell. With the next breath I took, I had the sense that Hunter was in my room. His distinct odor of soap and clean laundry filled my nostrils. Still, I knew that he was in another house, halfway across town.

I feel like you're here with me. The words were Hunter's. I wondered if he was experiencing the same thing I was.

The spell, I asked, *did it work?*

According to the council, Ciaran hasn't moved for twenty-four hours, Hunter replied. *A Seeker will move in on him tomorrow. And then there's the matter of our magick. Mine completely disappeared Thursday night.... This is the first glimmer I've of it all day.*

It feels wonderful. The words drifted through my mind, sending chills through my body. I wasn't sure whether they were mine or Hunter's. But it didn't matter.

At the center of the pinkish void, a small ball of silvery flame flared and began to pulse. It flared brilliantly until the entire space was lit with dazzling whiteness. It warmed me, as if I were standing with my face to the sun.

You are so brave. The words, the words, mine or his? *I love you.*

I didn't send any more thoughts. It seemed unnecessary. Hunter's presence was all I had wanted . . . and now I felt like I was surrounded by it, almost engulfed by it.

I knew what this light was. It wasn't Hunter's energy or mine. It was something beyond the two of us—something greater than the sum of two halves. This light was the energy between us, the power of *mùirn beatha dàns*, soul mates.

14

Heal

October 5, 1971

I tried to talk to Sam about what's been happening, but I never got the chance. The minute I mentioned the Harris Stoughton book, he became furious. He demanded to know whether I had destroyed it, and when I said I hadn't, he started shouting.

I was already on edge, and having him yell at me set me off. I told him that he should have burned the book himself. He was the one who stole it, he was the one who brought it home, he was the one who tried one of its spells even after I told him the book was evil. I was sick of trying to help him! As we stood there screaming at each other, I was suddenly struck with a splitting headache, a piercing, stabbing pain.

Sam threw up his hands and stormed out of my room. I followed him, still yelling—and so I saw what happened. As he reached the top of the stairs, the mahogany table in the hall gave a violent lurch. It slid as if the entire house had tipped on its foundation and slammed into him.

"Sam!" I screamed.

Sam clawed at the banister, but he couldn't stop himself from falling. He tumbled down the entire stair, head over heels. When he reached the bottom, he lay perfectly still for a moment, his leg twisted behind him. He looked up at me for one moment, then turned his head to the side and vomited.

"Sam!" I screamed again, then ran to call an ambulance. I knelt beside him while we waited for it to arrive, but he didn't open his eyes again. I felt numb as I rode in back with him to the local hospital. Luckily the doctors say that he's only got a broken leg and a mild concussion. He'll be all right. With a fall like his, they said, things could have been much worse.

Much worse—if things had been much worse, he'd be dead.

This can't go on. I know what happened with the table—I did it. I did it, and I can never do anything like that again.

I won't let another person die because of the Curtis witchcraft.

—Sarah Curtis

I woke up feeling fully rested. My body no longer felt achy or tired—I hadn't felt so alive in what seemed like weeks. I glanced at the clock, expecting it to read somewhere close to noon.

Seven-thirty A.M.

Just then I heard the gentle hiss of the shower, and I knew my sister was stepping into it. It was early Sunday morning. The pale light was just beginning to peek through my curtains. I could sleep as long as I wanted. Sighing happily, I lay back against my pillows and closed my eyes.

Then I opened them again. I was wide awake.

I thought about the night before—the beautiful, magickal way I'd been able to experience being with Hunter. It had felt so wonderful to have him with me that I would have thought the whole experience had been a dream, if it hadn't seemed so real. Beyond real—almost *more* than real, if such a thing was possible.

Mary K.'s shower ended. I waited a few minutes, but she didn't come into my room to wake me up for church. I thought of the smile she'd given me the night before.

I heard the familiar sound of my father's slippers as he padded down the stairs into the kitchen. There, then, was another thing I had missed—my family.

I threw off my covers and walked over to my closet. I pulled out a gray flannel skirt and a red sweater. Quickly I pulled on my clothes and brushed my hair.

I was going to church.

"Hi," I said as I walked into the kitchen.

My mother looked up from the paper she was reading. "Morgan," she said, her eyebrows lifted in surprise. She took in my outfit from head to toe, then smiled. "You look very nice," she said.

I grabbed a Diet Coke from the refrigerator. "I thought I'd come with you to church this morning."

My dad stared at me from where he was standing by the sink, his coffee cup lifted halfway to his mouth. He set it down on the counter. "Well, well." A pleased grin spread across his face. Looking down at his bathrobe, he said, "I guess I'm lagging behind."

Dad took his coffee and headed upstairs just as Mary K. came down. "What are you wearing?" she asked, staring at me.

"Morgan is coming to church with us this morning," Mom said, as if it was the most obvious and normal thing in the world.

"Oh," Mary K. said. Apparently this possibility hadn't occurred to her. "Great!" She grinned at me and went to the refrigerator. "You want toast?" she asked.

The normalcy of the question seemed like something from another time. "Sounds good," I said, sitting down at the table. In fact, it sounded better than good. It sounded like the best thing in the whole world.

Stepping into the church was like visiting an old friend, welcoming and familiar. There was the spicy smell of the incense our church uses and the odor of faded roses as I passed by Mrs. Beacon's pew. The strains of organ music drifted over the congregation. Mom's friend, Mrs. Lu, turned and gave me a big smile as we slipped into the pew behind hers. I smiled back and waved to her three-year-old daughter, Nellie, who giggled.

When it came time to take communion, I leaned over to

my mom and said, "I think I'm going to skip this." I just didn't feel right about it—somehow taking communion seemed like a definite commitment to Catholicism. Even though I appreciated the beauty of the service, I wasn't about to stop practicing Wicca. I was glad that my family loved coming here, and I loved it, too—but Wicca had chosen me as much as I had chosen it, and I wanted to find a way to keep both of my religions in my life.

I half expected my mom to frown or look disapproving, but she just squeezed my knee and followed my sister and father to the front of the church. A short while later the service was over.

A new level of calm swept over me as my family and I stepped outside. The sky was a clear blue, and a few small clouds tumbled across it. I was glad I had come.

"Mom, Dad," Mary K. said as we walked to the car. "Would it be okay if Morgan took me to the hospital to see Alisa later?"

My mom looked sideways at my dad, who nodded. Parental telepathy. "I guess it's all right," my mom said.

I smiled at my mom, and she smiled back. Of course, she would never refuse to allow Mary K. to see a friend in the hospital, but she could have insisted on taking Mary K. there herself. I felt like she was finally beginning to see how hard I'd been trying.

"Thanks," Mary K. said. But she wasn't looking at my parents. She was looking at me.

My boots clattered as we walked down the long corridor in the hospital toward Alisa's room. The hospital was quiet, and I found it kind of unnerving. Mary K. had seemed really eager to leave right away once we got home, so I didn't bother changing, and now I felt overdressed and awkward. Every step I took made me sound like a lumbering elephant.

Mary K. looked down at the small red-and-white teddy bear she was clutching against her chest. She had insisted that we stop at the drugstore before we came so that she could pick up a card for Alisa, and the teddy bears had been on sale. Bringing the bear was the kind of thing Mary K. was really good at—the kind of thing I never would have thought to do. "It's so weird," Mary K. said as she checked the door numbers. The nurse had told us that we'd find Alisa in room 341. "We've been in two hospitals this week."

Personally, I thought that the animal hospital was more comfortable and homey than this sterile, silent place, but I didn't say so.

"I'm glad Dagda's okay," Mary K. went on. "I hope Alisa will be, too."

"She will," I said. My voice conveyed much more certainty than I felt.

Mary K. gave me a sideways look but didn't reply. I wondered what she was thinking. I had no idea whether she knew how close to death Dagda had been. Did she realize that Erin had healed him?

"Three forty-one," Mary K. announced as we walked up to a door at the end of the hallway. It was half open. There was no noise coming from inside except for the steady beeps and whirring of machinery.

My sister looked at me uncertainly, and I realized that she was frightened. "It's okay," I told her, and rapped lightly on the door. There was no response, so I pushed it open a little farther. "Hello?" I called softly, but there was no reply. I was secretly relieved. The last thing I felt like doing was making polite conversation with Alisa's family. I nodded at my sister and stepped inside. Mary K. followed me.

Alisa's bed was at the far end of the dim room, near windows that were shrouded in curtains. She was either asleep or unconscious, and Mary K. sucked in her breath when she saw the machines clustered around her. Alisa's hair was limp on the pillow, and below her closed eyelashes were dark circles. Her cheeks were sunken and pale, her lips chapped and peeling.

How could someone get so sick so quickly?

Mary K. hesitated, then placed the teddy bear on the small table next to Alisa's bed, propping the card up against it. "So that she'll see it when she wakes up," she whispered to me.

"Do you want to wait awhile?" I asked.

Mary K. nodded. "If you don't mind," she said.

"Sure," I said, looking back at Alisa. I could only glance at her for a few seconds before I had to turn away. She looked horrible.

There was a yellow chair next to the side table, which I lowered myself into. In spite of its hideous color, it was big and comfortable. I patted the empty space next to me— there was more than enough room for Mary K. to fit. "Do you want to sit?"

"Yeah . . ." Mary K. was staring at Alisa, not moving. She seemed to be in her own world, pondering something. Suddenly she turned to me. "I'm going to get a Coke," she said. "I saw a machine in the front hall. Do you want anything? A Diet Coke?"

There was a strange edge in her tone, as if she were nervous. I wondered whether she was upset about the way Alisa looked—she certainly was a pitiful sight. "Are you okay?" I asked. "We don't have to stay here if you don't want to."

"No, no," Mary K. insisted. "I want to. I just . . . want a Coke."

I frowned at her. Her tone was strange and tense, as if she wanted to tell me more than she was saying. But—what? "Do you want me to come with you?" I asked.

"No—that's okay. I'll be right back. I mean," she said quickly as she raked a hand through her hair, "I mean I'll be back in a few minutes. The soda machine is near the entrance. It'll take me a few minutes to get back." Mary K. glanced at Alisa, then at me, and in that one glance I understood.

Mary K. wanted to leave me alone with Alisa.

She thought I could heal her.

Before I could even protest, Mary K. was out the door. Her footsteps retreated down the hall, first quickly, then more slowly. I guessed that she remembered she needed to take her time to get the soda.

I glanced at Alisa and had to suppress a shudder. She was so very sick. And I wasn't even the one who had healed Dagda—Erin had done that! I knew next to nothing about healing, even with Alyce's knowledge inside me. I wished Erin were there with me. I didn't know whether she could heal Alisa, either, but she sure as hell knew a lot more about it than I did.

I sat on my hands, swallowing the sob that was rising in my throat. But what if I can help her? I wondered. How can I sit here and do nothing when Alisa might be—

Don't think it, I commanded myself.

—dying. The word stung my consciousness like a fresh burn. I pictured Mary K.'s face. I tried to imagine what I would tell her. You see, Mary K., I know enough magick to fight dark forces, but not enough to help your best friend. . . . My vision blurred, and I rubbed my chest where it had begun to ache.

Alisa drew in a ragged, shuddering breath, then moaned. My stomach dropped. "Please don't," I whispered. Alisa grew quiet, but that didn't make me feel better. I had to do something to help her. Even if I couldn't heal her, maybe I could do a spell to take away some of the pain. Quickly I reached out and took her hand.

Immediately the cool, steady pulse of the heart rate monitor began a high-pitched scream. I dropped Alisa's hand and jumped back, my heart pumping wildly. What had I done? I hadn't even touched the machines! Without thinking, I screamed, "Mary K.! Mary K.!" I should have called for a doctor, but I didn't even think of it.

The door was flung open and a tall African American nurse exploded into the room, pushing a cart full of machinery. "You're going to have to get out of here," she said to me as a doctor hurried in behind her and rushed to check Alisa's monitors.

A chill breeze blew over me—I felt like the temperature in the room had dropped forty degrees. Goddess, help me! I thought. Alisa's body shook with convulsions.

Mary K. appeared in the doorway, looking tense and pale. "What happened?" Her wide eyes fastened on Alisa's machines, which were still going crazy. "Oh my God—what *happened*?" She stared at Alisa in horror.

I steered her out the door. "I don't know," I said as Mary K. tried to peer past me. Another nurse ran down the hall and pushed past us into Alisa's room. "Look, the nurse said we should get out of here," I said as calmly as I could, fighting my panic. Every nerve in my body was screaming.

"But we can't just leave," Mary K. protested. Her eyes were filled with tears.

"We're in the way," I said. "Mary K.—I'm sorry."

I was. I was so sorry. But I didn't know what to say. I had barely touched Alisa's hand, and I hadn't even been using magick at all.

Something had happened—but what? And why? I couldn't have caused that, I told myself. I didn't even do anything! But even if it was true, I couldn't change the fact that Alisa had just crashed horribly. That she was very sick and maybe dying. And that I couldn't do anything to help her.

As we walked down the corridor tears flowed down Mary K.'s face, a silent, steady stream.

There was nothing I could do to stop them.

15

Lift

October 8, 1971

I'm so weak, I can hardly write this. I've told Mom
and Dad that I have a bug so they won't bother me, but
that's a lie. I've been in bed for over twenty-four
hours. I can hardly sit up. And I can't stop crying.

I had to do it. Sam is still in the hospital, and I'm
the one who put him there. Who would be next? My
mother? My father? Me?

So last night I pulled the Harris Stoughton book
from the shelf. It took only a moment to find the
spell I was looking for—the same one I'd discovered
accidentally the other day. The spell to strip one's self
of magick.

I crept up to my room and prepared everything, the

black candle, the cauldron. At first I was afraid that I wouldn't be able to pronounce the chants correctly— they were written in a language I didn't know. But as I started speaking, I found that the words flew off my tongue. For a moment I thought that the ceremony wouldn't be so bad.

I was wrong.

After a few minutes I began to feel like there was a weight on my tongue. Something slimy. As I continued the chants, the weight slipped down my throat, into the pit of my stomach, as if I'd swallowed a snake. It stayed there and started to grow. I kept chanting, but the weight grew and grew, choking me. It spread farther, down my arms, down my legs, until I felt like my entire body was filled with a giant, black serpent. I was gagging on it, gasping for air. The weight pressed me against the floor, crushing me. I thought my spine would crack, but it didn't, and soon the weight turned into a searing pain. Then, thankfully, the whole room went black.

I woke up on the floor of my room, feeling like a tree that's been hit by lightning. Alive on the outside but dead on the inside . . . rotting away. I'll never use my magick again. I hardly even know what I am.

And I still have the book. I've hidden it under my mattress until I can decide what to do with it. I can't bring myself to destroy it, and I can't let it fall into the wrong hands.

I can't think about this now. All I want to do is sleep. Forever.

—Sarah Curtis

I was just about to crawl into bed when I heard the call. *Morgan.* The instant the word sounded in my mind, I knew that it was Hunter. He was sending me a witch message. I reached for the lapis lazuli by my bed. Lying back, I focused my energies and placed the smooth stone on my forehead. At the next heartbeat I felt Hunter, as if he were within me.

We have Ciaran.

For a moment they were words without meaning. I had spent the last several hours worrying about Alisa, terrified that I'd somehow hurt her, so it took me a moment to remember that there were other terrors in my life. Then images came into my mind, images of my birth father being bound by the *braigh*, of him crying out in pain, and I knew that Hunter was telling me that Ciaran had been appre-hended by the council.

A thousand emotions rained down on me—relief, first, but then anger, and pity, and fear. And other feelings that I couldn't even identify. Ciaran's dark magick frightened and revolted me, but he was my *father*—the closest blood rela-tive I had ever known. And when I remembered what I knew of witches who had had their power stripped—David Redstone, who had suffered horribly, or even how awful I'd felt when my power was only reined—I felt a horrible dread in the pit of my stomach. My father, my evil father. Captured. And utterly changed.

He will be stripped of his magick soon, Hunter's voice said in my mind. *First, he must stand trial. But Morgan, apparently he had a few things in his possession that led the council to conclude that he definitely was targeting you for attacks.*

I frowned. *What things?*

Hunter was slow to respond. *The council won't release all*

of the information, but they said that he had a strand of your hair in a small box in his breast pocket.

I sucked in my breath, wondering how Ciaran could have gotten a strand of my hair. But of course, it would have been easy. We spent plenty of time together. He could easily have found one of my hairs on his own jacket, for example.

They've also pulled in Lenore Ammett, Hunter went on. *According to her own Book of Shadows, she doesn't need proximity for telekinesis.*

My chest felt hollow. That was it, then. It was true. My own father had practically tried to kill me. Why? I wondered. What could he possibly gain by hurting me? *Morgan,* Hunter went on, *now that Ciaran is in custody, I think we should lift the deflection spell. There's no telling what might happen to him if he is stripped while still under the spell—and there's no need for it anymore, anyway. Erin is here, and she agrees with me.*

In a few moments I saw Erin's familiar face and twinkling eyes. She was sitting in a room surrounded by candles. Her face was lit with a golden glow. I felt the delicate bones of her hands in mine, and I knew that she and Hunter were holding hands. They were ready to begin the circle.

I had to blink back tears. Although I had feared that Ciaran might have been behind the strange accidents all along, somehow finding out for certain didn't fill me with relief; it filled me with sadness. I'd known he could be incredibly cruel, but a small part of me simply didn't want to believe that he was capable of hurting me. He was my birth father, after all. My only living parent. To know that he had actually tried to harm me, even knowing I was his daughter, was almost incomprehensible. And I couldn't understand why.

Can we have the circle without Sky and Alyce? I asked.

Sky has already left, Hunter replied, *and Alyce is busy with the store. But it doesn't require as much magick to release the spell as to put it in place. The three of us can do it.*

All right, I said. *But first I have to tell you something.* I took a deep breath. *Alisa is very sick. She's in the hospital. Mary K. and I went to see her this afternoon, and she had some kind of crash. I'm worried.* I didn't tell him that I might have been responsible for what had happened. I simply couldn't allow myself to think those thoughts.

That's terrible, Hunter replied. I could feel his concern, then confusion as he added, *Do you think we should send some healing spells her way?*

No, I don't think that's such a good idea. Even though I felt certain that I hadn't actually performed any magick that afternoon, that Alisa's crash was just a coincidence, the idea of doing a spell for her was terrifying. What if we ended up hurting her? I couldn't take the chance. *Alisa quit the coven,* I explained. *I don't know if she would want a spell done for her. And I wouldn't want to do anything against her wishes.*

All right, Hunter conceded, even though I could tell he wasn't entirely convinced. *Let me know how she's doing, won't you, Morgan?*

Of course, I promised. I inhaled deeply, bracing myself for the task to come. *Let's begin,* I said with Hunter's voice.

Erin began a low hum at the back of her throat, then, in a voice that was almost a whisper, she began to chant.

"Let us now unwork the magick that encircles the blameworthy,

Leave him to his own strategy,

Just or fell."

*   *   *

The words went on, and the magick that welled up in me was like cool, clear water, fluid and bracing. I waited for Erin to pull out Harris Stoughton's book, and I was surprised to realize that she wasn't going to. She didn't even seem to have the book with her. Instead, she reached for a large white dish and a white teapot. With a steady hand she filled the dish with steaming liquid. My nostrils were filled with the scent of mint and rosemary, and I nearly laughed to realize that my connection with Hunter was so strong that I could actually *smell* what he smelled. Reaching into a green velvet pouch beside her, Erin pulled out a handful of something and crumbled it into the water. The water shimmered for a moment, like the ocean in the setting sun. There was a light hissing sound and the scent of lavender, then Erin looked up and smiled.

"We have released the witch from his own restraints." Erin sounded as happy and relieved as I felt. "He will no longer be his own victim."

I inhaled deeply, still taking pleasure in the beautiful smells that lingered around me. Undoing the deflection spell had been as beautiful and easy as putting it on had been ugly and horrible. I felt wonderful now, even though the magick hadn't been directed at me. I was safe now—Ciaran couldn't threaten me any longer, and my magick was intact.

Morgan, thank you, Hunter's voice echoed in my mind.

For what?

There was a moment before he replied. *For everything,* he said finally. *For everything,* he repeated, soft as the sound of water flowing over smooth stones. In the next moment he was gone.

The lapis lazuli made a slight click as I placed it back on

the nightstand and turned off the lamp. I love you, Hunter Niall, I thought as I pulled the comforter up to my chin. I looked out my window, into the depths of the starry sky.

"I did it." Bree leaned against a bank of lockers, clutching her books to her chest. There were dark circles under her eyes, as if she hadn't slept well.

"You talked to Robbie?"

Bree gave a faint nod.

"How did it go?" I asked. It was five minutes to the first bell.

"Badly," Bree said. "But better than I thought it would."

"So are you . . ." I didn't know how to finish the sentence.

"We're still together," Bree replied, tucking her silky hair behind one ear. "He was hurt, though. Really hurt about the stuff with Matt." She looked at me, her eyes rimmed with red. "That was the worst part. I've never—"

"I know," I said. "It's okay."

"He said that he loved me." Bree's voice was small and fragile, like a little girl's teacup. "I'm glad I told him, even though it wasn't easy."

We stood there a moment, not saying anything.

"I guess I'm afraid," Bree said finally.

I thought about Bree—about all the nights she ate dinner alone because her father was out of town on business. I thought about the brother she hadn't spoken to in over a month, the mother she hadn't seen in years. Bree knew about difficult love. No wonder she was afraid. "Robbie is special," I told her. "And you're strong."

Bree nodded, as if what I'd said was something she knew already—something she'd forgotten. She squeezed my hand, then let it go. "You're strong, too."

The bell rang, and we were swept down the hall toward homeroom in a churning sea of students. Neither one of us said anything more. Neither one of us had to.

16

Letting

October 14, 1971

I couldn't hide it from them forever. Even though I tried.

My parents wanted to take me to see John Walter, the best healer in our coven. I knew he'd tell them the truth, so finally I had to admit what I'd done. My mother cried for two days, and my father stopped speaking to me altogether. My parents had always told me that there was nothing I could do that would make them stop loving me.

But I guess I found the one thing.

There's nothing I can do about it now. I couldn't bring my magick back even if I wanted to. And I don't want to. Even though I'm still weak from the ceremony, I would rather feel pain myself than run the risk of putting someone else in danger. I know that Wicca is dangerous. Beautiful, but dangerous. I just wish that *someone would talk to me, would try to understand why I did what I did. Don't they understand that I've lost even more than they have?*

I write this from a Greyhound bus bound for Houston. It was the farthest place from Gloucester for the smallest amount of money. Even so, it took most of my cash — I've only got twenty-three dollars and thirty-seven cents in my pocket . . . what's left of my life savings. With that, and a small bag of clothing, and the Harris Stoughton book wrapped in a black cloth (it's no danger to me any longer, and how could I leave such an evil book with my family?), I begin my new life.

I keep trying to tell myself that this kind of change is exactly what I need. That nothing has changed in my family for centuries and that I'm a pioneer, off to explore new worlds. I'm not really buying it, though.

It might be easier if I had some idea of where all of this would lead. But I don't.

I guess no one ever really does.

—Sarah Curtis

"Morgan?" Mary K.'s voice echoed up the stairway. I put my book aside and stood up. I had been lying on my bed, reading my English assignment, with Dagda curled comfortably in the curve of my waist.

Mary K. called up again, with more urgency this time. "Morgan!"

"What? What is it?" I stepped out of my room and

peered down the stairs. Mary K. was standing at the bottom with a huge grin. "What's going on?"

"There's somebody here that you might like to see."

"Who?" I started walking down the stairs. Hunter? I thought hopefully. But no, I would have sensed his coming. Who else could she be talking about?

When I got to the bottom of the stairs, Mary K. was alone in the foyer. Was she playing a trick on me? "Well, who—"

I broke off. Alisa was sitting on the couch in the living room, looking small and pale. Her hair was pulled back in a ponytail, emphasizing her gaunt, delicate face. She looked up at me nervously. "Hi, Morgan."

"Wow, Alisa." She looked like she was still weak, but she was *there,* sitting in my living room, talking to me. I walked over to the couch and perched beside her. "I'm so glad you're okay. How do you feel?"

Alisa shrugged. "Depends when you ask me, I guess." She pulled her hands into her lap, and I could see that she was holding the red-and-white teddy bear that Mary K. had brought to her hospital room. "I still feel weak, and I still have aches and dizziness every once in a while." She smiled a wan smile. "But I'm getting better. I'm well enough to leave my house, and that feels great."

Mary K. perched on my dad's armchair. "Do they know what made you sick?"

Alisa shook her head a little sadly. "Nobody seems to have any idea," she said. "After you two left, I got really bad, and the doctors were pretty worried. They told my father to start preparing for the worst. But after a few hours I just seemed to get better. And around midnight, I woke up really thirsty and asked the nurse for a glass of juice. I mean"—she gave a little laugh—"I'd been unconscious for, like, days, and I just up and asked for some apple juice out of the blue. The nurse was in shock."

"Wow." Mary K. looked at me as if to say, "Isn't that crazy?"

"I know," Alisa went on. "The doctors say it was a really bad virus and that the worst of it just had to pass through my system before I could start getting better." She looked at me meaningfully. "But the fact is, they don't really know what made me sick—and now they don't have any idea what made me better."

The way she was staring at me made me uncomfortable, and I looked away, out the window. Did she and Mary K. think that I'd cured her? But I hadn't. "Alisa, I—"

"Anyway," Alisa interrupted me, "I just wanted to say thank you. For coming to visit me in the hospital, I mean." She looked down into her lap and stroked the tiny red-and-white bear. Even though she was better, I still sensed a sadness in Alisa. I wondered about the family problems Mary K. had mentioned before.

"You're welcome," I said softly. I reached over to squeeze her arm. She seemed so down, and I still felt this weird protectiveness toward her. I wondered if I was starting to get maternal urges or something.

As I touched Alisa's arm, there was a crash. Alisa jumped. We all looked up to see that a framed photo had fallen off the mantel across the room. Frowning, Mary K. jumped up and picked it off the floor. "That's weird," she murmured, holding up a photo of our family around the tree last Christmas. "Must have been a draft."

I stared, frozen. There was no reason for that picture to

fall off the mantel. No reason, that is, except the strange telekinetic incidents that had been following me. But that was Ciaran, I told myself. And Ciaran's in custody. He can't be doing this to me.

Was it possible that it was just a weird accident? Maybe I was making something out of nothing. If it had happened anytime before the past couple of weeks, I wouldn't have thought twice about it. It was just that so much had been happening lately . . . anything even vaguely out of the ordinary seemed suspicious.

Mary K. gingerly picked up the broken glass that surrounded the picture. As I watched her, I had a more frightening thought: What if it wasn't Ciaran who had been behind those incidents? What if it was someone else—someone else who was after me, and still on the loose?

"Um, I'd better get back to my homework," I blurted, standing up. "Alisa, I'm really glad you're feeling better. I hope I'll see you back at school soon."

"Thanks."

As I left the room, my eyes fell on the photo. Mary K. had propped it, still in the broken frame, on an end table while she picked up the glass. I shuddered when I saw how it had broken. Deep cracks had formed that set Mary K., my mom, and my dad in one section. In the other section was me, alone.

I sprinted back up to my room.

But before I even had time to think about what had happened, Mom knocked on my bedroom door. "Do you have a minute?" she called.

"Sure," I said as my mom opened the door and walked in, holding a sheaf of papers in her hand. I sighed. I could smell a lecture coming on. I knew what the papers were—it was the extra-credit assignment I'd written for Mr. Powell. He'd just handed it back that morning, with an A—that meant the full twenty points of extra credit. I'd been so excited about it that I'd left it out on the kitchen table for my mom to see, but now I remembered. She hadn't been so thrilled that I'd chosen to write about the persecution of witches. No doubt she wanted to tell me that this wouldn't be an appropriate application essay for Saint Anne's.

"Morgan," my mom said as she settled at the edge of my bed, "I like to think I'm a reasonable person."

Usually, I said mentally. But I didn't say anything out loud; I just nodded.

"That's why I—" But she couldn't finish. She just looked at the paper and shook her head.

"Look, I didn't mean to upset you," I said finally. "I just left it out because I thought you'd be glad that my grades are coming up."

"I know," my mom said slowly. "And you were right—I *am* glad." She flipped through the paper. "This is very well written, Morgan. You must have done a lot of research for it."

"A lot," I agreed. "But it's not hard when you're researching something you're really interested in."

My mom nodded and pursed her lips. "I always told you girls that I'd never stand in the way of things you were interested in," she said. "At the time, I thought that was such an easy promise to make." She looked down at the paper again. "Morgan, I think your father and I made a mistake when we considered sending you to Catholic school."

For a moment I thought I'd misheard her or hallucinated or something.

"That was the wrong solution," my mom went on. "I guess

we—or I guess I—just overreacted. "I . . ." My mom stopped to take a deep breath. "I hope you know that I'm just afraid for you, Morgan. I love you, that's all," she finished in a whisper.

I felt a wave of relief wash over me. She was serious—no Catholic school! Thank the Goddess! And with that wave of relief came a rush of love and gratitude for my mom, who was putting aside her fear and allowing me to explore something she didn't understand. I leaned over and took the paper from her hand. "Thank you so much," I said softly. "I know Wicca frightens you. But it's part of me, Mom. I can't change it."

My mother was silent for so long that I thought perhaps I'd upset her. But finally she said, "You're right." She sighed and shook her head. "Morgan, I'm your mother, and I want you to be happy. I was concerned when I saw your grades suffering. But now you've shown me that you're bringing them up. You've even proved that your interests and your academics can peacefully coexist." She looked at me. "I don't want to be the kind of mother who tells you what to believe. I swore to myself that I'd never be like that, and I intend to keep that promise. No matter how hard it is."

I leaned over and hugged her, breathing in the light, sweet smell of her perfume. It occurred to me how much I had missed her—how much I had missed my whole family—in the last few weeks. Now I was safe, Ciaran was in custody, and I had my family around me. I felt warm and happy. My mom kissed me on the forehead. "I think that this hard work deserves a little reward," she said. "What do you suggest?"

I lifted my eyebrows and grinned. "The end of my grounding period?"

"How about a phone call?"

"Good enough," I said quickly, scrambling out of bed. Dagda let out a mew of complaint.

"Where are you going?" my mom asked.

I turned and grinned at her. "To go call Hunter."

"Ah," she said with a smile. "Well, tell him I said hello."

"I will," I called over my shoulder as I practically ran down the stairs. I couldn't wait to tell him the good news about Alisa—I couldn't wait to tell him everything. I was in such a hurry as I punched in Hunter's number on the cordless phone that I messed up twice. I took a deep breath and tried again.

Hunter answered on the first ring. "Morgan, I'm so glad you called," he said.

I laughed for what seemed like the first time in weeks. I hadn't spoken to Hunter in days, and his voice seemed delicious to me. It was true that the mind melds we'd been having were great, but there was something so comforting about hearing his voice on the phone, so normal, that it almost made me giddy. "I guess there's no point in trying to surprise you with a phone call," I said lightly. "Guess what! No Catholic school!"

There was a moment of quiet on the other end of the line. For a second I wondered whether he'd heard me. "Morgan, love, that's brilliant. Is it because you've brought your grades up?"

"It is," I said happily. "Oh, and Alisa's okay! She stopped by earlier."

"Oh, excellent."

I paused, thinking about Alisa's visit and the picture falling. Should I tell Hunter about that? Or would he just think I was paranoid?

"Morgan—" Hunter began. There was something in his tone. What was it? Concern? Fear?

"What is it?" A feeling of dread spread through the pit of my stomach.

"I've heard from Sky."

It took a moment for the news to sink in. "What did she—"

"She's found some leads," Hunter went on. "In fact, she believes my parents are not in France."

"No?" I felt a sudden, horribly selfish wave of relief. Did that mean Hunter wouldn't have to go to Europe to search for them?

"No," Hunter replied. "She believes they're in Canada. Quebec. It would explain the French. I'm going to head up there myself, as soon as possible."

The room started to tilt crazily, and I had to hold on to the counter for support. "But—but—the council—"

"I've spoken with the council," Hunter said. "Morgan, Ciaran is in custody. Selene and Cal are gone." He paused. "I've asked permission to investigate the Canada leads. There's no reason for me to be here now." He sighed. "Don't you see? You're safe now. There isn't anything left for me to do in Widow's Vale."

Had he really just said that? "Thanks a lot," I said bitterly, swallowing the tears that were welling up in my throat.

"That isn't what I meant, and you know it," Hunter said quietly.

I did know. But it hurt anyway. "How long will you be gone?" I asked.

"It's hard to be sure," Hunter replied. "It could be a few days or a few weeks. Or longer. It depends on what I find."

Of course. That was what I was afraid of. The image I'd seen when I scried, the image of Hunter waving farewell, entered my mind, along with the feeling of dread I'd felt when I first saw it. Was it possible . . . was it possible that he might *never* come back? Don't think that way, I commanded myself, but it was too late. I thought of the picture falling earlier, how frightened I had been. Had something so small really seemed so important just a few minutes ago?

"Just how reliable is Sky's information?" I demanded. The moment the words were out of my mouth, I hated myself for saying them. But I couldn't stop. "What if you're heading into some kind of trap?"

Hunter didn't reply. He didn't have to. We both knew that Sky would never have told Hunter he should go to Canada unless she had some overwhelming evidence.

I pulled out a chair and sat down at the breakfast table, my forehead in my palm. This can't be happening, I thought dizzily. Now that I was safe, Hunter was leaving. I tried to focus on my breathing, on pulling the fresh air into my lungs and letting the old air go. For a crazy moment I wished that I could be in some sort of horrible danger. It was a very strange thing, to realize that I would rather have my life in jeopardy with Hunter than to be safe . . . without him.

"Morgan," Hunter said. His voice grew quieter. "We're *mùirn beatha dàns*. You know I love you completely. But you also know how I feel about my parents. You wouldn't want me to pass up this chance, would you?"

Yes, I thought. I opened my mouth to say it, but I couldn't. How could I tell him that? What would it do to our love?

"No," I whispered. "I want you to find them."

"I knew that was what you would say." Hunter's voice was a caress.

I inhaled. I exhaled. I ran my fingers over the ridges of the cotton place mat. It felt impossibly normal to me, incongruously simple.

Out of nowhere, the words Alisa had spoken over a week ago echoed in my mind. *I wish things could stay the way they are.* For a brief moment I'd been safe, my family had been happy, and I'd known who my *mùirn beatha dàn* truly was. And now he was leaving me. I remembered the vision I'd had, the one in which Hunter had waved good-bye, and I tried not to think that this separation was permanent.

Trust me. The words hadn't been spoken, yet they seemed to be all around me, spinning lazily like dandelion fluff on a summer wind. I looked out the kitchen window. The night was dark, and the moon was out. I couldn't see any stars, but I knew they were there. I could picture them, waiting patiently, their light cutting through the infinite darkness. Fire had never looked so cold to me.

Trust me.

What choice did I have?

"I do," I said.